LEARNT

LEARNT

A NOVEL BY
EDWARD M. BALDWIN

Dear Ron,
May you enjoy this as
much as I enjoyed
writing it!

Best regards,

Jazlo & Lossi Publishing

Jacksonville, FL

Jazlo & Lossi Publishing
1704 E. 24th Street Suite 102A
Jacksonville, FL 32206

ISBN 978-0-9794074-4-4
Library of Congress Control Number: 2007929357

First Edition

Attention schools, universities, colleges, and educational organizations: Quantity discounts are available on bulk purchases of this book for educational or gift purposes. Special book exerpts can also be created to fit special needs. For more information, please contact: Special Sales Department, Jazlo & Lossi Publishing 1704 E. 24th Street Suite 102A, Jacksonville, FL 32206.

Acknowledgements

There are too many people to thank for helping with this book, but my earlier readers were a tremendous influence: my wife Liz, Jeanice Lue, Jennifer Brigman, Marshall Moreland, Sheri Boltz, Korey Godsey, Jennifer Henderson, Brad Cunningham, Rachel Lovely, Jeff Take, Amy Hurley, De Ann "Frenchy," "Cat" from Red Lobster, James Nipper, Connie Downs, Thomas Yarger, Kim Jackson, Alex Abdul, Matt Ellison, April Vannatta, and dozens of others who will kill me for not mentioning them here.

To everyone involved, big or small, thank you so much. We did it.

For my mother.

Standard English (stăn'dərd) n. The variety of English that is most widely accepted as the spoken and written language of educated speakers in formal and informal contexts and is characterized by generally accepted conventions of spelling, grammar, and vocabulary while admitting some regional differences, especially in pronunciation and vocabulary.

dialect (dī'ə-lĕkt') n. A regional variety of a language distinguished by pronunciation, grammar, or vocabulary, especially a variety of speech differing from the standard literary language or speech pattern of the culture in which it exists.

proper (prŏp'ər) adj. Appropriate. Suitable.

Prologue

MR. GUMBLE'S FIRST DAY AT LINCOLN High School, and he's showing courage. He knows he's already the students' third teacher this year. That's fine, but he's here now. Of course, there's only one reason why a man of his stature, a former community college professor of twelve years, would lower himself so far as to teach in a school like Lincoln. Some may say it's the money, but lack of money is far more accurate. Besides, Mr. Gumble has bills and a savings account that won't allow him the privilege of being particular about his place of employment right now. Mr. Gumble needs a job—yesterday.

As he sits at his desk with a nervous twitch in his left knee, waiting for his first class to appear, he reminisces about the college life, when students waited for him to walk into the classroom—no, waited for him to present himself. For their sage to finally come forth. But now, thanks to two vindictive students, one video camera, and one too many on-duty whiskey sours, his scholastic sovereignty has been stripped away. Now, it is he who's doing the waiting. And while he waits for his students to arrive, he also waits for his left knee to stop twitching.

Why the twitch? *Because he's utterly terrified.* Nothing a touch of brandy couldn't handle, but not a good idea for the first day on the job.

Yes, he's scared. Besides his two years spent at the Saint Joseph Christian Academy, a horrid experience that was more than a few slices shy of heaven, he hasn't had much practice with adolescents. After all, they're nothing but kids, really. He's accustomed to dealing with adults, people who take their future seriously.

Throughout the entire first period—his planning period—he waits at his desk, wondering what to do with himself—and his knee. He glances at the clock for the hundredth time, not knowing what else to do because he has already done everything. He has already arranged their desks to his liking, counted the textbooks, mounted his motivational signs throughout the classroom. Their first assignment has been on the board for forty-five minutes, right underneath his immaculately written "Professor Oliver Gumble."

They need to know he's no mere teacher. Their first two teachers—those they reportedly ran off after just six weeks of school, details not forthcoming—may have been ordinary teachers, but he'll let these upstarts know from the very beginning, he's not just a teacher. He's a "retired" Professor of English Literature, with a Master's degree to prove it.

Another glance at the clock—twelve minutes left.

How he wishes his planning period was in the middle of the day instead of the very first class period. An outrage, to be sure. After all, whoever heard of starting a game with the halftime? Who starts an opera or a play with the intermission? Ridiculous.

Mr. Gumble broods about his class schedule for only a few seconds more—at least, so it seems to him—but the bell rings anyway, and his heart lurches.

They're coming.

He checks the top of his desk. It's as neat as it was thirty minutes ago. Everything is in order. Not much to do on the first day, anyway. Just some get-to-knows and a preliminary assessment of their skills. His modified syllabus will suffice to make their acquaintance, and, as for their initial assessment, that's already written on the board below his name: pages seventeen through twenty-two of their composition textbooks. Child's play, even for them.

Abruptly, the door begins gushing students, and with them comes the noise. Loud, unrestrained, threatening noise. Instinctively, Mr. Gumble—no, "Professor" Gumble—fidgets to his feet and wonders why in the hell he's so afraid. After all, he's a veteran educator, for chrissakes. They're just—*kids*.

The room becomes deafening as it fills to capacity. The professor grabs his syllabi, not knowing they'll prove worthless. The students have already turned to their own internalized manual, which explains in chapter six how to deal with a third teacher. In fact, their curriculum was set long before Professor Gumble ever thought he'd lose his comfortable college gig.

"Okay, let's take our seats, everyone," he says nervously. His request is ignored, but the snickering, jeering, and laughter more than prove that he is indeed in their spotlight.

"Hey, ya'll! Check out dat Mr. Rogers jacket he got own!" announces a voice from the back of the classroom.

"Damn! We got Mr. Rogers up in nis bitch?"

Professor Gumble holds onto his syllabi firmly with both hands, but the papers still shake. His nerves are getting the better of him. His head swirls with thoughts, but the penalty for student profanity is the last thing on his mind.

"C-can we take our seats, please?" he returns, surprised at the tremble in his voice. He clears his throat. "Everyone needs to have one of these," he informs them, holding the syllabi over his head with both hands, still firmly.

No response. Not even a smart comment. He is no longer in the room, and the adolescent commotion within the classroom consumes him. This strikes a chord deep within him, and he suddenly realizes that for the first time in his career, he'll have to yell at a class.

So be it.

"Will everyone sit—*DOWN!*" he cries, perhaps a bit too loudly. A request coated with frustration, close to a demand, but it feels good just the same. Besides, they were asking for it.

A rather tall, lanky, black student rushes forward like an NBA guard, and brings his face within a foot of the professor's. "Who da hell you yellin' at, bitch?"

The room quiets. Heads turn to the front of the classroom.

And so it starts.

To the professor, the sudden silence is more threatening than the noise. Never in his life has he been more terrified in a classroom. "Excuse m-me?" he stammers, complete with batting eyelashes. "What did—?"

"I said who da hell you yellin' at, *bitch!*"

Subtle beads of fear form on the professor's forehead. He swallows hard. Says nothing.

"He was yellin' at *you!*" chimes a voice from across the classroom.

"Make him apologize, yo!" offers a voice with a Spanish accent.

"Dass what his punk ass *bettuh* do!" answers the NBA guard, spitting whenever he says words beginning with the letters *p* or *b*. "You don' juss come up in my class disrespeckin' me!" he says, slapping his chest for emphasis. He inches closer to the professor, and the room grows even more silent. It takes everything that the professor has to remain planted in his spot. "Ah'm wait'n fuh you ta apologize," he growls.

The class starts up with the appropriate uh-ohs and laughter. Even though the professor is standing in the center of the room, he has been backed into a corner, like a frightened forest creature, caught in the center of a noisy interstate, paralyzed by indecision. He hasn't felt this way since—when? Playing his computer chess game? Is it his move? What harm can there be in a simple apology anyway? Just a simple apology, and he can get on with teaching the class, right?

Every grinning face within the classroom says otherwise.

"Kick his ass!" erupts from a muffled voice, and is followed by more giggles and snorts.

The professor suddenly realizes how wrong he's been all of these years. The Saint Joseph Christian Academy was indeed a slice of heaven—a huge slice.

"Mr. Rogers is dissin' you, man!" another voice adds.

"Slap dat stupid ass look off his face!" adds another voice from the far corner.

The professor fiddles with his syllabi, trying to hide his trembling hands. At the moment, that's all he can think to do. *Mask the fear*. And feeling he could very well die at any moment, he does a fairly decent job.

The first of five classes, and he's already had his halftime.

Chapter 1

My knees are killing me, but I've got to keep going. I try not to think about them, but have you ever tried clearing your mind while you're in pain? Trust me, it's not easy. On top of that, the sweat's starting to bother me now, getting into my eyes, and the cut over my right eye is stinging. We've been at it for sixteen minutes. Never realized how much time existed in sixteen minutes, but I try not to think about it.

This is my first day of karate. It's supposed to be the toughest. Hard to believe anyone can get used to doing this stuff, that you can get better at ignoring the pain. I'm fifteen, but you wouldn't believe it by looking at me. I'm also overweight and out of shape—*that* you'd believe. After just three minutes of this torture, my left knee started making this snap-pop sound with every kick. A snap on the way out, a pop on the way back.

Snap. Pop.

Snap. Pop.

Everyone heard it; I know they did, but no one looked at me. They kept looking straight ahead. Maybe it's something they hear a lot with the new people. Maybe they're remembering their own snap-popping days behind those sweaty poker faces, or maybe they're just good at hiding grins.

They call this the "front kick." I call it torture number two; number one was the left leg. We're on the right leg now, which is a good thing. My right seems to be stronger and have less to say, although I can tell by the way it feels that it's just waiting for the right time. Still, it's holding out a bit longer than the left. The left gave out fast. *Too* fast. I had to stop before the switch. Can't remember if it was the "snap" or the "pop" that had the final word. I'm thinking "pop." My right is proving to be a tad stronger—not by much, just a tad, which is strange considering I walk on both legs equally. Something to ponder, but I'm too tired for pondering.

The teacher, Mr. Travers, said to do this properly takes "focus." I wondered what the hell he meant by that. I mean, focus on what? The pain in my knees? Now, I don't give a damn. Besides, I've already decided it's best not to think about it, not to focus.

I'm trying like hell not to count. Counting made it worse for my left leg, even though I lost count around forty-eight. This time, I just look around the room. It's easy to maintain the rhythm and pace of the class by following the symphony of grunts. So, I decide to take a mental inventory of my surroundings. Maybe if I'm lucky, I can catch a thought train out of here.

I don't move my head, just my eyes. The flag with the big red dot in the middle is the center of attention as far as decor is concerned, tacked flush on the front wall. It also gets all of the attention when class starts, our feet together as we bow our heads. And I'm told that it'll receive additional homage when class ends. I guess the dusty American flag always stays in the left corner, hanging from its pole. Been a while since I've said the Pledge of Allegiance, but I'm starting to appreciate how non-physical our pledge is. What country have we pledged allegiance to with our bowing? Was it China or Japan? I don't know much about either country, but I just bowed to one of them. You'd think I'd at least *know* which one, but I wasn't told. I bowed because the teacher required it.

Above the entranceway is a sign bearing a yin and yang symbol. I can't make out the words from where I'm standing—or should I say, where I'm flailing my right leg. It looks like someone wrote it by hand. Probably Mr. Travers. Everyone calls him "Sensei," but to me he's Mr. Travers because I don't know what the hell "Sensei" means. Again, I wasn't told.

The right wall is one big mirror, but we don't get to face it; we have to face Mr. Travers. The mirror makes the room seem bigger than it really is, which is about the size of a tennis court. On my side of the room, there's a rack with a lot of vertical standing poles in it. They look like broom stick handles, but they're longer. Some are black. Some are brown. All are made of wood. I count twenty-one, but there are only thirteen of us here, excluding Mr. Travers. Five of the poles have chucks hanging on them, the impressive kind that look like two polished nightsticks, held together by a shiny silver chain. Chucks held together by a rope look so cheesy.

Anyway, I guess you have to learn the pole before you can learn the chucks. Should be the other way around. Chucks are cool. Besides, you can't carry a pole around everywhere you go. Can't take it to school. Can't take it to Arcade Stadium without people looking at you funny. Girls look at me funny anyway, always whispering and giggling, but that's okay; I own the Stadium. There isn't a video game in the Stadium I haven't mastered. Let them laugh. They're sluts anyway, not a virgin among them. Arcade Stadium's just a warm-up for when they're old enough to get into dance clubs.

. . . *Pop.*

. . . *Pop.*

There goes my right leg, popping as I snatch it back. The extension is still silent, no snapping—yet. I think I can hold out until we switch to something else, and I'm hoping like hell it's not back to the left.

Perspiration has officially claimed these pajamas. Even my underwear is soaked. Good thing the floor is carpeted. Otherwise, my bare feet would be sliding all over the place, splashing in a pool of sweat. It would be so much easier to just leave, walk out with what little knees I have left. After all, it's Friday. I could go hang out at the Stadium, but if I did, Mom would hit the roof. Karate was her idea, not mine. She's convinced that this is good for me, that the Northshore Karate Institute will make me a better person, a different person. I've had too many fights at school, and my grades prove it.

By the way, the school said I'm "emotionally handicapped." That's fancy talk for not having it all upstairs. They keep saying all of these things about me, but they don't know me. Don't *want* to know me. All they ever want to know is test results and attention span, like it matters. During the last conference, Mom told them that my emotions were just fine, partly because she can't keep coming to my school whenever they call. Having to leave work for a conference takes away from her paycheck, and that cuts into her partying money. She ran out of sick leave and vacation days a few months ago. Nowadays, she claims a "family emergency," but that's not a paying category.

She said that if Dad were still alive, I'd be different. She said that I'm always looking for attention. Yeah, right. Fat kids in school have no problem getting attention, no problem getting into fights, but nobody wants to hear that.

Two days ago, I had a fight that got me sort of kicked out of school, which also got me a small cut over my right eye, thanks to Mom's long-nailed slaps. Nine of them—slaps, not nails. She stopped when she saw the blood—on me, not her. Still, I stayed in the same spot, waiting for more, even after she went into the living room to watch television.

I've never been kicked out of school, so it took me by surprise. Now, I gotta go to a new school a week from Monday, one that'll take a student like me. You'd think I'd be back to square one, but my record comes with me. The good thing about this is that Mom gets the chance to work for five days without wondering whether I'll get into trouble. I get a guaranteed week with no fights, maybe not even at home.

I have a guy named Logan Ellis and a few of his friends to thank for these latest troubles. I can still hear Logan and his dumb-ass friends.

Hey, fat boy!

I should've told him to blow me. Either way, the results would've been the same.

You could get a group rate at Weight Watchers!

I didn't say anything, but they always take silence for fear. That's the real problem; I'm never afraid.

Damn! You can pinch a lot *more than an inch!*

Why did he have to touch me? They always have to either touch you or jump in your face to the point where they're spitting on you. Logan wasn't so funny after I busted his nose and split his lip. My Biology book came in real handy that time. The school called it assault. Yeah, whatever.

Yesterday, Mom finally told the wrong friend about her problem child, the kind of friend who doesn't know how to mind her own business. She told Mom about a husband who teaches a "discipline." That's the word that did it. Next thing I knew, Mom's on the phone getting the details, and here I am, kicking in a set of oversized, soaked pajamas.

. . . *Pop.*

Snap. Pop.

There's the snap. I'm thinking, a few more kicks and my right leg's gonna fall right off, but we finally get ready to switch to something else. Everyone's back to standing at attention—feet together, hands to the side. I just stand, barely.

"Let's begin our reverse punches!" Mr. Travers yells to us.

I'm thinking, *Reverse punches?* I am *not* gonna ask.

"Kenny, just follow along the best you can!"

Okay. So Mr. Travers is used to reading faces. A regular psychic, but I wonder if he knows I'm the closest to the door, even on this side of the room.

Now we're standing with our feet apart and knees slightly bent, as though someone's supposed to crawl through our legs on hands and knees. Mr. Travers calls it the "horse stand," but horses don't stand like this. Looks like we all have to go to the bathroom.

The half grin is startled from my face when everyone starts yelling out loud with each punch, beating the hell out of nothin'.

Kee-yah!

Right fist goes out, the left one snatches back to the hip.

Kee-yah!

The fists trade positions. So do mine, but I don't say anything—no shout, no grunt, no nothing. Hell, I'm tired. Don't have anything left to shout with, even less to shout for. I'm here for my mom. Not exactly the greatest source of inspiration.

This is supposed to teach me how to behave, how to fit in, and how to do all kinds of other bullshit things that'll prove I'm not a discipline case, but I don't see how. This is like regular school, but instead of desks, there's a dotted flag in the front, a pole rack with chucks, and the biggest damn mirror I've ever seen. The ceiling's a lot higher than the ones in school, probably for swinging poles around, but even though there are no books to read, no homework, it's more same than different. I could tell when I first walked in.

"Hello, Kenny," Mr. Travers said to me, "I'm Mr. Travers—'cept all of my students call me 'Sensei.' Your mom told me you were coming today. I see the gi fits okay. When she stopped by, she asked for the largest I had." Then he looked at me funny and said, "You ready?"

I just nodded at him. He came across friendly enough, but all teachers do until they get to know you. So I just nodded. No smile, no frown, just a nod.

"Take off your shoes and socks," he said, sort of like an order, but not quite, "and put 'em in the back of the dojo."

I glanced at the back of the room where everyone was stretching on the floor. They were already staring at me, without so much as a smile.

Then, Mr. Travers put a hand on my shoulder and said, "Everyone! This here is Kenny Houston! He's gonna be joinin' us this evening!"

They always have to announce you. And it's always followed by a few mumbled, almost patronizing hellos.

"After you put your shoes up," he said, still giving me his stupid grin, "start stretchin' out with the others. We're startin' in a few minutes."

I placed my shoes in the back of the room, then turned to find an empty spot on the floor, knowing that I wasn't gonna "stretch out." I just didn't want to be the only one standing. Besides, everybody here's pretty flexible. There was no way in hell I was gonna make myself look any worse. So I just sat and waited in a vacant square yard, feeling all eyes attacking me at once as their conversations died down.

They didn't talk to me then, and they're not talking to me now. They're busy punching and yelling, facing straight ahead, while I throw my punches from the back of the class.

Mr. Travers conducts class as if it's the military, but in the military, everyone's equal—no individuals, no specials, no sore thumbs. This is *not* the military. There are four rows, four people in each, but there are thirteen of us. I'm in the back forming my own row. Just another coincidence? Of course it is. And after class is over, people will mistake me for Bruce Lee.

Supposedly, all new students are issued a pair of pajamas, a white belt, and then placed in the back. Believe it or not, that's what I was told. Too funny—haven't learned a damn thing and already I've earned a white belt, the only one in the room. Already I'm an individual, a special, a sore thumb. And after I've finished this Chinese torture session, I'll be an *extremely* sore thumb—Thumb Lee.

I don't really know what a white belt's supposed to mean, but I know it's opposite of a black belt. Black means you've got lethal hands and feet, and that you can kill with no weapons, no textbooks, and you get respect. You don't have to worry about what people think about you. You don't have to hear snickering behind your back, and you can walk the halls of school or go to Arcade Stadium without a care in the world. You don't have to hope your mom is in a good mood when you get home, or listen to her yell and complain about how much you eat.

There are two people in the front row who have black belts. One's a Chinese-looking guy, the other's a black. I guess that's one chink and one jungle bunny you don't wanna mess with. I'm just a white belt, born and raised. I don't know what I did to earn it, but I'll probably be one for the rest of my life. All the reverse punches in the world can't help me.

BEFORE KENNY BEGINS ANOTHER TRAIN of thought, his left shoulder starts throbbing. He tries to ignore it the way he ignored his legs, but to no avail; the pain is there to stay, to taunt and keep him company throughout the exercise. *To convince him to quit.* But he knows he can't quit, despite the painful shoulder. He has to keep going, even though every left punch reminds him where the exit is located.

Suddenly, without warning, his right shoulder joins the assault, and after another minute of punching, a tear makes its way to his chin, and is forced to fall by the relentless streams of sweat. Kenny is in agony. He's had enough, but he keeps punching, searching for strength and endurance he doesn't have. In his mind, he's now shouting with the rest of the class.

Just when his arms are ready to fall off, to submit to the saturation of lactic acid forming in his muscles, the unexpected happens. It starts at the pit of his stomach, and races upward like the mercury of a thermometer dipped in molten lava. So abrupt is the eruption that Kenny doesn't make it to his hands and knees in time. The first spew decorates a portion of his right forearm and both his hands, due to a futile attempt at suppressing the inevitable. Surrendering to his body's regurgitation, he stares helplessly at the carpet as it tries to soak up his vomit. When he realizes the onslaught isn't over, he closes his eyes, and more of his lunch splashes its way to the carpet, leaving a long strand of saliva hanging from his gaping mouth.

With his eyes still closed, he finally notices the silence in the room. The punching and yelling have stopped. Kenny tightens his eyes. Throughout much of his life, he has endured mockery, taunts, and ridicule, but never has he felt so utterly mortified and defeated. He feels the redness in his face, and even though his wave of nausea ebbs away, he doesn't open his eyes, and he doesn't move. Instead, he braces himself, preparing for the all too familiar barrage of teasing and laughter, hoping with all his might that no one touches him.

"Kenny, you alright?"

He opens his eyes and finds himself inside a circle, with Mr. Travers bending over with his hands on his knees. No one else says a word, to him or each other. Other than the faint shuffle of karate uniforms and the gentle hum of the fluorescent lights, it's silent, but Kenny refuses to look at anyone. His eyes remain on the bare feet surrounding him.

Mr. Travers' voice comes closer. "It's alright, son. You ain't the first to throw up in my class. How ya feelin'? Can you stand?"

Kenny wants to cry, but doesn't. He wants to get up and run out, but can't. He finally manages to stand, still looking at Mr. Travers' bare feet.

"Continue with your punches everybody!" yells Mr. Travers, pointing toward the front of the room. Everyone in the class returns to his and her assigned place and resumes punching. Mr. Travers has to raise his voice a little in order for Kenny to hear him over the shouting.

"You go on home now," says Mr. Travers. "You had a good first day. The next class will be at six o'clock on Monday. My son'll be teaching that one. He's a second-degree black belt, but he's only a couple years older than you, so you should have a lot in common. I'll tell him to take it kinda easy." He looks at the carpet. "Don't worry about this, Kenny," he says, masking his irritation. "It's alright. Think you'll be able to make it Monday?"

Kenny doesn't *want* to make it. Listening to the shouts of the class, he's quite aware that he doesn't belong here, but he's also aware that he has no choice. As he looks at Mr. Travers' face, he thinks of his mother. What would she do?

He doesn't know what she'd do, but he can imagine, and with his imagination comes the realization that he'll be here. He'll be here or face the unknown.

Holding back the tears, Kenny responds with the strongest voice he can muster, given his present state. "I'll be here," he mutters.

Thumb Lee must return.

Chapter 2

PAMELA HOUSTON PULLS INTO HER DRIVEWAY at 6:40 P.M. She's running over an hour late. Normally, she's home before the evening news, especially on Fridays, but a stop at the grocery store was long overdue. She hates shopping for food, but there's hardly anything in the cupboard, and even less in the refrigerator. Because of Kenny, she works hard to keep it that way. She still has enough pancake mix, eggs, and sausage to last *her* through next week, but she remembered that yesterday her son had eaten his last grapefruit and fat-free granola bar. This morning, she gave him two eggs—scrambled without oil or butter, of course—and she cursed herself out loud as she poured them onto his plate.

After parking her pampered Acura three feet shy of the closed single-car garage, she grabs her purse and keys with one hand, the grocery bag with the other, and makes a beeline toward the front door with an feigned sense of urgency. Her new neighbors, Carl and Tonya Jacobson, are kneeling in their front yard, trimming hedges. Pamela takes exaggerated strides, trying to avoid having to exchange pleasantries.

She doesn't make it.

"Heeey! Hi you today, Miss Houston? I see you done went grocery shoppin'!"

Pamela glances back three steps short of her front door, and she sees Tonya standing in a pair of dirty overalls. She's also wearing a pair of new garden gloves and holding a pair of shiny garden shears, her back now to the hedges. Her husband continues with his work, sculpturing and clipping at a steady, comfortable pace, refusing to acknowledge Pamela's presence.

"Yeah! Just a few things I needed!" Pamela answers back, and then practically lunges for her door as she readies the house key. She unlocks the recently installed deadbolt and then hears Tonya utter something else, but she can't make it out because of the rattling keys and the crumpling of the grocery bag.

She pretends not to hear Tonya, and, instead, flashes her neighbor a forced smile, steps inside her house, and closes the door. Even from twenty yards away, Tonya hears the lock as it slams into place.

"T'own even know why you waste cho' time wit 'uh," chuckles Carl, keeping his eyes on the hedges. "Dat lady don' wanna talk ta you."

Tonya returns to the hedges. "So what, Carl? I got mannuhs even if *she* don't."

Carl shakes his head. "She'own won't cho' mannuhs."

Tonya frowns and throws her hands on her hips. "Hi you know what dat lady won't?"

"I ain' say I did," Carl shoots back, still concentrating on the hedges. "I said I know what she *don't* won't, an I can tell she *doesn't* won't nut'n na do wit cho' mannuhs."

"Well Carl, you can at least show h'uh dat chew *got* some mannuhs, whethuh she won't 'em uh not. Wha's da sense in ackin' like she ack?"

Carl glares at his wife. "An waste my mannuhs own somebody like h'uh?"

"Wha's da difference? Mannuhs is mannuhs."

Carl gives a quick snort and shakes his head. "Naw, honey. I save my mannuhs fuh people like you, watch dis." He stands and gives a slight bow. "Mrs. Jacobson, will you please go in na house an git me some ice tea?"

"I'll ice tea you awright," she declares, then pulls off a glove and throws it at him before heading toward the house.

"Thank you, Miss Tonya," Carl snickers as he turns back to the hedges. "Thank you very, very much."

PAMELA STANDS IN THE KITCHEN and takes a melodramatic breath. It's been three months, but she still hasn't felt comfortable about her new neighbors. She's never had much experience dealing with blacks, and she resents being forced into such a position.

She recalls how much the neighborhood has changed, how much her life has changed in the last eight years. It seems such a short time ago when she and Warren decided to leave the glorious state of Kentucky, seeking better job opportunities here in Florida. In Lexington, Warren's position at a construction site had come to its final lap, and for the first time in four years, new opportunities were running scarce, right when they needed money most. They had enough saved to sustain them for about six months, but a wife, a seven-year-old son, and another on the way meant a break in cash flow was out of the question. Warren had to find more work, and soon.

At the close of his current job, word was getting around that Jacksonville, Florida was in the process of going though a major face lift—new roads, better bridges, five-star hotels—to better accommodate a city with an NFL franchise. Supposedly, it had become a contractor's paradise. The news was raising eyebrows, and after Warren checked a few leads, the grass definitely seemed greener. Besides, what did they have to lose? So three weeks after giving the landlord of their quaint two-bedroom house a written notice, they headed south in a mid-sized U-haul, loaded with all their belongings and fueled with high expectations.

They arrived in the sunshine state around 11:00 P.M. and stayed in a cheap motel. Neither slept very well, even though the driving was shared. Having a son wedged in the middle forced the passenger, as well as the driver, to maintain an upright position throughout the entire trip. At 10:30 A.M., they grabbed a quick bite at a nearby Waffle House. Afterwards, they moved into a semi-affordable two-bedroom apartment. They could've rented cheaper, but only with blacks living to the left, right, above, and across the way.

At first, the move seemed to be a mistake. Jacksonville was indeed rebuilding, but Warren found it difficult to penetrate the fraternity of the local unions, where seniority ruled with an iron hand. After a while, Pamela decided to do her share of job hunting, despite her husband's disapproval, and within three days, she was hired as a telemarketer at Florida Transtech. Starting pay was nominal, but it was a job. It helped with the bills, and after a few months, allowed Pamela to buy a used Dodge from one of the hundreds of We-Finance car lots splattered across the city, and she couldn't be gladder. She always thought of taking a bus as unbecoming, a stab in one's social status, and was all too eager to throw away all of her accumulated bus schedules.

Eventually, Warren's experience with operating Caterpillar equipment landed him a job with a company notorious for strip malls, fast food restaurants, supermarkets, and the occasional movie theater. The pay was less than he was used to, but what was lacking in pay was promised in longevity.

Finally, everything started falling into place. It wasn't long before their combined income provided hope of, one day, saving enough for a down payment on a house. And at the end of their lease, three months after the birth of their daughter, Amanda, that's what they did, the same house where she and Kenny now live.

She tosses her purse and keys on the kitchen counter and slowly removes the items from the grocery bag, the way a person does when in deep thought.

She thinks about better times, when she always had a man in the house, when there were no black neighbors, when she didn't have to deal with a troublesome son, or the constant phone calls from school, or teacher conferences. Those were the good times, before all of the firm discipline, all of the screaming. But those times are gone, struck down by a black man in a stolen vehicle, a black man who didn't belong in her neighborhood, in her world. Amanda was only four months old.

After counting the grapefruit, Pamela yanks open the refrigerator, which holds a carton of eggs, two heads of slightly browned lettuce, a half of a cucumber wrapped in foil, three Weight Watcher dinner packs, a jar of light mayonnaise, and three cartons of orange juice. She places the grapefruit in the bottom drawer, next to five small containers of low-fat yogurt, and then she does a quick recount.

In the cupboard are several cans of fruit cocktail and sardines. A can of string beans is nestled between a bag of white onions and an almost empty container of olive oil. She places twelve cans of Healthy Choice soup—all chicken noodle—in front of the fruit cocktail. Other than an open box of pancake mix and a bag of rice cakes, that's all that's there.

She places two boxes of low-fat granola bars on top of the refrigerator. The emptied box from yesterday still rests on the counter. For a moment, she stares at it incredulously, then she tosses it into the trashcan. Obviously, Kenny purposely left the empty box on top of the counter, despite her rules about neatness.

This is how he tests her.

A frown twists Pamela's face, and she sighs as she thinks of how she'll deal with him later. She still doesn't know what went wrong, why her son decided to become the monstrosity she now shelters. She remembers how active and vibrant Kenny used to be with Warren. They were always playing in the yard, running and wrestling and laughing. That all ended with the crazy black driver. Nowadays, Kenny just sits around doing nothing, refusing to stay out of trouble or make friends. *Refusing to be a normal kid.*

Kenny was ten before she took serious notice of his weight, thirteen before she decided to talk to him about it. The conversation eventually turned into a bitter, one-sided argument, filled with harsh words, and it ended with her sending Kenny to his room without dinner. That night decided the fate of their relationship, even though Kenny never said a word. She did all of the talking, and eventually, all of the yelling.

Nevertheless, she knew her son was ignoring her, taunting her, challenging her competency as a single mother as he sat quietly, staring at the floor. Well, that night she accepted the challenge, and she decided to do whatever it took to get Kenny back on track. *It would be for his own good.*

However, shortly after she began rationing his breakfast and dinner, Kenny provided a new challenge by becoming disruptive in school. He was testing her on a different scale, but making the results more public. Her frustration was matched only by her shame as the phone calls turned into conferences. At one conference, the term "emotionally handicapped" was brought to the table. She wanted to laugh at the school idiots. What did they take her for? She knew that labeling Kenny meant labeling her as well. Those sneaky, stupid assholes! Yes, her son had become a handful, but he was only being rebellious and clever. They were just too wrapped up with all of their fancy terms to see it.

Well, Kenny may have fooled *them*, but she's no retard. She won't be so readily defeated. She's seen what single mothers found on talk shows are reduced to, begging the host and audience for help that never comes. She will be different.

She eyes the clock on the microwave and gasps; she had no intention of being so late. She grabs the last item from the grocery bag, a bottle of Stoli vodka, and takes it with her into the bedroom, undressing as she closes the door.

*　　　*　　　*　　　*

That's just great. Mom's still home. It's 7:20, almost dark, and she's still home. She's usually gone by six o'clock, but she's home now. That's just terrific. She's probably running late, unless Hank's coming over here tonight. But he never comes on Friday, only Saturdays. Practically the entire neighborhood knows that. You can hear his four-wheeler for miles, but always Saturday nights. That's the way it's always been: Mom *goes* on Fridays, Hank *comes* on Saturdays. They've been seeing each other for over a year as far as I know, and he's never picked her up on a Friday.

But maybe, just this once, he did. Maybe Romeo's trying to

impress her with a little spontaneity, or maybe he won't be able to show tomorrow. Maybe Mom *isn't* home. If that's the case, I won't have to explain why I'm home so early.

Yeah, and maybe there's a note on the fridge right now that reads: "Help yourself." Who am I kidding? When do things go my way? Never. That's why I couldn't keep up with the class; that's why I threw up all over the place; and that's why I know she's home.

I could stay out of sight for a while, wait until the right time to go inside, a time that says I didn't skip out of class early, but there's nowhere to wait in a neighborhood like this, not without causing suspicion among the Neighborhood Watch enthusiasts. They've really been on the ball since the Jacobsons, the third group of blacks, moved in on the block. They seem friendly enough, but then again, so do we.

Guess I'll just go on in, weather the storm long enough to make it to my bedroom. Besides, I'm too tired. Can barely stand for another minute, let alone another hour or so.

AS KENNY WALKS UP THE DRIVEWAY, he starts piecing together what he'll tell his mother should she ask. He knows she will. The martial arts class was supposed to last until seven o'clock, and he was to come home immediately. Not by bus, not by hitching a ride— by foot. Ever since he was thirteen years old, his mother has made him walk home, as long as she didn't consider the distance to be abusive. She told him it was for his own good. Now, no matter where they go together, Kenny always tries to pay attention, always tries to remember his way home, just in case. The Northshore Karate Institute is six miles away, just a stroll for him, even with his aching knees, but he knows he's home way too early.

He approaches the front door with an unconscious stealth and takes the house key from his duffle bag, the one with the sweaty, stained karate uniform. Then he zips it closed to contain the odor. He inserts the key into the door and slowly turns it, forgetting that the click of the new lock can be heard even when his room door is closed. His mother opens the door with a ferocious yank. She's wearing a pair of tight-fitting shorts and a bikini top. Yet only her heels and make-up say that she is indeed leaving.

"Stupid! You scared me half to death! I thought somebody was pickin' the lock!" she roars, then her surprised expression turns to one of suspicion. "What are you doing home so early?" she asks, her voice dropping to a cold monotone.

Kenny isn't ready to answer, so he doesn't. After all, she has taken *him* by surprise. He just stands in the doorway, fidgeting and thinking, knowing that his silence is working against him.

Pamela folds her arms. "Kenny, I asked you a question," she growls. She stands as if she doesn't want him inside, not until he answers.

"Somebody gave me a ride home," he finally murmurs as he slumps into his submissive posture, his eyes on her feet. "I told them I didn't need it, but they wanted to take me anyway. I *told* them I didn't need it."

"Don't you raise your voice to me, boy."

He knows that he hasn't. He hasn't for a very long time, but he also knows better than to say otherwise, so he keeps silent.

"Who brought you home?"

"Some of the guys from class."

Pamela sneers at her son suspiciously. "Well, the next time somebody wants to bring you home, you just tell them that you want to walk, tell them that you *have* to walk, to get rid of some of that flab. Tell them that! They'll understand then. You got that? Can you remember that?"

"Yes." As soon as the word leaves his mouth, he closes his eyes, realizing that he has slipped under fire.

She grabs the strap of his duffle bag. "Yes, *what*?" she yells.

"Yes . . . ma'am."

"Get in this house!" she croaks, taking one step to the side. Kenny slides inside, being careful not to brush against his mother with any force, being careful not to rub her the wrong way. "You're gonna respect me, Kenny," she continues. "You'll respect me if it kills you. You hear me?"

"Yes, ma'am."

Pamela's eyebrows shoot to the ceiling. "Did you say 'yes, ma'am?' That's what you said, right—'yes, ma'am?'"

Confused now, Kenny doesn't answer. He has no idea where this episode is going, but he's positive that it's going somewhere—he smells the vodka.

"Let me show you something," she says, motioning for him to follow her into the kitchen. "Come *here*!" He joins her in the kitchen where she stands next to the trashcan, holding the lid in one hand. "What do you see in here?"

Kenny looks inside the trashcan, but has no idea what the correct answer will be, what response will get him to his bedroom. "Garbage," he mutters, almost in the form of a question. Her slap leaves his left ear ringing.

"Don't get smart with me!" she hisses. "I don't have time for your bullshit! What's that on top?"

Still not knowing what she's talking about, he has to look inside the trashcan once more. "The granola bar box?" he asks, with a small tremble in his voice. Never has he wanted to be more right. All he wants to do is get to his room, take the weight off of his knees and feet.

"Riiiiight, a granola bar box," she says mockingly. "Where was it before it got to the trash?"

It finally hits him. He's being accused of not throwing away an empty box, but he knows he's innocent. Obviously, she had given him the last granola bar yesterday, and he wasn't about to approach a box of granola bars planted on the kitchen counter. He thought it was bait. How was he to know the box was empty? She's the one guilty of leaving the box out, but he knows the vodka says differently. He doesn't have a chance. Two against one.

"You're always testing me, Kenny," she says, in the tone a judge might use during sentencing. "I don't know why, but you love to test me. I ask you to do one thing, you do another. We agreed a long time ago that you should start walkin' off some of that weight. What do you do? You grab the first damn ride that comes along! You leave trash everywhere, fight at school all the time. How do you expect to ever make friends if you're gonna fight with everybody? Hell, even your body don't wanna mind!" she declares, waving the can lid just inches from his face. "I give you nothing but healthy food. Look here . . . !" she says, snatching the refrigerator door open. "Look at this! Just look! You got stuff for salad! You got grapefruits! I get you all kinds of health stuff! But you keep . . . gaining . . . *weight*! How much do you eat at school? You can't be eating *that* much in thirty minutes, but you know what? Go right ahead." She pokes him in the forehead with an index finger. "But between me and this karate class and whatever else it takes, Kenny, you're gonna learn some"—she pauses to find the word—"*discipline*!

"So . . ." she says, slamming the refrigerator door, ". . . every time you get a ride home, you don't eat. Every time you leave your mess around, you don't eat. And if you get into a fight with anybody at this new school you're going to, you don't eat. If I'm lucky, I won't have to go grocery shoppin' for you so damn much. Besides, skipping a meal here and there might do you some good." She takes a deep breath. "Now . . . do I make myself clear?"

"Yes, ma'am."

"Good," she says, smiling now. "We'll start tonight. You don't eat because of taking that ride home."

An unexpected silence rips through the kitchen. She waits to see if he has any rebuttals, any words of protest or defense. Kenny has everything and nothing to say. The phone interrupts the moment. Pamela drops the trashcan lid on the floor and prances to the living room, grabbing the phone as if she'd just polished her nails. The kitchen phone was torn off the wall after her heated discussion with Kenny's ex-principal at Susan B. Anthony.

"Hello? Yes, baby, I'm on my way now . . . well, what do you think I'm wearing?"

Kenny knows by his mother's sudden lifted spirits that she's talking to Hank. He collects the lid and places it on the trashcan, another trap dismantled. He tries, but can never find all of them.

He wants to go to his bedroom so badly but stays in the kitchen. He knows his mother isn't finished with him, isn't satisfied.

After she hangs up the phone, Pamela runs to her bedroom. In the center of the kitchen floor stands Kenny, waiting. Five minutes go by. He waits. Another five minutes go by. He shifts his weight to the other leg. Three minutes after that, Pamela rushes from her bedroom to the kitchen, trying to fasten an earring in her earlobe.

"Open the refrigerator," she commands, still fumbling with her ear.

Kenny obeys with a gentle tug on the door.

"I've counted everything in there, Kenny. *Everything.* I've also counted everything in the pantry. Don't be stupid. You can eat in the morning. You may not believe this now, but it's for your own good." She closes the refrigerator door and places a hand gently on his shoulder. "How was the karate class?"

"It was good," he replies, knowing that anything but a positive answer would risk another episode. If not now, later.

"That's good. Mommy loves you." She kisses him on the cheek and heads toward the door. "I won't be too late," she says, and then slams the door.

Kenny listens to the sound of her heels as she runs to the car. In less than twenty seconds, the sound of the car fades as she races off to God knows where. It's now safe for him to take the weight off of his knees and feet. Safe for him to go to his room. To lie down. To get some rest. To cry.

Chapter 3

ONCE AGAIN, COLD WINDS CLEANSE the night air. The outside temperature is far from freezing, but for the true Floridian, it's an uncomfortable chill. It's the time of year when thermostats are lowered during the day and raised at night. Tentative spring.

For several hours, the chilly breezes have been making their way into Kenny's open bedroom window, washing over his uncovered body. He lies face up on his bed, wearing nothing but boxers. He's spent half his life in Florida, but has always preferred the cold. Lately, since the implementation of his mother's "walks," he has learned to revel in it.

His alarm clock sounds at 12:30 A.M. Eight minutes go by before he hears it; he's still tired. Nevertheless, he grunts to his feet, staggers across the room, and peers out of his window at the still vacant driveway. On Fridays, his mother's routine is to come home no earlier than four in the morning. It's his routine to see if she sticks to hers.

She's still gone. She usually gets home just before it gets light outside, but you can't be too sure . . . not with her. With the window open, I'll hear her when she pulls up. Wherever she goes, she never spends the night. Wish she did.

A damn granola bar box! Now she's trying to starve me for the things that *she* does. That's a new one, but I should've seen it comin'. Senility's startin' to kick in. Sooner or later, I'll probably get blamed for that, too.

Why does she do it? Why does she hang onto me when she doesn't even want me? I'm not her son; I'm her problem. When she looks at me, all she sees is a fat, violent retard; a fighting Dumbo who's always slipping up big time. Far too many slip-ups for a mother to be proud of, but she hasn't been my mother for a very long time.

I can't even remember the last time we did something as a family, but we haven't been a family since . . . the incident. We've never been happy together with just the two of us. All of my good memories, memories of playing and acting crazy with Dad, are before the incident. We were always horsing around, clowning and going at each other no matter how tired he must've been from working all day. Once, I baptized him with a full pitcher of water while he was reading the paper. Got him good, too. Soaked the paper, the couch, and the floor, but not a voice was raised. I ran outside when he started refilling the pitcher, but he still got me back. Mom never joined our escapades, but she never complained either, never went psycho. She'd just warn us about breaking things.

Shortly after the incident, she became a different person. Not sad or anything like that, just *different* somehow, like she'd been kidnapped by aliens from outer space, and I'm now living with an imposter, and not a very good one.

She didn't cry at the funeral. She held it in, and we've never talked about the incident to this day, but, like I said, we never really talk about anything. She may not miss Dad, but I do. I was in my room napping when it happened. I was awakened by the squeal of the tires and the awful crash in front of the house. That's where it happened, right on our sidewalk. Both Dad and Amanda died instantly—at least, that's what we were told. The car had flipped on its side, but the guy driving the car wasn't even scratched—a black guy at that! Guess how many times Mom and I said "nigger" that year.

Dad's death got her a lot of money, and she started buying things and going places. She took me everywhere she went when I was younger, but it was only because she didn't want to leave me behind. *Why not?* I could always tell she didn't want me around. In the beauty salon, I was always given the same seat, the one on the other side of the wall that separated those being fixed up from those waiting to be fixed up. It was the seat out of her view, the one that said I didn't belong to her. At the grocery store—I'm talking about when she used to do real grocery shopping—she always told me to wait for her at the entrance, and there I stood, without even a seat.

The mall wasn't so bad. Whenever we went there, she'd give me ten bucks to stay in Arcade Stadium while she shopped for two hours. I felt like a puppy on a leash, but playing games helped me ignore the feeling. Unfortunately, ten dollars only lasted for about an hour, and then I'd have to wait another hour or so for her to come by and collect me. The first time I decided to catch up with her in the mall, after blowing the ten bucks, she raised my leash to twenty bucks. Twenty bucks kept me at the Stadium for at *least* two hours. Mom once commented on how strange it was that I never made friends there. Strange to her, but not to me.

She still says she loves me, but she says a lot of other things too, shit that sticks. She says I'm worthless to her, just a mouth to feed. I can't do the yard the way she likes, clean the house the way she likes, wash the car the way she likes, make the grades, lose the weight, or stay out of trouble. I can't do anything, no matter how much she gets on me, no matter how much I try—and I really do try, just because.

I don't know . . . maybe if I started doing things right, things would be normal—whatever the hell "normal" is—but to tell the truth, I'd be happy with just getting my mom back, getting rid of the alien. I miss my mom about as much as I miss my dad. The incident killed one but took both. I'm on my own now, living with an alien. No family, no friends.

Never did make any friends. Don't recall ever getting the chance. I remember the day I told Dad about how the kids made fun of me in school, calling me "chubby" and making pig noises and stuff. He told me that they were jealous little nothings, and that if people aren't friendly to me, I can't ever call them a friend. He also told me to ignore them if I could but fight back if I had to. *Never fight, always fight back.*

That was fourth grade. Back then, I never had to fight; ignoring them was enough, but now, it's different. Now, I can't walk away; they won't be ignored. No way.

Couple of years ago, Mom decided to join their ranks. One night, she started lecturing and advising me on my eating. She complained about how I just sat around the house, not making friends, not acting like a normal kid. *The alien had arrived!*

I didn't say anything, just listened. I was too surprised. Then she started calling me names like everybody else does, and she got really mad. I was mad too, but I was also scared. I didn't know what the hell was happening! That wasn't Mom! Next thing I know, she's making me walk and making me starve. She even cleaned out the kitchen. The alien won't be ignored either.

AFTER STANDING IN FRONT OF THE WINDOW for a few more moments, enjoying the caress of the night air, Kenny takes a long, hot, massaging shower. After he finishes, he makes certain the bathroom floor is dry, the faucet isn't dripping, and everything is in its place, before turning off the bathroom light and slipping into a new pair of boxers. He then goes to the kitchen, where he fixes a tall glass of ice water. He remembers to fill the ice tray before returning to his room, drink in hand.

He flicks on the bedroom light and places the glass on the nightstand. Then he walks over to his closet and pulls out a huge television box. It's filled to the top with books, and he has to give it four good drags to get it halfway out of the closet.

Ever since losing his father and best friend, he has read books.

No more playing.

No more laughing.

No more going outside.

Just reading.

For years, his only friends have been the likes of Edith Wharton, Nathaniel Hawthorne, and John Steinbeck. He has walked home with Alice Walker, William Faulkner, and Charlotte Bronte. He's fallen asleep with such voices as Richard Wright, Ernest Hemingway, and even Shakespeare still in his head. It doesn't matter to Kenny. He'll listen to any author who cares to talk to him. For the past few days, he's been with Daniel Defoe.

He grabs *Robinson Crusoe* from the top of the stack and tosses the novel onto the bed. Then he stretches his arm toward the corner of the closet, the same corner where the television box was, and retrieves two shoe boxes. He opens the Nike box and removes two candy bars and an opened pack of doughnuts. From the Adidas box, he takes a half scoop of Kool-aid mix from a container, dumps it into his water, and places the lid back on the can. From the same box, he also takes one of five packs of cookies. The bottoms of both boxes are filled with money and game tokens. He removes five dollars, then returns both boxes to the corner of the closet. Afterwards, he tucks the money inside his duffle bag.

Tomorrow, his mother will give him twenty dollars to spend at Arcade Stadium while she entertains Hank. Including the walk time, Kenny will be gone for more than five hours, and his mother knows it. On occasions when she wants even more private time with Hank, she'll give her son thirty dollars. She knows how much Kenny loves the arcade. What she doesn't know is how skilled he has become, far more skilled than the little boy she used to abandon with a twenty-dollar leash. For years, twenty dollars has been way too much money for Kenny, but he has never said a word.

The fighting Dumbo is no idiot.

Chapter 4

S ARAH PARKER SUSPECTS SHE WAS THE ONLY one
walking toward the dining table. In fact, she's certain of it. She
believes that Tony was heading for the love seat, and his mother,
Mrs. Avery, was heading for the recliner, but now they follow Sarah to
the table. They're treating her like a guest, and *that* she doesn't want.

"We don't have to sit at the table," she says, hoping they'll take her
up on her offer. "Let's have breakfast the way you two normally do."

"We g'own all have breakfas' right at dis h'yuh table, sweethar'd,"
insists Mrs. Avery, trying to conceal her embarrassment. "Dass what
decent folk do, an Ah'm as decent as da nex' person."

"Oh please forgive me, Mrs. Avery. It wasn't my intention to come
across as . . . condescending," says Sarah, the desperation in her voice
sounding loud and clear. "I just want you to feel at ease. There's no
reason to be uncomfortable in your own home."

Mrs. Avery pauses for a moment as if considering Sarah's words.

All Tony can do is smile. The way Sarah uses words like "intention"
and "condescending," as easily as he uses "yeah" and "no," is one of
the hundreds of reasons he loves her. At the university, he'd heard his
share of phony intellectuals who'd dish out multi-syllabic words, trying
to impress by using pretentious, academic voices. Wannabe aristocrats
who would strain their brains to say "hello" in ten words or more.

Sarah is the real thing, bred from a family found in the upper middle-class portion of the socioeconomic spectrum. Well read, well versed, and trained in every etiquette rule imaginable—before Sarah, he had no idea there was so many—making it easy to dub her as a snob. When they first met, he knew she was a snob. It took him two study sessions and a first date to conclude he was judging a book by its cover.

"Tell ya'll what," says Tony, "why'own cha'll two sit at da table, while I sit own na couch." He turns to the love seat, knowing his mother will never allow it.

"Boy, git cho' behine na dis table," demands Mrs. Avery. "Dese grits gitt'n cole."

Tony returns to the table and signals to Sarah that it's okay to be seated. She doesn't understand the grin on his face but sits anyway, timidly.

"I apologize for any—"

"Ain' no need da apologize," Tony says, realizing Sarah may be feeling uncomfortable. "If it was juss me an Mama h'yuh, we'd be sitt'n ovuh nex' ta da TV. It was out uh habit dat we was head'n fuh da livin' room."

"Well, we can still—"

"No, honey," declares Mrs. Avery. "We fine right h'yuh." She bites into a slice of bacon. "Besides, I cane be watchin' no TV. I need da siddown an talk ta my fewchuh daught-in-law. Tony wrote so much about chew while he was in college dat I feel I already know ya, but we still got uh lot ta talk about."

"In uh way," adds Tony with a smile, "us head'n fuh da TV is uh sign dat we *do* feel comfthable roun' ya."

Mrs. Avery rolls her eyes. "Don' pay him no 'tention, baby," she says assertively. "Ah'm na one should be apologizin'. It was bad mannuhs. Been so long since I had somebody in h'yuh, dass all."

"Oh, I do understand, Mrs. Avery, but it's my ardent wish that I not be treated as an outsider. Perhaps I've been behaving as an outsider. If that's—"

"Na don' go talkin' crazy," Mrs. Avery interrupts. She places a hand on Sarah's forearm. "You my son's fiancée. Ain' exactly family yet, but as close as anybody g'own git. Na eat cha food," she says, pointing at Sarah's plate. "Dis yo' firs' time eat'n grits, an I'own won't cho' firs' time na be cole. Don' *nobody* like no cole grits."

The unforced nature of Mrs. Avery's kindness leaves Sarah with few words. The more she gets to know Tony's mother, the more she likes her. She's like no other Sarah has ever known. She gives Tony a smile, and he responds with a quick wink.

"What chew wankin' 'bout?" Mrs. Avery asks her son.

"Nut'n, Mama." Tony attacks his scrambled-eggs-with-cheese.

"Dass all you g'own eat? Why you ain' git no grits? You ain' even got no bacon. You'own like grits an bacon no mo'?"

"Eggs an toas'll do me juss fine, Mama. Ah'm gitt'n ready da go ta da paurk. I tole Bone an Cletus I was g'own play ball wit 'em nis mornin'. Cane be playin' own uh full stomach."

Mrs. Avery crinkles her nose in a frown. "Why you gotta see dat ole devilish Bone? Boy what'n no good when you was h'yuh befo', an he sho'nuff ain' no good na. He ain' *nevuh* g'own be no good, Tony. I'own even see why Cletus be roun' 'im all la time."

Tony doesn't respond. In high school, he was a star debater, but he rarely wins an argument with his mother. Mrs. Avery's words drift in the silent air, and then Sarah initiates small talk by making an inquiry on the proper ways to eat grits. As Mrs. Avery launches into a seminar on grits, Tony's thoughts find their way back to his mother's comments. She has never understood her son's attachment to Bone, but neither has Tony.

He first met Bone on the courts one day when he and Cletus were just kids. They were playing twenty-one, a basketball game that's never played one-on-one, especially in *their* neighborhood. Too many players, not enough balls. Bone appeared from nowhere and asked to join in. He was much bigger and older, the perfect specimen of a bully. What choice did they have? Bone could've just taken the ball away from them. His asking was merely a formality. Their "yes," survival instinct.

But Bone never took advantage of his rank. He treated them as equals, a humility that fertilized a relationship that, over the years, withstood all the warnings and finger-shakes Tony's parents had to offer. Tony and Cletus learned to like Bone, despite the talk of the neighborhood. It had always been an unlikely, yet resilient friendship.

When Tony's father died, Bone was there for him, watching over him, keeping him safe from bullies, allowing Tony the freedom to study and make the grades without harassment. Mrs. Avery had always pushed Tony to do well in school, but she never knew what it took, how risky it could be to stand out, to swim against the current.

From an adversarial point of view, Bone understood Tony's dilemma better than anyone. In school, Bone was someone to contend with, the enemy of all "potentials," an over-achiever's nightmare, a title he maintained until dropping out.

"Hey, boy! Wha's wrong wit chew?"

Tony blinks absently at his mother, raising his eyebrows. "You talkin' na me?"

"I say, is you ready?"

"Ready fuh what?"

Mrs. Avery drops her fork on her plate. "You ain' h'yuh uh thang I said."

Sarah clears her throat. "Your mother wonders whether you're prepared for the rigors of being a school teacher."

"If *you* cane pay attention na grown folk," says Mrs. Avery, "why should da chill'un pay attention na you?" She rolls her eyes. "Sitt'n nare daydreamin'."

Tony finishes his last bite of toast. "I was juss thankin', Mama, dass all."

"Thankin' 'bout what? 'Bout hi dem kids g'own run all ovuh ya?"

"No. I was thankin' hi I should be goin'—G'yuh you girls uh chance ta git ta know each othuh bedduh."

"Lookadare, Sarah," Mrs. Avery says. "Ain' been h'yuh uh whole day, an he already leavin' his mama."

"Mama, I'll be back in uh couple hours." And with that, he kisses them each on the forehead, gives Sarah another wink, and heads out the backdoor, leaving the burglar bar door unlocked.

"Dat boy is somp'm else," says Mrs. Avery, warding off the silence.

Sarah smiles, her eyes still on the door. "Yes. Something else entirely."

Mrs. Avery offers a mild chuckle. "Chile, wha's uh girl like you doin' wit uh boy like mine?"

Sarah places a hand on Mrs. Avery's forearm. "Enjoying every minute of it, I assure you."

Mrs. Avery's smile widens.

They finish their breakfast with pleasant, light conversation, talking about such things as the Florida weather, life in the South, and the experiences Sarah and Tony had at the University of Virginia—their study sessions, their dates, their leisure pastime. Eventually, Mrs. Avery provides confidential information concerning Tony's wonder years, info Sarah more than readily accepts. By the time their talk ends, they are sitting side by side on the love seat, heads buried in a photo album.

Afterwards, Mrs. Avery decides to shower before cleaning the kitchen. When Sarah hears the sound of running water coming from the bathroom, she takes the opportunity to drink in her surroundings. The modest, two-bedroom house isn't half the size of her parents' home, but it's well kept, and no space is wasted. The walls are neatly cluttered with pictures and portraits. And every corner, shelf, and small table holds a treasured ornament, an interesting artifact, some personalized trinket. The home arouses all of Sarah's senses, not unlike the way Paris or Hong Kong alerts the awareness of the average American tourist. Tony's house—no, his *life*—is foreign territory to her, an undiscovered country, but she embraces it the way one would a trip to Tahiti—a permanent trip.

When she takes the dishes into the kitchen, she sees that there's no dishwasher, so she fills the sink with soapy water and submerges all the dishes, just seconds before Mrs. Avery comes around the corner, startling her.

"Honey, what chew call yo'self doin'?" Mrs. Avery asks. She's wearing sweat pants, a University of Virginia t-shirt, and a towel wrapped around her head.

Sarah continues scrubbing a plate with a pot scraper, not looking at Mrs. Avery. "I thought I'd start on the dishes, make myself useful. You've been so considerate with—"

"Chile, sit cho'self down," Mrs. Avery says with a grin. "Ain' no guess uh mine g'own be doin' no dishes. I'll take care uh dat. Leave 'em lone."

Sarah stays with the dishes. "No really, Mrs. Avery, I don't mind. Besides, I shouldn't be considered a guest. In a few months, I'll be your daughter-in-law. I'll be family, and—"

"Until you an my son walk down nat aisle, you uh guess in nis house, young lady. Na g'own siddown an let dat breakfas' you ate digest. G'own na," she says, shooing Sarah away.

Sarah keeps her eyes and hands in the sink. "Mrs. Avery, I *insist.*"

Mrs. Avery takes one step back and raises an eyebrow. "Oh, you do?" she says, smiling now. "Well, since you insis' so much, why'own chew insis' own lett'n nat fry'n pan soak fuh awhile. Itta take you fuh'evuh ta clean it na, even wit uh pot scrapuh." Then she heads for Tony's bedroom, where Sarah slept while Tony spent the night on the couch. "Baby girl say she *insis',*" she says, shaking her head. "Tony done messed roun' h'yuh an foun' hisself uh bonafide woman."

"Mrs. Avery, I've already made the bed this morning, if that's where you're heading. If I'm to become a member of the family, I might as well act the part, don't you think?"

Mrs. Avery comes back around the corner and stands in the doorway again, one hand on her hip, the same chuckle in her voice. "Tony's been family longuh dan you, an I still haff ta git own nat boy 'bout makin' nat bed."

Sarah finally makes eye contact with Mrs. Avery. "Well, Mrs. Avery, I'll definitely have a talk with him about that."

"You *do* dat." She heads toward the love seat. "An if you g'own be uh par'd uh dis family, you bettuh star'd callin' me 'Mama.'"

A warm sensation flows through Sarah, right before the smile comes to her face. Suddenly, she realizes that Mrs. Avery's been wanting to treat her like a daughter all along, to make her feel at home.

That's what decent folk do.

Chapter 5

BEFORE TEN O'CLOCK, THE PARK IS always quiet. Sometimes, birds rustle through the trees that shade the basketball court, but not today. It's totally silent, save for an occasional breeze navigating through the trees' upper branches.

Tony's the only person in the park. A few minutes ago, a morning jogger entered through the front entrance, hugged the perimeter of the baseball field, and exited through the torn opening in the fence at the back of the park.

The echo of Tony's dribbling is almost hypnotic to him, adding to the sense of serenity. By releasing the ball with a high arc, he makes another free throw—six in a row. He feels good knowing he hasn't lost his game. At the university, before becoming wrapped up with Sarah, he played at least twice a week with a few of the guys who were usually found on the campus courts. But those games never compared to those he remembered playing on this court. Here, a code of knees and elbows had always been prevalent. A foul wasn't a foul, it was a complaint, and all players were expected to keep their complaints to a bare minimum. Only a wuss gripes, and nobody likes a wuss.

As he concentrates on his next free throw, he fails to notice the three figures snaking up behind him.

"G'yus dat ball, punk!" cries Bone as he snatches the ball on the up-dribble.

"BONE? Aw man!" screams Tony. He latches onto Bone in a vise-like hug, pinning Bone's arms to the side and making him lose the ball.

"Damn! Can uh nigguh breathe?" Bone grunts.

Cletus recovers the ball and starts dribbling through his legs. "Da college boy done came home!"

"Cletus Waters!" exclaims Tony. They exchange their patented handshake, and then give each other a macho embrace. "Damn, I missed ya'll!"

"I could'n believe dat was you own na phone lass night," says Cletus. "Home fuh good, huh?"

"Yeah, man, home fuh good."

"'Bout cracked one uh my ribs, nigguh," says Bone, pretending to nurse his left side.

"Sorry, Pops," Tony says. "Ah'm juss kind uh glad da see ya'll." He finally glances at the third member of their party. "Darryl, lass you?"

"Hey, Tony," says Darryl. He drops Bone's duffle bag and taps fists with Tony. "Wha's up, dawg?"

"*You*, man!" Tony says, and then looks at Bone. "Yo' brothuh done got big!" And then back at Darryl, "Looka chew, Darryl! 'Bout tall as me. What grade you in na?"

Cletus puts an arm around Darryl's neck, almost choking him. "Darryl g'own be uh seniuh nex' year."

"Go head own, Darryl," says Tony. He gives Darryl a quick slap in the stomach. "Ain' no tellin' whey it could lead." And then to Cletus, he asks, "So, what chew been doin' na lass fo' years?"

"I got uh job workin' at da warehouse own Jenkins St."

"Jeffuhson Papers?" Tony says incredulously. "Must'uh took you fuh'evuh ta git uh job in nat place."

"An don't chew know it. Dey finely called, dough. I work da forklif' na."

"Oh, so you rollin' in it na, huh? I know whey da go if I need some pocket change."

"Yeah right," says Cletus as he shoots a jump shot, all net, "you bettuh try Lotto."

Tony bounces his head up and down. "Well, looka h'yuh. Cletus still got game."

"He *thank* he got game," says Bone. "Still cane hang wit me."

Tony takes a hard look at Bone's expensive sweat suit that's much too nice for sweating. "I see you ain' doin' too bad fuh ya'self eithuh, Pops," he says. "Looka chew. Got uh nice watch, jewelry—da whole nine. Whey you workin'?"

"Ah'm self-employed," says Bone, and then motions for Darryl to toss him the ball.

"Listen na him," says Darryl. "Talkin' 'bout he self-employed."

"Dass right, nigguh! Th'o me da damn ball!"

Cletus sighs and shakes his head. "He slangin', Tony."

Tony eyes Cletus suspiciously. "Slangin' what?" Then to Bone, "Rocks? You uh drug dealuh?"

"Street pharmacis'," corrects Bone, staring Tony down. No smile, no frown, but a look that says—what? Tread carefully? Tony isn't sure.

"You ain' no drug dealuh," Tony finally says with a forced chuckle, but he knows by Cletus' expression that it's no joke. Bone keeps staring at Tony, still no smile or frown. Tony glances from Cletus to Darryl, and then back at Bone. "What . . . What chew doin' sellin' drugs?" he manages to ask.

"Makin' mo' money dan all ya'll put togethuh," claims Bone, and with that, he snatches the ball from Darryl, takes a shot from the free throw line, and misses. Darryl fetches the ball and passes it back to his brother.

Tony glances back at Cletus, and Cletus looks away. "Damn, Bone. . . ." Tony says.

Bone takes another free throw shot and misses again. "Damn Bone *what*?"

Tony pauses for a second, then shrugs and says, "Whatevuh. It's yo' life. It's juss good da see ya'll again."

Bone grins. "It's good da see you too. You *know* you like uh son na me." He turns to his brother. "Darryl, I used ta take care uh dis boy. Tell 'im, Tony."

Tony forces a smile. "He ain' ly'n." He motions for Darryl to toss him the ball. "School would'uh been somp'm else if it what'n fuh Pops."

Bone releases a snort. "Kids used ta be pickin' own Tony, try'n na git dat ass, Darry. He had uh *lot* uh kids try'n na whoop dat ass."

"Why dey messed wit chew?" asks Darryl.

"His grades," Cletus adds. "Tony always did make good grades, an all la teachuhs liked 'im, too. Dass worse dan putt'n uh sign own ya back."

"Yeah, Darryl," adds Bone, rubbing Tony on the top of the head, "an his mama was strick own nat homework, too. I was strick own everybody leavin' 'im 'lone. What'n his fault his mama made him stay in na house all la time—all lat studyin', an homework, an housework, an yard work. Shit, Tony was uh workin' fool. His mama was har'd, boy—I tell ya." He eyes Tony. "Ah'm surprised yo' mama let chew come na see us na. Don't chew haff ta re-roof da roof uh some shit? Pick some cotton?" Then he chuckles and says, "An she nevuh did like us anyway. Hi you escaped dis time?"

"Nevuh liked *you*," corrects Cletus. "She ain' got no problem wit me."

"Well, Ah'm uh grown man na," Tony states firmly. He makes another free throw. "I ain' got ta be sneakin' out da yar'd no mo'."

"Daaamn!" exclaims Darryl, laughing. "Sneakin' out da yar'd?"

Bone chuckles louder. "Darryl, his mama used ta say, *you ain' leavin' dis yar'd 'til you finish dat homework.*" Then he nudges Tony on the shoulder. "Da whole block could h'yuh 'uh."

"She'own know dat ch'all like family," says Tony, but he doesn't appreciate the humor.

"So you leff da yar'd fuh dese fools?" asks Darryl, still laughing.

"Yeah, but he brought 'is homework wit 'im," adds Cletus, a comment that causes everyone to laugh even louder.

Tony stands with his hands on his hips, trying to force a smile. "She was juss lookin' out fuh me. Try'n na be uh mama an uh daddeh ain' all lat easy."

"Whey yo' daddeh?" asks Darryl as if surprised that Tony has a father.

Tony shrugs. "He g'own."

"G'own whe'uh?"

"His daddeh was shot," explains Cletus. "Hi ole was we, Tony?"

"Seven."

"I was eleven," adds Bone, dribbling the ball. "His ole man caught two in na chess an one in na leg when somebody broke in ney garage."

"Fuh awhile, Tony was havin' nightmares about it," recalls Cletus.

"Yeah," adds Bone, "he used ta h'yuh gunshots in 'is sleep all la time. Membuh dat, Tony?"

"Yeah . . . I remembuh."

"Soun' like yo' daddeh needed da be strapped," says Darryl.

Tony looks at Darryl with a slight frown. "He *was* strapped. Mattuh fack, he shot da man *firs'*. Did'n kill 'im fass anuff dough. Da man got off seven shots, an still managed ta crawl out da yar'd. He finally died in na hospital, but my daddeh died right dare in na yar'd."

Cletus nudges Darryl on the shoulder. "You been livin' in nis neighborhood long anuff ta know you'own shoot at nobody wit'out gitt'n shot back at."

"If you wanna proteck yo' family," adds Tony, "you git burglar bahs uh somp'm. You'own juss buy uh Smith an Wessin thankin' you uh bad ass. Da man wit da Glock's uh bad ass, too."

"We g'own play some ball uh what?" asks Bone.

Tony takes a deep breath. "Dass what *Ah'm* sayin'." He rubs his hands together. "I need da take ya'll la school befo' Mama come up h'yuh talkin' 'bout it's lunchtime. My fiancée cane keep 'uh busy fuh'evuh."

"FIANCÉE?" exclaim Cletus and Bone in unison.

"Damn, nigguh!" Bone shouts. "When was you g'own tell *us*?"

"You gitt'n married?" asks Cletus.

Darryl chuckles. "Well, lass what it mean na have uh fiancée—you git married."

Cletus turns to Darryl and grabs his crotch. "Marry dis."

They all laugh, and it feels good.

"I would'n be able la fine uh rang small anuff," Darryl fires back.

More laughter.

"Awright . . . you got me," Cletus says, but he gives Darryl the finger, and then looks at Tony. "What she look like?"

Bone grins. "She fine ain't she? You nevuh did mess wit no ugly women."

"Tina," murmurs Cletus. Then he slaps a hand over his mouth as if the name slipped out.

"Tina who?" asks Darryl, and then quieter, "*Hyena* . . .Tina?"

Bone slaps a hand over his mouth as well. "Oh damn! I fuhgot all about dat bitch!"

Darryl's eyes become golf balls. "No! No! Nooo! Tony, dey ain' talkin' 'bout *dat* Tina! I know dey ain' talkin' 'bout *dat* Tina!"

Tony shakes his head and places his hands on his hips. "Tina what'n ugly," he mutters.

"Shit!" Darryl gasps. Then he joins Cletus and Bone in their laughter and frolicking.

"She *what'n* ugly," Tony insists. He tries to hide his irritation. Tina was just a friend, but he feels he should defend her anyway.

"Dat lady . . . *hairy*, Tony!" says Darryl, coughing now.

"As hairy na as she was den!" adds Cletus.

"An she used ta put own all lat lotion!" adds Bone.

Cletus gives Bone a high-five. "Made 'uh look like uh wet dawg!"

"Damndes' thang I evuh did see," adds Bone as he clutches his ribs, laughing. "Uh German Shepherd wit uh Jerry curl!"

Tony waits until the laughter subsides and then says, "My fiancée's name is Sarah, and believe me, she doesn't look anything like Tina. Not to say anything derogatory toward Tina, but they are night and day." He says this in Standard English, with flagrant articulation.

"You met 'uh in college?" asks Darryl.

"Yes."

Bone's attitude shifts. "So what do 'Sarah' look like?"

"She's about five-foot-four, pretty, and she's one of the—"

"Wha's wrong wit chew, Tony?" asks Bone, obviously annoyed.

Tony looks at Bone oddly. "There's *nothing* wrong with me."

"So why you talkin' nat talk?" Bone hates it when "black talks white," as he calls it, and Tony knows it.

"Talkin' what talk?" asks Darryl.

Cletus knows the question is a rhetorical one but answers anyway, trying to keep the mood light. "Whenevuh Tony used ta git serious about somp'm back in na day, he always talked dat school-book English. He was own na debate team in high school."

"He star'd talkin' *white* is what 'e be doin'," says Bone.

Cletus groans at Bone's words, certain that even after five years, it's still the wrong thing to say to Tony.

"I'm not talking white," Tony says, frowning now. "If yu'd like me ta tawk wide, I'd be more'n happy ta accomidate cha, young feller. Ya peckerhead sum'bitch. . . ."

Bone doesn't join the explosion of laughter. "Den wha's wrong wit chew, Tony?" he asks, more irritated now.

"Not a thing, Pops," Tony says, still in an incongruous tongue. He wants to switch from Standard English back to English, but he knows that Bone won't let him.

"What she look like in na face?" asks Cletus, still giggling from Tony's impersonation.

"She uh redbone?" asks Darryl.

"Not exactly."

Brimming with agitation, Bones says, "Damn, nigguh! What she look like?"

Tony sighs and gives Bone a quick, pondering look. This isn't the setting he had in mind. "Sarah has a pretty face," he finally says. "She has long, brown, curly hair. Hazel eyes. Her teeth—"

"WHAT?" interrupts Bone. The ball lands on his foot and rolls off the court. No one takes notice as it nestles in the grass.

"She white?" Darryl asks.

Tony doesn't answer. He fetches the ball, dribbles to the free throw line, and prepares for a shot—and the onslaught.

Cletus clears his throat. "Tony . . . you marryin' uh white girl?"

"Nope," he replies. "She's all woman." He misses his first free throw.

"Well . . . I'll . . . be . . . *damn*," says Bone. "Dis nigguh done ran off ta college an back, an na he like white women."

"I don't like white women," argues Tony. He retrieves the ball, avoiding all eye contact. "I like kind, sweet, pretty women. It's her parents' fault she's white. They said it runs in the family."

Cletus and Darryl manage to keep their laughter down to a snicker, but it doesn't prevent Bone from glaring at them. He plants his hands on his hips. "Damn, nigguh, I thought I raised you bettuh dan nat."

Tony stops dribbling. He knew the news would be a surprise, but never an issue. After all, they had always accepted *him*, regardless of his success in school. Cletus and Bone were always able to see past his grades, his accomplishments, the disfavored book cover his academic life had become. He looks directly at Bone with challenge in his eyes. "What's that supposed to mean?"

"Yeah, wha's dat supposed ta mean?" snickers Cletus.

Darryl decides to assist in the fomentation. "Yeah, bruh. Wha's dat supposed—"

"Ya'll know what Ah'm talkin' 'bout," fumes Bone as he steps toward Tony, just short of a breath's length. "All lem good grades you made. You'd thank you'd have sense anuff ta stay own yo' side uh da fence."

"Every fence has its gate," Tony murmurs. He avoids all eye contact. Bone's words are starting to dig deep, and Cletus and Darryl's joking isn't helping the matter.

Darryl nudges Cletus but keeps his eyes on his brother. "He foun' uh gate, Bone!"

"Ya'll stop trippin'," Bone says. "Da fence ain' *got* no gate." He gives

Tony a side look. "You eithuh jumped it, uh crawled unduh it." When Tony doesn't respond, he adds, "Dass what it *is*. Dis white girl got cho' ass crawlin'."

As the two instigators' bellowing approaches hysteria, Cletus manages to throw another log onto the fire. "Damn! She got chew crawlin', Tony? Say it ain' so, man! Say it ain' so!"

"I told you," Tony says. "I found a gate." He watches Cletus and Darryl enjoy the moment, laughing it up, while he stands in a thick fog of tension and irritation.

Bone glares at Tony incredulously. "What gate? Ain' no gate! Ain' . . . no . . . damn . . . *gate*!"

"Then we built one," says Tony, hoping with each response he'll find words that will suffice, that will end this session while his demeanor is still sociable. He's feeling badgered.

Bone eyeballs Tony as if dumbfounded. "What?"

Darryl snickers as he tilts his head toward Cletus. "Built one? How you do dat, Cletus?"

Cletus shrugs and grins at Bone. "I'own know. How you bill uh gate, Bone?"

"Tony out uh his goddamn mine," grumbles Bone. "You cane juss bill uh gate. Hi in na hell you g'own juss bill uh gate?"

Tony shrugs. "Sure you can. All one needs are the right tools."

"So what we talkin' h'yuh, Tony?" snickers Darryl. "Hammuh an nails?"

"More along the lines of dinner and a movie," replies Tony.

Cletus nudges Darryl. "I guess da nailin' came latuh dat night."

The comment even takes Tony by surprise as he joins in with a small, but welcomed chuckle.

"Yeah, ya'll keep own laughin' wit da Unca Tom," retorts Bone.

The laughter stops.

The dribbling stops.

Cletus and Darryl finally realize that Bone is serious, that he has been angry the entire time. Being called an "Uncle Tom" by another African-American is almost the equivalent of being called a "nigger" by a white person—a black-on-black offense—and Bone sounds as if he means it.

"Oh—what?" Bone says, challenging the sudden silence. He's satisfied in finally gaining their attention. He turns back to Tony. "Sistuh's ain' good anuff fuh you? Is dat it, Tony?"

"Bone!" warns Cletus. "You gitt'n out uh han', man."

"Dat man can like any culluh he won't," adds Darryl.

"It's not *about* color!" snaps Tony. His temper now hangs by a silk thread.

Bone lurches forward, satisfied by Tony's outburst. "Den what da hell is all lis shit about, Tony?" he asks, in a tone warranting safe distance between speakers.

Cletus stands coiled, ready to step in if necessary.

"It's about what I like!" Tony shoots back. Then he takes a deep breath to try and regain his composure. "Jesus—some people like red apples; some people like yellow apples; I just want one without worms. Why is that so difficult to understand?"

"Hey, less all juss hole han's an sang some ole Negro Spiritual," offers Cletus.

Bone ignores Cletus and stays focused on Tony. "Preach own, nigguh! I'own give uh damn what chew say 'bout apples, an worms, an whatevuh! I still say you done fuhgot what it mean na be black!"

The silk thread breaks. "FORGOT?" huffs Tony. He steps a little closer to Bone, but not too close. "I never *knew*! Tell me, Bone! What does it mean to be black? Just what in the hell does it mean?"

"It mean knowin' what country you livin' in, nigguh! Whey you thank you at?"

"So, a passing grade in Geography makes you black? I earned an *A* in Geography. I guess you don't get any blacker than that, right?"

More snickering from Darryl and Cletus.

"Oh, so you thank dis shit funny, Tony?" Bone sneers.

"No. I think *you're* funny. I'm not saying we don't have racial issues to contend with, but I refuse to sit on my ass my entire life bitchin' about what the white man's doing. And besides, whatever he's doing,

Sarah has nothing to do with it. But you tell *me* something, Mr. 'Street Pharmacist'—why aren't you a real pharmacist? Did the white man tell you not to go back for your GED? Not to get a real job like Cletus? Not to go to college? Hell yeah, it's tough being black—shit yeah. But it doesn't hold you back. So what's holding *you* back, Bone? What's holding the street pharmacist back? Does being black mean having a good excuse to fail? A good excuse not to try and get—"

"It mean stickin' wit cho' own kine, nigguh! An lookin' out fuh yo' own people!"

"Oh, and I suppose you only sell that shit to white people! Is *that* what you want me to believe?"

Cletus steps in. "Fellas, dis gitt'n way too serious." He takes the ball from Tony. "Damn, Bone, leave da man alone. He can marry who he wanna marry, as long as he happy." He turns to Tony. "You happy, Tony?"

Tony returns Bone's intense glare. "Ecstatic."

Darryl claps his hands together and steps forward. "Okay, so less play some ball. Tony say he g'own take us ta school, but all I been seein' is uh bunch uh free th'os."

For a moment, no one says a word. Tony and Bone seem poised for battle, their staring contest still engaged, and then, suddenly, Bone decides to yield. "G'yuh me da ball, Cletus," he demands. "Come own, Tony. Take me ta school."

Tony regards Bone curiously, but eventually shrugs with a sigh of relief. "Oh, you ain' finta try me one own one," he says with a deflated smile. "You ain' *nat* crazy."

"Juss me an you," says Bone as he dribbles the ball.

Cletus backs up to give them room. "Go easy own 'im, Bone. He been away fuh awhile."

"He been away *too* long," says Bone. "His head's all messed up. I bet his game's messed up, too." He shoves the ball to Tony. "Check!"

Tony refrains from further comment. Bone's *check* sounds more like an *en garde*. "Check," he mumbles, then tosses the ball hesitantly back to Bone.

Bone rushes in with a strong dribble, knocking Tony down to score a lay-up.

Tony springs back to his feet, frowning. The tactic exceeds anything he remembers. Bone is playing by new rules. "What chew doin'?"

"Dass two," Bone says and dribbles back to the starting position. "Take me ta school, Tony—Check!"

Tony sighs as he tosses the ball back. "Check."

"You can take 'im, Tony!" says Darryl.

"G'yuh 'im some D, Tony," adds Cletus.

Bone rushes in the same way as before and scores another lay-up. "Fo'- zip," he says. "Take me ta school, Tony—*Check!*"

"I'own know dis game," says Tony. He tosses the ball back, but this time, when Bone rushes in, he's greeted by a good shoulder block that knocks him on his ass. Tony quickly gathers the ball and makes a lay-up. "But Ah'm uh fass learnuh—two fuh me."

Cletus and Darryl burst into laughter.

"Shut up!" warns Bone and then returns his focus to Tony. "Come own, nigguh," he hisses. "Less see what chew got."

Tony tosses the ball to Bone. "Check."

Bone shoves the ball back. "*Check!*"

Without dribbling, Tony scores a jump shot from where he stands. "Two plus two is fo'," he says with a smile.

"Daaamn!" says Cletus, placing a hand over his mouth.

Darryl starts jumping all around the edge of the court. "He takin' you da school, Bone! He said he was g'own take you da school! You in uh maff class na! You h'yuh dat? Two plus two is fo'! Two plus two is fo'!"

"Shut up, nigguh!" snaps Bone. "Befo' I buss yo' *ass* fo' times!"

"Maff *an* Gym class," corrects Tony.

Bone stands erect from his defensive stance. His eyes become two horizontal slits. "So da educated nigguh thank he smartuh dan everybody?"

Cletus flops his hands to his sides. "Damn! He juss jokin', Bone!"

"Well, don' be jokin' wit me!" Bone barks back. "I ain' nobody da play wit!" He steps to Tony. "You thank since you done went off ta college dat chew smartuh dan me?"

Tony sighs. "No. I think not selling drugs makes me smarter than you." He looks at Cletus. "Cletus, Ah'm g'own head own home. You wanna come?"

"Come own, Tony!" pleads Cletus. "Fuh'git about dis fool! Less play some ball!"

"Me an you can play latuh," says Tony, ignoring Bone. "I won't chew ta meet Sarah."

"Stay off ma basketball coat," Bone warns.

Tony's head whips around. "*Yo'* coat? Lass time I checked, dis basketball coat was da *city's.*" He turns to Darryl. "Nice ta see you again, Darryl. Keep dem grades up."

"You got it, man," says Darryl as they tap fists. "Tell yo' mama I said hey."

"You heard what I said, nigguh," growls Bone. No one noticed him retrieve the gun from the duffle bag, the 9mm Taurus now aimed at Tony's face. "Stay off . . . ma coat."

Tony doesn't think about dying, nor does he think about his fiancée, or even running. His only thought is how disappointed his mother would be in him, should Bone decide to pull the trigger. He sees the expression on his mother's face. Vivid. Distracting. So distracting that he doesn't even realize he has stopped breathing.

"Git dat thang out uh his face!" yells Cletus. He carefully grabs Tony by the arm. "Less go, Tony."

Tony takes four backward steps before turning around and walking out of the park with Cletus. He never glances back, but he still sees the barrel of the gun, pointing at his forehead.

Check.

Chapter 6

TONY'S WALK HOME TAKES LONGER than his walk to the park. The neighborhood is up and about now. Children are playing in the streets; elders are rocking on their porches; cars are cruising slowly up and down the roads, stereos blaring; and many people call out to Tony when they see him and Cletus strolling by.

The temperature is almost at its noon high, but Tony easily endures the heat. He says a few words to every child who waves him down. He leans inside the window of every car that honks and stops, and he stands at the step of every porch that calls his name. Thanks to his mother, the neighborhood has known for some time that he was coming home, and many eagerly express how glad they are to see him again. Every smile, every handshake, every tapped fist, and every kind word comforts him like a homemade quilt that's been handed down from generation to generation.

Cletus keeps up with Tony's lazy pace. They haven't said a word since leaving the park. "You awright, man?" Cletus finally asks.

"Hi long he been dealin'?" Tony asks, abruptly. He doesn't look at Cletus, and he doesn't stop walking.

Cletus shrugs. "I'own know. 'Bout two years, I guess."

"Two years . . . an you still hangin' wit 'im. . . ."

"Man, you know Bone."

"I'own know Bone na Drug Dealuh," Tony shoots back.

"Come own, Tony. He ain' nat much different dan when you leff."

Tony stops and looks directly into Cletus' eyes. "You tell *me*, Cletus. What would happen if I *did* set foot back own nat coat?"

Cletus' mouth opens quickly, but nothing comes out. He honestly doesn't know, and isn't about to give an answer that would put Tony in danger. He has seen Bone pull his gun on Tony, and he has seen Tony pull his fancy talk on Bone. Until today, both were inconceivable, and he now realizes how much more he may not know.

"Dass what I thought," murmurs Tony as he starts walking again.

Cletus wants to say something, but has no idea what would be appropriate. "So what chew g'own do?" he finally asks.

Astonished, Tony looks at Cletus, as if he has just asked whether the earth is round or flat. "Ah'ma stay da hell off dat coat—what chew *thank?*"

Surprisingly, the comment causes them both to release a small chuckle that immediately disappears. Tony feels a trace of guilt because this is no time for laughter. He has lost a friend today. A week will pass before he realizes that he also lost his basketball.

Trying to improve Tony's mood, Cletus says, "So tell me 'bout dis Sarah."

"Aw man. It's so much ta tell, I'own even know whey da star'd."

Cletus shrugs. "Star'd from na beginnin'."

Tony goes silent for a moment and then says, "We met uh couple uh years ago in my Intro da Ed class."

"She g'own be uh English teachuh too?"

"Naw. She uh Special Ed majuh."

"She g'own teach retar'ded people?"

Tony frowns a little. "Naw. I mean, dey'own *haff* ta be. I'own know. *She* g'own be da Special Ed teachuh, not me."

"What cha'll doin' in na same class?" presses Cletus, confused now. "Should'n Special Ed teachuhs be takin' *special* classes?"

"Dey *do*," Tony replies. Still, he knows by the look on Cletus' face that a more thorough explanation is needed if the conversation is to go any further. He stops again. "See, uh lot uh da classes, *everybody* gotta take. In uh lot uh ways, uh teachuh's uh teachuh, an if you g'own teach *anythang*, dey got classes you g'own haff ta take no mattuh what chew g'own teach. Don' ax me why, dey juss *do*."

Cletus pauses a moment as if allowing Tony's words to sink in. "So hi ya'll hooked up?" he finally asks.

Tony starts walking again. "Well, we ain' hook up right off da bat. At firs', I ain' even like 'uh. Da firs' day uh class, she come walkin' in na classroom all propuh, like she got uh book own top uh h'uh head uh somp'm. She sat right nex' ta me."

"Den you put da moves own," Cletus says with a grin.

Tony smiles. "Naw. She ain' even *look* at me Ah'm try'n na tell ya. Star'ded talkin' all sadiddy wit dis girl behine me, right? Like she juss *all* lat. Ain' even look at me."

"Sitt'n right nex' ta ya?"

"Dey'own talk ta ya, 'less you talk firs'. You git used ta it. But damn, she ain' even *look* at me."

"See? You shoulda went ta Mo'house."

"Mo'house ain' g'yuh da bess scholuhship."

"Okay. So you sitt'n nare, an she dissin' ya—"

Tony shakes his head. "Naw. She what'n *dissin'* me."

"Well, she what'n *talkin'* ta ya."

"I tole ya, *nobody* talk ta ya."

Cletus frowns. "Well damn, Tony! Hi ya'll got togethuh?"

"Da professuh had uh habit uh makin' us split off in na groups. I hated when professuhs did dat, but dass hi we worked own uh lot uh thangs in nat class," Tony explains. "Da firs' time na professuh tole us ta make groups, I look aroun' na room na see what group Ah'ma squeeze in, right? Nobody looked at me. Hell, everybody already *had* dey group befo' da professuh said anythang—hell, since da ferse *day*. Den, all uh sudden, Sarah tapped me own na back an tole me I could join ney group, but I could tell by da look own ney faces dat she ain' bothuh axin' nem firs'."

Cletus snorts. "Dey ain' won't chew jumpin' nat fence."

"Dat ain' *even* funny."

"Yeah it was."

Tony playfully shoves Cletus away. "*Anyway*—da nex' time we had da make groups, it's juss me an h'uh, right?—an anothuh girl who was kine uh nice. Da othuh three ended up in othuh groups. Da professuh had ta han' pick people ta even out da groups," Tony shakes his head. "An ney g'own be teachuhs. Ah'm suhprised dey ain' draw straws uh somp'm."

"So, Sarah liked ya?"

Tony shrugs. "I'own know. I thank she was juss bein' nice. She helped me feel mo' comthable," he says thoughtfully. "She star'ded talkin' na me even when we what'n in groups. Little by little, we got ta know each othuh, 'til one day I axed 'uh if she won'ted ta study togethuh."

Cletus gives a wicked smile. "'Course she said yeah, right?"

"Yeah, but guess whey we studied at."

"In na library?"

"Naw."

Cletus grins. "At cho' place—da dorm?"

Tony laughs. "Naw! We went ta h'uh house."

"Dass good, ain' it?" asks Cletus, still grinning.

"H'uh *parents'* house."

The grin vanishes. "H'uh what?"

"Yeah."

"Dey was dare?"

Tony smiles. "Whey you *thank* dey was g'own be?"

"Oh, well I was thankin'—"

"Yeah, I *know* what chew was thankin'." Tony chuckles and gives Cletus another shove. "It what'n like dat."

"So, ya'll juss studied?"

"Yeah."

"In h'uh room?"

"Come own, man."

"Awright, awright," concedes Cletus. "So what h'uh parents do when ney saw *you* comin'?"

"Dey ain' do *nut'n*."

"Dey what'n suhprised?"

"Dey ain' *look* suhprised."

"She must'uh tole 'em."

Tony shrugs. "Maybe. I what'n thankin' 'bout it," he admits. He stops walking. "It felt funny, dough. I was real nervous uh somp'm. I'own know."

"Fuh what?"

"Standin' own na porch, wait'n fuh h'uh ta open na doh—dass when it hit me."

"What?"

Tony's eyes lock with Cletus' eyes. "When was da lass time *you* set foot in uh white person's house?"

Cletus doesn't answer. He has never been in a white person's home, but he tries to imagine what it looks and smells like inside. Most of his imagery comes from television shows and movies—this, he knows—but he rationalizes that, in reality, there can't be much difference. Except for the sofa being in the center of the room—as seen in practically every sitcom—similarities between Hollywood and real life must exist. "What it looked like inside?"

"Oh, it was nice," says Tony. "Dey got uh big two-story house—all la bedrooms upstairs. Dey got uh gran piano sitt'n—"

"Was da sofa in na middle uh da room?" Cletus interrupts.

"What room?"

"I'own know—da livin' room, I guess."

"What about it?"

"Whey dey *sofa* was at?"

"In na livin' room," says Tony. "Dey got three. Two in na livin' room, an one in na den."

"But whey dey was *at*?" presses Cletus.

"Who?"

"Da *sofas*."

Tony frowns. "What? You lost me. Whey da who—?"

"Nut'n . . . dass awright, man," says Cletus, not wanting to sound stupid. "What happened nex'?"

Tony shrugs. "We studied. An check dis out—dey got dey *own* library."

"What?"

"In na house. Dey got uh room nass uh small library. Dass whey we studied."

"Daaamn."

"Dass what I said when I firs' saw it. 'Course, I ain' say it out loud."

"What dey *do* fuh uh livin'?"

Tony shrugs again. "H'uh daddeh's uh doctor—uh neurologis'. Somp'm na do wit da nervous system. H'uh mama work in uh lawyuh's office, but she ain' uh lawyuh uh nut'n. I'own know what chew call 'uh. Sarah tole me, but I fuhgot."

"Dey ain' ack funny uh nut'n?"

"No."

"*Nut'n?*"

"No."

"Da whole time?"

"Da whole time," assures Tony. "I even ate dinnuh wit 'em afthuhwoods."

"So, da fo' uh ya'll juss—"

"*Five,*" corrects Tony. "She got uh brothuh, too."

"*Big* brothuh?"

"Naw. He 'bout Darryl age."

"Hi *he* was?"

"He was awright. We got along. He got uh *big* comic book col-lection," Tony recalls. "Got all la good ones, too." He pokes Cletus in the shoulder with an index finger. "You know dat boy got uh *Batman* numbuh one hundred. He got it fuh his birfday."

"Daaamn. He got Spawn?"

"Dat boy got *all* la Spawns."

"So, all ya'll sat aroun' eat'n an read'n comic books?"

Tony shoves Cletus away. "Oh, you funny," he says. "We ate at da dinnuh table."

"An all ya'll talked togethuh . . . like *nut'n?*"

"Like nut'n."

"What ch'all talked about?"

Tony waves at a woman who's watering the flowers in her front yard, then turns back to Cletus. "Dey mostly juss axed me questions about *me*. Stuff like, why I wanna be uh teachuh, whey Ah'm from, an all lat kine uh stuff."

"H'uh daddeh axed you all lat?"

"*Everybody* was axin' me stuff. It made me feel good, too, 'cause I ain' know *what* ta ax dem. Even Sarah was axin' me stuff—fuh h'uh *an* h'uh brothuh."

Cletus gives Tony a double take. "Fuh h'uh brothuh?"

"Oh, I fuhgot ta tell ya. H'uh brothuh deaf."

"Deaf?"

"Yeah. She was translat'n fuh 'im," explains Tony. "Dass why she goin' in Special Ed."

Cletus tilts his head slightly. "Ta teach deaf kids?"

"Ta teach kids dat need special teachuhs, but mostly deaf kids, yeah."

"So, she g'own be bettuh dan na average teachuh," states Cletus.

"In uh lot uh ways, yeah."

"Bettuh dan you?"

Tony smiles. "She *already* bettuh dan me. Nices' person in na worl', too." He pauses for a moment and then says, "Kevin's probbly got uh lot ta do wit hi nice da whole family is."

"Damn, Tony. Who's Kevin?"

"Oh, h'uh brothuh."

"What he got ta do wit dem bein' nice?"

"Sarah tole me 'bout some uh da mess dey done put up wit juss 'cause Kevin cane h'yuh. People ackin' funny, treat'n Kevin different." Tony shrugs. "Da way I figguh, dey done had dey share uh people judgin' Kevin by what he cane help, dat dey done learnt not ta do it. It's gotta have *somp'm* na do wit it."

"So, dey said ya'll can git married?"

Tony contorts his face. "Damn! Slow down, man. When I firs' went ovuh dare, it what'n even uh date uh nut'n. We was juss studyin'."

"Okay, you done loss me again," admits Cletus.

They both wave at a car that honks as it drives by.

"It what'n uh date," Tony repeats. "We juss studied. Nobody, not even Sarah, thought dat we'd end up dat'n. It what'n in ney mine."

"But it was shonuff in *yo'* mine," says Cletus with a smile.

"You damn right," chuckles Tony. "You thank Ah'ma follow some ugly girl home?"

Cletus grins. "What about Tina?"

"Oh, you *real* funny today," says Tony as he feigns a backhand.

Cletus ducks. "Awright, man. Well, cut th'ew all la bullshit. Hi ya'll hooked up?"

Tony shrugs. "Afthuh 'bout da forf time we studied at h'uh house, I juss axed 'uh out."

"Juss like dat?"

"Juss like dat."

"An she juss said yeah? No problem? Did'n even thank about?"

"She axed me what took so long."

"An nass it?"

"Dass it." They both go silent for a moment, and then Tony says, "We star'ded spinnin' uh *lot* uh time togethuh. If we what'n goin' na da movies uh dinnuh uh juss fuh uh walk, we was studyin'. We star'ded gitt'n along *real* good."

"I guess ya'll did. Hell, ya'll gitt'n married. She muss be got some good stuff fuh you da be gitt'n married."

Tony frowns. "Man, you ain' gotta go dare."

"What? You hitt'n it, aint cha?"

Tony responds with silence.

"Ah'm sorry, man," Cletus finally says. "I ain' mean na be disrespeckin' you an yo' ole lady."

After a few steps, Tony says, "I know, man. It's juss dat it ain' like dat. It's kine uh har'd da explain." He takes a small breath and pauses, groping for the right words. "She juss make me feel good when Ah'm aroun' 'uh, ya know?" He shrugs. "I'own know."

Cletus gives Tony a quick slap on the back. "Ah'm happy fuh ya, man."

Tony smiles as he walks, his eyes aimed at the ground. "Dare was dis one time own uh date, she axed me why I did'n soun' like I was from na South. I tole 'uh dat I could, an so she axed me ta show 'uh. Dat was uh *big* mistake," he says with a chuckle.

"What?"

"I could'n do it! I ain' even thank about it when she firs' axed me, but when I star'ded to, I could'n."

"Why not?"

Tony starts laughing. "Hell, I'own know! It felt funny, fuh one thang. Don' ax me why, but it did. Plus, I ain' even know what ta say. What da hell was I supposed ta say? An she was lookin' at me like I was gitt'n ready ta do uh magic trick uh somp'm. Da whole thang struck me funny, so I juss star'ded laughin'. Then she axed me what was funny, an I could'n even tell 'uh *dat*."

Cletus isn't sure he understands either, and for a moment, he wonders what Bone would say to this. "So, she'own know what chew soun' like fuh real?" he finally asks.

Tony regains his composure. "Yeah she do. I let 'uh listen na one uh ma phone calls ta Mama. Know what Sarah said afthuh I hung up?"

"What?"

"Dat I got uh wonduhful accent." Tony starts snickering again.

"Well, lat juss mean I got uh *wonduhful accent* too," adds Cletus with a laugh.

"Boy, looka h'yuh," says Tony. "I 'bout fell out when she said dat." He settles down again and looks directly at Cletus. "She make me feel good, Cletus. I'own know. I cane explain it."

"Maybe you ain' *supposed* ta be able la explain it."

Tony turns his eyes back toward the ground and takes a deep

breath. "I spent uh whole semestuh savin' fuh uh rang," he admits. "I axed 'uh right befo' da Christmas holiday, an she ain' say, 'Yeah,' she said, 'Of course.' You h'yuh me? *Of. . . course.*"

"Made yo' day," says Cletus, smiling.

"Boy, looka h'yuh—Ah'm h'yuh da tell ya," says Tony, grinning back. "I spent my lass two years cookin' par'd-time in uh restaurant an savin' money."

"But what 'uh family had da say? Dey g'own come ta da wedd'n?"

Tony stops walking. His house is less than a block away. "Cletus . . ."

"What?"

". . . dey *payin* fuh it."

"Daaamn. I bet dat suhprised *you.*"

"Hell yeah! 'Specially when I thought about hi much I owed 'em fuh all la food I ate at dey house."

"What?"

"Dey pretty much fed me th'ew da lass two years uh college. Mama say she what'n suhprised."

"So, I guess it ain' bothuh yo' mama none."

"You know hi Mama is," says Tony as they start walking again. "She juss worried 'bout what dis *worl'* g'own do more dan anythang, but she definitely don' mine. She would'n even let me send h'uh uh plane ticket ta ma graduation. She said I should star'd savin' as much as I can na."

Cletus shakes his head with a smile. "Yo' mama juss don' like fly'n, nass all."

"You know it. I'own know *who* she thank she was foolin'. Cane nobody git h'uh in uh plane. But she what'n g'own leave Miss Annie anyway."

"Yeah, I fuhgot about Miss Annie," Cletus admits. "She ain' doin' too good from what I heard."

"She ain't, from what Mama say. Anyway, I ain' wanna maurch since Mama what'n comin. So, Sarah took da Sprang semestuh off, so she could come down h'yuh an see 'uh. She g'own be h'yuh fuh uh few weeks."

"Well, when ya'll gitt'n married?"

"I won'ted ta wait 'til Sarah graduated, but she say she g'own finish h'uh lass two years h'yuh at UNF, afthuh we git married. She wanna git married dis summuh. Dass why I came back. I know people h'yuh, an I knew I could fine work at Lincoln. Dey *always* hirin' from what Principal Hernandez tole me."

"Our ole principal? Well, why you don' work dare at Prudence Crandell?"

Tony shakes his head. "Prudence Crandell don' have no openin's in English, but Principal Hernandez knows da principal at Lincoln. All it took was uh phone call. He said dey g'own handle all la papuhwork when I get dare, but dey won't me ta star'd Monday."

Cletus shakes his head. "Hell, Tony. Even Booker T. Washington woulda been bettuh dan goin' na Lincoln."

"Dass uh skill centuh," Tony fires back. "I'own wanna teach at no skill centuh."

They enter the gate located in the back of Tony's yard, but they go around to the front of the house. Tony's mother doesn't take kindly to guests using what she calls the "nigguh doh." They pause at the front steps.

"Ya know, Tony, Lincoln ain' got no bettuh since you leff," warns Cletus. "Dey always hirin' 'cause teachuhs always *leavin'*, an fuh good reasons, too."

"I know, but I'own wanna live off uh Sarah's bank account. I need uh job. I ain' g'own stay dare long. Juss g'own pay ma dues, finish out dis year. Hopefully, by next fall, I'll be done foun' somp'm bettuh. I'd like ta work at Chamblin, uh maybe Dean Clifford uh Sojourner Truth. Besides, I *did* go ta college, ya know. I learnt hi da deal wit *some* thangs in ma Classroom Discipline course."

Cletus chuckles. "I hope yo' ass learnt hi da fight, college boy."

Tony grins and knocks on the door. A few seconds later, the door opens, but the burglar bars don't.

"Oh! They're everywhere," says Sarah. "Just one moment!" She disappears into the house.

Tony aims his surprised look at Cletus, who's equally surprised. The next thing they hear is the sound of Mrs. Avery's voice, followed by the jingling of keys approaching the door. It takes Sarah a few awkward seconds to find the right key before she finally opens the door.

"We were hoping that you'd return soon," she admits, and then she gives Tony a quick kiss, ignoring his sweaty face. She looks at Cletus for the first time and says, "Hello."

Cletus clears his throat. "Hey." Not knowing what to say next, he maintains his initial smile.

"Sweetie, dis Cletus," Tony says. "Cletus—Sarah."

Sarah beams. "Cletus Waters. It's a pleasure to finally meet you. Tony has spoken of you a great deal."

Cletus' eyebrows rush to his hairline. "He . . . *have?*" he manages to say, and then, turning to Tony, he adds, "I hope he haven't told you nothin' bad."

"All positive," Sarah says. "I assure you." She backs into the house. "Well, come inside! You two must be roasting in this heat. The humidity makes it almost unbearable."

When Sarah heads back into the house, Cletus grabs Tony by the arm. "You ain' tole 'uh nut'n bad, did ja?" he whispers.

Tony grins. "I'own 'membuh," he says, and then he clears the three steps with one hop.

Cletus locks the burglar bar door behind them, and then he hangs the keys on a nail located on the left of the door frame. They follow Sarah to the den, which used to be the back porch before the late Mr. Avery modified it, during the summer before he was killed. As a porch, it could barely accommodate two rocking chairs. Now, it houses the loveseat, recliner, and the small dining table where breakfast was served. The furniture was bought by Tony's father, and it has never been rearranged.

Mrs. Avery rests on the love seat, holding a plate that bears a final bite of a sandwich. "We was hopin' you git back h'yuh befo' long," she says. "Hi you, Cletus?"

"Ah'm okay, Miss Avery."

"Yo' mama doin' okay? I ain' see 'uh in church lass Sunday."

"Yes, ma'am. She went ta Moun' Zion lass Sunday."

"Oh, h'uh sistuh church?"

"Yes, ma'am."

"I need da git out dat way one uh dese Sundays," Mrs. Avery says thoughtfully. "Been uh while since I done heard Pastuh Williams preach."

Tony notices that his mother is wearing her walking shoes. "Mama, you gitt'n ready ta go somewhere?"

"Me an Sarah gitt'n ready ta walk up ta Miss Annie's. We was try'n na wait own *you*."

Tony glances at Cletus, and then back at his mother. "Mama, le'me hang wit Cletus fuh uh lu' while. I'll see Miss Annie latuh own."

Mrs. Avery's eyes widen a bit. "Boy, you bettuh g'own fix you one uh dese san'wiches so we can come own h'yuh," she warns, and not too gently. "Miss Annie been wait'n uh long time na see you."

"Come own, Mama," pleads Tony. "I wanna talk wit Cletus fuh uh lu' while. I'll see 'uh latuh."

Sarah smiles. She's never seen Tony pout before, and she thinks it's cute.

Unfortunately, Mrs. Avery thinks it's anything *but* cute, and she gives him a glance that could easily be misconstrued as the Look of Death. "What I juss tell you, boy?"

Sarah carefully steps in. "Ma-*ma*, they probably haven't *quite* finished their male-bonding." She moves over to Mrs. Avery, faces the two men, folds her arms, and raises one eyebrow. "I'm sure Tony will meet us there *shortly*. If he doesn't, he'll have both of us to contend with."

Tony looks from mother to fiancée, and then back to mother. "Right! Dass what I meant, Mama. I'll be right behine ya'll."

Mrs. Avery frowns at him for a moment, and then says, "Don't chew keep us wait'n fuh'evuh own you, Tony."

"I won't, Mama," he says, and then kisses his mother on the cheek. "Juss tell 'uh, Ah'm own na way."

The Look of Death melts away. "Help me up from h'yuh, boy." Mrs. Avery grunts to her feet and says to Sarah, "I'll be back in uh minute, baby girl. Ah'm juss g'own wash ma face an hands real quick."

"Take your time, Ma-*ma*," Sarah says. "I'll whip up the sandwiches for these two gentlemen."

"You ain' got uh do dat," says Tony. "I can—"

"Oh no, no, no! I insist."

"Dare she go again," chuckles Mrs. Avery. "Ya'll bettuh back up *na*." She places her plate in the kitchen sink and heads for the bathroom, still chuckling and mumbling about Sarah's insistence.

"What chew makin'?" asks Tony.

"Ham and American on wheat," Sarah says. "We don't have Swiss." She looks at Cletus. "Is that all right? Ham and American?"

"Yes, ma'am," he says with a nod and a smile.

"With lettuce and tomato?"

Cletus takes a seat at the dining table. "Dat soun' good ta me."

"And mayo?"

"Yep."

When Sarah goes into the kitchen, Tony takes her by the hand and leads her around the corner into the living room. He gives her a tender kiss. "I love you, Miss Parker, soon to be Mrs. Avery," he whispers.

She throws her arms around his neck and kisses him again. "Not soon enough," she whispers.

Tony grins. "You and Mama have obviously been getting along."

She caresses the back of his neck. "As only girls can."

"One suggestion for the future," he says.

"And what's that?"

He brings his lips closer to her right ear and says, "You can place the emphasis on the first 'ma,' or have no emphasis at all, but never, never, *never* place the emphasis on the second 'ma'."

"Mama?"

"Exactly."

They kiss again before releasing each other, and Sarah finishes the sandwiches seconds before Mrs. Avery returns. She sets the plated sandwiches and two glasses of milk on the table. "Enjoy," she says, smiling at Cletus.

Cletus grins back. "Thank you. Dis look *real* great." He scoops up the sandwich and pushes the plate to the side.

Mrs. Avery stands with her hands on her hips, shaking her head. "I declare, Tony. Dis girl g'own spoil you rott'n."

The two women say their good-byes to Cletus before heading for the front door. Again, Tony reassures his mother that he won't be long, and after he watches them disappear down the sidewalk, he locks the burglar bar door and hurries back to the den. Cletus has already finished half his sandwich.

Tony sits with his arms folded. He looks at Cletus as if waiting for him to say grace.

"What?" Cletus asks with a stuffed mouth.

Tony sucks his teeth. "What chew *thank*?"

Cletus takes a few seconds to swallow before replying. "Ain' no worms in nat apple, Tony," he finally says, shaking his head. "No worms at all." Then he packs the rest of the sandwich into his mouth.

Tony smiles. "She make uh mean san'wich, too."

Chapter 7

KENNY READS THE DIGITAL CLOCK on his nightstand. It's 2:27 P.M. On Saturday, routine has it that if he doesn't shower by three o'clock, or show in some other way that he's getting ready to leave the house—combing his hair, tying his shoes, fumbling with his duffle bag—his mother will conduct an episode. Hank usually arrives around four o'clock, and Kenny is to be nowhere in sight. He will know what time to return home by how much money his mother has placed on the kitchen counter.

Twenty bucks or thirty, he wonders.

He knows that the money is already waiting for him, and he knows that his mother is dressed like a loose teenager and is now waiting for him to leave the house. The sooner, the better. She no longer has to remind him of what day it is. The need for words vanished long ago. For some time, Saturday has been a carefully orchestrated routine.

He's spent the last two hours cooped in his room, reading about the exploits of Robinson Crusoe. Crusoe has just discovered footprints on the beach and is beginning to put into verse his waves of paranoid delusions. Despite Kenny's ascending interest in the novel, he dog-ears the page and places the book inside his duffle bag. He isn't about to endure one of his mother's episodes for a marooned moron on an island.

He gathers a few clothes from a drawer. As he heads for the bathroom, he glimpses his mother lounging in the living room, watching television. She's wearing *the* blouse and *the* miniskirt. He knows that her outfit is different from the one she wore last night, maybe even different from the one she wore last week, but he doesn't remember in what way.

Something on the television has won her attention. She doesn't notice him or his involuntary frown. Kenny quickly glances inside his mother's bedroom. The door is usually closed but is now wide open. He isn't surprised to see that everything has been put in its proper place. The bed's made; the clothes are off the floor; the glasses have found their way to the kitchen. It's definitely Saturday.

He enters the bathroom and leaves the door cracked. After turning on the shower, he nudges the shower curtain into the path of the warming water for more noise. Then he strips out of his boxers and steps into the shower. After wetting his hair, he grabs the soap, holds it just above his head with two fingers, and lets it drop noisily to his feet. He does this twice more before finishing his shower. After dressing, he gives his hair three quick whisks with a brush and grabs his duffle bag.

On his way to the kitchen counter, he announces, "I'm leaving."

Pamela ignores her son as she continues aiming and clicking the remote at the television. The remote never leaves her hand whenever she's watching television. Kenny has never touched the remote, but he knows all about it. He isn't allowed to touch the precious television when his mother isn't home, and he refuses to watch it when she *is* home. So he cannot remember the last time he has watched a television program, but he doesn't care. For a long time, reading has suited him just fine, and it gives him a solid excuse to stay in his bedroom. That's why he's familiar with the remote. When the television was bought two years ago, after a violent thunderstorm claimed their late 19-inch, the owner's manual made its way to his bedroom. He doesn't remember how many times he's read it, but he probably knows more about the remote than his mother ever will.

Kenny takes the money from the counter—twenty dollars, which means that she wants him home around nine o'clock. From an experience he'd rather forget, he knows to be back before ten o'clock, but not before nine o'clock.

"I'm gone," he says, starting toward the door.

"What have you been eating?" she asks, not looking away from the television.

Whether his heart stops beating or starts beating three times faster than normal, he doesn't know, but he feels it in the heart first. The first thought that races through his mind is the fact that he's only two feet from the door. Two feet or two miles, there's little difference; he's not going to make it. He turns to her and swallows. "Ma'am?"

His mother keeps her eyes on the television, but she's frowning. "You didn't eat breakfast or lunch," she says, and then she glares at him. "Why aren't you hungry? What have you been eating?"

He swallows again. "I *am* hungry—*very* hungry," he says, his pulse racing. "I haven't eaten anything because I thought you said I would eat tonight—the ride yesterday, remember? I thought you said I had to wait until tonight, because of the ride home."

She stares at him for one of the longest minutes of his life, wondering how he could possibly forget that she told him to wait until breakfast. Then, she turns back to the television, but he sees that she's still in the same train of thought. Finally, she looks back at him, grinning now. "Alright," she says cheerfully. "I almost forgot. I'll have dinner wait'n for you when you get home. You have fun, okay? Mommy loves you."

As she turns the volume back up and starts surfing the channels, Kenny stands at the door watching her, being careful not to watch too long as he turns the knob.

He wants to slam it. He wants to yank it so hard that the knob comes with him, but he closes the door behind him with a faint click and then takes a deep breath. Of all the things she's said to him— and *will* say to him—those final three words always carry the most peculiar impact, like a punch that slips through the skin, finding its true target. He remembers how his mother used to say those words in the past and how he used to believe her. As he starts his eight-mile hike to the mall, he wishes it was she who was saying them now.

She kills me sometimes—no, I take that back—she kills me *every* time she says that shit. *Mommy loves you.* Well, that's just great, Kenny. The psycho, alien bitch from outer space loves you. I guess she shows it the way all of the people from her world do—Moranus, planet of the assholes. And it's easy to find, too. Just hang a left at Pluto, head straight down the Psycho Belt, and look for the third planet on your other right. You can't miss it. It's shaped like a nut, and it's the only planet that spins in the wrong direction.

She knew damn well I was supposed to have breakfast. Did she call me? Hell no, she didn't call me, but she loves me, right? She loves me. She loves me. *She loves me.*

Oh, of course. Here it comes, right on schedule. Exactly what the counselor ordered, right? As if walking down the street with tears in my eyes is gonna solve anything. In public, too.

Stupid.

Stupid.

Stupid.

So she loves me. What's so bad about that? Absolutely nothing. Get a grip, Kenny. Kids are *really* starving in other countries. Or didn't you know? So count your damn blessings! You're a lucky boy!

Yeah, I'm a whole lot of other things too, but I haven't figured most of them out yet.

Once, a while back, I was playing with this frog. Actually, I was harassing it, nudging it with my foot, and it was hopping left and right, trying to escape, jumping all over the place, not knowing which way to go.

Then, along came this bug. I don't know what kind of bug it was—one of those flying kind that makes a lot of noise when it flies. It landed just in front of the frog. And this is what really gets me—the frog's running away from my foot, right? But it finds the time to stop and eat that bug! Doesn't even think about whether or not it has time, it just does it. So then, I realized that the frog never *was* afraid of my stupid foot. I don't know. Maybe it was. But I gotta tell you—it really ticked me off to think that it wasn't; so, I tried to kick it a hundred yards. I tried to teach it to respect a foot—I say I "tried" because I ended up stubbin' my damn toe instead. Hurt like hell, too. I dropped straight to the ground, clenching my teeth, my fists, everything. My whole body went tense. The frog looked at me for a second before it hopped off. Now I know what a frog looks like when it's giggling its ass off.

I don't figure there's a moral to the story since it really happened, but the way I see it, I'm either the foot, the frog, or the fly. Don't know which for sure. But like I said, I'm a lot of things that I haven't figured out yet. On some days, I'm more one than the other, but I don't think that counts as a moral.

When it comes to morals, children's books have the best. Grownup books have decent stories but can have some of the dumbest morals—if they have any at all. You take some of the books that I've read—they were okay stories, but don't look for morals; you won't find one. Some people might think they're "topnotch," but I don't really think so, not if you're looking for a good moral.

Take *The Scarlet Letter*, for instance. The moral of the story is simple—marry the man you really want to be with. That way, if your husband dies, you still won't be willing to jump at the first man that looks your way. You'll be heartbroken for a long, long time. You'll be a hundred years old before thinking about hanging out with a new guy on the weekends. And if your husband was to come back, you'd be happy because you wanted to be with him in the first place. Not a bad moral, just not a good one. The thing is, you should already *know* that.

The Native Son is another example. What's the moral of *that* story? If you're a black man, don't get caught killing a white woman? *Well, duh!* Everybody knows killing is wrong, even blacks.

The moral to Hemingway's *The Old Man and the Sea* is either "don't go fishing alone if you're too old" or "don't be surprised if things don't go your way." What the hell kind of moral is that? Makes you not wanna be old *or* go fishing. Besides, you don't have to go fishing to learn that life can be a bitch. All you have to do is get up in the morning. Just try to get through a day without getting into trouble, you'll learn it.

When I was a kid, my favorite book was called *The Little Red Wagon*. I really loved that story. I had other kid books too, like the one about the little engine, the one about the cat, and all of that stuff, but *The Little Red Wagon* was the best. Mom must've read it to me a million times, but I never got tired of it.

It's about this little boy who had a little red wagon, but the boy had like a zillion other toys, too. The book never told you how the boy got so many toys, but he had tons of toys. In his bedroom, toys were on the bed, under the bed, in the middle of the floor, and everywhere else in the room. And in the corner of his room, the little red wagon was sitting with a sad face, and in the wagon were even more toys. There was stuff like teddy bears and trains and yo-yo's and all kinds of junk hanging out of the wagon. It was stuffed with toys, but you could tell by the way the wagon looked that it wasn't very happy.

The wagon was sad because the boy never played with it—never took the wagon outside like he did with the other toys, never took any of his friends for a ride in it, nothing. The wagon still looked brand-spankin' new because it was neglected. The little red wagon was sad because he didn't feel loved.

Well, one day, the wagon decided to leave the little boy. It went down the street, over the horizon, looking for someone who would love it. Eventually, it came to a house that had a little boy in the yard who was playing with a toy truck. When the little boy saw the wagon, he ran right up to it and started playing with it. The book never said what the boy did, but obviously, whatever "playing" with a wagon was, the little red wagon loved it, and they played for hours.

After a while, the little boy was called in for lunch, and he left the wagon and the toy truck outside. Then, it started raining, really coming down hard, and the little boy ran outside, scooped up the truck, and ran back into the house. He didn't even look at the wagon. The wagon got all wet and muddy, and it didn't take long for it to get the same sad look on its face. So, on it went again, over the horizon, looking for someone who would love it.

Next, it came across two boys who were playing catch with a Frisbee. When they saw the little red wagon, they ran right up to it—just like the little boy with the truck—and claimed it as their own. They took turns riding and pulling each other all over the neighborhood, but the thing is, they were too rough with the wagon. Being careless, they pulled the wagon over holes and bumps, and they didn't even bother to slow down. Finally, when a wheel came off, they didn't want the wagon anymore. So, they left the wagon on the side of the road. By this time, it was scratched up, dented, and had a broken wheel, and the sad look returned.

As if that wasn't bad enough, it turned out to be trash day. The people in the neighborhood had all of their trash cans next to the curb for the trash men to pick up. Well, the little red wagon happened to be sitting right next to a group of trash cans when the trash truck came chugging down the road, and sure enough, they thought the little red wagon was trash. They snatched it up and threw it in the back of the trash truck. The trash men didn't even notice how sad the little red wagon was, like they didn't even care.

Well, it just so happened that the boy who kept the wagon in his room had been looking for the wagon, ever since it left. He came riding up to the trash truck on his bike, and he didn't look very happy when he asked the trash men if they'd seen a little red wagon. The trash men told the boy that the only wagon they'd seen was one that nobody would want, and they took the wagon from the back of the trash truck to show him. The boy looked at the wagon that was full of scratches and dents, missing a wheel, and had a banana peel stuck to it, and yelled with a big smile, "That's my wagon!" The trash men handed the little boy the wagon, and the boy gave the wagon a big hug and told the wagon how much he missed it.

At that point, the wagon had a very happy look on its face. The final page of the book showed the wagon back in the corner of the little boy's room, toys stuffed in it just like before. The wagon still had its scratches, still had its dents, and was still missing a wheel, but it had a big smile on its face because it knew that it was in a place where it was "indeed loved," as the book put it.

No guessing there. The moral of the story slaps you right in the face.

Wish I still had some of those books. Mom was saving them for when Amanda grew up, but she threw them away. She got rid of everything that reminded her of Dad or Amanda—pictures and everything. It always kills me to think about how she threw out *my* books. Of course, I'm too old for them now, but they were still mine.

DESPITE HIS DISGRUNTLED THOUGHTS ON adult literature, Kenny fishes *Robinson Crusoe* from his duffle bag. Taking his all too familiar trek with a book partially shrouding his vision causes only a few stumbling steps. During the day, he takes the longer route to the mall because of the congestion on the Interstate. His shorter route at that time, which leads through six lanes and no median, can take up to thirty minutes before a not-so-decent opening presents itself. So, he takes the longer route for the sake of time rather than safety. On the way home, blitzing the highway, followed by a brief pilgrimage through thin forestry, proves the more efficient gauntlet.

When Kenny reaches the mall's parking lot, he shoves the novel back inside his duffle bag. With a sigh, he heads for his usual entrance to the mall, which is already cluttered with a dozen adolescent loiterers. The nudges, gestures, and giggles start long before he's close enough to hear them. He ignores the explosion of laughter, carefully making his way through the crowd and into the mall. Once inside, he takes his usual left turn, even though the Arcade Stadium is to the right, and he walks straight to Farley's New & Used Bookstore. He steps inside and stands next to the magazines, the way he always does when Mr. Farley is busy with customers.

After finishing with the customers, the partially bald, totally gray-headed Mr. Farley squints at the figure standing near the magazines. "Kenny? That you? I didn't see you come in."

"I didn't wanna bother you while—"

"If I told you once, I told you the truth, you're never a bother to me, son." Mr. Farley makes his way around the other side of the counter and places a hand on Kenny's shoulder. "How's life treat'n ya? You doing okay?"

"I'm alright."

In his seventy-four years, Mr. Farley has had his share of hardship. Years ago, he developed a talent for recognizing it in others. Yet, over time, he has learned to accept Kenny's answer. At one point, his prying decreased Kenny's visits considerably—visits Mr. Farley has come to enjoy dearly. It was a while before Kenny returned to his weekly schedule, and Mr. Farley cherishes their precarious relationship too much to jeopardize it again. He concluded that his nightly prayers would have to suffice, and he's been praying for Kenny every night for over two years. "That's good, that's good," he says, rubbing the top of Kenny's head with an age-trembling hand. "I'm awright too—Oh! I got one for ya!" He makes his way back around the counter, reaches underneath the register, and retrieves a used hardcover book.

Kenny rests his elbows on the counter to get a closer look, and then he frowns at the title. "*Wuthering Heights?*"

Mr. Farley shrugs. "I don't know why, but I can't get rid of it." He tries to inject a little sorrow in his voice. "People don't appreciate the great ones like they used to."

Kenny nods as if hearing this for the first time, instead of the fifty-first. "What's it about?"

Mr. Farley smiles. "Now, you know better than to ask me that, Kenny. Find out for yourself." He hands Kenny the book. "Go on back to the table. I'll be there in a minute."

Kenny places the book in his duffle bag. "Well, can you tell me if it's one of your favorites or not? You've told me *that* before."

"You're trying to be sneaky again," says Mr. Farley, grinning. He points a wrinkled finger at Kenny. "All I can tell you is that this one definitely belongs in a class by itself. I'm tellin' you, son, it's *topnotch!*"

For the first time this week, Kenny laughs.

Chapter 8

"**S**OMETIMES, SHE CAN BE IN ONE UH H'UH feisty moods, but don' let dat fool ya, honey—she uh nice lady," explains Mrs. Avery as she and Sarah walk down the intermittently cracked sidewalk, heading to Miss Annie's house. "She got uh funny way wit people sometimes. It can take some gitt'n use to. Juss don' let it bothuh ya. She'own evuh thank what chew *thank* she thank."

"I'll keep that in mind," says Sarah with a nervous smile. "But if she's a friend of the family—"

"Oooh, she uh lot more dan nat, baby," says Mrs. Avery, grinning as she links her arm with Sarah's. "She uh good frien' uh da whole neighbuh'hood. *Everybody* know 'uh."

"The entire neighborhood?"

"Pretty much."

Sarah finds this somewhat impressive, considering the "neighborhood" is identified as everyone within a half-mile radius. "How did she come to know so many people?"

"She was h'yuh firs'."

"First?"

"Uh-huh."

"By 'first,' are you saying that she was the first to move into the neighborhood?"

"I'own know 'bout all lat, but she was h'yuh befo' any uh us was."

"Us?"

Mrs. Avery stops abruptly and looks at Sarah incredulously. "Da black folk, baby. You mean na tell me Tony ain' tell you Miss Annie white?"

"No . . . he didn't."

"He talked about 'uh didn' 'e?"

"Well . . . yes . . . quite often, but . . ."

Mrs. Avery chuckles as she starts moving again. "Well, I guess unless you come out an ax, he ain' have no reason na tell ya, so I'll tell ya—she *white*." She glances at Sarah. "Whituh dan you, as uh mattuh fack," she says, smiling. "Whituh dan you."

"And she was here . . . 'first,'" repeats Sarah, thoughtfully.

Mrs. Avery chuckles again. "Well, I guess I shoulda said she was da lass ta go, but she ain' g'own nowhe'uh yet."

Sarah smiles hesitantly.

"An she say she ain' nevuh g'own go—'I ain't leavin' until the Lawd take me away.' Dass what she say."

They've gone just under a half-mile when they finally reach an attractive two-story, gray house trimmed in white, the finest on the block. The paint is fresh; the lawn is green; the hedges, though in need of trimming, show little sign of neglect. The neighboring houses, also two-story dwellings—although each level is rented to two separate families—show signs of wear and tear. They are a sharp contrast to Miss Annie's house, which glows with rejuvenation and a deep proud history.

For a long time, Mrs. Avery has been a part of that history. Though a regular for six other houses on the other side of town, she has been Miss Annie's maid for the last fourteen years, free of charge. She places a key in the heavy oak door, and after a resounding click, it swings open without the slightest squeak. "It's me, Miss Annie!" she calls. She motions Sarah to enter first. "An I got somebody fuh you da meet!"

The house smells of pine. In the living room sits a handsome sofa, loveseat, and chair, each draped with an elegant, hand-sewn, miniature quilt. A sturdy mahogany coffee table bearing a fresh bouquet of flowers is the centerpiece of the carefully positioned ensemble. Beyond the living room is the dining area, which sports a cherry wood table with six chairs. The table has six place settings, complete with polished utensils and sparkling glasses. An equally impressive cherry wood china cabinet rests against one of the dining room walls, and a beautiful painting—the frame, also cherry wood—of the Last Supper is on another.

Sarah stands in awe as she eyes the countless artifacts. As with Tony's home, no space is wasted, but Miss Annie's house is much larger, easily holding four times the number of whatnots, curios, and oddities. In their midst are shelved figurines of African-American culture, commemorative plates of the Civil War, and various religious icons. The staircase facing the front door has a mechanical chairlift mounted on the wall, opposite the railing. Above the chairlift's path is the ascension of several portraits, including both Kennedys and Martin Luther King Jr. At present, the chair is positioned at the bottom of the stairs.

"She muss be in na den uh somewhere," mumbles Mrs. Avery. "She cane git up dem stairs wit'out h'uh rockit seat."

"Mama!" gasps Sarah, giving Mrs. Avery a scolding grin.

"Well, lass what it look like," Mrs. Avery says in a half whisper. "You'd thank she was try'n na shoot ta heaven uh somp'm—Oh, an I see Tony done talked ta you about dat 'Ma-*ma*' thang."

Sarah stands with her mouth agape, speechless.

Mrs. Avery heads down the hall leading to the den. "Miss Annie! Whey you at, Miss Annie?"

"Sheronda, Ah'm back here!" answers a voice from beyond the dining area, in the kitchen. "And stop all of yer hollerin' in ma *house!*" demands Miss Annie, giving her best impression of a tough and ornery old lady.

Suddenly, a white-haired woman, garbed in a thick bathrobe and slippers, exits the kitchen with the help of a walker.

Mrs. Avery throws her hands on her hips. "Lady, what chew doin' in nat robe?" she asks with warmth in her voice but a small frown on her face. "I tole you I was bringin' 'uh ovuh."

Miss Annie tightens her lips. "Ma robe's clean and ma slippers're clean. Hair's as neat as it's gone git . . . 'sides, I ain't goin' nowheres." She finally turns to Sarah. "So . . . this here's Sarah," she says, but in a tone that says she'll hold off on the cartwheels.

"Yes, ma'am," replies Sarah uncertainly.

Miss Annie keeps a straight face as she makes her way to the sofa. "I had to come down and feed the cat," she complains. "The darn thang's been meowin' all day." She places the walker on the side of the sofa, and then sits down with an exaggerated grunt. "The bowl was empty."

Mrs. Avery sucks her teeth. "Miss Annie, you need da stop it. Dat big ole bowl I got fuh dat cat don' *evuh* be empty. It might git low, but nevuh empty."

"Well, she must've been tellin' me it was gittin' low," Miss Annie argues. "She follered me right to the kitchen, and when I filled it up, she started eat'n. Now, what *that* tell ya?"

"Dat tell me, you reminded dat devilish cat whey da bowl was."

Miss Annie turns to Sarah. "Would you like somethin' to drink, Sarah?"

"No, ma'am . . . thank you."

"Sheronda, would you go git Sarah and me some lemonade, please?" she asks, keeping her eyes on Sarah.

"You *got* lemonade?"

Miss Annie smiles. "No, ma'am, but while you makin' us some, I can talk to this young'un who's wantin' to marry ma boy."

Sarah lifts an eyebrow. She feels ill-prepared to be alone with Miss Annie, and she doesn't like the way the old woman is eyeing her suspiciously.

"I tell you what," says Mrs. Avery, "Ah'ma go in na kitchen an git cha'll some Kool-aid. Den, I'll go straighten up ya room fuh ya. Hi 'bout dat?"

"Why thank ya, Sheronda," replies Miss Annie, sarcastically.

Mrs. Avery gives the old woman a smirk. "Oh, you are sooo welcome, Miss Annie." Then, without warning, she lassoes Miss Annie's neck with both arms and kisses her on the side of her forehead.

"Come own, chile!" exclaims Miss Annie. "Yer messin' ma hair!"

"An I love you *too*," says Mrs. Avery. She gives Miss Annie another peck on the forehead, winks at Sarah, and then is off to the kitchen.

For a moment, silence sweeps into the room. Miss Annie eyeballs Sarah, studying her carefully. "Well, have a seat, chile," she finally says, motioning toward the love seat, opposite the couch.

Sarah forces a smile. "Thank you."

"So ya marryin' ma boy?"

"Yes, ma'am."

Miss Annie leans forward. "Honey, you can drop the 'ma'am' business. I know you from the north—whereabouts? Richmond was it?"

"Actually, I'm from Charlottesville . . . ma'am."

"That still Virginia?"

"Yes, ma'am. It's northwest of Richmond."

"I got family in Richmond," Miss Annie mumbles. "I ain't seen hide nor hair of any of ma blood relatives fer God knows how long. They done abandoned me. You ever been there?"

Sarah swallows nervously. "Yes, ma'am. I have an uncle in Richmond."

"An they say 'ma'am' in Sharlieville, or wherever you said you was from?" asks Miss Annie, irritated now.

Sarah places her hands on her knees and sinks into her seat. "Although using 'ma'am' is considered a southern trait, we northerners have been known to use the term a time or two . . . ma'am."

Miss Annie waves a hand. "Suit yerself."

Sarah shows her teeth in an attempt to smile, but Miss Annie isn't fooled.

"You call yer folks 'ma'am' and 'sir'?"

"No, ma'am. They've always found it too formal for family. My brother and I've addressed them as such, depending on the conversation or circumstance, but it's never been mandatory. It's too impersonal."

Miss Annie aims a wrinkled index finger at Sarah. "It shows respect," she argues. "Shouldn't young'uns respect their mama and papa?"

"Absolutely," Sarah answers nervously, "but . . . I was taught that respect has to be earned—"

"*Earned?*"

"Well . . . yes, ma'am." She hopes she hasn't said anything wrong.

"They brang you into this world, ain't that enough? They feed ya. They clothe ya. Don't that count fer nothin'?

Sarah nods uneasily. "Yes, ma'am. . . ."

Miss Annie tilts her head to one side. "I can tell you gotta problem with what Ah'm tellin' ya. Go ahead, spill it out," she demands.

Sarah rubs her hands together, feeling more uncomfortable by the minute. "Well . . . it's just that . . . a child never asks to be brought in the world. As for the caring of a child . . . it's a parent's duty, regardless of the child's respect, or the lack thereof." She swallows hard. "Isn't it?"

Miss Annie releases a grunt as she sits back and glares at Sarah. Sarah wonders what's taking Mrs. Avery so long.

"That's what's wrong with all la children today," Miss Annie grumbles. "They don't respect nothin'." She leans forward, as if to give Sarah confidential information. "How you gone raise a chile like what chew talkin' about? Earnin' respect and all kinds of . . . If you spare the rod, yer *gonna* have trouble with yer young'un. You take a switch to 'em every time they git outta line, you'll git some respect," she says with an affirmative grin and a nod.

Sarah suddenly takes an interest in the floor.

"Yes indeedy," continues Miss Annie, smiling now. "You light 'em up when they disrespect cha, and you'll git it right back." She leans back in her seat. "What chew say?"

Sarah forces smile. "Well . . . forcing a child to be obedient . . . isn't the same as respect," she says cautiously.

Miss Annie frowns. "How you figger?"

Sarah swallows again. "A child may do what he or she is told," she says warily, "but it's really due to fear—of the 'rod,' as you say—not due to respect." She shrugs, and then immediately wishes she hadn't. "Um . . . respect and fear . . . well, they aren't the same."

Mrs. Avery glides in with a small tray bearing two glasses of Kool-aid, and Sarah couldn't be more relieved. "Dis yo' glass h'yuh, Sarah," she says as she places a coaster on the coffee table. "Miss Annie cane have dat much sugah, so I had da add some in yours."

"Sheronda, what chew did to Tony whenever he didn' mine?" asks Miss Annie.

Mrs. Avery eyes the old woman suspiciously because she knows Miss Annie better than anyone. "What?"

"When he was growin' up, how did you make 'im behave hisself?"

"I whooped his behine," she says with a curious look.

"An did it work?" asks Miss Annie, now beaming at Sarah.

"You bettuh believe it worked," Mrs. Avery says and then focuses on Sarah. "What cha'll talkin' about?"

Sarah shrugs. "We're discussing a child's respect for his parents." Because she feels more comfortable with Mrs. Avery present, she asks, "Would you say that Tony behaved due to fear or respect?"

"Oooh, I see whey ya'll lat," says Mrs. Avery, smiling now. "Well, he was definitely scared. He knew what was wait'n fuh 'im if he evuh got in na trouble—an it was wait'n fuh 'im too—I ain' play. He knew it. I did *not* play. An you cane help *but* respeck uh butt whoopin'."

"I ain't sure," mumbles Miss Annie, "but I don't thank yer heppin' me none."

"Well, Ah'm juss sooo sorry," says Mrs. Avery. "I thank Ah'ma take my no-helpin' self upstairs, git cho' room straightened up." And with that, she makes a few quick comical faces behind Miss Annie's back, causing Sarah's grin to broaden. Then she gives Sarah a remember-what-I-told-you face before heading upstairs, tray in hand.

"Don't make me take a switch to *you*, Sheronda!" Miss Annie yells over her shoulder. Then she turns back to Sarah. "What was she doin' behine ma back to git chew gigglin' so?"

Sarah places a hand over her mouth. "I . . . I don't think I'm at liberty to say."

"Well, I guess I can't be talkin' much about raisin' a young'un, seein' as how I never had none of ma own."

"You make some good points," assures Sarah.

Miss Annie fans Sarah's comment away. "Aaah, yer just sayin' that. Still, considerin' how good yer upbringin' was, I guess yer folks knew what they was doin'."

"Well . . . thank you."

She fans at Sarah again. "I call it like I see it."

"Well, the way *I* see it," Sarah says, "your method seemed to work for Tony."

Miss Annie eyes Sarah carefully, and then takes a sip of her Kool-aid. "I never laid a finger on that boy." She lowers her voice. "To be honest wit chew, I used to hate it when that boy would fine trouble. I couldn't stand to see him whooped. I used to tell Sheronda to take 'im outside, but I could still hear 'im, and it always broke ma heart to hear that boy screamin' and carryin' on."

"You really love him," Sarah says, nodding and smiling.

Miss Annie stares at Sarah long enough to make her smile disappear. "The only person that loves 'im more," she finally says, frowning again, "is God and that angel upstairs cleanin' ma room." She pauses for another moment, eyeballing Sarah again, and then asks, "What's yer story, chile? What a nice white girl like you doin' with ma boy? Sheronda's one of the sweetest people you ever could meet, but sometimes that work against 'er. She ain't about to say nothin' to hurt yer feelin's none, but I ain't about to sit back and watch ma boy git hurt, and I know she wouldn't want that either. Now . . . you tell me—give it to me right—what's this all about?"

Sarah's heart sinks to the floor. She feels as though she has been blind-sided by a collapsing building. As she clambers to the surface of this mental ton of bricks, she thinks of Tony. Thoughts of him ease the impact—a little. At the same time, she's returning one of Miss Annie's pauses. Miss Annie waits patiently, as if pausing is part of the game.

"I want him," Sarah finally says, as calmly as she can.

"Want 'im?"

"Yes, ma'am."

"Fer what?"

"For me."

Miss Annie takes a deep breath and readjusts herself on the couch. "Do you even *love* 'im?"

"Without question," says Sarah, gazing at the old woman incredulously.

"Why?"

"At this point, you know more about him than I do. Do you really need to ask?"

Miss Annie's pause returns, but so does her smile. "What do yer folks say about you marryin' a black man?" she finally asks, sounding as if she's ready to say "checkmate."

"They don't."

"Don't what?"

"They don't say anything."

"Well, what do they *think* about the idea?" she asks, frowning again. "You must know what they *think*. What do they think?"

"My parents have always wanted me to be happy," Sarah states matter-of-factly. "They *think* Tony makes me happy."

"Well, do he?"

Sarah pauses and takes a deep breath. After a moment, a radiance comes to her face. "Yes," she finally says, "he does." After another pause, she adds, "When I first saw him, he was just another cute guy. The University is filled with cute guys. Tony was just another guy. We were in the same class, and he was very bright, an ideal study partner, so we started studying together. The rest was . . . automatic. The more I learned about him, the more I liked." She shrugs and grins. "I can't really pinpoint it," she says thoughtfully, "but at some point . . . I realized what he meant to me."

"Mmm . . . and what was that?" asks Miss Annie, listening intently.

Sarah shrugs again. "Everything. It's as if he filled a void I never knew I had," she admits. "At any rate, I can no longer smile fervently at what the future may hold, if it doesn't hold his face smiling back at me."

Miss Annie stares at Sarah for another moment. Then she takes another sip of Kool-aid and sighs. She sees that Sarah is feeling uncomfortable with the conversation. "I can tell you got a good nature about cha," she says with a stiff brow. "And I don't doubt that y'all care fer each other." Then, she shakes her head. "But the *world*, chile—the world still ain't ready to see ya'll holdin' hands."

Sarah looks back at the floor as if the words she wants to use are found there—broken. "We've already discussed the world," she mutters, obviously disturbed by the conversation. "And we've discussed the issues and challenges that come with it." She faces the old woman and shakes her head. "The world isn't responsible for our happiness—we are."

Again, Miss Annie shakes her head. "What about the children?" she asks earnestly. "They won't belong on either side."

Miss Annie's words cut deeply, but Sarah maintains her composure, despite her growing agitation. "That's a pessimistic opinion," she mutters. "Optimistically, our children will be . . . *familiar* . . . with both—not both 'sides,' but both *cultures*." She says this with concern written all over her face, oblivious to her fidgeting hands. "The idea of sides," she continues hesitantly, "consummates a *we* versus *they* attitude—a feud." She looks down at the floor, unable to think clearly while watching Miss Annie. "In that respect," she says softly, "neither I nor Tony identify ourselves as being on a 'side.'"

She struggles to compose herself, but her mind races with jumbled thoughts. "Why should our children . . . it frightens me sometimes . . . to think that everything I thought . . . people and such—my brother's deaf, and I can remember . . ." She stops suddenly. Her words are too shattered, trampled by emotions she can no longer control.

She exhales, indicating her frustration and her inability to continue. Even if she could, she doesn't want to. She can well imagine some of the bridges that may or may not come. To think of them ahead of time is to cross them more than once—at least, mentally. She knows some may come more than once, while others may never come at all. For Tony, she'll cross every one, without regret. She loves him that much. But she'd rather wait and see than find and conquer.

Miss Annie watches Sarah unblinkingly. Suddenly, the tough and ornery old woman feels a twinge of shame. She knows the young couple will have to endure more than enough trouble, without having to suffer questions and comments from friends and loved ones. To be prejudiced is simply to prejudge, and only now does she realize her folly. Her mind was already made up before Sarah arrived, before she was even born. Now, finally meeting Sarah, she knows better. She doesn't even remember what she was trying to accomplish. "I wish there were more people like yerselves," she finally mutters. "This world can be . . ." Looking at Sarah's face, Miss Annie catches herself. Then says, "It scares me to think about ma boy gitt'n hisself into such a fix." She rubs her wrinkled hands together, uncomfortable for the first time. "But I can tell by talkin' to ya . . . he ain't have much choice in the matter." Then she shakes her head again. "I just wish . . ." Again, she catches herself.

Miss Annie turns away from Sarah as she carefully grunts to her feet. Sarah instinctively reaches with a helping hand, but Miss Annie snatches her arm away. "I don't need no help!" she yells, and then, seeing Sarah's painful expression, she adds, "Not yet, anyhow. Let me get a few more years on me, like when ya'll give me some gran' kids. *They* can help me . . . maybe."

Sarah stands up as well, not knowing what to say or do. Her eyes start to water, but she doesn't know why. She fights to hold it in.

Miss Annie sees Sarah struggling with her feelings. She spreads her arms. "Come here, chile." As they embrace, Sarah is surprised by the strength of Miss Annie's delicate arms. "Ma boy picked good," Miss Annie mumbles as she gently rocks Sarah from side to side. "Ma boy picked *real* good."

Whether the hug is a response to her misty eyes, Sarah doesn't know and doesn't care, but she knows how good it feels. She watches her first tear land on the back of Miss Annie's robe. When the next one falls, the doorbell rings. "That must be Tony," she murmurs, but she doesn't let go.

Miss Annie tightens her embrace. "He can wait, honey," she whispers. Her eyes water. "He can wait."

Chapter 9

FOR THE MOMENT, PATRONS INTENT ON buying a new or used book will have to spend a few minutes browsing in other stores and shops, or maybe waiting it out on a bench, watching the mall rats scurry about—Mr. Farley is busy right now. The steel mesh at the entrance of *Farley's New & Used Bookstore* has been pulled down, positioned just below knee height. A handmade cardboard sign rests on the floor, right underneath. In red marker, it reads: "Sorry, back in 30 minutes." The sign is old and tattered, but legible. Those customers who peer through the mesh catch a view of Mr. Farley enthusiastically waving his hands about while talking and laughing with Kenny.

Kenny never has much to say, and Mr. Farley has become wary of asking him too many open-ended questions, particularly those likely to strike a nerve by his probing too deeply. During their conversations, Mr. Farley is always prepared to overshadow a bad question with a better one, an impersonal one. Preferably, a question that can be readily answered with a "yes" or "no." Of course, questions about the books Kenny reads are also safe. Mr. Farley doesn't mind doing most of the talking. His years provide him with enough to talk about for the both of them. Kenny may not be a talker, but to Mr. Farley, he's the best listener he has ever met.

"And so there I was," says Mr. Farley, "sitt'n and wait'n on a squirrel to fall for my trap."

"With a box propped up by a stick?" asks Kenny.

Mr. Farley raises an index finger. "And the string attached to the stick, it was pretty long. It let me hide behind a tree that was about ten yards or so away from the trap."

Kenny nods. "So you had a box with a stick and some string?"

"Don't forget the acorns, too," adds Mr. Farley. "A trap ain't a trap without bait. Anyways, I was ready to snatch that string as soon as a squirrel went for the acorns."

"How did you know they would want acorns?"

"'Cause that's all I ever seen 'em munching on—acorns. I tried a few myself, but I didn't see what was so great about 'em."

Kenny snickers. "You *tried* some?"

Mr. Farley shrugs. "Well, yeah! When I was little, I'd try just about anything—once." He leans in closer to Kenny. "You mean to tell me you never tried an acorn?"

"I don't think I have," replies Kenny, shaking his head.

"Well, you should," suggests Mr. Farley, rapping his knuckles on the table. "Who knows? You might be just the type of fellow that'd like 'em."

"I don't know," says Kenny, still shaking his head. "I think I'll take your word on how they taste."

"*My* word?"

"Yeah."

Mr. Farley frowns. "You can't take my word on how they taste, I was only five years old!"

"So?"

"*So?*—So your taste buds git different when you git older. Things when you're five don't taste the same when you get as old as me."

Kenny measures Mr. Farley for a quick second and then asks, "Have you tasted one since?"

"No way! Once was enough for me. I don't like the taste."

"But I thought you said—"

"Anyways! I had the box propped up with a stick, a long string tied to the stick, and five acorns positioned under the box."

"Right," gasps Kenny through his snickering.

Mr. Farley smiles as he waits a moment for Kenny to regain his composure. "You with me?"

"Okay, okay . . . a box, a string, and five acorns," Kenny finally manages.

"And I was hid'n behind a tree," reminds Mr. Farley.

"Right—the tree."

"Well, I must've been hid'n there for about thirty minutes or so, but the squirrels wouldn't take the bait. They wouldn't even come near it. And for a five-year-old, wait'n for thirty minutes or so is like wait'n for days."

"So what did you do?"

Mr. Farley shrugs. "I just kept wait'n. I didn't know what else *to* do."

"For how long?"

"Well . . . forever! It felt like *two* forevers! Then, all of a sudden, my pappy comes walkin' toward me. I could tell by the way he was comin' that he knew what I was up to. He came steppin' kind of gentle-like," explains Mr. Farley, making a walking gesture with two of his fingers. "Then, he asked me real quiet-like—'What're you doin', son?' And I said, 'I'm trying to catch me a squirrel.' I said it real serious, too."

"You must've been serious to wait so long," says Kenny, smiling.

"Oh, I was *very* serious, very determined," admits Mr. Farley, rubbing his hands together. "I knew I'd catch one if I waited long enough. I mean, I had the perfect plan, right?"

Kenny isn't so sure, but still says, "Sounds good enough."

"You better believe it was good enough! I was really smart for a five-year-old—at least, I thought I was." Mr. Farley lowers his voice. "But then Pappy asked me just one single question to change all of that."

Kenny leans forward, listening intently. "What?"

"To change how smart I thought I was."

"What was the *question?*" asks Kenny, playfully slapping a hand on the table.

"Oh . . . the question. . . ." Mr. Farley says, trying to keep a straight face.

"Yes, the question," says Kenny, leaning back in his chair.

Mr. Farley scratches the top of his balding head. "What *was* that question?"

"Come on!" pleads Kenny. He whisks a quick hand through his hair. "Don't tell me you don't remember!"

"Give me a minute," says Mr. Farley, still scratching his head as a smirk comes to his face.

Kenny shakes his head. "You're wrong, Mr. Farley, that's just *too* wrong." He tries to give his best look of disappointment.

Mr. Farley slaps the table with both hands. "Oh, *now* I remember!"

Kenny calms down. "What did he say?"

Mr. Farley raises an index finger. "It was a question, one question."

Kenny sighs with a grin. "Okay . . . what was the *question?*"

Mr. Farley clears his throat and says, "My pappy's eyes stayed on my trap, and he said, 'Son, why would a squirrel bother with your five acorns when there's about a zillion of 'em laying all over the ground?'"

Kenny's eyebrows shoot to his hairline. "Don't even. . . ."

Mr. Farley nods. "Yep. There was acorns everywhere," he says with a shrug, "but I never gave 'em much thought. My acorn trap was sitt'n right smack dab in the middle of acorn heaven."

"Don't *even* . . . !" repeats Kenny, laughing now.

"I learned two things that day," Mr. Farley says, but pauses to give Kenny a moment to control himself.

Kenny snaps back to attention, almost miraculously. "And what was that?" he asks. "Two morals?"

"I guess you can call 'em that."

"What were they?"

"One—a trap is only as brilliant as the trapper."

Kenny snickers. "I'll have to agree with that."

"And two—my pappy was a brilliant teacher."

Kenny's smile fades at the mention of the four-letter word. "*Teacher?*"

"Yeah, you see, he didn't tell me that what I was doin' was stupid. Instead, he let me tell myself." He leans toward Kenny. "But to be able to call yourself stupid, you have to git a little smarter first. You have to be smart enough to *know* you're stupid, and you have to be smart enough to know *why* you're stupid. A good teacher don't tell you these things. He helps you figure it out for yourself, like a coach."

Kenny tilts his head the way a dog does when hearing a strange sound. "So . . . the more you realize how stupid you are . . . the smarter you get?" he asks, and then he snickers again, trying to hold in his laughter.

Mr. Farley scratches the top of his head. "Well, when you say it *that* way. . . ."

They explode in a fit of laughter, complete with wheezing and table-slapping.

After a few minutes, Mr. Farley glances at his watch. "Well . . . once again, we've kept the customers wait'n longer than we should've." He scratches the top of his head. "Same time next week?"

Kenny's more familiar straight face returns. "Probably."

It's his usual response, but it's as good as it gets. Mr. Farley always expects him but has learned not to be too disappointed whenever Kenny fails to show. In his heart, he believes that Kenny shows up whenever possible, and that only extenuating circumstances, the kind Mr. Farley believes to be beyond Kenny's control, keep them apart.

After raising the steel mesh and placing the sign back behind the counter, they exchange their usual parting words. Typically, Mr. Farley expresses his enjoyment of the visit and his high anticipation of the next one, while Kenny murmurs a "S'long" or a "Take care." The final hallmark of Kenny's departure—his taking approximately ten steps before glancing back and waving—is something Mr. Farley waits for before tending to the customers who saunter in.

This is the part I really hate. I can't stand to see him look so sad. I feel sorry for him, there all alone. That's why I like stopping by. It makes him feel better. I don't think he has anybody that cares for him. His wife's been dead a long time and he doesn't ever mention anything about family, only in the past tense, like with his dad and the acorns.

A box, a stick, and some string—that was a good one, a *really* good one. I don't think he'll ever run out of stories, and he never tells the same one twice. That's pretty good for his age. You'd think he'd end up telling me one that's already been told by now, but he hasn't yet. Even if he did, I wouldn't tell him. He doesn't need me telling him how stupid he's getting. Like he said, that's a teacher's job. I'm just glad I can make him feel better, even if it's only once in a while. Once in a while is better than never. "Never" can really hurt sometimes. "Never" is hard on a person. "Never" sucks.

I finally get to Arcade Stadium, and the place is as crowded as always. I like standing in the entranceway for a minute or two, to check out all of the aspiring video masters. Most of the people here are regulars, which means most of them know not to challenge me. On any game in here, I've put most of them to shame. Like I said, I own the Stadium.

It's a really big deal to be able to hold your own in a place like this. From the outside, if a person is looking in, it's only an arcade room. That's probably how most people who don't play video games see this place—just an arcade. Nothing could be further from the truth. This is a digital, technologically advanced battleground. Regulars like me are the warriors, but there are no sides to take. It's every man for himself. People who come in and pump in a few tokens to pass the time are considered innocent bystanders, not even amateurs. Usually, a regular will let a bystander play alone, let the machine do the damage. Other times, a bystander can really catch hell from a regular, and it all starts with an innocent enough question: "Mind if I join in?"

A good warrior like me doesn't take pleasure in muscling a bystander.

It's the lousy warriors—the grunts—who make the bystanders suffer. The grunts aren't good enough to earn respect from people like me— and yes, there are some warriors even I have to respect. Even I slip up once in a while, and a good warrior can take advantage of it, but never a grunt. So, some grunts choose to pick on bystanders to get respect, but that's no good. Bystanders don't come back much, and they take the respect with them.

Some grunts haven't even earned respect from the machine. If you can't defeat the computer on a regular basis, don't even think about challenging a good warrior. You'd be free lunch. Every game has a pattern, and if you've got half a brain, you'll notice it, but it takes some of the other half to take advantage of it. Playing a person's different because people can change on you, just when you think you've figured them out. But they have to be smart enough to *know* when they've been figured out. Then they can change again, keep you guessing.

That's the enticing thing about messing with bystanders. Most will keep trying the same stupid strategy—stupid because it's been figured out but keeps showing up. They keep doing the same stuff and are amazed when it doesn't work the fifth time. (Talk about brain dead.) With people like that, you *know* you'll be on the game longer than with playing the computer. How much longer depends on the amount of money a bystander has, and whether he's been baited properly. That's the part that takes a little talent—baiting. But when done right, it doesn't matter whether you're a grunt or a warrior—you become a hustler.

With video games, the trick to good baiting is winning by the smallest margin. If a bystander thinks that he came close to beating you, he'll pump in more tokens to do just that. I've seen business- men complain about running late for appointments because of a good baiting. I've seen husbands blow up on their wives who keep telling them not to play anymore, to just give up. But the thing is, if they've been baited correctly, they can't.

Baiting doesn't work on girls as well as guys. It must be an ego thing, but it could be that girls are smarter. When you think about it, it's hard to be smart and macho at the same time.

It's also hard to be macho all by yourself. That's why playing video games at home isn't the same. You've got to learn to perform in the middle of a crowd of strangers egging your opponent on, trying to give him the motivation to beat you, each waiting to be the one to take you down, to show you up in front of everybody. The best way to learn how to play under pressure is by playing under pressure—period. And the biggest pressure comes when everybody wants to beat you.

The hottest game out now is a fighting game called *Conflict*. Everybody likes to play it, but it's even fun to stand and watch someone else play it. There's only six fighters, but they each have unique personalities and fighting styles. There's an overweight guy named "Stomp." He moves the slowest, but he's also the strongest. "Shy" is a sweet-looking girl who fights sneaky. She looks innocent, but don't let that fool you. There's another girl named "Spice." She's dressed in a leather miniskirt, heels, and fights real mean. She's not as fast as Shy, but she's stronger. "Jock" looks like a football player or a bodybuilder, and he stands like he's wearing a cape or something. "Brain" is the smart one. He looks like a geek, a teacher's favorite. He isn't strong or fast, but he has the most effective moves, as if he's studied and practiced more than anyone. "Coolio" is the opposite of Brain. He looks and acts like a troublemaker, the kind of guy girls really go for. He dresses good and has flashy moves, but he has absolutely no endurance. He looks as if he drinks and smokes, but the game never shows him with beer or cigarettes.

Only six characters. Other games have a lot more, but the two things that make this fighting game so hot is how real the characters seem—most people can relate to at least one of them—and the taunts. Each character has an endless arsenal of taunts—except Brain doesn't really taunt; he lectures. It takes a while to master even one character. I've mastered every character on every game in here. I'm the best—so far.

Right now, there are five *Conflict* games in here, all occupied. I walk over to the one that's being played by a little boy I've seen before.

He's playing the game with Coolio, which is everybody's favorite, but I don't care for him.

"You wanna play me?" the little kid asks, without even looking at me. I can tell by how he asks that he knows something about my game, but little kids don't care much about losing. Their egos aren't fully developed yet.

I shake my head. "Naw, I'll watch you play," I tell him. He appreciates it too. I can tell.

"I've seen you playin' people before," he says. "You're good."

"Thanks."

He glances at me really quick then back at the game. "How do you do that thing with Stomp?"

"What thing?" I ask. I'm impressed that he's talking to me and playing the game at the same time. He's actually pretty good for his age.

"I saw you beat Coolio using Stomp," he explains. "Even his butterfly kick couldn't beat you. Can you teach me how to play with Stomp?"

"Yeah, if you want," I say. I'm surprised. Not many people like playing with Stomp.

The little kid says, "After this game. Okay?"

"Okay."

He's already beaten Shy and Stomp, but now he's having a hard time with Jock. In fact, he's about to lose.

"He always does this to me!" he yells. "I hate Jock!" He takes it kind of hard, serious, but then again, everybody does—even me. "That's awright," he says. "Show me how you play with Stomp." He pumps in the tokens and fires the game up. "Show me some things I can use against Jock too," he advises. Then he steps to the side and motions for me to take over the game. The screen flashes the usual request: "CHOOSE YOUR PERSONALITY!!" I pick Stomp.

First, I try to show the kid all the moves that shouldn't give him much trouble to remember. He gets all excited when I fight Jock. "Yeah! That's what I'm talkin' about! Take *that*, Jock! That's awesome!"

I start smiling. He's killing me with his comments. He really has it in for Jock.

After I defeat the game twice, the kid takes over. I offer to pay him back his tokens, but he doesn't wanna take it. Instead, he shows me all the money he's got, and I think to myself, *that's some leash*, but I don't say it out loud because I don't know how he'd take it.

He's playing with Stomp, and he's liking it. He's carrying on, getting all excited. When Jock comes up, he gets real quiet, real serious. I feel sorry for him when he loses.

"Man! I almost had it!" he says. He gives the game a little shove, but it doesn't even budge under his small weight.

"Keep at it," I tell him. I sound like a boxing trainer or something. "You'll get it."

He keeps at it, too. He keeps losing to Jock, but each time, the kid gets better and better. All he needs is time. Time runs out when a guy I've never seen walks up with a sleazy-looking girlfriend.

"You playin' him?" he asks me. He's referring to the kid, but he doesn't look at the kid.

"No," I tell him, and then I step to the side, the way all spectators tend to do.

He doesn't say anything else as he drops some tokens in, interrupting the kid's game, which is rude if you don't ask. The screen reads in huge letters: "YOU ARE BEING CHALLENGED!!" Then the game starts playing the thumping music that it plays whenever a second player joins in, with a bass that makes you think of King Kong's heartbeat. It works, too.

"You ready for me, little man?" he asks the kid as he looks over at his girlfriend. The kid simply nods as "CHOOSE YOUR PERSON-ALITY!!" flashes on the screen. The guy picks Jock, and the kid picks Coolio. I don't really blame him.

"Let's do it, little man," the guy says, but he's still looking at his dumb girlfriend. He never looks at the kid.

The guy is good, not the best of warriors, but definitely not a bystander. The kid holds his own decent enough, but the guy is better.

What sucks is how he taunts the kid while he's playing, treating him like he's a little baby or something, as if the taunts in the game aren't bad enough. But I give the kid credit; he doesn't quit. Every time he loses, he pumps in more tokens. The guy is loving the kid's tenacity; it gives him more time to show off in front of the girl.

All of a sudden, the kid picks Stomp.

"*Stomp?*" the guy says, laughing out loud—forcing it, really. "You gonna try and beat me with Stomp?"

The kid doesn't say anything. He just waits for the guy to choose personalities.

"This is gonna be good, baby," the guy says, looking at the sleazy girlfriend again. He's a real asshole. "Little man wants to use Stomp. Let's do it, little man."

The guy beats the kid worse than ever. The kid needs a lot more practice with Stomp.

"You can't beat somebody like me using Stomp, boy!" He gives his girlfriend a kiss, and then looks down at the kid. "Who you gonna play with next? Brain?"

Nobody plays Brain. Like I said, he doesn't taunt; he lectures. But I learned him anyway because you never know what you need until you don't have it. The kid picks Stomp again. I guess he figures if he's gonna lose, he might as well get the practice.

"Stomp *again?!*" the guy yells, laughing. Everybody in the place can hear him. He's really showing off. "You can't be that dumb! Didn't you see how I ate your lunch?"

The kid points back at me. "*He* can play Stomp really good."

That's all he says. He isn't trying to start anything, just making an innocent comment. Funny how these things happen.

"Well, damn! He *looks* like Stomp!" the guy says, but he's still looking at his girlfriend. "And everybody knows that Stomp is the sorriest. He's even sorrier than *Brain!*"

They play again, and the kid loses, almost the same way.

"I *told* you, boy!" the guy says, carrying on like a fool. "I'm bad! You can't hang, little man! Especially using somebody as sorry as Stomp!"

"*He* can," the kid says, pointing right at me, and he says it with a worried look, a look that says, *Don't make a liar out of me.*

The guy looks me up and down. "Let's see it, big man," he says, and then he grins at his girlfriend.

The kid reaches in his pocket and holds out some tokens for me.

"I got it," I tell him. Then I grab a handful of tokens from my bag. It's sitting on the side of the machine where the girl is standing, so I turn my head a little. I don't wanna seem as if I'm looking at her legs. The guy mumbles something to the girl, but I don't pay it any attention.

"Let's do it, big man," the guy says, but he's still looking at his girlfriend. He's starting to irritate me.

I choose Stomp. The guy gives a stupid giggle, widens his stance a little, and then it begins. He has some decent moves, but I saw most of them when he was playing the kid. It's over before it really begins. I probably break a personal record, but I don't say anything. I let the machine do the work. Stomp has some pretty mean taunts, particularly if the fight ends quickly. The kid helps a little too because he can't stop snickering.

The guy's mouth drops open. "What the hell . . . ?" Obviously, he's just experienced defeat from Stomp for the first time. He isn't looking at the girl anymore. He looks at the screen, listening to the taunts he's never heard before.

"I wasn't with it that time," he finally says, still not looking at the girl. "Let's go again."

Before I can say anything—which I wouldn't do anyway—he's pumping in the tokens. This time he chooses Coolio. "Coolio's who I really play with," he says as he widens his stance again. "Let's do it."

I pick Stomp again, and almost catch my recent record. The guy isn't too happy now, especially since a crowd is forming around us. Stomp's taunts aren't heard too often, and they start attracting attention. Now, the guy is baited by the crowd.

"Come on. Let's do it," he says again. He still doesn't look at the girl.

"You're wastin' your money!" the kid tells him, smiling like he's at a birthday party. "You don't got it!" The kid's words make it harder for the guy to back down. The girl's watching, and so is everybody else. This is the point where intellect gets mugged by ego and macho.

"Let's do it," the guy says again.

We play a few more games, all of which I win with no trouble at all. Once, I even defeat the guy using Brain. The crowd's really into it now. They're not used to seeing Coolio being handled by the personalities I select. Even the guy's stupid girlfriend giggles.

"Damn!" the guy says, and he gives the machine a kick. Everyone can tell he hurts his foot because he winces, but he tries to hide it. The crowd laughs. Even I smile, but only a little.

"Dammit! Dammit!" the guy says over and over again. "Let's do it! Come on! Again!"

He's really lost it, and I can smell trouble. "I don't wanna," I say to him. "You can play by yourself." I'm giving him a way out.

"I'm ready! Come on!" He's trying not to look so worked up.

"Baby, it's just a game," his brainless girlfriend says to him. She's totally clueless.

"He uses cheap moves!" the guy says. I don't mind the accusation, but he gives me a little shove while I'm reaching for my bag. Not a real threatening shove, but a shove just the same. Now it's my turn not to back down in front of everybody. I shove him back.

His fist comes so fast that I barely have time to flinch. My jaw starts throbbing. That's the only thing that tells me where his punch went after I closed my eyes. I shove him again, this time as hard as I can. He goes down after slamming into someone in the crowd. He surprises me by how fast he gets up.

The crowd isn't helping much. They provide taunts like every crowd does. They also spread out a little to give us some room. I glance at my bag. When I see the kid standing next to it, it makes me feel a little better. The kid looks at me with the same look he gave me when he first put me into this mess—the worried look. I start wondering where the hell the manager is. Grownups are never around when it counts.

The guy kicks me in the stomach, but I don't feel it much. Obviously, he still has Coolio on the brain. He's actually trying to fight like him. He backs up to try another kick, but when it comes, I *see* it coming. I grab him by the leg and snatch him off balance. He hits the floor—hard. I start stomping on him like Stomp does in the video game, but I'm not thinking of Stomp. I'm wanting to leave, but I don't want the guy to come at me again before I can get to my bag. I also realize that I'm making a statement for everybody who's watching.

"Okay! Okay!" the guy yells, all curled up on the floor, trying to protect his vital parts. So I stop, even though my pulse is racing.

The crowd starts murmuring the word "stomp" until it turns into a chant. I go for my bag, but the kid is already holding it out for me. He's even zipped it up. "I'm gonna start practicing real hard with Stomp," he says to me.

I take my bag, and I want to say something to the kid, but I want to leave even more, so I do. I pass the manager reading a magazine at the entrance as I start through the mall. I take a deep breath. With each step, the "stomp" chant grows more faint, but I can still feel my heartbeat at the tip of my fingers—chanting.

Chapter 10

TONY TAKES THE LAST COOKIE from the plate, and after offering to share—everyone refuses—he stuffs the entire cookie in his mouth, a technique he's perfected since childhood.

"Sarah, I'm gonna give you the recipe," says Miss Annie. "You definitely gonna need it. This boy know he loves his chocolate chip cookies."

"He ain' try'n na hide da fack eithuh," says Mrs. Avery, frowning and shaking her head. "Eat'n like da cookies g'own jump off da plate an head out da doh. Dem cookies ain' finta go nowhe'uh."

"I like *yo'* chocolate chip cookies," mumbles Tony through a packed mouth.

Mrs. Avery frowns. "Boy, don' sit dare talkin' wit cho' mouf full!" she exclaims. "You makin' me look like I ain' raise you wit no mannuhs!"

Sarah and Miss Annie exchange glances, but keep their snickering to a minimum.

"Lookadare," says Mrs. Avery. "Dey laughin' at chew." She collects the plate and the three glasses. "Dey should know bettuh dan na be laughin' at me. So I *know* dey laughin' at chew." Then, she disappears into the kitchen.

Tony swallows hard and then grumbles, "Mama, we all family h'yuh."

"Yeah, but Ah'm na only one who g'own git blamed fuh hi you eat!" she calls back. "An you cane fool me. You juss showin' out in front uh Sarah. You cane fool me, boy. Yo' mama know bettuh. Always remembuh dat—yo' mama *know* bettuh."

Sarah and Miss Annie explode into a fit of giggles.

"Man . . . hi she soun'?" mumbles Tony, frowning now.

Miss Annie leans forward. "Chile, whatever make them cookies taste good to you, you keep right own doin' it."

"That's right, honey," adds Sarah. She places a hand on Tony's knee. "You keep right on ensuring your food doesn't escape, and every morsel is accounted for."

Miss Annie explodes again, and Sarah and Tony follow suit—Sarah more so than Tony.

"I guess you juss g'own haff ta school me own hi da eat cookies someday," he says, smiling.

"I wouldn't think of it," replies Sarah. "I find your Neanderthal approach attractive. It makes me crave a chocolate chip cookie better than any TV commercial could."

"I just like watchin' ya eat 'em," admits Miss Annie, grinning. "It makes me feel like I can cook!"

"You *can* cook," agrees Tony. "Always could."

"Well, I don't have ta cook fer ya no more," Miss Annie says. "You gitt'n you a wife." She adjusts her position on the couch. "It make me feel real old, havin' you all married an such. And yer a teacher now, too. Where you gonna be teachin'? Prudence Crandell? Chamblin?"

Tony's smile disappears. "No . . . Ah'm g'own be at Lincoln fuh uh lu'while."

Miss Annie stares at Tony hard, causing him to feel like a kid again. "Lincoln?" she finally asks incredulously.

"Yes, ma'am."

"You mean to tell me, you got all that college on the brain, and you wanna go teach at Lincoln?" she says with a frown.

Tony shrugs. "It's juss fuh na. Ah'ma fine somp'm bettuh, probbly in na Fall."

"Then, why not wait fer Fall?"

Tony sighs. "I need the experience."

"You can git ex'perence in the Fall," Miss Annie shoots back.

"Not *this* kind of experience," replies Tony. "Besides, we're getting married this summer, and I kind of like the idea that, as a husband, I'll have a source of income."

She gives Tony one of her all too familiar pregnant pauses, taking her time before responding, but Tony is used to it. "I see you ain't lost yer other talk none," she finally says, smiling again. "I guess I'm talkin' to the teacher now, huh?"

Tony gives Miss Annie a lopsided grin as he takes Sarah by the hand.

Miss Annie cocks her head to one side. "Well . . . I guess you know what cher doin'," she says, and then looks at Sarah. "What chew say, Sarah?"

Sarah nods. "He knows what he's doing." Then, she gives Tony's hand a firm squeeze. He kisses the back of her hand.

Miss Annie tilts her head to the other side. "It's funny hi you two look a heap better together in person than you ever could in a person's head."

Tony leans closer to Sarah. "Just in case you're wondering, sweetie, that's a bona fide compliment, coming from Miss Annie herself. Hard to tell, isn't it? But you get used to it after a while."

"Git use ta what?" asks Mrs. Avery, re-entering the room, drying her hands with a cloth.

"Git use ta Miss Annie," Tony says.

Mrs. Avery chuckles. "I done tole lis chile 'bout Miss Annie. You ain' gotta worry 'bout Sarah—I done tole 'uh."

Miss Annie's eyes narrow. "Told 'er what? What cha'll sayin' about me behine ma back?"

"Why, *nut'n*, Miss Annie," says Mrs. Avery. "I juss tole 'uh what uh nice person you is, dass all."

"I *know* that's a lie," Miss Annie grunts. "Sarah, you wanna know somp'm about me, you come to *me*. Anythang else is hearsay."

Sarah nods. "Yes, ma'am."

"Yes, ma'am," Tony and his mother repeat together.

Mrs. Avery places her hands on her hips and sighs. "Well . . . I done didja room, an I done tidied up da kitchen. I even put mo' water in nat cat's water bowl, so you ain' got ta worry 'bout dat cat. It'll be awright 'til I git h'yuh tomorrow aftuh church. Na, you g'own git some rest. We done already kept cha up longuh dan we shoulda."

"There you go, bossin' me around again," Miss Annie grumbles. When she struggles to her feet, Tony and Sarah also stand. "Come own, baby," Miss Annie says with open arms. When Tony steps forward, she fans him to the side. "Not chew! My *other* young'un."

Sarah raises her eyebrows and places a hand on her bosom. "Me?"

"Well, I sure as heck ain't callin' Sheronda a young'un!"

Everyone laughs except Mrs. Avery, who stands with her hands on her hips, slowly shaking her head. After hugging Sarah and Tony, Miss Annie finally turns to face Mrs. Avery. "Come here, precious."

Mrs. Avery sucks her teeth. "I was g'own *say*. . . ." She embraces Miss Annie and then gives her a kiss on the cheek. "Na, g'own git in ya chair."

Miss Annie fans a hand and grumbles, "Don't worry none about me, Miss Sheronda. Ya'll just be careful, bein' in these streets this time of night."

"I brought da c'ah," says Tony. "I figguh'd dey what'n g'own wanna walk all la way back, so I drove."

"You musta been thankin' 'bout Sarah," says Mrs. Avery. "You know I'own mine walkin'."

Miss Annie escorts them to the door, despite the disapproval of her three visitors. Once outside, Mrs. Avery turns the deadbolt with her personal key to the house; Miss Annie doesn't usually bother.

"Cole as it is, Ah'm glad you *did* bring na c'ah," says Mrs. Avery as they near the car. "I'll git in na back."

"Absolutely *not*," says Sarah incredulously.

Tony snorts, shaking his head. "Ain' no way you g'own keep us h'yuh all night, lookin' at chew try'n na cram in na back of uh hatchback."

Before a debate can ensue, Sarah springs into the backseat. Mrs. Avery reluctantly, albeit silently, climbs into the car as Tony turns the ignition.

"Not too fass," says Mrs. Avery as Tony pulls away from the curb.

Tony sighs. "Yes, Mother."

"Yo' daddeh's c'ah don' evuh seem like it's g'own quit runnin', huh?"

Tony shrugs. "I ain' have no problem out uh it *yet*." He pets the dashboard. "It's been good da me."

For a moment, everyone quietly listens to the hum of the engine, as if waiting for the car to contradict Tony at any minute. Then, Mrs. Avery glances over her shoulder at Sarah. "So what chew thank uh Miss Annie?"

"I like her," replies Sarah.

Mrs. Avery grins. "Yeah, but chew ain' like 'uh at firs'."

"What do you mean? I just—"

"Dass awright, baby girl," chuckles Mrs. Avery. "I tried da tell ya, she somp'm else when she wanna be. At one time, I almost came down nem stairs aftuh ya."

"You could *hear* us?" asks Sarah with amazement.

"Yeah, I could h'yuh ya. An when I heard hi she was gitt'n you all worked up, I was comin' fuh ya befo' you decided ta git up an run out da doh! But when I got uh lu'ways down na stairs, she decided ta git h'uh head back own right. So I went back ta cleanin'."

"I had no idea. . . ."

"I *know* you didn'!" Mrs. Avery says, laughing now. "You hadja head all droopin'. I said da myself, Lawd, looka h'yuh at what Miss Annie putt'n own nis girl! You juss looked *pitiful!*"

Mrs. Avery slaps Tony on the shoulder, causing him to release the laugh he's been trying desperately to subdue. Sarah sits in the backseat, her mouth agape, as the two in front incoherently express their apologies, though through the rapture of snorts, wheezes, and giggles.

"Don' let it bothuh ya, sweetie!" Tony gasps. "I done been nare many uh times! I know hi ya feel!"

Sarah joins in the laughter but says, "I can't believe you're laughing at me!" Then, she grabs Tony by the ear.

"No, baby! He *DRIVIN'!*" Mrs. Avery yells, with such a jolt that it startles Sarah and Tony.

"S-sorry. . . ." stammers Sarah, snatching her hand back.

Tony raises his eyebrows, and then holds the steering wheel with two stiff arms. "Ooookay," he says. "Reducing speed to twelve miles per hour. For the safety and comfort of our kinetically-troubled passengers, please keep your hands to yourselves until the vehicle has come to a complete stop, and thank you for scaring us half to death."

Sarah snickers with a hand over her mouth, while Mrs. Avery resists the urge to also grab Tony by the ear.

"I'm so sorry, Mama," gasps Sarah, almost choking now. "He caught me off guard."

"I ain' payin' him no 'tention, baby," says Mrs. Avery. She cranes her neck to face Sarah. "Why'own chew ax Mistuh Man ovuh h'yuh 'bout all lem whoopin's he use ta git?"

Tony's grin disappears. "Mama, dass cole."

Mrs. Avery chuckles. "Yeah, laugh *na*, Mistuh Man."

Tony catches Sarah's eye in the rearview mirror. "What did she say about me?"

"She said you were a miniature man of mayhem. That you had a nose for trouble, and a taste for its flavor."

Mrs. Avery folds her arms. "He wouldn've had *half* da trouble dat he had, if he woulda stayed away from nat devilish Bone growin' up," she says, looking straight ahead. "By da way, hi did it go wit cho' long time buddy-buddy in na paurk?"

"Okay," replies Tony, solemnly.

Mrs. Avery notices Tony's change in mood, but she decides to leave it at that. She allows Tony's response to echo inside the car for the rest of the trip home.

Mama knows better.

Chapter 11

KENNY FINALLY ROUNDS THE CORNER of his block at 9:26 P.M. Even from a hundred yards away, he sees the Confederate flag that covers the back window of Hank's oversized pickup. He slows his pace and takes a deep, deep breath, ignoring the simulated smoke caused by the forty-four-degree night air. He hopes the temperature has brought down the swelling on his mouth, his mark of defiance; he does not feel up to another confrontation today. Fatigue has claimed him, and his knees ache.

Nestled in his duffle bag, underneath the towel he uses as a sweat rag, rests illegal sustenance—five candy bars, three packs of cookies, and a sliver of beef jerky. As he walks up the driveway, he shakes and squeezes the duffel bag. The food is still quiet, still safe.

He enters the house, forcing a cough, and closes the door with a modest slam—his only proof that he isn't trying to be "sneaky." The muffled sounds coming from his mother's closed bedroom door hesitate, but only for a moment before starting again. Kenny can easily distinguish his mother's laughter—the high-pitched, trilling cackle with the giddy tone. The unmistakable sound of too little to eat and too much to drink.

Most of the lights are still on. In the dining area, the glass-top dining table is covered with a thin coat of cigarette ashes and blotches of spilled beer and vodka. An orange juice carton acts as the table's centerpiece, while an overflowing ashtray rests close to the edge. Tomorrow will be a usual day of his mother complaining about the musty second-hand fumes, while Kenny plays the silent and meticulous house servant, a role he never gets right.

He walks into the kitchen and spots the granola bar on the counter. It's the only thing out of place. When he looks in the refrigerator, he finds a bowl of chicken noodle soup and a half slice of grapefruit, each covered with plastic wrap. Like the granola bar, they also stand out, independent of their refrigerated counterparts. Items still joined with their package must *not* be tampered with—ever. Fruits are not to be sliced or peeled, and cans are not to be opened. Only those rations placed in plain view are considered sanctioned.

He isn't hungry. After storming out of Arcade Stadium, he shared a table with Daniel Defoe at the mall's food court. Only after killing a few chapters of *Robinson Crusoe* did he consider it safe to go back to the game room. The guy, his girlfriend, and even the kid were gone, and there was no sign that there had ever been a disturbance. Still, he decided to finish the remainder of his time playing in solitude, waving off all challengers.

He takes the food from the refrigerator, the granola bar from the counter, and then heads to his room. Even with his door closed, he still hears Hank and his mother laughing and shushing. He hides the granola bar and his smuggled supplies in the closet, and then starts on the cold bowl of soup as he resumes with *Robinson Crusoe*. By the time he finishes the grapefruit, *Robinson Crusoe* has only two chapters left to offer, but he decides to take the bowl back to the kitchen, toss the peelings in the trash, and turn in for the night.

He strips to his boxers and then climbs into bed. The voices in his mother's bedroom have been replaced by the sounds of noisy box springs and a restless headboard. Kenny pulls the covers over his head, satisfied that he has survived another day. Surviving helps keep the bad dreams away, and Kenny hates when nightmares rob him of true rest. His thoughts drift to Mr. Farley, and in less than five minutes, he's sound asleep.

*   *   *   *

IT'S THE EXPLOSION OF AN OPENING DOOR that causes Kenny's eyes to flutter open—barely. With a dormant consciousness, he gazes in the darkness of the covers still over his head. Two seconds after hearing the faint click of his light switch, the covers are ripped off of him.

"Geyyup, Kenny!" his mother slurs. She giggles as she stands over her son, wearing nothing but a flimsy robe. Hank stands in the doorway, totally nude. She jabs at Kenny with an index finger. "Let Hanky see wha' I'm talkin' about!" she commands.

Kenny doesn't move fast enough. He's momentarily preoccupied with the pain of the light in his eyes. He shadows his face with an outstretched hand.

"Geyyup!" his mother yells. She grabs his hand and yanks ferociously. Then, she glances back at Hank. "See, this another thing I tellin' you about!" she slurs.

"Get up, *boy!*" thunders Hank. "Don't cha hear ya mama talkin' to you?"

Although there's laughter in Hank's tone, the bass in his voice startles Kenny. Now, he's almost fully awake—almost. Somehow, he manages to clamber to his feet, but his vision is still blurred.

His mother lifts his t-shirt, exposing his stomach. "Lookit this!" she giggles, grabbing Kenny by the stomach. Her nails sink in, threatening to break the skin. "What can you do about it? He don't eat hardly nothin', and he still's growin'!"

Hank steps into the room. "Damn, boy!" he bellows. "What *you* need is some good ole exercise! Can yer big ass give me even one push-up?"

Pamela almost loses her balance when she closes her eyes in

laughter. "Push-up my *ass*," she snorts. "Tha'll be the day! Wha' you talkin' push-up?"

"Lemme see some jumpin' jacks!" Hank laughs. He grabs Kenny by the wrists and tries to lift his hands over his head, but Kenny snatches his hands away.

His mother grabs him by the throat and tries her best to muster a serious tone. "Don't you try . . . show out, Kenny! Don't try to show . . . *out!*" she hisses, groggily.

"Look at his eyes 'bout to pop!" laughs Hank, pointing.

When Hank's arms encircle Pamela's waist, her giggling returns, but she still has Kenny by the throat. Then, she finally notices the bruise on Kenny's mouth. "Wha' is this? You been fight . . . fight'n *again?*"

Now, Kenny is totally awake, but he doesn't respond. It's pointless; the scent of stale alcohol violates the air. Right now, any answer is the wrong answer.

Without warning, Pamela pounds her son with clenched fists. "You be fight'n again! You been fight'n . . . *again!*" she screams over and over. The force of her sudden onslaught catches Kenny off balance, and he stumbles back onto his bed. His mother straddles him immediately, her nudity flashing from underneath her robe, as she continues her raving and pounding, almost in tears. Other than closing his eyes, Kenny does nothing to shield himself from her fogged rage.

Hank snatches Pamela up with one arm. "Woman, you got time fer all that later!" he croaks. "Hell! We ain't got all night!"

Pamela's bloodshot eyes glower at Kenny with unparalleled revulsion and fury. *"WHAT'S THE MATTER WITH YOU?!"* she screams, as Hank leads her back into her bedroom.

For fifteen minutes, Kenny lies on the bed completely motionless. Only when he hears his mother and Hank's laughter and giggling does he decide to switch off his bedroom light and close his door. He glances at the clock—1:04 A.M. He collapses on his bed, face down. His crying brings no sniffles, no noise, just tears.

By tomorrow, his mother won't remember a thing, and he knows it. He also knows that if he still has the bruise, it will betray him yet again. Right now, he doesn't care. His mind aches along with his body. He doesn't want to think about tomorrow, nor does he want to think about the Northshore Karate Institute on Monday, or the new school he has to go to, a week from Monday—Lincoln High.

When the sounds of the noisy box springs and headboard return, he pulls the covers over his head, still crying. After ten minutes, with tear-stained cheeks, he's asleep again.

And then come the nightmares.

Chapter 12

MATTHEW HAS ALWAYS LOVED HER, since the first day of school, but their conflicting schedules make it difficult for him. He constantly watches for her in the halls, between classes, and has even slipped notes and dollar bills in her locker, professing his love for her, though he has never signed them. Matthew is only fifteen, and by adult standards, he doesn't know very much, but he knows he loves her. He would do anything to be in a regular class with her, a class other than homeroom, preferably a class without assigned seating. But for the past five months, he's been forced to settle for the ten minutes they share each day in homeroom. Further complicating his aching hormones is the fact that she sits four seats directly behind him. Even during their ten minutes together, he has to settle for the sound of her voice as she responds to the roll call.

. . . Elizabeth Arnold . . .

Here.

To him, no one says it better.

His only moments of reprieve have been those few instances when she has gone to the front of the classroom to sharpen her pencil, a vision of teasingly false mental refuge. And even though he's inhaled a different perfume each time she's passed, he has remembered most and loved them all. Each time, he has exhaled slowly, realizing how cruel life can be.

As chance would have it, today is his lucky day. Elizabeth whisks by, just moments after responding to her name during Miss Atkins' roll call. Another fragrance is added to Matthew's nasal shrine, and his eyes follow Elizabeth to the pencil sharpener mounted on the wall.

As his eyes drink in every ounce of her physical features, he decides that today is *the* day. Today, he'll show his feelings for her. Out in the open, when she's on her way back to her seat, he'll give her a sign of his love, a sign that says he's the answer to all of her past queries. A sign that says he's the one.

After Elizabeth grinds her pencil for an extra thirty seconds, she brings the newly sharpened lead within an inch of her bright red lips and then blows away the excess, the way Eastwood would blow a smoking gun—eyes slanted. She pretends to ignore the small whistles and kissing noises emanating from various parts of the classroom. She heads back to her seat, skirt threatening to rise with every step.

Matthew also ignores the verbal ogling. He stays focused on his love. He doesn't want to squander such a rare opportunity, a chance to come forward and identify himself. As she nears his desk, he brings his eyes to her face, the way he always does, without moving his head. As usual, she doesn't return his stare as she prances on, hips flailing, totally oblivious to his existence. As she passes him, Matthew makes his move. With talon-like fingers, he quickly grabs her by the left buttock and squeezes gently.

Elizabeth spins around to face Matthew, a boy she's never seen before. "What the . . .?!"

Matthew glances up at her and gives his warmest smile.

Elizabeth's astonishment turns to rage. She tightens a fist as best she can, given the length of her nails, and slams it down on Matthew's shoulder with all her might. By the time she realizes the same hand holds the pencil, it's too late.

"*AAAURGH!*" he screams as the pencil penetrates his shoulder.

Startled by his outburst, many students jump to their feet. Even

Elizabeth is shaken by Matthew's piercing yelp. She stumbles back, dislodging her pencil from his shoulder, but she now wields it like a knife, like a weapon.

"SONUVABITCH!" Matthew roars. He knocks his desk over to stand. "Bitch, I'll kill you!"

He takes a step toward her, but she convinces him to keep his distance by raising the pencil in a stabbing position. Her heart races as she notices the blood on Matthew's shirt sleeve, spreading downward.

"Elizabeth, put that pencil *down!*" yells Miss Atkins. The tone of her voice adds to the commotion of the class, to the adrenaline of the situation. "Matt! Everyone! Stay away from her! Elizabeth, I said put that pencil down!"

Elizabeth wants to comply but can't. *Matthew wants to kill her.* Everyone in the classroom has retreated to the walls, even before Miss Atkins' warnings. Some have scampered to the front of the classroom, threatening to leave. But Matthew doesn't budge from his cat-like stance. He's prepared to lunge at Elizabeth as soon as the opportunity presents itself.

Miss Atkins doesn't know what else to do. Of course, approaching Elizabeth is the furthest thought in her mind, but she isn't sure if code allows her to follow her instinct—*flee to safety*—so she simply stands in place, watching, paralyzed by her inability to make a decision.

Samantha Doyle, one of her "better" students, is the first to think of the "crisis alarm" button. "Miss Atkins!" she calls. "The button! *Press the button!*"

It's not Miss Atkins' fault. It could happen to anyone. Besides, it's only her second year teaching. She doesn't have the reflexes of a veteran teacher—not yet. That comes with time. During lunch period, they'll assure her of that in the teacher's lounge.

*   *   *   *

THE AMERICAN FLAG FLIES HIGH UPON a silver pole. It doesn't budge despite the small breeze that caresses Tony's face. He takes the steps of the front entrance to Lincoln High three at a time. He's fifteen minutes late. He misjudged the morning rush hour traffic, and the fender bender he passed didn't help, thanks to all of the rubbernecks. This isn't how he envisioned his teaching debut years ago.

The double doors are closed but unlocked. He snatches open the right door and is startled by an extremely muscular police officer who's escorting a girl from the building in handcuffs.

"Excuse me," says the officer.

Tony watches as they walk down the stairs, the officer gently holding the girl by the elbow. Only when they reach the bottom step does the girl's sobbing become audible, as if the outside ground brings new clarity to her situation. Tony is momentarily transfixed, unaware that he's still holding the door open for them, unaware that he's still running late. His stupor is broken by a sharp voice from behind. "Can I help you?"

Tony spins around to face a short, stout woman wearing a Lincoln High polo shirt, a skirt well beyond her knees, and tennis shoes. In her right hand crackles a two-way radio, and around her neck, resting below her sternum, dangles a clump of keys and a whistle. "I'm running late, but I'm Tony Avery," he says with a nervous smile, "the new English teacher."

The woman nods, unimpressed and brings the walkie-talkie to her face with a well-honed smoothness. "Principal Ryker, sir?" she calls. She takes her eyes off Tony as if to look for something more inter-esting. Tony stands glued in awkwardness, nervously swinging his leather briefcase—a graduation gift from his mother—as they wait for a reply.

"Yes, Dean Phillips," a voice finally responds.

"He's here, sir."

Another uncomfortable patch of silence.

"Thank you, Dean Phillips . . . Take him to my office . . . I'll be there shortly."

"Yes, sir," she says, and then glances back at Tony. "Follow me."

Tony has to walk faster than normal to keep up with her; she's quick for a woman of her size. "Is Mr. Ryker angry?" he asks. "He sounded angry."

"Principal Ryker takes *his* job seriously," says Dean Phillips, plowing ahead.

Tony takes a quiet, deep breath as he follows her through the empty halls in silence.

The neatness of the Main Office mirrors the condition of the school grounds—immaculate. Even though he hasn't seen many Main Offices, he knows the place is silent for a Main Office. Persons dart in and out with the purpose of worker ants, but without so much as a murmur. Everyone is focused on something, has something important to attend to.

Dean Phillips approaches a woman who's obviously absorbed in the clipboard she's holding. "Mrs. Madison, this is . . . the new teacher," she announces. "Sir, this is Mrs. Madison, our vice principal."

Mrs. Madison, a woman in her late thirties, takes her time with the clipboard before bothering to look up. "Hello, welcome to Lincoln," she finally says with a rehearsed flavor. Then she turns to the dean. "Dean Phillips, will you take these copies to Miss Atkins?"

"Yes, ma'am."

"And be sure to inform her that I will see her during her planning period."

"Yes, ma'am."

Vice Principal Madison turns back to Tony. "Enjoy your stay at Lincoln, Mr. . . . ?"

"Avery," Tony says, losing his smile.

"Glad to have you, Mr. Avery," she says, and then glances at the clock before scurrying out of the Main Office.

The pending silence is broken by the tapping of a keyboard in the distance. Tony looks to the back of the Main Office where Principal Ryker's secretary continues to type, even though she's been staring at Tony the entire time.

Dean Phillips clears her throat. "His office is over there," she says, pointing. "It's unlocked. Wait for him inside, but leave the door open."

She barely hears his "Thank you very much" before she darts out of the Main Office. The crackle of her walkie-talkie and the jingle of her keys fade quickly.

Tony exchanges a cordial smile with the secretary before stepping into the principal's office. The appearance of the office does little to ease his apprehensions for being late. Plaques, diplomas, and certificates are properly spaced; the desk is organized and tidy, and even the waste basket shows signs of pampering. This isn't the office of a man who tolerates excuses.

He walks over to the shelf behind the desk. A family portrait shows that Principal Ryker is a father of at least four children. Beside it rests a group photograph indicating that he's a former police officer.

"Fourteen years on the force and I never had to use my firearm," admits Principal Ryker, standing in the doorway. He eyes Tony curiously. "Mr. Avery, correct?"

Tony steps back to the other side of the desk. "Um . . . yes." He points at the principal's pictures. "I was just—"

"Have a seat, Mr. Avery," the principal says. He removes his blazer and hangs it on the coat rack behind the door. A walkie-talkie crackles on his belt.

Tony sits in one of the two oak-finished chairs facing the principal's desk. He feels Principal Ryker's eyes pierce the back of his skull as he closes his office door. "What seems to be the problem, Mr. Avery?" He places the radio on his desk and melts into his plush leather chair. He clicks an ink pen as he stares at his new English teacher, obviously disappointed.

"I . . . you mean my being late?"

Ryker makes an affirmative expression and continues to click his pen.

Tony clears his throat nervously. "I didn't know traffic would be so bad," he says, straining to maintain eye contact. "I apologize . . . it won't—that is . . . if I can—"

"Mr. Avery, I expect students to arrive on time," Ryker interrupts. He moves the radio from his right side to his left. "When students come to school, I expect them to be here before the first bell rings. They know this; the bus drivers know this; the parents driving their kids to school know this. When the kids switch from one class to the next, I expect them to do so in a timely manner—in other words, Mr. Avery, without being late." The principal takes a deep breath and places the pen in the right corner of his top desk drawer, then folds his arms. "How can I expect this from them *without* expecting it from my teachers?"

Tony shakes his head. "You can't."

Ryker raises an eyebrow. "Excellent answer, Mr. Avery," he says, then adjusts himself in his chair. "You know, Principal Hernandez spoke very highly of you—debate team, chess club, honor society, full academic scholarship, even a perfect attendance record during your last two years of school. He went on and on about what a terrific student you were, but never once did he mention that you were black."

Tony shrugs. "I guess it must have slipped his mind. After all, that was five years ago."

Ryker ignores the remark as he reaches into another desk drawer and retrieves a folder containing Tony's paperwork. "We have about three hundred black male teachers in Duval County. Of that number, only sixty or so are *not* coaches. You're a rare commodity, Mr. Avery. One would think it worth mentioning, is all I'm saying. I don't anticipate your being at Lincoln very long."

Tony accepts the folder and forces a smile. "Anything's possible."

"This morning, we had an incident, Mr. Avery," Ryker continues. "A girl stabbed a boy with a pencil during the homeroom period."

Though at a loss for words, Tony's face says it all.

Ryker pauses before continuing, as if for dramatic appeal. "What's even more disturbing," he says, tapping his fingers on the desk, "is that she actually took the time to *sharpen* her pencil beforehand."

Tony has absolutely no idea what he's supposed to say. Dozens of thoughts dance in his mind, too entangled for him to unravel even one statement or question.

The principal smiles for the first time. "It is very fortunate that your first period is also your planning period, Mr. Avery." He rises to his feet, and so does Tony. "Your mentor will give you the New-hire Induction Program workbook that must be completed during your first year. But your schedule is in this packet, along with the attendance sheets and Lincoln's English curriculum. The curriculum is fairly simple. Basically, you'll be prepping them for the English portion of the Aptitude Measuring Exam."

"Aptitude Measuring . . . ?"

"The AME test, Mr. Avery. Those students who pass it are placed back in the mainstream, typically back to the school they came from. Complete the paperwork and leave it with Miss Edwards before you leave today."

"Miss Edwards?"

"My secretary, Mr. Avery." The principal collects his blazer and radio and opens the door. "In your packet, you'll also find a copy of my list of expectancies. Read them, Mr. Avery."

Tony swallows. "Okay."

Ryker narrows his eyes at Tony before leading his new teacher to the far end of the Main Office. "Miss Edwards."

The secretary removes her hands from the keyboard. "Yes, sir?"

"This is Mr. Avery, our newest English teacher. See to it that he finds his classroom. Give him a map and highlight the way to his room from here."

"Yes, sir."

The principal grips Tony's right hand. "Enjoy your stay at Lincoln, Mr. Avery," he says, and then he strolls out into the hallway. Tony stands at Miss Edwards' desk, but he continues to stare at the entrance of the Main Office.

"You'll get used to it," Miss Edwards whispers with a smile. She retrieves a school map and a highlighter from her desk drawer.

"What's going on?" whispers Tony, relieved to find a real human being.

She starts to speak but decides to highlight the map when Mrs. Madison enters. After the vice principal disappears into her office, Miss

Edwards signals to Tony that she has written something at the bottom of the map, and then she dutifully returns to her work, tapping away at the keyboard, indicating that the conversation has ended.

Tony glances at the map, and then back at Miss Edwards. "Thank you," he says, taking a few backward steps toward the office exit. She responds with another quick smile but doesn't look up.

According to the map, his classroom is on the third floor. Again, Tony glances at the bottom of the map where Miss Edwards has written "Expectancy #8." He sighs before ascending the stairs two at a time.

The third floor has noise. Not the crackle of radios, the clicking of high heels or the rustling of papers, but *real* noise. Immediately, Tony registers three teachers—two by their raised voices, the third by a loud rapping sound, quickly followed by his demands for silence. As Tony rounds the corner of the hall leading to his classroom, other adult voices are heard yelling, pleading, threatening, and preaching. Their voices are submerged in an ocean of adolescent chatter and tossed with every wave of disruption.

Tony is afraid. Of what, he cannot say. But this feels nothing like the nurturing and reassuring environment of his internship. Perhaps his anxiety stems from the realization that he is indeed on his own, that good and bad decisions are solely his to make. Perhaps his fear stems from the harsh face of autonomy.

The door to his classroom is locked, and he doesn't have a key. "Of course," he mumbles.

When he turns to go back to the Main Office, he spies two custodians—one carrying a mop, the other carrying a half-full garbage bag. They watch him curiously, mumbling to each other.

The one carrying the mop waves at Tony to get his attention. "You need da git in nare?" he asks. His voice easily slices through the noise.

Tony glances at the locked door and then back at the two men. "According to the map, this is supposed to be my classroom."

They approach Tony, still eyeing him curiously. "The new Inglesh teacher, eh?" asks the garbage wielder. He speaks with an islander's accent.

Tony nods. "Yes—Tony Avery," he says with an outstretched hand.

The mop carrier grabs his hand first. "Ah'm Marshall Moore, but everybody calls me 'Cap.' Dis young'un right h'yuh is Malik. Don' worry 'bout his lass name—you would'n be able la say it anyway."

The islander ignores Cap and shakes Tony's hand. "Malik Ktanambu," he says.

"Pleased to meet you, Malik," Tony says. "That's a very nice accent—Jamaican?"

"Born un raised in Trinidad, but spent *time* in Joh-maica," Malik says with a smile. "So, you replacement far ole Mr. Gumble?"

Tony shrugs. "I guess so. They didn't tell me."

The custodians exchange a glance, and then Cap says, "I'll let chew in, but don' tell Mr. Rykuh I did it. We ain' supposed to wit'out his say-so, but I believe ya." He shakes his head. "Ain' nobody juss g'own up an claim Mr. Gumba class."

Tony thanks him and then asks, "Are his students *that* bad?" He tries not to sound alarmed.

Cap unlocks the door and says, "Dey *all* bad own na secon' an third flo'."

"Seniors're on the fust floor, Mr. Avery," adds Malik. "You don't notice noise 'til da second and thud floor, yes? To make it from dees school is to make it to *fust* floor, my friend."

"Mr. Gumba juss up an leff in uh huff one mornin'," offers Cap. "Ain' nobody seen 'im since. Dat was right befo' da Christmas break. Dey ain' been able la fine nobody dat'll stay. Substitutes won't even pick up da job no mo'. Fuh da pass munt, dey been jugglin' everybody aroun'—teachuhs, coaches, counseluhs—all of 'em been in an out uh dis classroom. Ah'm surprised dey ain' snatched me up yet."

"Good luck, Mr. Avery," says Malik. "You'll do fine." He smiles at Tony, but he doesn't sound convincing.

Cap pokes Tony's shoulder. "Juss don' let 'em git ta ya, man."

"Thanks again," Tony says. He can tell by the way they walk off that he'll be the subject of their conversation for the day.

The chalkboards are clean, but the walls are covered with signs and posters offering grammatical hints, behavioral tips, and words of motivation and encouragement. Mounted on the front of the teacher's desk is an NBA poster sporting the phrase "Dare to Dream." The blinds on the windows are closed, and their cords are tied at an unusual height, out of reach. Hanging underneath the clock is a handwritten sign that reads: "Time will pass, how about you?"

Tony sits at the teacher's desk—*his* desk. It's covered with carved messages, none of which express a student's love for a teacher. He opens his packet and thumbs through everything until he finds the principal's list of expectancies entitled "Ryker's Expectancies." Expectancy number four warns against "idle, pointless socializing on school time," and suggests that such "fruitless habits" be reserved for lunch and after-school hours. Expectancy number eight covers "attendance and punctuality" while number fifteen mentions "bus detail." The list ends at number twenty-seven—"patrol and surveillance."

After glancing over the packet and signing everything of relevancy, he places it in his briefcase. According to his schedule, he has four minutes before the bell beckons him to come out of his neutral corner. His heart is racing; his palms are moist; and his thoughts are scattered, but he remains calm by controlling his breathing.

Again, he glances at the clock—three minutes left. He removes a blank sheet of paper and a marker from the desk drawer, and writes in bold black letters: Time is either invested or spent.

Now, the clock has a new sign. He rips the old one in half and tosses it into the waste basket. When he sits back down, the bell rings, and his pulse skips a beat. He tries to swallow, but his mouth and throat are dry, and the effort is almost painful.

The halls become a roar.

They're on their way.

Chapter 13

MR. PALMER NO LONGER SEES A THING. In fact, it's been over five months—the beginning of the school year, to be exact—since he's had what educational textbooks call "with-it-ness," the state of being aware of your surroundings at all times, a teacher's knack for knowing. Mr. Palmer no longer has with-it-ness; he relinquished it. What choice did he have? They never found who wrote the note; they never found who vandalized his car; they never found who phoned his home, despite his unlisted number.

Of course, there were inquiries, but the pursuit was never real. The investigation was just routine documentation, a pacifier. Mr. Palmer has learned his lesson; he no longer sees a thing. Not in his classroom, not in the halls, and not as he stands in the boys' restroom at the beginning of his PS duty—which teachers secretly call "BS duty." For him, patrol and surveillance will never be the same, but he feels that the students like him for it—finally.

The students used to harp on his appearance, but making cracks about his weight and sloppy demeanor soon lost its luster. They no longer bother. The Social Studies teacher has become a shadow. In some ways, they give him a subtle hint of respect—that is, small apparitions of it, fertilizer for his favoring delusions—but they still call him "the B-1 Palmer" regardless of his vicinity.

The male students pour into the restroom. Some occupy stalls and stand at urinals, some don't. Rodney Coleman almost lights the cigarette in front of Mr. Palmer before walking into his usual stall. As soon as he clicks the lock, James Cotner flies into the restroom in a huff. Although all stall doors are closed, he knows exactly where to find Rodney.

"Rod! Check it out, yo!"

"Hole own, damn!" replies Rodney. He flushes the toilet, but keeps the stall door locked.

James slaps the door. "We finely gotta teachuh! Gumbo's class! He black, man! He *black!*"

"Only somebody like you'uh be crazy about dat! Leave me alone!"

"Bettuh dan havin' somebody like dat jive ass Mr. Tuddles!" replies James as he glances at Mr. Palmer. "You won't somebody like dat jive ass Mr. Tuddles? Mr. Whitebread?"

"Whatevuh you say, Mr. Malcolm Luther Mandela!" Rodney replies. He flushes the toilet once more before he emerges from the stall. Then he glances at Mr. Palmer. "Damn, Powuh—you cole. B-1 still standin' nare, nigguh. You juss don' be givin' uh damn."

Mr. Palmer pretends he doesn't hear, as best he can.

TONY REMAINS SEATED AS THE STUDENTS ENTER the classroom in groups of twos and threes, each talking about something worthy of an excited and raised voice. The classroom grows in attendance and noise. Some take a seat, others continue standing, but their conversations don't miss a beat, even when things are said that cause the group to glance at Tony.

"Hey, what's your name, yo!" yells Jose Perediaz from the back of the classroom. The noise dies a little.

"My name?" asks Tony, smiling. He recognizes this greeting as an opportunity to build rapport, and he's anxious not to squander it. His smile broadens.

Jose mumbles something to his group, but is obviously overheard by the rest of the class as the room erupts into a fit of laughter and stomping.

Tony loses his smile.

"Yeah, yo!" replies Jose, his Spanish accent more pronounced. "I'm asking you what *your* name is!"

Tony springs to his feet. "Hold on . . . I'll write it on the board."

"Yeah, you *do* that!" Jose snaps.

The class erupts again.

When Tony turns to face the board, his back to the class, another comment penetrates through the verbal rumble from a different part of the room, still too low to decipher. Only the tone and the responding eruption indicate the spirit of the statement. Tony writes "Mr. Avery" on the board with extra pressure, breaking the chalk in half. The late bell has yet to ring, and he already feels a twinge of irritation.

Jarek Mitchell and his two confidants, Corey Watson and Jacob Pauls, enter the room with a moan. They take the three desks in the back corner opposite Jose's group. Jarek pulls out a deck of cards.

"Wha's up, Mr. Teachuh!" exclaims Rodney, entering the classroom. He's followed by James, who's chanting lyrics of a song and timing the verse with the rhythm of his stomping feet.

"Avery," Tony replies.

"What?"

"My name is Mr. Avery."

Rodney smirks at the man standing behind the desk. "'S'cuse me, Mr. Teachuh *Avery!*" he snaps. Then he heads to the back of the classroom, and the class explodes again.

"Ya'll g'yuh da man some respect!" James says. "Da brothuh try'n na do his job!"

"Uh-oh!" exclaims Keith Reynolds. "Ya'll done fired up Powuh!" He jumps on a desk and thrusts a fist at the ceiling. "Hey, Powuh! Powuh ta da people, yo! Ah'm wit it!"

The class roars.

"Quiet please!" Tony says. He tries to be heard using a civil voice.

"Please get off the desk!"

Marcus Lafavor and Roland Hess lunge into the room after the bell sounds.

"We got uh new teachuh?" Roland asks.

"Guess so," Marcus replies. He waves a hand at James. "Hey, Powuh! You likin' nis, ain't cha?"

"That was the bell, everyone!" says Tony, trying to slice through the ruckus. "Please take your seats!"

Marcus glares at Tony from head to toe and then turns back to James. "Hey, Powuh! Wha's wrong wit cha boy?" he yells. Then he ignores Tony along with the rest of the class.

"Hey, Powuh!" snickers Rodney. "He soun' juss *like* Mr. Tuddles, boy! *Two* slices!"

"Kiss my ass!" James shoots back. He takes a seat and starts a rhythm on his desk.

Lisa Boyer peels away from the class and approaches the teacher's desk, then walks behind it to stand next to Tony. "Mr. Avery, you cane do nut'n wit dem," she says, not missing a beat with her gum smacking. "Dey ain' g'own listen. You won't me ta do somp'm fuh ya? Take somp'm ta da office uh somp'm?"

Tony forces a smile. "No . . . thank you. Now, please . . . take your seat."

"You won't me da take da roll?" she persists. "I can do da roll fuh ya."

He wills another smile to his face. "You would be helping me a great deal if you would take your seat right now."

Lisa shrugs, struts away, and blends back in with the subtle chaos, joining a conversation with the familiarity of never having left.

Tony frowns. "May I please have your attention!"

A few glance at the front of the room as if Tony is a momentary distraction. James is one of the few who's seated. He beats on his desk without talking to anyone, drumming another tune. Jarek, Corey, and Jacob are on their second hand of a card game—seven card draw.

Richard Brigman has been seated the entire time, his head buried in his folded arms. His snoring is camouflaged by the noise. Davon Williams is one of the few who gives Tony any resemblance of attention, but the majority of the class remains standing, talking, laughing, and even shouting.

Tony almost laughs at the notion of sending an entire class to the Dean's office. "I need to call the roll, people!"

Marcus looks at their new teacher wannabe. "We all h'yuh!"

"I don't know that for sure," says Tony.

"Well, we know dat—*fer sure*," snaps Marcus. "An Ah'm tellin' ya we all h'yuh!"

The class explodes.

"What is your name?" Tony asks.

A series of "uh-ohs" quiets the class to some extent.

"Why you need da know *my* name? What *I* do?"

"What is your *name?*"

The class quiets down more. They recognize the possibility of an entertaining confrontation, something Marcus has vast experience with. He's one of the school's leading performers in that regard, and Tony is taking the bait.

"I would *tell* ya ma name," starts Marcus, the class growing even quieter, "but I ain' allowed da talk ta stranguhs, an ney'own git no stranguh dan *you!*"

The class explodes into a fit of screaming, stomping, and high-fiving. Tony believes that in another role, he too, would laugh, or at the very least, crack a smile. Unfortunately, he's not in another role. But still. . . .

"That's very humorous, Mr. What-can-I-do-to-attract-attention-to-myself-because-I-don't-receive-enough-of-it-at-home."

The card-dealing pauses; the percussions cease, but the snoring continues as the room erupts, showing the lack of loyalty toward Marcus. Tony's verbal reflex pays off—sort of.

"Teachuh try'n na rank own ma boy!" exclaims Roland. "Git 'im Marcus! Show 'im what time it is!"

Rodney looks over at James. "Hey, Powuh! Marcus 'hue-ma-russ!'" he laughs.

"Hey! Who changed da clock sign?" a voice rings out.

"I'own git it!" answers another.

"Like time is money?"

"Spending."

"*He* probably did it."

"Invessin' yo' money."

"It's da same!"

"I still don' git it."

"Okay, check dis out, yo!" starts Marcus, the room plummeting to silence. "Dat crack had uh luh flavuh ta it . . . juss like uh triple-stuffed Oreo dass been out uh da pack too long, but hang wit us, we'll git rid uh some uh dat fillin' fuh ya!"

The class hits the ceiling, but falls with almost the same suddenness, anticipating Tony's reply. Only the sound of snickering in the back of the room and Richard's snoring can be heard.

Tony speaks in a low, even tone. "If I don't hear your response, you're absent, and your inability to hear me call your name is no excuse." He clears his throat and calls roll.

"Barbara Anderson . . ."

A mixture of groans and laughter fills the room.

"She ain' h'yuh, Mr. Avery," says Lisa. "She ain' *nevuh* h'yuh."

The class continues moaning, talking, and laughing, but Tony maintains his low voice.

". . . Lisa Boyer . . ."

"Dass me!" she says, smiling and waving her hand enthusiastically. At this, the class laughs even more, but Tony doesn't change his tone.

"He cane hang, Marcus!" exclaims Roland.

". . . Richard Brigman . . ."

"Dass him sleep," says Lisa, pointing.

"Girl, why'own chew shut up!" snaps Marcus.

"Don' tell huh da shut up!" says Faith Dunn. "*You* shut up!"

". . . Rodney Coleman . . ."

The class pauses for a moment, some glancing at Rodney.

". . . James Cotner . . ."

"Ah'm h'yuh, man," says James, frowning. He starts another beat on his desk.

". . . Faith Dunn . . ."

"Here," says Faith, raising a hand.

". . . Keith Fryer . . ."

Rodney finally raises his hand. "Ah'm h'yuh, man—Rodney Coleman." He takes a few steps forward. "Dass me. Ah'm h'yuh."

Tony keeps his eyes on the roll. "No, you're absent. Michael Gray . . ."

"Here," says Michael. A few students take their seats.

"Hi you g'own maurk me absent, an Ah'm h'yuh?" Rodney asks, frowning now.

". . . Roland Hess . . ."

"Here," says Roland, taking a seat.

". . . Brandon Harris . . ."

"You maurk me absent, it's g'own look like I was skippin'." complains Rodney. "I ain' skippin'! Ah'm *h'yuh!*"

"Right h'yuh," says Brandon, raising a hand in answer to the roll call.

"Man, I ain' cleanin' no toilets an all uh dat because uh somp'm I ain' do!" insists Rodney. "Ah'm h'yuh!"

Cleaning toilets? wonders Tony, but he doesn't ask. He continues with the roll. ". . . Victor Lawrence . . ."

"He ain' h'yuh," says Lisa, now standing beside Tony, peering at the attendance sheet.

By the time the roll is done, Rodney has pleaded his case twice more and has kicked a desk, but Tony never falters. Even with his heart racing, Tony is determined that Rodney is no longer in the room. Part of him wants to tell Rodney it's alright, that he'll mark him present if he only settles down, but he doesn't know if such a move would loosen the grip he seems to have on the class at the moment; he feels it would. So, at the moment, he doesn't know what to do, and Rodney is in his face, a crossroad with an attitude.

Tony looks at the floor and controls his breathing.

"Am I h'yuh uh what?" asks Rodney. He takes another step closer. Tony doesn't look up. The rest of the class chimes in:

"Rod gitt'n ready da swang own 'im."

"Yeah right."

"What he doin'?"

"Swang own 'im, Rod."

"Look at 'em."

"Rod ain' crazy."

"He 'bout ta cry."

"Why he ain' sayin' nut'n?"

"Damn."

"Who?"

"Rod *is* crazy."

"He look so stupid."

"Let da man talk, ya'll."

"Check out da shoes, ya'll. Check out da shoes."

"G'yuh 'im some tissue. He 'bout ta cry."

"Dey bofe look stupid if you ax me."

"He wait'n fuh us ta shut up."

"Oooo—an high-waters too."

"Why he ain' sayin' nut'n?"

"Dass uh shame."

"Ain' nobody *ax* you."

"He trippin."

"He gitt'n ready da ride out, ya'll."

"Powuh, wha's up wit cho' boy?"

"What he thankin' 'bout?"

"He ain' *got* nut'n na say."

"He look so stupid."

"Why he *my* boy? Kiss my ass."

"He meditat'n, ya'll. He gitt'n ready da karate somebody."

"He ain' goin'."

"Prayin'—I say prayin'."

"Somp'm."

"Swang own 'im, Rod."

"Yeah, right. Rod don' know no karate."

"Five dolluhs say Rod ain' g'own swang."

"He ain' crazy."

"I'd fall out."

"He prayin', ya'll."

"Look like he 'bout ta cry."

"Dass what Ah'm sayin'."

"Hurry up and git to the Amen."

"Ya'll crazy."

"Damn."

"Man, Ah'm h'yuh," says Rodney as he spins around to take a seat.

"Rod crazy, ya'll."

"Dey *bofe* crazy."

"You absent, Rod. Might as well git cho' ass up an leave."

"Hey ya'll, did he call my name?"

"Damn."

"Yeah. He called you. I'own know if you said nut'n."

"Ah'm h'yuh."

"Whey my five dolluhs at?"

"Who said dat? I ain' absent *nut'n*."

"Why you lookin' nis way? It what'n me."

"Nigguh please."

"I'own owe you no five dolluhs, nigguh. We ain' shake own it."

Tony clears his throat, brings his head up, and raises a hand. The class becomes silent, mostly out of curiosity, and again, snoring is heard. "If you listen to nothing else, listen to this," Tony says, his hand still in the air. "First of all, as a student, you're supposed to raise your hand if you want to talk to the teacher. Therefore, I will do the same when I want to talk to the class."

Mild snickering follows as Tony paces the front of the room. "I've just decided to treat everyone here as an adult—an adult in the real world. This classroom is now a part of the real world."

"Real world?"

"Hunh?"

"I tole ya'll dis nigguh crazy."

"What?"

"This changes some things," continues Tony. "For instance, I will *not* waste my time and the time of the students in here on writing referrals. No referrals will be written in this class. This is now the real world."

"What chew mean you ain' g'own write no referrals?" asks Marcus, warding off the mumbling and snickering. "Wha's dat supposed ta mean?"

Tony frowns at the question. "Marcus—right?"

"Yeah."

"It means what it sounds like it means, Marcus."

"So . . . no mattuh what we—"

"If you don't do what you're supposed to do on the job, your boss won't keep sending you to the office. Your boss doesn't keep writing you up on a referral." Tony scans the faces. Only snoring is heard. "If you don't do what you're supposed to do in college, your professor won't keep sending you to the office. Your professor won't keep writing you up on a referral."

There's an undertone of soft laughter, but Tony ignores it as he continues pacing. "Therefore, if you do *not* want to act the way you're supposed to in this class—and I'm not about to spell it out for you because you *know* what I'm talking about—I will *not* send you to the office. I will *not* write you up on a referral. You will soon be in the real world, on your own. What better place to practice being in the real world than in the classroom?"

"Oh, so you juss g'own—"

"I'm talking, Marcus."

Some snickering is heard, but the class generally remains quiet. Tony continues pacing. "From now on, just like any adult in the real world, I expect you to do *only* what you want to do."

Silence.

"You are adults now, responsible for your *own* lives. If you don't want to be in this class, don't come."

"You won't write us up?" asks Marcus.

"I will *record* your absence," Tony says. "That's *my* responsibility as an adult, but if you don't want to be here, I don't want you here."

"So, you don' care if—"

"I care about every student in here; I'm supposed to. But if you're on the other side of that door," he says, pointing at the door. "You're *not* a student in here."

Marcus frowns. "So . . . if we leave, whey we supposed ta go?"

Tony walks behind the teacher's desk, places both hands on it, and leans forward as if preparing to whisper to the class. "Why should I care?" he finally says.

"'Cause you da teachuh," Lisa offers.

"I thought teachuhs was supposed ta care," adds Roland, mockingly.

"I am your new English teacher," Tony announces. "I'm here for you, and I *do* care about you." He looks around the room, and then says, "But I will not care about you . . . *for* you."

The room quiets, and Marcus is at a loss for words.

"This is a room for students, ladies and gentlemen. If you do *not* want to be a student in here, then do what any other adult in the real world would do and be—some—place—else. Adults don't make a habit of doing what they don't want to do. If you want to be an adult—fine. Let's be adults, starting today."

The class remains silent. Marcus is now the only one still standing. He feels the discomfort but ignores it. "Dass stupid," he finally says. "Grownups do thangs dey'own wanna do."

Tony smiles. "Like what?"

"Like *what?*" Marcus says, sounding as if his new teacher is a fool. "Like uh lot uh thangs—work, fuh instance. Uh *lot* uh people don' wanna work, but dey go 'cause dey ain' got no choice. Dey got ta pay bills an stuff."

Many others express their agreement with their obstinate classmate.

"There are a lot of things adults don't *like* to do," corrects Tony. "For instance, many adults don't *like* to go to work, but they go. Many don't *like* to pay taxes, but they pay. Many don't *like* to go to college, but they go. Many don't *like* to floss their teeth, but they floss. Many don't *like* to pay for what they take out of a store, but they pay." Tony raises his eyebrows. "Now . . . why is that, Marcus? Why would a person do something that they don't like or even feel like doing?"

"'Cause dey haff to."

Tony smiles; the class giggles, but their attention is steadfast.

"Come here, Marcus."

Marcus steps back. "What? Man, what I do na?"

"Absolutely nothing. Come stand next to me, I want to illustrate something."

There's giggling and snickering, but Marcus complies, timidly.

"Why did you come *that* way?" asks Tony.

"What?"

"Why did you come to *this* side? Why didn't you come to the *other* side?"

Marcus eyes Tony as if his new teacher is trying to be funny. "Dis way quickuh," he says, frowning.

A few laugh.

"Was the other side available to you?" Tony asks. "Could you have walked to the *other* side?"

"Yeah, but like I said, dis way quickuh," Marcus fires back.

Tony grins. "How do you *know* it's quicker? Did you take the other way before?"

"Look at it—it's obvious," answers Marcus, motioning with his hands, exaggerated irritation in his voice. Giggles report here and there.

"So, is it safe to say that when faced with a choice, you have a tendency to choose the 'obvious'?"

"Dass uh trick question, ain' it?"

The class laughs.

Tony smiles. "No. It's not."

Roland stands and says, "If it's *obvious*, hell yeah you g'own take it."
He sits back down. "I mean, damn. It's *obvious*, ain' it?"

The class laughs again.

Tony raises an eyebrow. "And you are . . . ?"

A series of uh-ohs fills the room.

"Ah'm Roland. Me an ma boy dare, we like partnuhs in crime, like
thunduh an lightnin'.'"

"Mo' like salt an peppuh," Lisa mumbles.

More laughter, louder this time.

Roland stands and turns before the class, arms stretched out. "Oh,
why uh white man cane git no respect? Boy, ya'll g'own make me run
off an join na Clue Clucks Clan one uh dese days!"

The class explodes, and even Tony chuckles. "Why don't you come
join your friend," he says.

"You know what, I thank I'll *do* dat," says Roland. He looks at Lisa.
"So I can git away from Miss Otch ovuh h'yuh."

"Miss Otch?" says Lisa, jerking her neck.

"Yeah, first name 'Bea'—Bea-otch!"

The class erupts as Roland walks behind Tony's desk. "I came na
short way, too," he says. "Da *obvious* way."

More laughter.

Tony folds his arms. "I noticed. So, I ask you again," he says, this
time, to the entire class, "is it safe to say that when faced with a choice,
we have a tendency to choose the obvious?"

Many mumble their agreement along with Marcus and Roland.

Tony lifts an index finger. "Now . . . do you *have* to choose the
obvious?" He points at Marcus and Roland. "*Could* they have gone to
the other side?"

"Yeah, but goin' na othuh way woulda been stupid," adds Marcus.

Tony walks around to the front of the desk, leaving Marcus and
Roland standing behind it. "A person has a job that she absolutely

hates, but she needs to pay the bills; she needs to put food on the table for her children. Should she keep the job, or should she quit and never go back?"

The class pauses.

"That's stupid too, yo," Jose finally says. "She don't got no choice. It ain't like she—"

"Yes, she do!" snaps Lisa. "She got uh choice!"

"She ain' *got* ta go ta work if she'own won't to," adds Faith.

"So, what's she gonna do?" asks Jose, mockingly. "Let all her kids starve?"

"She *could*."

"Sho' could."

"Right, that *is* an option," interjects Tony. "Not the more *obvious* of the two, but still an option. But as Marcus has pointed out, *not* choosing the obvious—going the other way—can be stupid."

The class pauses again.

Tony folds his arms and takes a deep breath. "There is very little that we *have* to do," he says. "Very little—aging, for instance. Aging is not a choice. Breathing—we all have to breathe. In fact, it's impossible to commit suicide by holding your breath." He looks around at all of the faces staring back at him. "What else?"

They all look at each other—some thinking, others waiting. Something is murmured, causing a muffled giggle.

"Come on . . . what else?" eggs Tony.

"Being born?"

Tony points at the girl in the second row, third seat. "What is your name, ma'am?"

"Jasmine . . . Woods."

"You are absolutely correct, Jasmine," says Tony, smiling now. "We had no say in our mother's decision to have a child." He motions for Marcus and Roland to have a seat, and then he takes a deep breath, arms folded. "Make no mistake, people—adults do what they *want*. It's just that sometimes a good choice—the short way, the *right* way—can seem sooo obvious that the alternate route is overlooked; it's as if it's not even there. Other times, the alternate route, as Marcus pointed out, seems stupid."

"*Is* stupid—I said 'is.'"

Tony nods. "My apologies, Marcus—*is* stupid." A whisper is heard, followed by a giggle, but Tony ignores it. "But what about people who *choose* the alternate route? Why would a person choose *that* way?"

"Dey stupid."

"Ignorant."

"Dey'own know no bettuh."

"I'own know."

"Dumb."

"Dey won't to."

"Dey crazy."

Tony raises a hand. "I heard 'stupid,' 'dumb,'—I think I heard someone say 'crazy.'"

"I said 'crazy,'" admits Davon.

"So nigguh?"

"Good fuh you."

"Ya'll be quiet."

"Who you thank—"

"They're all good answers," interrupts Tony, raising his hand again, "but another reason a person might take the less obvious is because they don't know where it leads; they don't know the consequences—and, oh yes, there's a consequence at the end of *every* choice. Another person takes the long way," continues Tony, gesturing toward the path neither Marcus nor Roland took, "because the more obvious route *isn't* so obvious."

Again, the class chimes in:

"Like I said—ignorant."

"Dey dumb."

"Dat don' mean ney ain't crazy."

Tony raises his hand. "Regardless of *why* we choose what we choose," he interrupts, raising his voice almost to a shout, "can we *now* agree that, as adults, we have choices?"

Half agree, half remain silent, but all are attentive.

Tony glances at the clock, astonished at how much time fifty minutes is not. His grimace intensifies. "From now on, ladies and gentlemen, this classroom will be reserved for my adult *students*, those adults who want to learn. I cannot stress this enough—if you do *not* want to be here the way an adult student is supposed to be, then be someplace else. Where? Wherever you *want* to be. It's *your* life. Choose your *own* path."

The snoring has stopped for some time now; the cards have been put away; the room is still silent.

"We started on a sour note," says Tony, his voice now at an even tone as he glares at Rodney Coleman. "Tomorrow, let's take it from the top. I will spend time getting to know my students, finding out where we are in our studies, where we need to be, and how we're going to get there. For those of you who are *serious* about being a student rather than a well-liked, disruptive, entertaining class clown who probably can't even spell 'smart choice,' please remember to bring pen and paper the next time you come to class."

Tony walks back to his desk, and again, leans on it, assuming the whispering stance. "As for those of you who choose *not* to make the obvious choice—for whatever reason you may *think* you have— farewell . . . good luck . . . and remember, I'm here for you if you ever *choose* to change your mind."

Lisa raises her hand.

"Yes?"

"What if one uh da dumb ones come in h'yuh an ney'own wanna leave? What chew—"

"I will send one of my *students* to the office, where they will find someone who will come back and remove the 'dumb one' from our class—obviously."

Tony maintains his stern, slightly irritated demeanor. He sits and jots down notes without ever looking up. In the back of his mind, he wonders what instructional sins he has committed. The class mumbles softly among themselves, but it eventually reaches the volume of normal conversation. Most talk about their new teacher, their new predicament, but without getting too loud.

When the bell rings, the students file out without a single good-bye. Tony takes a deep breath and massages his temple. He has survived his first class.

Four more to go.

Chapter 14

ON THE TOP RIGHT CORNER OF TONY'S lunch tray rests collard greens or spinach; he isn't sure which. He'll eat the salad, chicken, and roll, but he'll play it safe and stay away from the scoop of over-shredded, overcooked leaves.

He leaves the thunder of the cafeteria and enters the teachers' lounge. He's surprised to hear robust conversation and laughter. The room is the size of a typical classroom, and has four vending machines he wishes he had known about. The sink area sports a large microwave, and there's an ice cream machine. Two of the four long tables are empty. The table closest to the door is filled with teachers, while the table in the far corner is where the custodial staff sits.

Malik and Cap, seated with three other gentlemen, wave the new teacher over. Tony places his tray in front of a vacant seat at the teachers' table, one located between two jabbering educators, before obliging.

"New Inglesh teacher still wit us, I see," says Malik, smiling. "Just four more weeks, un Cap owes me one dollar."

The table enjoys a quick chuckle. "D-Don't chew listen na dis fool," stammers Cap, smiling. "I what'n doin' nut'n but talkin'."

"Dass all you *evuh* do, Cap," adds the largest and oldest-looking member of the group. He addresses Tony. "If you wanna know anythang about anythang, Cap's da man. He'll even tell ya about cha *self.* Am I ly'n, Jay-Jay?"

The young man wearing jewelry and cologne says, "You ain' ly'n, Coach." Then the table enjoys another chuckle, Cap included.

"So hi it's goin' so far?" asks Cap.

Tony nods. "I think it's going okay, Cap," he says. "Maybe even enough for you to lose that dollar."

The table erupts. "Say it right, Mr. Avery!" the coach says. "Look out na!"

"I don't blame you, Cap," adds Tony. "My third period class gave me the scoop on how many people have come and gone since Mr. Gumble's disappearance."

"Three in less dan uh munt," Cap says. "But dat don' mean nut'n. You got it."

"I was wondering which number was right," Tony says. "I was told everything from three all the way up to seventeen."

"Dey was probally count'n substitutes too," Jay-Jay offers.

"At any rate," Tony says, "even some of my *students* have voiced an opinion on how long they think I'll be here."

"Ta be honest, man," the coach adds, "pretty much everybody's been talkin' 'bout chew. When you was late dis mornin', dey thought chew what'n comin'—me included. But chew h'yuh na, an nass all lat mattuhs. You go'own do yo' job, an fuhgit about all lese gamblin' fools. You evuh need anythang, you juss ax fuh Coach Bryant, awright?"

Tony grins. "I really appreciate that."

"Ain nut'n ta it," the coach says. Then he waves at everyone at the table. "I'll see ya'll gentlemen latuh." He says a few words to those at the teacher table before he throws his lunch trash away and leaves the lounge.

"Well," Tony says, "thanks again for getting me in my classroom this morning."

Cap shakes his head. "Don' even worry 'bout it."

"You enjoy your lunch, Mr. Avery," Malik says. "And we be seein' you around, yes?"

"You can count on it," replies Tony. "In fact, go ahead and put me down for a dollar," he says, laughing with Cap.

A few teachers join the chuckle as Tony returns to his tray.

A small, thin man dressed in coat and tie, sitting across from Tony, asks, "So, how are the little devils treating you, Mr. Avery?"

"Just fine, Mr. . . ."

"Tuddles."

Tony smiles. "Oh, *you're* Mr. Tuddles."

A few snicker, the rest at the table smile.

"So, you've heard of me already," says Mr. Tuddles. "Why am I not surprised?" He rolls his eyes and takes a swallow of his tea. "So, am I the only one finding his way on their slander list?"

"Actually," says Tony, "there's a Miss Atkins. . . ."

"That would be me," says Miss Atkins, raising her fork, but still looking at her salad.

Tuddles frowns. "Well, of course they'd want to drum up *all* about the dreadful occurrence today," he grumbles. He takes another sip of tea. "In fact, I wouldn't be a bit surprised if some are plotting to do one better this very instance."

A chunky man drinking a Slimfast says, "Mr. Avery, not everyone at this table shares Mr. Tuddles' obnoxious hatred for the kids."

"You're absolutely right, Mr. Genrich," Tuddles says. "The rest of you choose to loathe them in silence."

Everyone voices their disagreements with a friendly banter while Tony listens, partly enjoying his lunch.

Tuddles smirks. "So, it is I alone who has . . . Oh, why do I even bother?" he says. "Mr. Avery, allow me to introduce you to all of the sudden nay-sayers at the table. Starting at the far end, we have Miss Atkins, our esteemed history teacher and most recent prey of our would-be-scholars-gone-amok. She *did* have a position waiting for her next year at a private school, all the way down in St. Petersburg, but I guess now she will—"

"I didn't say anything!" laughs Miss Atkins, a hand covering her mouth.

"Well, well, well," says Tuddles, lifting his eyebrows. "Now, beside her is Mrs. Moreland—math teacher."

Mrs. Moreland points her fork. "Okay now, Mr. Tuddles."

"Well, other than doing His will," Tuddles says, pointing upward, "there's no other logical explanation for how or why she endures— twelve years, mind you. She gets *some* respect, but not enough worth mentioning. Her students don't study the least bit, either."

"I got *some* that do," Mrs. Moreland protests, glaring at her talkative colleague. "You don' know all uh my students, Mr. Tuddles."

Tuddles shrugs. "Generally speaking, Mrs. Moreland," he says. "Mr. Avery, it's worth mentioning that Mrs. Miller, who isn't here today, can rightly be called a failing replica of Mrs. Moreland. For she, too, is here due to God's compelling hand, but she has yet to get their attention for more than five minutes at a time, let alone their respect. More zealous, mind you, than Mrs. Moreland, she's even been known to interrupt a grammar lesson or two to spout Bible verses. Anything to try to curb the chaos, right?"

Mrs. Moreland points her fork again. "Now Mr. Tuddles, I juss don't *wanna* do that sort of thang, that's all," she says. "But, I tell you what . . . if it works, maybe it wouldn't hurt for *you* to start try'n to use some—"

"Excuse me? What is it they call her?" Tuddles says, raising his chin.

The question settles it.

"Mr. Avery, I'm Larry Zimmerman—history teacher," the man seated to Tony's left says with an extended hand. "Please ignore this raving lunatic. How are your classes so far? Any problems yet?"

"No . . . no problems. . . ." answers Tony, forcing a smile. Then he waves at the four departing custodians.

Tuddles smirks, eyeing everyone at the table. "I'm only being upfront with what Mr. Avery should expect from these . . . *students*," he says.

"I appreciate that, Mr. Tuddles," says Tony, not knowing what else he should or shouldn't say.

"As well you should," says Tuddles, smugly. "Now, where was I? Oh yes, Mrs. McBride here teaches science with just—"

"*Tries* to teach," corrects Mrs. McBride. When a few give her a quick glance, she says, "What? He should know . . . I mean, really. These kids are some of the most . . . He should know what to expect."

After taking another sip of tea, Tuddles says, "Absolutely—my sentiments exactly." He looks around the table. "How many new-hires have we lost already this year?" he asks.

"I'm Mrs. Kendall, Mr. Avery," says the woman seated between Mr. Zimmerman and Mr. Palmer. "Don't get me wrong, but I've been here for six years now, and believe me, it takes some getting used to. The only thing you can do is cover the chapters with them, correct their homework—the homework of those who do it, anyway—you can give curves, whatever. You just learn to do what you can for the ones who want to learn something. Don't expect too much, and you'll do fine. I know what they say about expectations and all of that, but the name of the game is survival. You've got to be careful not to drive yourself insane."

"What do you teach?" asks Tony.

"Math—or like Mrs. McBride says, I *try* to, anyway."

Genrich clears his throat. "Basically, what you want to do," he says, "is find those students who deserve a shot at the AME test."

"The test for returning to normal schools?" Tony asks.

Tuddles folds his arms and mumbles, "Schools with extracurricular activities, instead of heightened security measures."

"It's the only thing we use for mainstreaming," adds Zimmerman.

"I've got information on it in my packet," says Tony. "But I thought *every* student tested."

Tuddles gives a sarcastic giggle. Others glance around the table or shift in their seats.

"There was a time," Genrich says. "But we've found that it's more . . . *practical—*"

"'Practical.' Now there's a word," Tuddles interrupts. "What he's trying to convey is that four years ago—our final attempt at mass scholastic chivalry—only six percent of more than twenty-one hundred students passed the test, and that was one of our strongest years. Now, each teacher recommends only those students who *may* have a snowball's chance in hell."

"*That* many fail every year?" asks Tony, astounded.

"Well, most pass the MLE test," says Genrich. "It doesn't get them out of here, but it gets them to the next grade."

Tony nods uncertainly. "So . . . most end up getting their diplomas from Lincoln instead of a quote-unquote normal school?"

For a moment, the table is silent. Then Tuddles says, "That's one of the many drawbacks to hiring new teachers so frantically, without so much as an interview." He sighs. "They don't tell them hardly anything before they get them in here."

"What's the point of having a hoax interviewing process?" asks Genrich. "This place needs teachers—*bad!* Whoever so much as looks in our direction—*boom*, they're hired." He glances at Tony. "Not to say anything about you *personally*, Mr. Avery."

Mrs. Kendall speaks gently, almost apologetically. "Mr. Avery, they don't receive high school diplomas here. They haven't for many years now. They receive a diploma equivalent certificate."

"I don't understand," Tony says. "Diploma equivalent? What does that have to do with . . . I mean, how does that—"

"They've found that it's best to help them strengthen their self-esteem," Genrich offers. "It's not exactly a diploma per se, but at least it shows that they've completed *something*."

Tony surveys the faces around the table. "So, you're *not* a high school?" he asks, rather confused.

"Well," says Genrich, "technically, we *are* a high school."

Tuddles shakes his head. "Isn't it amazing some of the things they can forget to mention to their teachers?" he asks sourly.

"We're a dumping ground," mumbles Mrs. McBride.

"Now that's not nice ta say," says Mrs. Moreland. "It's juss that with all that's going own downtown . . . an the politics—we know 'bout the politics . . . an people disagreein'. . . ."

"Oh, come now, Mrs. Moreland," says Tuddles, swirling his glass of tea. "I concur with Mrs. McBride—we *all* do. We know we have the students no one else wants, that no one else *needs*. All pretenses aside, they're here to fail in solitude."

"*And* to help other schools have a fighting chance in the GPA war," adds Mrs. McBride. "School supplies, funding—lots of things are based on it."

"Wow," says Tony, not knowing what else to say. And why shouldn't he draw a blank? His mind is still on lunch. "That's really something," he adds, wondering what reaction they're hoping for. "Really something to think about."

"At one point," Tuddles adds, "there was even talk of creating a middle school equivalent of Lincoln, but, according to certain influential big wheels downtown, we've given them no indication that this program works. So, what do they do? They drop the middle school idea entirely, but somehow Lincoln still stands—as is. Now, middle schools make sure they 'pass' all of their problem students to the high schools—which, in turn, pass all of their problems onto us."

"I thank Mr. Avery's had enough negative talk for one day," says Mrs. Moreland. "Ya'll act like you're try'n na scare him away."

"That is definitely *not* my intention, Mr. Avery," Tuddles assures. "Please don't think you're not welcomed; you really are."

Tony grins. "Well, to be honest," he says, "it's nice to know that you *do* talk among yourselves. Earlier this morning, I was starting to think I was on Candid Camera or something."

No one so much as bats an eye at the remark.

"Didn't you receive a copy of the expectancies?" asks Zimmerman.

Tony scans the faces staring back at him. "Yeah, I've got a copy in my packet."

Palmer stands without a word, dumps his tray, and leaves the lounge.

"We're not supposed to discuss the 'Ryker's Expectancies' list," whispers Tuddles. "But let's just say we don't call him 'The Third Ryke' for nothing."

"I believe that's my cue," says Mrs. McBride, standing with tray in hand.

"Ah'm right behine you, girl," Mrs. Moreland adds.

"Me too," adds Miss Atkins.

Genrich checks his watch. "Well . . . it's about that time anyway," he says. He grunts to his feet.

"How long has he had these 'expectancies'?" Tony asks.

"Before *my* time," says Mrs. Kendall.

"Since he firs' got here nine years ago," says Mrs. Moreland, dumping her tray.

"He used to be a police officer," adds Zimmerman.

"Still *would* be," Tuddles says, "if it weren't for his being sorry on the draw. He's been shot on three separate occasions."

Tony's mouth drops open. "Shot?"

"Once in the shoulder, and I believe the other two were in his right leg," says Tuddles.

"No, the second time he was shot in the leg," corrects Zimmerman. "But the last time was in his right side, just below the waist. Someone must've given him some good advice on starting a new career—we're guessing his wife."

"Lucky us," mutters Tuddles. He rises to his feet.

Zimmerman stands and says, "Anyway, keep it under your hat, alright?" He glances at Tuddles. "Ryker still thinks we don't know about it. Anyway . . . see ya around."

They exit the lounge, leaving Tony alone, thinking how odd it is for teachers to address each other so formerly, using last names only. A far cry from his experiences as an intern.

He works at finishing his lunch, but doesn't enjoy the silence for long. The next group of teachers file in. Tony says his hellos, but he's determined to leave before the episode starts anew. Ignoring the growing conversation, he slams his tray repeatedly on the inside of the trashcan, thankful he didn't try the green stuff, but he wonders what he's gotten himself into, what he's taken a bite of instead.

The day is half over, but he already has a headache.

Chapter 15

My knees feel a little better now. They're still a little stiff, but they don't ache as much. I have a few miles yet before I reach the karate school, but if we have to do more kicking—and with my luck, we'll kick all evening—it shouldn't be as bad as the first time. Still, I'm not gonna kid myself. I know I won't feel like walking back home—not that I *ever* feel like it, because I don't. Walking home is never *ever* a happy-happy trek.

They must've laughed their asses off after I left last Friday. I wonder who had to clean the carpet. Mr. Travers never called Mom to tell her what happened, but I would've sworn he would've. Still, I know if I do it again, I can hang it up; he'll definitely call, and Mom'll be ticked—*really* ticked.

Even with the discount, I know she's paying Mr. Travers money she'd rather keep. She hates spending money on me. I can see it in her eyes, every time I see her come home with groceries. Even though practically everything is generic brand, it's still too expensive; the stuff is for me. The only money she gives without so much as a gripe is the token money for Arcade Stadium, but that money's not really for me, either.

Sometimes, I wish I could go back in time, make everything okay again. All I'd have to do is tell Mom and Dad not to take that walk with Amanda. I'd let them know a crazy-driving nigger was going to be on the loose that day. That would solve everything. Well, almost everything—I'd still have to go to school.

Nigger. I know Mom uses the word with Hank all the time, but I don't remember Dad saying it. Maybe he did; I just don't remember it. Guess I wouldn't say "crazy nigger" just in case Dad wouldn't like it. Mr. Farley sure doesn't like it.

"African-American" is just too damn long, so I try to say "black" whenever I can remember, but I keep slipping up. Mr. Farley says that one day I'm gonna slip in the wrong place, and I might not have anybody around who'll pick me up. Too funny. And it's not like there's a bunch of blacks at my school, because there isn't. I see them at the Stadium all the time, but they usually keep to themselves—mostly. And they're always calling each *other* "nigger." Too funny.

I wonder how many will be at Lincoln High School. I never got into trouble with a nigger before, so I probably won't have many fights. Sure, I've heard things, but when I really think about it, I just don't know. Based on the books I've read, they don't seem all that bad for the most part. Weak maybe. Religious—definitely, but not bad. Not really.

The one black in Mr. Travers' class doesn't look weak, even without the black belt. I wonder what he looked like *before* karate. Probably the same. He definitely *looks* like he's been ripped all his life. Maybe if I work really hard at it, that could be me in thirty years, but right now I'd be thankful for making it through the night without vomiting on anyone.

Mr. Travers said his son is teaching tonight. He also said his son's close to my age and that we may have some things in common. That'll be the day. He's teaching, and I'm throwing up. He's probably the perfect specimen—a fit, lightning-fast black belt. Probably has tons of friends, and even if he had enemies, they wouldn't be a problem. He can probably take most people out without breaking a sweat, but, of course, it would be an act of "self-defense." That's the discipline part of it, and discipline keeps you out of fights. Discipline also keeps you from having to walk home, making unhappy treks.

Yeah, we'll have tons in common.

BY THE TIME KENNY REACHES THE NORTHSHORE Karate Institute, he almost regrets making the trip wearing his karate gi. The thick cotton is very damp down the center of his back and under his armpits, but he'd rather deal with that than change at the school again, in front of jeering classmates.

If he wasn't afraid to find his mother waiting at a stop one day, he'd take the city bus. Maybe Lincoln High is closer to the karate class than his house is, at least he hopes. If not, he'll opt to ride the school bus home and walk to the class from there. The round trip is only twelve miles, but he'd like it to be shorter, considering how tough the kicks and punches have turned out to be.

He finally arrives at the karate school. Judging from the two cars parked outside, he's one of the first to show. He enters the school and glances around the "store area," as it's called, where various martial arts trinkets, videos, and weapons are sold. He hears Mr. Travers' voice coming from the workout area located in the back room.

Kenny steps in the doorway and places his duffle bag at his feet. He watches unnoticed as Mr. Travers and the Asian-American black belt student discuss a topic obviously concerning self-defense techniques. Mr. Travers mimics various movements with an invisible opponent to better illustrate his point.

"Then, you should take the knife hand and take it back like this," Mr. Travers says, "and then you pivot on the ball of ya foot like this."

The student effortlessly imitates what he sees.

"Right," continues Mr. Travers. "Just like that." The instructor maintains his contorted stance, but he looks slightly uncomfortable. "Then, you flip the wrist at this angle, step across, and then take the knife away with your free hand. It should almost fall out of the adversary's hand."

In the middle of executing the final steps of his newly-learned intricate maneuver, the student and the instructor finally notice Kenny standing in the doorway.

"Hey, Kenny!" says Mr. Travers. "Good to have you back!"

Kenny nods, but stays put.

Mr. Travers waves him in. "Come on in, come on in. I was just showin' Melvin here a few things. Testin's comin' up in a couple of weeks, ya know," he says with a wink. "You remember Melvin, don't you?"

Kenny nods his head as Melvin offers a smile and a handshake. His strong, yet non-threatening grip doesn't go unnoticed.

"Go ahead and put your shoes in the back," says Mr. Travers. "You know, stretch out and stuff. Melvin, show him some good stretches. Nothin' too advanced."

"I'd be happy to," Melvin says. "Are you feeling okay today, Kenny?"

Kenny shrugs uncomfortably. "I'm okay."

"Real good, Kenny," says Mr. Travers. He places a hand on Kenny's shoulder. "I've gotta git going in a few. I just need to take care of somethin' in the store first, but my son and everybody else should be here in no time. Meanwhile, ol' Melvin here'll help git you ready. Okay?"

"Okay."

"Good. Real good. And I'll see you again on Wednesday, Melvin. Don't let Kenny overdo it." He points at finger a Kenny. "You hear me, Kenny? Take it *easy*."

Kenny nods and then looks at the floor. He releases an inaudible sigh when Mr. Travers walks out.

"There's nothing to be ashamed of about last Friday, my friend," says Melvin. "It shows you're really trying, and that's always a good thing." On the word "good," he taps Kenny's shoulder with his fist.

Kenny removes his shoes and places them, along with his duffle bag, in the back of the room, then joins Melvin in the center of the floor. Melvin shows him several beginning stretches, giving Kenny a thorough explanation on the importance of stretching and the difference between muscles and tendons, stressing that tendons don't stretch. He also covers the importance of the warm-up, and he explains how neglecting these preliminaries can lead to serious injuries.

The way Melvin expresses himself relaxes Kenny. His tone is comforting and sincere. His choice of words—positive, even encouraging. He constantly tells Kenny how well he's doing, and Kenny feels a little better about being in the class.

Mr. Travers leaves with a final wave and good-bye, and it is then that Kenny realizes that Melvin is obviously a trusted student. It is also then that he notices the yin and yang sign from the night before, and he makes a mental note to read it before leaving.

Other students enter the school. Some come already in gi; others disappear behind the skimpy changing wall before claiming a spot on the floor to stretch. They all speak upon entering. The room gets steadily louder, but the instructor for the evening has yet to arrive.

"How long has Mr. Travers' son been doing karate?" asks Kenny, feeling more comfortable with Melvin now.

"Sempai?" asks Melvin.

"Who?"

"I'm sorry. 'Sempai' is how we address Sensei's son," explains Melvin. "He's a third dan, an upper-level black belt. He's been in the arts for thirteen years now—since he was four."

"Then he's only two years older than me," says Kenny.

"He's only seventeen, still in high school," says Melvin. "How old are you?"

"Fifteen."

"Then, I guess you're right. He's got you by two years."

"What does 'Sensei' mean?"

"It means 'teacher.'"

"What about 'Sempai?'"

"A Sempai is like an older brother, a role model for the rest of the students in the school. We're all like a family."

"Are you a Sempai?"

"Not yet, but I'm working on it," Melvin says, smiling. Kenny is asking questions most new students don't ask. Usually, new students want to know how quickly they can get a black belt.

"So, he's like a master?" Kenny asks.

"Not quite, but as close as you can get to being a master without being one. I don't think it'll be much longer before he becomes a master. He trains hard."

They continue with their conversation a little while longer, until Melvin retreats to his own spot where he performs his very advanced, very impressive warm-up routine. His final words of comfort and assurance leave Kenny feeling optimistic about his future with the school.

The room is packed now, more so than it was last Friday, and everyone is stretching and jabbering away, even with Kenny. They ask him all types of general questions—his age, his hobbies, where he lives—and every now and then, someone tells him how good it is to have him back. With his spirits rising, Kenny is suddenly feeling up to it. He feels ready for the task at hand. Maybe karate won't be so bad after all.

Finally, the atmosphere livens another notch with the announcement of their Sempai's arrival. When he enters the school, all students spring to their feet and bow. Kenny's one of the last to stand, but he's eager to bow as well, until he finally sets his eyes on Mr. Travers' son. His heart sinks to his stomach as he stands and watches the entire class bow to the same guy from the game room, the one with the sleazy girlfriend, the one with the quick temper, the one who fights like Coolio.

It takes a few seconds before Sempai notices the only figure in the room refusing to bow to him. He returns Kenny's astonished look. Over his left eye is a bandage, compliments of a well-placed stomp—two insignificant stitches.

Without looking at anyone again, Kenny goes to the back of the room and grabs his shoes with one hand, his duffle bag with the other. Just before he exits, he glances up at the yin and yang sign over the entrance: ALWAYS LEAVE STRONGER THAN YOU CAME.

Suddenly, the walk home is much longer than six miles.

Never *ever* a happy-happy trek.

Chapter 16

READING AND WRITING IS WHAT THE test measures most. The AME test isn't really concerned with any other ability—not math, not science, not history. That fact continues to wash over Tony's conscience as he sits at his desk and waits for the first bell to ring, the signal for round two, the start of his second day. The students' academic salvation rests on the shoulders of the Language Arts teachers. Somehow, Tony feels it's no coincidence that most students' weakest subject also serves as their educational rite of passage.

The test's format is extremely demanding in its simplicity. Students are given two articles, each averaging five hundred words. At the end of each article, students have seven multiple-choice questions and an open-ended question for a writing prompt. They are to answer the open-ended questions by writing no less than five paragraphs, a short essay. The students must refer to the article by making inferences in their essays. The questions are worded in such a way that any other type of answer ignores the question entirely. The quality of their answers indicates their reading comprehension, and, of course, their writing must be focused and grammatically sound. For the most part, students are kept at Lincoln by two essays.

Tony realizes he needs to know a few things about his students.

He needs to know where they are in their abilities—how well they read, how well they write. Do they know the difference between a verb, adjective, and an adverb? What about a comma splice? Punctuation? Prepositions? How well do they understand subject-verb agreement? What is their vocabulary level? These are some of the questions that must be answered before he can begin. He must know where they are, to know where they can go. To find out, he will start with the basics.

When the bell rings, Tony flips the switch of the overhead projector, displaying a seating chart on the screen, and then sits at his desk. As the students filter in, Jose is the first to groan an opinion of the new seating arrangement. "Aw man, he must be crazy," he mumbles, but he locates his new seat and takes it with a sigh.

"I'own *thank* so!" exclaims Lisa as she enters the classroom. "Git out uh my seat, Keith!"

Keith Fryer, one of the least talkative students, gives a shrug as he turns to Tony.

"Ma'am, what is your name again?" Tony asks.

"Lisa," she says, and then finally sees the overhead. "Oh, we got uh seat'n chot na? I ain' see it. Why we gotta have assigned seats na?"

"Why do we *have* to have assigned seats *now?*" corrects Tony. "I'll explain in a minute."

"Why we have to be moved aroun', yo?" gripes Jose, his arms folded in defiance.

"He *said* he'll tell us in uh minute!" snaps Lisa, taking her seat.

Jose points at her, but he continues looking at Tony. "Was I talkin' to her?"

"No you weren't," answers Tony, leaning back in his chair.

Lisa's mouth drops open as she places her hands on her hips, but she barely subdues a smile.

Tony shrugs. "Well . . . he wasn't."

"Okay," says Lisa. "Dass awright." She slumps back in her desk, folds her arms, and chews her gum at a comfortable, steady pace.

Tony and Jose exchange a quick glance, and Jose adds a grin.

Jarek, Jacob, and Corey pause as they enter the classroom. With a sigh, they drag their feet to their new desks; no card game today. Jarek, the understood leader of the reclusive trio, places his textbook on the desk with an impact that accentuates his irritation. Not rewarded with even a glance from Tony, he sighs again before placing his head on his desk, face down.

When Marcus walks in alone, Tony asks, "Where's your friend?"

"Oh, he comin'," replies Marcus. He does a double-take at the sight of the overhead. "We got assigned seats na?"

"You *have* assigned seats *now*," corrects Tony.

Marcus rolls his eyes and finds his seat.

The class grows steadily in size and noise, but it's not yet out of hand, not rambunctious.

Rodney and James enter, leaving the scent of cigarette smoke in their wake. Tony chooses to ignore it, but with a small sigh and a frown.

"Aw man! Why you trippin'?" asks Rodney, seeing the new seating arrangement.

Tony eyes him with an almost bored expression.

Rodney looks back at James as he stands in the center of the room with no books, hands on his hips. "See dare, Powuh?" he murmurs.

James shrugs and takes his new seat. Rodney mumbles something else, but he follows his friend's example.

"What up, yo?" says Roland as he enters the classroom. He pauses when Marcus points him to his newly assigned desk.

When Roland's mouth drops open, Marcus says, "I know."

When the bell sounds, Tony finally springs to his feet. With a seating chart in hand, he walks around to the front of his desk to address the now loud class. He raises his hand in the air. "Okay everyone, listen up," he says calmly. A few give their attention, but the noise level remains the same. "Listen up," he repeats, hand still in the air, but with the same results.

He surveys the classroom and eyes the seating chart. "Jose!" he calls.

When Jose gives him his attention, Tony summons him to the front of the class with his index finger. Jose's groan and sudden approach to the front of the room causes his group to fall silent.

Again, Tony scans the classroom and glances at the chart. "Deborah!" he calls, and again, the index finger.

By the time he summons three others to the front of the class, students he considers to be lacking decibel control, the room is relatively silent. "Yesterday, I explained that I was going to raise my hand when I wanted your attention," he says. "Well, I raised my hand, but I didn't get your attention." He scans the faces. "Did we forget about the choices we talked about yesterday? Did we forget that we are now adults?"

Rodney mumbles something, causing snickers and giggles.

Without a change in expression, Tony summons him forward with his index finger, but he grabs a paper from his desk and walks to the door. He pushes the door wide open.

"Okay, man! Okay!" exclaims Rodney, smiling now. "Ah'm sorry, man! Come own, na!"

Tony's only response is an unflinching face as he continues to hold the door open. The class is silent. Their heads move back and forth from Rodney to teacher.

Rodney finally stomps to his feet. "What? We cane joke aroun' in class na? You cane take uh joke?"

Even though they are now face to face, Tony speaks a little louder than necessary because he feels that it *is* necessary—college textbooks call it *Vicarious Learning.* "This is an outline of what we're covering today," he says. He hands Rodney the sheet of paper. "I'll always have these for my students who will be absent for one reason or another."

"Come own, man!" pleads Rodney.

"If you care to try again tomorrow," continues Tony, "I suggest you go over this carefully. If not . . . good luck, Rodney."

"Good luck wit what?"

Tony stares at Rodney as if not believing the question. "Good luck with your *life*," he says, and he looks directly into Rodney's eyes, showing zero emotions—not anger, not frustration, not malice—nothing.

Rodney sighs. "Awright, man. I'll be quiet. I'll be good," he says, almost solemnly.

"Then I look forward to seeing you tomorrow."

"Whey Ah'm supposed ta go?" Rodney asks, now standing outside the door.

"I've already spoken to Dean Phillips," Tony says. "For a while, she's willing to grant certain students the opportunity to *rethink* their chosen path while just sitting in her office. Of course, her leniency won't last forever. But, as we talked about yesterday, you don't *have* to. As always, the choice is yours." And with that, Tony gently closes the door, leaving Rodney—pleading face and all—in the hallway.

Tony tells the five students still standing to take their seats, and then returns to the front of his desk and raises his hand. "Again . . . I will raise my hand whenever I want to talk to the class, whenever I want your attention. I don't mind your talking; I don't mind your joking; I don't mind your laughing, your playing, your singing, your gum-smacking, or whatever. But when I raise my hand, I want your attention. When I raise my hand, I want your attention. When—I—raise—my—hand—I—want—your—*attention*."

He pauses and scans the faces glaring back at him. Right now, he has their attention. "If you continue to talk after I've raised my hand and asked for your attention, that's telling me you don't want to *give* me your attention, you don't want to hear what I have to say." He folds his arms. "Well, okay. That's fine." He strolls over to the door. "If you don't want to hear what I have to say. . . ." He opens the door and looks back at the faces scowling at him. "Then I'll have to ask you to find somewhere else to be, find someone else to ignore."

Many of the students aren't happy, but they're quiet. Many don't like what they hear, but they're listening.

Tony continues to hold the door wide open. "The choice is yours."

He allows the uncomfortable silence to rip through the classroom for a good thirty seconds. To some, it feels like an hour, but he still has their attention. Finally, he closes the door and returns to the front of his desk. He takes a deep breath before he speaks again. "We'll avoid this ridiculous episode from now on," he says, then reaches around for his textbook. "Sometimes, I don't like making choices any more than you do."

He takes another moment to peruse the faces in the classroom. The students continue to watch him silently, most with expressions of disinterest.

"Before we start, are there any questions you'd like to ask me? Anything about me personally? You already know each other, and, thanks to this seating chart I've worked out, I'll get to know *you* as time goes by, but if you'd like to know anything about *me*—anything at all, feel free to . . . well . . . anything," he says with a shrug.

A few shuffle their feet, others fold their arms. Some glance around the room, wondering if anyone will dare.

Tony suddenly feels uneasy. "Alright," he says, clearing his throat. "Let's just plunge right in. The AME test is just around the corner, so we really need to get a move on."

Davon Williams raises his hand, causing everyone to focus on him.

"Yes . . ." says Tony—a quick glances at the seating chart—"Davon."

"I thought only two uh three people from every class was g'own take it."

"*Were going* to take it?" corrects Tony. "Well . . . I have no idea who's going to take it. Anyone can qualify," he says, unsure that "qualify" is the right word. "There's really no set number, no maximum amount of people who are allowed to take it."

Lisa raises her hand. "So hi many you g'own pick from nis class?" she asks, still smacking her gum.

"How many am I *going* to pick from *this* class?" corrects Tony. "Well, that's up to you to decide."

Silence.

"Any more questions?"

Some of the students eye each other, almost tauntingly.

"Open your textbooks to page fifty-four. And, let's see . . ." Tony peers at the seating chart. "Whoa . . . I have *two* Keiths in here—Keith

Fryer and Keith Reynolds. Okay . . . Keith Fryer, start reading from the 'Parts of Speech' section, please."

Keith appears irritated as he glances down at his unopened textbook.

Tony raises an eyebrow. "Keith?"

Keith looks up at Tony with a frown. "My eyes botherin' me," he finally murmurs.

Tony feels they've already lost enough time, so he calls on another. "Keith Reynolds, start us out."

Keith hesitates for a moment, but he complies. After Keith, Tony calls on Corey, who glances at Jarek as if he needs Jarek's permission before he complies. Jarek and Jacob roll their eyes and shake their heads as Corey reads with some difficulty.

Yesterday, Tony recognized the clique, but now he believes they communicate with no one else in the classroom. The three stick together exclusively. If they were the only white students in the class, maybe their behavior would be more understandable—maybe.

After Corey, Roland is called on, and after Roland reads, Lisa volunteers. Eventually, Marcus, James, Faith, and a few others cover several sections of the textbook relating to nouns, pronouns, verbs, adjectives, adverbs, and the like. Tony gathers from their expressions that the subject matter is about as familiar as porcupine mating rituals. Still, he trudges forward.

Afterwards, he places a transparency on the overhead. It contains a single sentence: "I can accomplish virtually anything when I try hard enough." After he adjusts the transparency, he turns to face the class and points to the screen. "Take out a sheet of paper and copy down this sentence."

Lazily, the class shuffles as students search notebooks for paper and pencils. Some have to borrow both.

"Underneath the sentence, I want you to number your paper from one to ten," he continues. He paces up and down the aisles, glancing over shoulders. "The sentence has ten words. All you have to do is write what these words are, according to the Parts of Speech. So, for number one, write whether the 'I'," he says, pointing at the screen again, "is a verb, noun, preposition, or whatever. For number two, write what 'can' is. For number three—'accomplish,' and so on. You have five minutes."

"Five *minutes?*" exclaims Marcus, breaking the silence.

Tony pauses in his manner, acknowledging all of the astonished faces. "Five minutes, Marcus," he finally says.

"What if we can't finish in time?" asks Deborah Weems. Lisa and Faith look at each other before they roll their eyes.

"Finish what you can," Tony answers.

The class moans and groans, but many put pen to paper. Tony returns to his desk, grabs another lesson outline, and walks over to Richard Brigman, who's been nodding the entire class period and is now fast asleep. Tony has to tap him twice to get his attention. "Here," he says, handing Richard the sheet of paper. "You'll need this. Let's try to stay awake from now on, or find somewhere else to sleep."

Richard frowns groggily. Walking away, Tony doesn't see the scowl, and by the time he returns to his desk and glances back at Richard, the frown has been replaced by the more familiar expression of disorientation.

"For homework, I want you to read the sections on direct objects and indirect objects, starting on page one-twelve," he says as he writes it on the board. "Do the exercises on pages one-sixteen and one-seventeen."

More moans and groans.

Moments after Tony sits back at his desk, the bell rings. The students jump to their feet, grumbling. To Tony's surprise, only about half the class turns in the assignment. He's at a loss for what to say as the students file out of the classroom. No one says anything to him—no good-byes. He hears many of the students talk about him more freely, once they leave the room. He isn't surprised to hear they don't like him—disappointed, but not surprised. What *does* surprise him is when he hears someone mention his name, right before saying "Uncle Tom."

Chapter 17

YESTERDAY, THE VOICES HAD NO NAMES. But today, as Tony makes his way to the teachers' table (after saying a few words to Malik, Cap, and the others at the custodial table) Mr. Tuddles' voice distinguishes itself from the others loudly and clearly. Currently, the table is enjoying a heated discussion fueled by Tuddles' timely quips, as well as the usual opinionated "facts." With the presence of Mrs. Miller, all members of the main table are accounted for—Tony being the tenth. A vacant seat waits, as if reserved just for him. With the conversation at full throttle, a few offer an acknowledging grunt or gesture to him, while Mrs. Kendall motions for him to take his place in the dining forum, right between Tuddles and Palmer. Zimmerman currently has the floor.

"I'm standing there trying not to lose it, but he wouldn't take them off," continues Zimmerman. "So, finally I tell him if he won't take off the headsets, he can leave. I know he heard me because he just smacked his lips—you know how they do it—and started swaying his head—you know—as if he can't hear me, humming and tapping on the desk."

"Why didn't you just take them?" asks Miss Atkins.

Tuddles snorts at the suggestion. "Never, never, *never* a good idea to touch them or their belongings," he says, raising an index finger.

"Especially when they switch to delinquent mode. I'd rather stand up to the 'Third Ryke' and his precious rules."

Palmer pauses before he takes another bite of his lunch, and Tony takes notice of the Social Studies teacher's discomfort with the conversation.

"I'd have to agree with you on that one," says Genrich. "The last thing you want to do is provoke them—in *any* way."

"Well, believe me," continues Zimmerman. "I may have only been here three years, but I'm not . . ." He pauses and glances at Palmer. "Well, you know . . . I've seen my share of mayhem. So, I let it go— wasn't worth it."

"The problem is we have to *pretend* to have some control even when we don't," offers Mrs. Kendall. "Until Mr. Palmer came along, we had no idea there was a limit on how many times you can use the button. I mean—*really!*"

"My sentiments exactly," says Tuddles. "After all, what's it there for if we can't rely on it *every* time?"

"You need to start relyin' on the Lord," says Mrs. Miller, but she doesn't look up from her salad. "I haven't had to use that button yet, and I git some of the same children, some of the same trials and tribulations."

Tuddles rolls his eyes, but doesn't respond. Everyone knows he wants to; he always wants to.

"What button are we talking about?" asks Tony, unwittingly breaking the silence.

"You don't know about the button?" asks Mrs. Kendall. "It's right next to your door, opposite the light switch."

"I thought that was the fire alarm," Tony admits. "It isn't labeled, but it looks like the fire alarm."

"That's definitely *one* way of looking at it," says Mrs. McBride, causing a few giggles.

"So . . . what is it?" asks Tony.

"False hope in some cases," quips Tuddles.

"It's an alarm system that was installed a few years back," says Genrich. "It was intended to decrease the response time to serious situations in classrooms. There was a time when Lincoln was pretty bad, had at least one major occurrence a day."

"Thompson," says Mrs. McBride as she takes a bite of her lunch.

"Right. A teacher was even stabbed, and to this day, no one knows who did it," explains Genrich.

Tuddles shifts in his seat. "*Someone* knows."

"It's gotten a little better since then," says Mrs. McBride. "But I'll bet Miss Atkins won't miss this place. Will you, Judy?"

Miss Atkins shrugs with a smile as she continues to chew her food.

"Where you headed, again?" asks Mrs. Moreland.

"Christian school, right?" asks Mrs. Miller. "All schools should be Christian schools. That's what's wrong with—"

"St. Petersburg, right?" Tuddles interrupts. "I hear it's very lovely down there."

"It's hard to bake a great pie when you can't pick your own apples," whispers Mrs. McBride.

Some suppress a snicker as Mrs. Miller mumbles something underneath her breath. Then she takes another bite of her salad, obviously irritated, chewing with renewed vigor.

"I can hardly wait until the day comes when this place is behind *me*," says Tuddles.

Zimmerman frowns. "Who are you waiting on *now?*"

"Microdisc, a software company in Lake City, remains promising, but I'd rather be at H & D Electronics. The pay is thirty-five percent more than what Microdisc is willing to part with."

Zimmerman responds by sucking his teeth.

"What I don't understand is," Mrs. Moreland says, "if you lost yo' other job because of downsizin', why you wanna go back to that kind of work?"

"Well, I'd rather take my chances in the so-called 'real world,'" explains Tuddles, "than in the supposed preparatory institute."

To this, Tony snickers before the group for the first time. Tuddles shoots him a puzzled look, unsure whether it's his comment or he who Tony suddenly finds amusing.

"Teachers lose jobs too, Mrs. Moreland," says Zimmerman.

"I don't think you have much to worry about, Mr. Zimmerman," says Mrs. Kendall. "It ain't like there's a whole string of teachers just dying to run over here and 'make a difference in the lives of America's promising youth.' Our jobs here are fairly secure."

"You got *that* right," mumbles Mrs. McBride. "If it wasn't for Principal Ryker, we wouldn't even have to worry about our evaluations."

"I *don't* worry about evaluations," Mrs. Kendall admits. "I give whatever class I'm evaluated with a party at the end of the week, if they act right. They scratch my back, I'll scratch theirs."

Most nod in agreement; Mrs. Moreland remains silent; Mrs. Miller sighs; Palmer takes another mouthful of food; Tony tries to eat.

"I tried awarding grades, but that doesn't work," snorts Tuddles. "It seems as if the only thing they'll respond to is what they can hold in their hand," he says, slapping the palm of his own hand.

"They're too stupid to take a free *A*," says Mrs. Kendall. "They're not motivated. Half don't care about grades, and the other half just . . . *ugh!*" She massages her temples. "I mean, what do you do? Why doesn't Mr. Ryker send them to William Wells Brown?"

Mrs. McBride shakes her head. "How long do you think a principal can keep his job after sending hundreds of students to William Wells Brown?" she asks.

"William Wells Brown is a *disciplinary* school, mass detention at best," adds Genrich. "There's no teaching there. Besides, Brown can only hold them for a maximum of thirty days. Then they're sent back to their own school, regardless of whether they've been 'rehabilitated.'"

"Lincoln's the *real* William Wells Brown," says Tuddles. "If you send students to Brown, they come back, but if you can show they're failing most of their subjects—well . . . need I say more? We're the *real* William Wells Brown, the *real* disciplinary school, and the entire county knows it."

"So, what do you do?" repeats Mrs. Kendall.

"We start a candy fund so it doesn't have to keep coming out of our own pockets," says Mrs. McBride.

The table erupts.

Mrs. Moreland smiles.

Mrs. Miller sighs.

Palmer chews his food.

Tony glances at the custodial table. He feels out of sorts, disoriented, even down. He feels the tides of despair washing over his consciousness, drowning his already waning focus and optimism. He's becoming more discouraged. He shouldn't have some of these emotions, but somewhere along the way he forgot this was a temporary assignment, one he'd hold only until next fall. He's starting to care beyond his initial intentions. So, as he tries to enjoy his lunch, he also tries to remember his goal—to teach at a much better school, in a much better environment, with a much better caliber of students. He tries to envision it—all of it, but somehow, it doesn't set his mind at ease.

Tony's low mood doesn't escape Mrs. Moreland's notice, but her loss for words renders her powerless. She's seen Tony's expression on dozens of new-hires. To her, it's only a matter of time before Mr. Avery becomes a statistic.

Miss Atkins waves her spoon to gain everyone's attention. "You know, I remember something about rewards and punishment and stuff like that in one of my college courses," she says. "I don't think giving candy or whatever is all that bad, from what I remember. It gives them something to shoot for, right?"

"Even if the powers that be *do* condone awarding them candy for doing what they should naturally *want* to do," says Zimmerman, "there's far too much that a college textbook can't teach."

"I concur," says Tuddles. "College has very little to offer when it comes to *these* misfits. How could *anything* prepare you for this place, this . . . educational facade?"

"Give me the book that shows you how to deal with Mr. Ryker and his rules," says Mrs. Kendall, smiling. "I, for one, would pay top dollar."

Palmer gets up from the table.

"Here, here," says Tuddles, ignoring Palmer and raising his cup of tea in salute. "Although, if faced with a choice, I'd prefer the juvenile-management manual."

"Oh, that reminds me," says Mrs. Kendall, beaming. "We won't have to worry about Carlton Winston for awhile."

"Suspended?" asks Mrs. McBride.

"Yep. I gave Mr. Winston his fifth write-up for skipping class, and as of yesterday, he's officially suspended."

Tony wonders if he's the only one who notices the irony.

"Good riddance," says Genrich. "I won't miss him."

"I'll shed my tears in private," mocks Tuddles.

Zimmerman sighs. "You know, there was a time when I thought bringing back swats would help." He shakes his head. "I was dead wrong about *that* one."

"Most of mine would *gladly* take swats rather than be held in detention," admits Mrs. McBride.

"Of course," adds Mrs. Kendall. "Detention cuts into their social time. Swats are over in a matter of seconds—*seconds!*"

"Like I said, how can you prepare for such curveballs?" says Tuddles. "As soon as you think you've figured them out. . . ."

The majority of the table grunts and nods in agreement, and then an unexpected silence settles over them. After everyone uses the pause as an opportunity to take a mouthful of lunch, Mrs. Moreland decides to whisk away the silence, but on a different note. "I don't know if any of ya'll heard yet, but Mr. Avery here doesn't seem to have any problems controllin' his classes. As a matter a fact, from what I hear, he does a better job than any of us do—he doesn't even have to raise his voice."

Tony stares at Mrs. Moreland, dumbfounded.

"I have some of your same students," she says, smiling. "They say you really know what you're doing, that nobody even *thinks* about givin' you a problem. Maybe you could share with us how you learned to deal with these kids."

Tony feels all eyes on him, even though most of the group are still chewing or sipping. He takes a moment to enjoy the silence because he knows it will be shattered shortly after his reply. "College," he finally says, then takes another bite of his lunch. His eyes remain fixed on his tray.

Mrs. Moreland's smirk blooms into a smiling sunflower.

And the silence stays awhile.

Chapter 18

KENNY PRETENDS NOT TO SEE HIS NEIGHBOR, Carl Jacobson, pull into the driveway after a long day's work. He even makes sure that his back is to his neighbor when Carl checks the mailbox, which is only a few yards from where Kenny is raking his yard, the last of his chores for the day.

Carl stands at his mailbox for a moment, thumbing through his mail without acknowledging Kenny. He's determined to return his neighbor's anti-social behavior with equal enthusiasm. After he gives his junk mail far more attention than it deserves, he maintains his feigned lack of interest in his immediate surroundings. Then he walks up his driveway, slapping the mail against his thigh, whistling a tune he's never heard before. He smells the sweet potato pie before he even opens the door.

"Somp'm smells good!" he says, gently closing the door behind him.

Luther Vandross plays on the stereo. He enters the kitchen where Tonya, her back turned, is placing a pie on the kitchen counter. Unsure of whether she knows of his presence, he remains quiet until her hands are empty.

"Don't be try'n na scare me, Carl," she says, her back still turned.

"Na see—I was juss standin' h'yuh minin' my own business—"

"I h'yuh ya, Mr. Minin'-my-own-business.'" Tonya removes her oven mittens, walks over to him, and melts into his waiting arms. "Hi was work?"

"Same as always—borin'."

"No sales?"

Carl snorts. "*Sales?* Baby, dey still got me an Donald goin' thew all uh da *ole* leads. It's gonna take us anothuh week uh so befo' we finish wit 'em, but ain' none uh 'em 'bout worth nut'n. We juss goin' thew da motions."

Tonya doesn't say anything, but she grips him a little tighter. On cue, Carl momentarily stifles his griping as they begin their daily, sixty-second embrace. It's been known to last much longer, but today they enjoy a minute as they listen to Luther. Carl is always the one to break the mood.

"I see we havin' sweet potato pie fuh dessert," he finally says. "Wha's da occasion?" He hopes he hasn't forgotten an important anniversary, birthday, or promise.

"Nut'n special," she says, returning to the counter.

He follows and wraps his arms around her waist, kissing her softly on the neck, and then he notices the two other pies next to the stove. "Why you cooked *three* pies?" he asks.

"Two fuh our neighbuhs," she says, and then glances back at him. "*Both* neighbuhs."

His arms recoil. "Na Tonya—"

"Don't star'd wit da 'Na Tonya,' Carl. Dey our neighbuhs whethuh you like it uh not."

"Na Tonya, you know I ain' got no problem wit George an Laura. Dey good people. But Tonya, why in na world would you bothuh bakin' nat lady an huh boy uh pie?"

"Because it *ain't* no bothuh, Carl. Besides, how would dat look? What?—I'm supposed ta cook uh pie fuh da Bentley's, but leave Pamela an huh son out? What would dey thank *den?* I'll tell you what dey'd thank—whatevuh dey *was* thankin', dey'd thank dey was right, an I don't won't dem ta *evuh* thank dat, because dey *ain't* right."

Carl takes a deep breath, shaking his head. He doesn't like it, but he doesn't want to put Tonya in a foul mood. "Awright," he concedes. "Kill 'em wit kindness—dat da idea?"

"Love thy neighbuh, Carl. It'own say nut'n 'bout lovin' na nice ones, but leavin' na mean ones wit'out uh pie."

"You right, baby," says Carl. Again, he wraps his arms around her waist. "You absolutely right."

A gentle peck ignites into a passionate kiss, but Tonya douses the fire. "Boo, would you do me uh small favor?" she asks.

"Anythang you won't, baby girl," he says and kisses her forehead.

"Take da Houstons dey pie."

Again, his arms recoil.

*   *   *   *

I've already cleaned the house, but when I finish with the yard, I need to find something else to do. It's always better to be doing something when Mom comes home, and now that any day can be the day she finds out I'm not going to the karate class, it's even more important than ever that I be on my guard, always looking like I'm doing what's expected. As Mr. Farley said, there are waves, and then there are *tsunamis*. I know when she finds out, there's gonna be a wave—a big one, but I don't wanna make it a tsunami if I don't have to. I don't wanna add wood to the fire by being caught not doing something else she wants me to do. I have to try to be the white slave boy that she wants, even though being the white slave boy that she wants is pretty much impossible for me. No matter what, shit happens.

Tomorrow's Wednesday—karate day. If the wave doesn't come today, I'll have to be gone when she gets here tomorrow, and then come back home around nine o'clock. The same on Friday, if the wave holds out. Sometimes I can't help but wonder what the wave would look like—how tall, how wide, how loud. Then I catch myself because worrying is about as much fun as a kite with no string. So, I force myself to think of video games, Mr. Farley, books I've read—even the dumb ones.

I'm tying off my last bag of grass like a good slave boy, thinking of the mother in *Little Women*, when something grabs hold of my left shoulder. I spin around just a little too fast, and I lose my balance and hit the ground.

It's Mr. Jacobson.

"Hey, I didn't mean to scare ya, young man," he says, and he's not holding back a smile or anything, so I believe him. Still, why in the hell did he have to walk up on me so quiet-like?

In one hand, he's holding a tin pan. Looks like a pie. He holds out his other hand to help me up, but he braces himself as if he isn't sure he can pull it off. He tries to hide his uncertainty, but not very well. When I get up on my own, he seems relieved.

"My wife made this pie fuh you and your mama," he says, holding it out to me.

This is a chess move, but I don't have time to think about it, so I take the pie. "Thank you," I say to him, but I forget to change my expression. He seems surprised when I say it, though. He smiles a little, and then looks at our yard as if he's looking to see what he can steal, but I don't think he wants to steal anything.

"You do a lot better job own your yard than I do own mine, that's fuh sure," he finally says.

Instinctively, I look over at his yard. "Your yard looks okay," I say. This time, I remember to change my expression, even though I'm starting to feel uncomfortable. Mom can pull up any minute. I don't know how she'd take me talking to him, and I don't really care to find out.

"We try," he says. "But it's gonna be awhile before we git it the way we won't it."

This time, I don't say anything. I just give a little nod as I keep looking at his yard.

"Well, I'll let you git back to your work," he says. "Enjoy the pie." Then he walks off.

He goes back up his driveway, gives me another glance, and disappears into his house. That's when I finally notice how good the pie smells. I don't recognize the smell, but it smells very, very good.

I drag the bag of grass against the house, then take the pie into the kitchen and set it on the counter. It doesn't look as if it's been tampered with. That's good. Mom needs to know that. She also needs to know that I didn't ask for this pie, but Mrs. Jacobson will cover that one. I don't know how Mom'll react, but I don't think today is a good day for the wave to hit.

*   *   *   *

WHEN PAMELA PULLS INTO THE DRIVEWAY, Kenny runs into the bathroom and grabs the bottle of bowl cleaner spray that's been waiting on the sink. He sprays down the sides of the toilet, rag in hand. He hears his mother enter the house; he hears her throw her purse on the kitchen counter; and then he hears the silence that says she's found the pie.

"Kenny!"

He reports to the kitchen, rag and cleaner still in hand.

"What the hell is this?" she asks, studying his eyes.

Kenny clears his throat. "Mrs. Jacobson made it for you," he says. "Mr. Jacobson brought it over to me while I was raking the yard." Saying this tells her that he did *not* answer a knock at the door.

She stands quietly for a moment, obviously in deep thought, still studying his eyes. "Okay," she finally says in a tone that says, "Carry on."

He's in the clear. No wave today.

He returns to the bathroom and hears his mother cursing and mumbling to herself.

Pamela kicks off her shoes and snatches open the knife drawer. She takes more than a moderate portion of the pie and places the slice on a paper towel. Then she takes the rest of the pie to the bathroom, where Kenny is on hands and knees, wiping the outside of the already clean toilet bowl. "Move," she orders.

He quickly stands next to the tub and watches as she slides the remainder of the pie into the toilet.

"Flush it," she commands, then heads back to the kitchen without looking back.

The white slave boy does as he's told.

Chapter 19

TONY IS PLEASED TO SEE SARAH AND HIS mother becoming closer with each passing day. At a glance, one would think they've known each other for years. The ease in which their camaraderie has grown has truly taken him aback. In fact, only the consistent disdain he receives from his students—their perpetually quiet animosity, their defiance toward his assignments, and their chronically malicious whispering—has surprised him more.

He has had no other confrontations since the Rodney incident on Monday, not even from Rodney. Indeed, by all standards, his classes are well-behaved. For the last five days, he has clearly outlined his expectations, and he's shown no sign of breaking any promises concerning "consequences," should anyone decide to challenge his being a man of his word.

He knows that what he said on Monday about the "real world" was perceived by most as a threat. So be it. However they may have misconstrued his message, it continues to work. Threat or no threat, classroom management is no longer an issue for him.

He suspects there's something else at work, an additional element convincing most of the students to behave accordingly, but he hasn't given it much thought. For the past few days, more pressing concerns have been tickling his brain: How does he get them to do their assignments? How does he get them to want to learn? How is he supposed to teach students who absolutely refuse to be taught? Even more—why does he care? Is it the challenge or the students? Is it a nagging notion of opportunity and responsibility? Is he using their response to him as an excuse? A scapegoat? A bandage for his injured sense of competence?

Sarah sees him as a caring teacher; his mother sees a talented son, but they have both noticed his poorly camouflaged blue moods. Each day, they've asked him how it went, and each day, he's answered with the same "just fine," each sounding less convincing than the last.

Moved by their mounting concerns about his flagging spirits, Mrs. Avery and Sarah conferred and concluded that it would be best to give Tony a total change of scenery, a chance to unwind and recharge before the onslaught of a new week. They agreed that a night on the town, away from Tony's usual brooding over lesson plans, would be the perfect prescription. Sarah also sees it as an opportunity to digest more of the South, a chance to partake in some of the more indigenous pastimes.

She always wanted to learn how to line dance. Laughing, Tony explained how that particular step had never made its debut on any of the dance floors he remembered. So, at that point, it was settled; they'd both experience an authentic part of the South for the first time—a country dance club. And even though Tony's enthusiasm didn't match Sarah's, his desire to please her remained as intense as ever. If her piercing hazel eyes asked, he'd probably mount a mechanical bull.

As they approach the entrance of the Ranch House restaurant, Tony sees the place that he's driven by dozens of times in a new perspective. Suddenly, he is, again, standing on Sarah's porch, waiting for the door to open, waiting to meet her parents for the first time.

Inside, they sit in the waiting area with several other people, waiting to be seated. The smells of steak sauce and fresh wood dance in the air. Boots can be tracked here and there by the sounds they make on the wooden floor, sounds which add to the already superb country western theme. The dining area is full. They have to wait for forty minutes before the hostess comes for them, and as they're led to their table,

Tony wonders if Sarah notices the many eyes that shoot daggers their way, conversations pausing at the sight of them. He also wonders if she notices he's the only person not needing a tan.

The number of cowboy hats is proportionate to the number of oversized pickups found outside. The parking lot can be mistaken for the site of a truck auction. A few trucks are covered with mud; some sport gun racks in the back window; many are adorned with the confederate flag. Tony tries to ignore his discomfort as it continues to tap him on the shoulder.

The hostess smiles as she hands them menus. "Your server will be with you shortly."

"Thank you," they say, but Sarah is the only one who returns a full smile.

The sounds of music and dance are heard in the adjoining room. A traditional saloon door separates the dance area from the dining area. Above the entrance is another pair of the many antlers displayed throughout the restaurant.

Tony motions toward the saloon door. "I guess that's where they do their dancing," he mumbles.

"It appears so," agrees Sarah, bubbling with anticipation.

Tony reads his menu and says, "I'll probably make a fool of myself once we get on the dance floor."

"We *both* will," says Sarah. "Remember, I've never done this either. I've only heard from friends how invigorating it's supposed to be. You don't have to go through with it if you'd rather—"

"I *want* to."

She leans over and gives him a quick kiss. The tapping on his shoulder becomes a tugging of the arm.

"They sure do have their share of steak entrees," he says, causing Sarah to pop her menu open. "T-bone, Rib eye, New York Strip—they even have filet mignon, and the prices are reasonable, too. I think I'll have steak."

"Very funny," she says. "All I *see* is steak, but shouldn't we order appetizers first?"

"We can order everything at once," Tony says. "It's better for the server."

Sarah almost forgot how Tony's working for a restaurant had taught him the finer points of dining out, but his response refreshes her memory of their only other semi-formal dining experience.

She smiles and says, "We also mention all of the condiments that we'll need when placing the order, right?"

"That's right," says Tony. "Especially if it's something out of the ordinary like—"

"Like Louisiana hot sauce?"

"I'm telling you, baby—servers can't *stand* that."

"Do tell," she says, tilting her head, noticing how Tony's eyes sparkle whenever he explains anything. She remembers that all waiters and waitresses should be called "servers," even though true etiquette suggests otherwise.

"I'm serious," Tony says.

"I know."

"You're laughing at me."

"I'm happy," she corrects. "I realize that working for a restaurant gave you more insight on what goes on behind the commercialized curtain. Now, continue. What else did you learn?"

"Things you don't want to know about."

"I'm waiting," she persists with a raised eyebrow.

"Have you decided what—"

She folds her menu. "Order for both of us. I trust your taste, now share."

After he looks at her for a moment, trying to gauge her interest, he shrugs and clears his throat. "The first rule to dining out is patience."

"Patience?"

"Patience. Most people have no idea how—"

"Hello. My name is DeAnn and I'll be your server this evening the special tonight is broiled rib eye covered with sautéed onions mushrooms and peppers would you like to start out by trying a few of our delicious appetizers this evening?" says a short blonde in a single breath. She wears a neatly tied flannel shirt, tight jean shorts, and a pair of white boots. She seems to have appeared from nowhere.

Tony gives her their entire order with polished cordiality, and DeAnn collects their menus and leaves with the same nimbleness as displayed with her abrupt arrival.

"Now," says Tony, "no matter how long it takes for our food to arrive, the rule is what?"

"Patience."

"Patience—right. And would you like to know why?"

Sarah stifles a grin. "Desperately."

"This is serious stuff," says Tony. He looks around as if preparing to disclose covert government information.

Sarah snickers. "I can tell."

Tony smiles at the hazels and says, "If you show that you're in a hurry—if you act as if you just *can't* wait another minute for your food, the server will let the manager know, who, in turn, lets the cooks know. Now—before you get a free meal by whining about your well-done twelve-ounce taking seven minutes to cook—"

"Seven minutes?"

"Yeah—*seven*." He leans forward and lowers his voice a little. "And the scary part is the fact that there are people who never even bother to think about how a well-done twelve-ounce sirloin can make it to the table in eight minutes."

"How?" asks Sarah, unaware that she, too, is whispering.

Tony leans back in his chair and strokes his chin. "Well, there are all kinds of ways it can be done once the kitchen manager decides to look the other way," he admits. He glances over his shoulder again. "The microwave, several heavy skillets, an extremely hot broiler with a bowl of water, and a spray bottle filled with vegetable oil on standby— a well-done steak can dry out on you when you're pressing all of the juices out; it turns into cardboard. So, if you dip the steak—"

"That . . . is . . . so . . . gross," Sarah says, covering her mouth with both hands. "How on earth can a person eat something like that and not know?"

Tony grins. "Well, if you're really not used to waiting a while for your well-done steaks. . . ."

"That's so gross!"

Tony shrugs. "So, if you're used to eating soggy cardboard, whenever you decide you *can* wait—the times you *don't* rush the kitchen by acting like you've walked into a fast food restaurant—you get a properly cooked steak." He grins and adds, "And those are probably the times when you say to yourself—'that was one of the best steaks I've ever eaten.'" He rubs at his stomach to accentuate his point.

They both enjoy a snicker before Tony regroups. He clears his throat, signaling he has so much more to expose. "Rule number two," he says, "and some people might want to slide this one up to the number one spot—no matter what type of service you *think* you're getting, be kind to your server."

"Well, they have a tough job," says Sarah. "I've never done it, but I can tell it's not as simple as some make it seem. It takes skill."

"Have you ever seen someone really rip into a server?" Tony asks. "The type of person who complains about everything from the service to the location of the restaurant?"

"Well, I've seen my share of grumps, if that's what you mean."

DeAnn returns to the table with their drinks, salads and the same smile. "And here's your Louisiana hot sauce," she says. She pulls the bottle out of her petite, almost insignificant apron.

"Thank you so much," says Tony.

DeAnn's smile broadens. "No problem," she says. "Your appetizers will be a few more minutes."

Tony shrugs. "Whenever," he says, trying to match DeAnn's smile.

After DeAnn leaves to tend to another table, Sarah says, "I think she likes you."

"You *want* your server to like you," says Tony. "Sometimes there's a reason why a server can take pretty much anything the customer dishes out, and still serve them with a smile."

"I do *not* want to hear this," says Sarah. "Not before I eat."

Tony nods and grins. "Okay, then. Rule number two—be kind to your server simply because he or she *is* your server. Only an idiot, a person needing a second pebble in his head to spark a thought, would irritate someone who's bringing him something he's about to put into his mouth."

"To be honest," says Sarah, "I've never looked at it from that perspective, but now that you mention it. . . ."

Tony reaches for his glass of water and takes a few swallows. "The things you learn while working in a restaurant," he says. "And I'm not saying all servers will do something to your food if you mistreat them. For the most part, they'll only return to the kitchen and complain about what a lousy table they have—but not all of them."

Sarah eyes her salad suspiciously and asks, "What are some of the more common complaints you remember?" She takes a timid bite of Romaine.

"Running them a lot is a big one," he says. "Staying in their section well after you've finished your dessert is a no-no." He takes a bite of his salad, and then his chewing slows as he recalls a particularly deeply-engraved memory.

"What?" asks Sarah, noticing his expression.

"No one wanted a black table," he says matter-of-factly. "The consensus was that black people don't tip."

"That's absurd," Sarah says, frowning. She takes another bite of her salad.

"That's what *I* thought when I first heard it," Tony admits. "But according to Vince—I told you about Vince, right? He was an okay guy—good server, too. According to him, black parties don't tip much—at least, not the expected percent. Vince said many will leave only a dollar or two, sometimes not even that. Of course, there were some who'd tip well—professional types and such—but for the most part, servers took a bigger chance when serving a black party."

Not knowing what to say, Sarah takes another bite of salad, but she keeps her eyes on Tony as he uses his fork to toy with a crouton. "There are many white people who don't tip either, Tony," she finally offers.

He shakes his head. "The ratio's different. The percentage of white people who don't tip isn't as great as that of black people." He takes another sip of water. "During the times when I sat at the bar after my shift, talking to the bartender, I started paying closer attention to black parties, especially the larger ones. I figured maybe the service had something to do with it or something, you know?" He pauses again, and then a lopsided grin comes to his face as he continues to play with the same crouton.

"What?"

He shakes his head. "You know, I had forgotten that before I started working there, I had no idea servers were paid only two dollars an hour," he admits. "And then, I remembered my prom."

Sarah stares at him, puzzled. "Your prom?"

"I don't remember tipping on my prom date," he admits. "That was the first time I went to a tipping restaurant, having to pay the bill myself. If I *did* tip, it was probably a dollar or so."

Sarah pauses before replying. "How . . . I mean, you took that job to earn enough money for this," she says, extending her left hand where the fruit of Tony's labor continues to sparkle. "You were twenty-one years old."

"Almost twenty-two."

"Are you saying that . . . ?"

Tony nods. "That's when I learned about tipping—*informed* tipping, anyway."

Sarah looks at him incredulously. "How . . . ?"

"Good question. I had to think about it myself," says Tony, laughing. "How old were *you* when you learned about tipping?"

Sarah thinks for a moment. "I . . . I don't know—*young*. My parents would always take . . . wait a minute." She tilts her head slightly. "Your mother grew up in the fifties, the sixties. . . ."

Tony nods.

Sarah's eyes pop open. "Segregation!"

"Segregation—right," says Tony, dropping his voice to a whisper. "But let's not shout that word too loudly, okay?"

Sarah takes a quick glance around and finds that they're being watched by an elderly party of four. "Oh . . . right," she whispers, causing Tony to chuckle.

"Mama said she never wanted to go into a restaurant when desegregation started up," he says. "She just couldn't see herself going into one—it was 'theirs.' She said in those days, if a white person was headed toward you on the sidewalk, the sidewalk became theirs—you had to move."

Tony pauses for a moment and takes another sip of water. "There was this one time when she was a little girl walking down the sidewalk. Two white girls, one bigger than Mama, were walking up behind her. Mama didn't notice them—not in time, anyway. The older girl knocked her down, and she chipped one of her teeth when she hit the sidewalk. She says that was the worst she'd ever experienced during those times, and she'll never forget it. Of all the things she's forgotten, she still remembers that day as if it were yesterday—at least, that's what she'll tell you." He shakes the ice in his glass of water and shrugs. "She was so used to being loyal to the segregation laws that even today, she'll still give the right-of-way to a white person on a sidewalk. Just habit."

"Well, that explains a lot," says Sarah. She reaches for her glass of iced tea. "How can one be expected to know etiquette . . . well, if you're not allowed in an establishment. . . ."

Tony picks it up, "If you're never allowed to play, why should you know the rules?"

"Precisely," Sarah says. "Or be expected to teach your children rules you have yet to internalize." She thinks for a second and adds, "How can you play their tune if you've never seen the sheet music?"

Tony explodes with laughter, causing many to glance their way. "Sheet music—that's a good one."

"You liked that one?"

"Yes—*that* was fresh."

"Fresh?"

"Fresh."

"Well, that's a little more than I can say for this salad," she says and crosses a knife and fork over her salad plate.

"The salad's usually made in the morning," says Tony. "And sometimes, it's even used the next day."

"You are *not* making this an ideal dining experience," she says, trying to hide her amusement. "I want you to know that. I wonder how your mother would fare with you as a dining partner, now that you've worked for a restaurant."

"We'd have to do some coaxing to find out. She's always preferred home-cooked meals."

"After some of the meals she's cooked for me, I can see why," Sarah admits. "She's an extraordinary cook."

They enjoy their meal in the comfort of frivolous conversation and the occasional intimate silence. They can feel their love grow with every beat of their synchronized hearts. With the tapping on Tony's shoulder gone, his discomfort long since faded, he's oblivious to everything in the room, except Sarah's piercing hazel eyes.

They bask in each other's company for a little while longer before relinquishing their table, but not without leaving an additional ten percent to Tony's usual amount of gratuity. He knows that to linger at a table is to take away from a server's potential earnings, and they have been very pleased with the service.

"It's time to dance some of these calories away," says Sarah, brimming with anticipation.

"I *will* embarrass us," he warns. "You *do* realize this, right?"

"There's nothing at all embarrassing about enjoying yourself," retorts Sarah. "I only wish I'd thought of buying you a hat and some boots; it seems to be the style here."

Tony gives her an incredulous glare.

"What?" she says. "You'd look cute."

They head for the saloon door, arm in arm.

Chapter 20

AT FIRST, THE MUSIC GIVES TONY REASON to pause, but after the first thirty minutes, he acquires a genuine appreciation for the songs being played, and, considering the dance steps, no other type of music would work as well. It doesn't take him long to catch on to the steps. To him, most are simple, but also surprisingly fun and invigorating.

Most of the dancers are regulars, and the synchronicity on the floor benefits from this fact. All feet move with the same intentions; every skip compliments every bounce, right on cue. Even the dozens of smiles have been painted with the same brush. The entire dance floor moves, sways, and prances under the notion of a common thought—enjoy thyself. No one stands out, not even Tony.

To her credit, Sarah also holds her own. Though not a born dancer, within the first hour, she was stepping with the best of them. Now, as Tony takes his third break, guzzling down his third Shirley Temple, she struts with feet that are far more confident and surer than they were two hours ago. She has only left the floor once, and as she switches from partner to partner, from one elbow swing to the next, she keeps her eyes on her fiancée, anxiously awaiting his return.

"I'm near reflume" is what she lip-reads as Tony points toward the men's room. After a flash of deductive reasoning, she nods, and Tony disappears with subtle haste. She wants to be at their table when he returns, so she gracefully excuses herself from the dance floor, causing a few cordially tipped hats. When she gets to their table, she downs one of Tony's Shirley Temples like Gatorade.

As she catches her breath, she glances around the festive room and notices a man staring at her from a few tables over. Obviously, he's been watching her for some time, because his date is annoyed with his averted attention. Sarah smiles uncertainly, but the man scowls back at her and takes another swig of his beer. She sees the malice radiating from his eyes, and a strange emotion shoots through her spine, so she returns her attention to the dance floor, uncomfortable for the first time this evening.

After a minute, she glances in the direction of the men's room. Tony's only been gone two minutes, but it seems much longer now. She still senses the man watching her, and she's suddenly afraid. Of what, she can't say.

Another minute goes by, but still no Tony. Sarah hears a commotion at The Watcher's table. The woman is expressing her agitation, and she doesn't care about making it public. Sarah hears the woman call The Watcher a bastard, repeatedly. Still, Sarah keeps her eyes fixed on the dance floor, occasionally glancing in the direction of the men's room.

"What're you doin'?"

Sarah doesn't know what startles her more—the deep raspy voice or the man's hand—*The Watcher's hand*—clamping down on her shoulder. She looks up at The Watcher with wide eyes, speechless.

"Ah'm talkin' to you," The Watcher says, raising his slurred voice. "Ain't you got no manners?"

The Watcher's date storms over next. She's wearing a suggestive, street corner outfit. In fact, her clothes—well, the lack of—actually divert Sarah's attention for a second. The word "harlot" enters Sarah's mind, but she pushes it aside.

"I thought you said you were gitt'n another beer," says The Watcher's date as she removes his hand from Sarah's shoulder. "You juss wanna start some mess."

The Watcher spins to face his date. "Why you defendin' 'er?" he asks. He looks as though he'd slap her if she spouts the wrong words. On the back of his jean jacket is a large, faded patch of the confederate flag.

Sarah's heart skips a beat.

"I told you!" says the woman. "I ain't defendin' nobody, but her business is her business! Besides, this ain't the place!" She says this without ever acknowledging Sarah.

Sarah doesn't know whether to stand or remain seated. It's an awkward situation, and her eyes are momentarily glued to the back of The Watcher's jacket. The emblem invokes nothing within her, but she wonders about Tony's reaction.

"Is there a problem here?"

Simultaneously, all three give their attention to Tony. Sarah relief is laced with anxiety. The Watcher eyes Tony as if measuring him for a suit. Tony stares back, suddenly wishing he was a few inches taller. He glances at The Watcher's date who, to him, is dressed like a floozy. He notices that The Floozy is trying to convince The Watcher to leave; she's gently tugging at his arm, but not saying anything. Even so, The Floozy stares at Tony as well, as if cursing him in her thoughts.

"Yeah," The Watcher says. "There's a problem." He jerks his arm away from The Floozy.

Suddenly, two more men flank Tony, one on each side. He has no idea where they came from. His heart sinks a little as he glances at Sarah, and his mind races. His only concern is for Sarah, but he knows he can't handle three men. Still, he braces himself, prepared to die swinging, kicking, biting, and probably yelling his head off.

"I don't think there's a problem here," says the man to Tony's left, returning The Watcher's stare. He sounds the way men do in Westerns just before they draw six-shooters. He's the older of the two, and big enough to bury three Tonys, but he's obviously more interested in ripping into The Watcher. He rests his forearm on Tony's left shoulder like they've been friends since first grade.

Tony's heart warms.

"Is there a problem here, Chad?" he asks the man to Tony's right.

Chad shakes his head. "I sure hope not, Amos." He resembles his larger partner in a way that only a younger brother could. "Be a damn shame to ruin such a nice evenin' like this."

"A *damn* shame," agrees Amos. Again, he trains his eyes again on The Watcher.

Despite the music and merriment, an awkward silence ensues before The Floozy, again, grabs The Watcher's arm. "Come on, let's go."

The Watcher pauses a moment, and then acts like he's leaving to please The Floozy. Chad actually snickers as they exit the building.

Amos turns to Tony. "I know you could've handled it, sir, but me and ma brother was kinda bored over there, and we juss could'n pass up the chance." He extends a hand. "Amos Garrett's the name."

"Tony Avery," says Tony, shaking Amos' hand heartily.

"Strong handshake," Amos says. "I like that. This here's ma brother—Chad."

"How're you," says Chad, extending a hand.

"Pleased to meet you," says Tony. "This is my fiancée—Sarah."

The two men tip their hats. "Ma'am."

"Hello," Sarah says.

"You two enjoy the rest of your evenin'," says Amos. He tips his hat again and motions to Chad to take their leave.

Tony grabs him by the arm. "Won't you join us for a while?"

Amos shakes his head. "Naw," he says, "we don't wanna butt in on yer night out."

"Please, we insist," adds Sarah.

Amos studies them, trying to determine the sincerity of their offer.

Chad clears his throat and says, "Well, I was head'n back on the floor, to tell you the truth. I got a ways yet before Ah'm as used up as ma brother."

"I'll join you!" yelps Sarah. She springs to her feet and kisses Tony firmly. "Back in a minute!" she says and snatches Chad to the dance floor.

"She likes her dancing," says Tony.

Amos slaps Tony on the back before taking a seat. "You reckon?" he chuckles.

As the evening ages, Sarah succeeds in coaxing Tony and Amos to the dance floor for a few final elbow swings, struts, and prances before the three decide to finish the night getting better acquainted. Chad decides to forgo retiring the night by way of Shirley Temples and beer. He wishes his brother and new friends a good night, and then leaves with a brunette under his arm.

Amos hears how Tony and Sarah met, Tony's new teaching assignment at Lincoln High, and their future plans—right up to the color of paint on their house and the number of children they intend to have. They, in turn, learn of Amos' failed marriage, his infatuation with jigsaw puzzles and grandfather clocks, and his modestly successful dental practice of seventeen years.

They enjoy each other's company for another two hours before calling it a night. Sarah and Tony lazily walk Amos to his pickup truck. It sparkles with a recent waxing. Tony notices the confederate flag license plate first, prominently mounted on Amos' shiny front bumper. When Sarah sees the plate, her smile wanes.

"That's a really nice truck," says Tony.

"Well, thank you kindly, Tony. You know, it cost me a pretty penny." He turns to the truck, inspecting his wax job, then looks back at Tony and Sarah. "It was really nice talkin' to you two," he says, trying to avoid saying good-bye.

Tony steals a glance at Sarah before replying. "We'll definitely keep in touch, Amos," he says, taking a step toward him and his truck. "You're good people. Maybe we can go bowling or something sometime."

Amos closes the gap between them to shake hands. "I'd really like that, ma friend." And with that, he tips his hat to Sarah with a final "ma'am," jumps into his truck, and fires it up. They give Amos a final wave, and he drives off with a honk of his horn.

As they head to the car hand in hand, Tony suddenly shakes his head and sighs.

"What's wrong?" Sarah asks.

Tony kisses the back of her hand and says, "I'm a terrible bowler."

Sarah wraps her arms around his waist. "Somehow, I don't think he'll mind."

Chapter 21

L AST NIGHT'S DANCING was refreshing for Tony, and today's earlier excursion with Sarah and his mother was welcomed, but now, it's back to business.

In college, writing lesson plans used to come easily for Tony. But now, seated at the kitchen table, he massages his temple, still at a loss; he has no idea what he needs to teach.

Ideally, in the great scheme of things, a teacher is to assess what the students know—determine their current academic prowess before plunging into a lesson. After all, why bother teaching algebraic equations when students can't add or subtract? Why bother with Shakespeare when Dr. Seuss remains a challenge? But Tony has yet to enjoy the benefits of even the most archaic of assessment tools. Multiple Choice, True & False, and Matching have all failed to solicit a significant response. His students refuse to work. Most of his handouts and quizzes are turned in with only a name. Some without.

Discipline isn't an issue. If he wants the talking to subside, all he needs to do is ask. Enter the classroom quietly, in a civil manner?—no problem. Find your assigned seat and stay there until the class period is over?—done. His students know and comply with the routines and procedures. Unfortunately, he won't be giving a test on behavior.

"Hi ma son doin'?"

On the inside, Tony leaps through the ceiling, startled by his mother's sudden appearance, but on the outside, he is calm and in control. "Ah'm okay, Mama." He leans back in his chair, but he keeps his pen poised over the blank page. "Juss try'n na git uh l'uh work done. Sarah sleep?"

"Sleepin' like uh baby," she says, frankness in her voice.

Mrs. Avery pauses for a moment. Then, she slides a chair out from underneath the table and takes a seat.

Tony doodles with his pen. The moment that was sure to come has finally arrived, and he couldn't be gladder.

"Mine if I sit wit chew fuh uh l'uh bit?"

"No," he says, shrugging. "I'own care."

His mother takes a deep breath. She doesn't know how to start. She's in unfamiliar territory, but she's determined not to let that stop her. Her son needs her, and she knows it whether *he* knows it or not. "Tony," she starts, with a tenderness only a mother could produce, "wha's goin' own in na school? Wha's happenin'?"

"Ah'm fine, Mama. Everythang's—"

"Tony, if I h'yuh anothuh *Ah'm fine* out uh you. . . ."

Tony gives his mother's snappy response a long-awaited smile of relief. Her facial expression of concern and irritation, matching the tone in her voice, goads him into providing an honest answer. "I really don't know what's going on. My students—most of them—won't do anything. Nothing. They just . . . I don't know. Were they like this before I got there? Is it the school? Is it the parents? I wonder sometimes. They have absolutely no motivation, Mama—*none*. It's as if they don't care. I don't get it. I mean, what am I—"

"Lowuh ya voice, Tony."

Irritation flashes across his consciousness. He's finally revealing himself—his frustrations, his doubts, his anger—and his mother is only concerned with how loud he expresses them.

Mrs. Avery sees it in his eyes. "I juss don' won' chew wakin' up Sarah."

Tony's expression relaxes. "I'm at a loss, Mama," he says, shaking his head. "I don't know. I just don't."

"Well, tell me wha's goin' own, Tony," she says, gently. She places a hand on his forearm. "Dey minin' ya? Dey behavin'? I mean—"

"That's the funny thing, Mama. I don't really have discipline problems. At first, there were those who tested me, regardless. They *did* too, but I didn't break. I mean, I showed them what I was about, what I would and wouldn't stand for. Right now, a lot of them think of me as a mean person, but I'd rather that than the alternative. Just like Professor Slaughter said, you can start out mean and become nice, but it's next to impossible to start out nice and then try to turn mean. He told us time after time, we're there to teach, not to make friends."

"Professuh Slaughtuh?" snickers Mrs. Avery. "Lawd Jesus. . . ."

"He teaches Classroom Management. Sarah and I took him together. He's a good man, and what he says is right on the money, but I need an assignment that will make them want to *do* something, Mama. They won't do anything. I still don't even know whether most of them can read or write. I mean, I try Round Robin Reading—no volunteers. I call a name—they just sit there, looking at me. What am I supposed to do? Write them up for not reading? I give them handouts—nothing. Most of them won't even write their names on the pages. Tell them that they'll fail? That should work, right? I mean—if you fail, you have to take the class over. Does that even faze them? Yeah, right. They don't care, Mama. They don't care. Why do they even show up? I don't get it, Mama. I just don't." He shakes his head as he resumes his doodling with increased vigor.

Mrs. Avery takes a moment to absorb Tony's words. She glances down at his paper. He's drawing a tree. She wonders what a psychiatrist would say about that. A tree of all things. "An it's been like dis since day one?" she finally asks.

Tony stalls before he answers, as if finishing the tree is more important. "The first couple of days, they talked," he says, still doodling. Then he shakes his head again. "They changed, Mama. I don't know."

"Tony, put dat pen down an look at me."

He does so with a sigh, but slowly, as if ashamed. He's also becoming more irritated.

"Na tell me, from na beginnin'," she says. "From na firs' day ta na."

With the same enthusiasm one uses when reading aloud a grocery list, he tells her how he introduced himself before every class. He tells her about all the Rodneys he had to deal with on his first day, and how he gained the compliance of every class soon after. He tells her how he spoke to the students as they entered and exited the classroom, and how they snickered and whispered when they weren't in his immediate presence. He tells her how he feels in the classroom.

The enemy.

The joke.

The outcast.

He's uncomfortable in the presence of his students. He feels as though he has a "kick me" sign stuck on his back, posted by the students, a sign only they see. The word "conspiracy" has moved up in rank to his immediate vocabulary, but he hasn't used it. He doesn't like going to school, looking at the dozens of difficult-to-read faces, and listening to the negative mumbling. Right now, he doesn't like any of his classes, and he doesn't like—no, *hates* being a teacher.

Mrs. Avery waits a moment before she says anything, as if she's stirring the information her son has served. Her expression hasn't changed. "Let me ax you dis . . ." she begins carefully, ". . . hi you talk ta 'em? You know, when you juss . . . talkin'?"

Tony hesitates due to all of the possible meanings to the question, and the new expression on his mother's face. He's still annoyed, but he doesn't know why. "I'm nice, Mama—at least . . . I *try* to be," he says thoughtfully. "As a matter of fact, I haven't raised my voice since Monday." He tilts his head, puzzled. "What do you mean?" He searches her eyes and recognizes her expression as discomfort, but nothing else.

"Tony . . . what Ah'm sayin'—Fuh instance, do you say *ain't* when you talkin' ta 'em? You know what I mean? Hi you *talk* ta 'em?"

The fog of confusion and annoyance thickens into a cloud of aggravation and disbelief. The thunder comes next. "Mama, I'm an *English teacher!*" he snaps. "How do you *think* I'm going to sound?" He fights the sudden urge to pace the floor. "I'm expected to teach these kids how to read. I'm expected to teach these kids how to write; how to be productive in society. I'm expected to set an *example*, Mama. How am I supposed to do that walking into the classroom sounding like—?"

It's her eyes that interrupt him. Her eyes reflect him and his words, and he suddenly sees himself as a stranger in his own home, a stranger who's just assaulted his mother. Her facial expression is one he's never seen before. There's pain, but something else he can't decipher, like an exposed scar that appears from nowhere. His eyes drop to the tree, and his heart drops to his stomach. He feels the pain of his words as they seep into his identity.

His mother breaks the uncomfortable silence. "Like me?" she mutters with a little smile. The smile is genuine, and this makes him feel worse. He tries not to think about the kinds of practice she's had, learning to smile no matter what.

"Mama. . . ."

"Baby, you ain' got ta say nut'n—I know. I *know.*" She pauses and then adds, "I know dat chew know who you *are.* I know you ain' ashamed uh yo'self—I know dis, Tony. An Ah'm proud uh ya, son. I am—*very* proud. You come uh long way. Da way you can talk na ain' come easy—I know. I remembuh all lem debate tournaments you used ta go to—used ta lose *all* la time. What dey called it? Abraham Lincoln somp'm?"

Tony swallows, and it hurts. "Lincoln-Douglas," he murmurs, a slight choke in his voice. He's still unable to look his mother in the eye, despite her motherly tone and firm, but gentle grasp of his forearm.

"Right—dass it. Lincoln-Douglas," she says, squeezing his arm a little. "Dey kep' takin' points off ya 'cause you what'n talkin' like dey do own na news—you know, like dem news people we see all la time. But chew worked at it an worked at it, Tony. I remembuh—sometimes real late at night. An you star'ded winnin'. You won uh lot, but do you remembuh what chew told me aftuh da firs' one dat chew evuh won?

What did you say ta me? You remembuh?"

Tony glances at the one plaque of the nine on the far wall, the one meaning the most to him, his first win. "Dey'own take you seriously unless you soun' like dey soun'," he answers thoughtfully, as if recalling someone else's quote.

"You what'n but fifteen, Tony. Fif—teen. But chew learnt somp'm nat day, an you still carry dat lesson wit chew. It's probally g'own stay wit chew fuh'evuh. Even na'day, if you talk about somp'm—somp'm nat chew serious about—you'll talk like dat, an you *should*, too. You *should* be taken seriously."

She pauses in thought, but only for a moment. "Ah'm glad da see dat chew can talk anyway you won't wit Sarah, too. Dat shows dat she like you fuh *you*. Ah'm happy ta see dat. I really am."

The silence returns for a long moment before he speaks. His voice sounds as fragile as a newly-betrayed heart. "Mama . . . I been ackin' like uh fool at school," he whispers. He places his face inside his hands, and then pulls down toward his chin, keeping his mouth covered. "I been so, so, so stupid." He remembers all of his actions as a teacher, all of his interactions with his students, all of his egotistical rectifications, his academically camouflaged insults, his blundering mishaps.

Mrs. Avery doesn't speak. She knows it's better to simply listen. Tony sits for a moment and stares at the tree, but the tree is no longer there.

"I star'ded out correctin' ney speech, Mama," he finally says, flatly. His face contorts as he recalls various incidents. "Since day one . . . I been tellin' nem kids hi dey should say dis an hi dey should say dat. I been comin' across . . . wrong. I been treat'n nem like . . . it's somp'm *wrong* wit da way dey talk"—he brings his eyes up to meet his mother's—"I been treat'n nem like . . . it's somp'm wrong wit da way"—he looks down at the tree, swallows, and then returns to his mother's eyes—"as if dare's somp'm wrong wit da voice dat raised me, dat tole me right from wrong, dat gave me"—he swallows again, and the first tear makes its way down his face. When his mother wipes it away, the gentleness of her touch is almost too painful to bear. He looks back down at the tree and says, "Da voice dat gave me comfort whenevuh I hurt myself, dat put me ta sleep at night, an"—He pauses to swallow the knot in his throat—"an da voice dat decided ta come in h'yuh . . . an talk some sense in uh educated fool . . . who . . ."

"Don't chew talk like dat, Tony," she says firmly. "Yo' mama ain' raise no fool, not by uh long shot. You h'yuh me?" She cups his chin in the palm of her hand. "You ain' no fool, Tony. You doin' what chew supposed ta do. Dem kids need what chew got ta give 'em," she says with a sigh. She pauses for a moment. "You juss need da let 'em know why. You *won'ted* ta learn hi da talk like dat, Tony. An hi da read, hi da write. Dey got ta wanna learn, too. Dass what chew need da do—give 'em uh *reason* na learn. If you bill up dey appetite, you ain' got ta shove nut'n down ney th'oat."

To this, Tony chuckles, and it feels good to do so.

His mother leans back in her chair. "You know hi dey say dat chew can lead uh horse ta warduh, but chew cane make 'im drank?" she asks.

Tony wipes at his nose and says, "Yeah. . . ."

"Well, what chew doin' lead'n uh horse in na firs' place?" she asks. "You supposed ta be rid'n it. An if you ride it har'd enough, it'll drank."

Tony laughs again, and his mother is pleased.

He shakes his head. "I done messed up wit 'em, Mama. Dey'own like me, an ney ain' got no *reason* na like me." He sees the tree again, but ignores it. " I would'n like me eithuh."

Mrs. Avery pauses for a moment as if deciding whether or not she should speak. "Tony . . . remembuh dat time when I was uh l'uh girl, an I got ma tooth chipped from fallin' own na sidewalk?"

He studies her curiously. "What'n you pushed?"

"Yeah, I was pushed—uh mean white girl," she grins. "I was so mad—turned out dat my mama worked fuh dat girl's mama. I ain' know it at da time."

"You ain' nevuh tell me dat," says Tony, mildly surprised.

"My mama ain' know it eithuh, not until I went ta work wit 'uh one day. She won'ted me ta play wit dat lady's daughtuhs. As soon as we saw each othuh, bofe our mouths flew open. I tole Mama dat dat was da girl, an na girl's mama paid da git my tooth fixed."

"Juss like dat?"

"Juss like dat."

"So ya'll played togethuh an everythang?"

"Yeah," she says with a thoughtful nod.

"You ain' tell me all uh dis," he says, shaking his head. "So you forgave 'uh?"

"Tony, people ain' always what dey star'd out bein'. Dat girl's name was Ann Simms—Miss Annie huh'self, an you know as well as I do dat we ain' got nut'n but love fuh each othuh."

Tony's jaw lands on the table.

"I nevuh tole you growin' up 'cause I ain' won't chew ta git uh attitude about somp'm nat's nut'n. Do right by dem kids. Dey'll come aroun'," she says and then grunts to her feet. "An if dey don't, at least you did yo' par'd. Don' be so har'd own ya'self. It'll be awright in na end."

"Uh lot uh 'em probably *still* won't study, Mama," he mumbles.

"Dass okay. You juss do *yo'* job as da teachuh. Dey ain' gitt'n paid da be students, so some might not. But chew gitt'n paid, Tony. You *won'ted* ta be uh teachuh. You dare by choice. Maybe uh par'd uh yo' job is makin' nem wanna be students. Let 'em know da *real* reason why dey need what chew got ta teach 'em. At least dey'll know what dey really passin' up. At least dey cane say dey did'n know, right?"

Tony nods as his mind races with ideas, strategies, and possibilities.

"Ah'm goin' na bed," she says as she shuffles off, satisfied with the conversation. "Try not ta stay up too late."

"Mama. . . ."

"Hm?"

"If I can just be half the teacher that you've always been. . . ."

"I love you too, son," she says, but she doesn't turn around. Her eyes fill with tears. "I love you too."

Tony spends the next five minutes or so thinking about how fortunate he truly is. Afterwards, he gets back on task—this time, with energy, focus, and the kind of passion a person has when working to make his mother proud.

Chapter 22

TONY SITS AT HIS DESK AND WAITS FOR the bell to start his day. Again, he glances at the copy of his new student's transcript. According to the information, Kenneth Houston isn't a very bright student, which isn't surprising since he's at Lincoln. What raises one of Tony's eyebrows is Kenny's profile. He's definitely a discipline problem. In fact, his disciplinary record makes most of Tony's other students seem tame. Tony takes another deep breath and rubs his eyes. He doesn't need a person like Kenny in the class—not now, not ever. Undoubtedly, he'll have to keep tabs on this one.

The bell rings, and the halls fill with the thunder of a five-minute stampede. As the students file in, their conversation wanes, the doorway acting as a dampening device. Faith Dunn and Lisa Boyer walk in with their usual smile and wave. They still seem to appreciate their new situation, their new teacher. Unfortunately, there aren't many like them.

Tony hears laughter in the hall, the kind that usually follows a slip and fall or a punch line. He knows the laughter well. Shortly after, Kenny walks in and pauses at the entrance. He looks at Tony as if he expects the teacher to say something.

Tony leans back in his chair and folds his arms. "What do you need?"

Kenny steps inside and looks about the classroom, and then back at Tony. "Are you the . . . teacher?"

Something about the way he asks brings a small frown to Tony's face. "Yes," he answers, blankly. "What can I do for you?"

"I'm Kenny Houston."

The laughter continues just outside the doorway, but they both ignore it.

"Heck naw," snickers Lisa.

Tony glares at Lisa and Faith, and their smiles disappear. Then he signals Kenny to approach his desk. "Let me see your schedule." After glancing at it, he hands it back and says, "Your seat is the sixth one in the third row from the window."

Kenny glances at his new seat, the one in the back of the class. Jarek and Jacob grin at each other from across the room. Kenny has to sit behind the final member of their trio—Corey Watson. Corey shoots them the finger.

Rodney and James enter the classroom and force a fit of laughter.

"You can save that for outside," Tony warns.

"Dat was Powuh—not me," says Rodney.

Kenny keeps his eyes on the floor as he heads to the back of the classroom. The snickers continue. Faith mumbles something to Lisa, causing her to laugh.

Marcus enters the room with Roland. "I tole you we had Fatso! What I tell ya?"

Tony stands, irritated. "He has a name, Marcus."

The class quiets down, but there's still snickering. Tony watches Kenny take his seat. He wonders what this new student, who is notorious for trouble, might do someday when he least expects it. Whatever Kenny does, he's sure it will be soon, but he doesn't want the class to set Kenny off on his very first day.

"His name's Fatso," mumbles Marcus as he takes his seat.

More snickering.

Tony frowns. "That is *not* his name, Marcus," he says, trying not to glance at Kenny.

The tardy bell sounds as Jose and Jasmine fly through the doorway. They gasp for air like they've just run the hundred.

"Sorry," Jasmine says as they take their seats.

Tony waits for the usual pre-class rustling to subside. He sits on the front of his desk, his heels lightly thumping the graffiti-scratched wood. "Before we get started, we have a new member of the class." He looks at Kenny with an obviously forced smile. "Would you like to introduce yourself?"

Kenny says nothing. He doesn't even blink.

Marcus raises his hand.

Tony rolls his eyes and sighs. "Yes . . . Marcus."

Marcus stands with a dictionary in his hand. "I juss wanna read dis definition," he says, then clears his throat. "*Fatso: a fat person—often used as a . . .* disparaging *. . . form of address.*"

The class explodes.

Marcus shrugs innocently. "Dass in na dictionary—don' look at me," he says, grinning. Then he takes his seat.

Tony waits a full thirty seconds for the commotion to end, and then he motions to Marcus to come forward. When he does, Tony leans over to whisper in his ear. "You will stop right now," he hisses, a cold threat in his voice. "You will also write a formal apology, a minimum of one full page."

"What I—"

"Take . . . your . . . seat."

Marcus stomps back to his seat. Roland flashes him a thumbs-up, but he ignores it. The snickering doesn't really end. Whispering is heard, but not located. Smiles are everywhere. The class is thoroughly amused. Tony sits on his desk, thinking. The class waits.

Finally, Tony looks over at James. "James Cotner—or should I say *Powuh*—bring me your dictionary . . . please."

James glances around the room, bewildered. "What I do?"

"Nothing. I just want to see your dictionary for a moment."

James reaches inside his desk for the dictionary, waiting for the punch line.

More snickering.

He walks to the front of the classroom and offers Tony the dictionary.

"Thank you," says Tony. "You may be seated."

James glares at Kenny as he returns to his desk. Kenny continues to show no response to his surroundings, not even a shift in his seat, but he keeps his eyes on the teacher.

Tony eventually shrugs. "That's what it says, alright . . . *often used as a disparaging form of address.*"

Again, the class explodes. Tony frowns at the disruption. Kenny frowns at the teacher, but he remains quiet and still.

Tony looks around at the smiling faces. "Well, I guess we can't really argue with the dictionary, now can we?"

High fives sound throughout the classroom, and the term "Fatso" echoes here and there.

"Let's see what else this book of wisdom has to say," Tony mumbles. His finger is already on the right page. "Ah . . . here it is."

The class quiets down a little.

"According to the dictionary, a book carefully chosen by the public school system, Marcus and over half the students in here are a bunch of niggers." He tries to pronounce the word with as much malice as he can mimic.

The class freezes. A teacher is heard talking next door. Distant traffic is heard outside, even though the windows are closed.

Tony places a finger in the dictionary and says, "Right here—page seven eighty-four—*Nigger: a black person—usually taken to be offensive.*"

The class remains quiet. Some reach for dictionaries.

Tony brings his face closer to the dictionary. "The second definition says *a member of* any *dark-skinned race—usually taken to be offensive.*" He scans the room. The smiles are gone. The melody of birds sounds over the distant traffic. "Well, well, well," Tony says, nodding now. "According to this book, this incredible source of information, a lot of people who thought they weren't niggers, actually are—including me."

He stresses the *r* sound every time he says "nigger."

The class remains silent. Some bury their heads in dictionaries, seeing the pages for the first time—first impressions.

Tony flips to another page. "Now this *is* interesting. According to this, a bastard is a person whose mother gave birth to him or her without being married." He looks around the classroom. All smiles have been collected and discarded. "Of course, there aren't any *bastards* in this classroom," he mumbles, thumbing through the dictionary again.

A few glance at Tammy Yates, who is four months pregnant. She looks at the floor. The sound of the pages bounces from the walls.

Tony taps his finger on a page. "This is one I really like. This is what I call a *good* definition. Who can tell me what word I'm defining—*an irrational attitude of hostility . . . directed against an individual . . . a group . . . a race . . . or their supposed characteristic?*"

No response. He didn't expect one.

"*Prejudice,*" he says softly. He closes the dictionary and jumps off the desk. "Prejudice is treating people according to how you see them, instead of according to how they *should* be seen. It's treating people according to who or what you *think* they are, not according to who and what they actually are—just people." He looks around at the faces and shrugs. "Just people."

He allows the uncomfortable silence to baptize everyone before he continues. "Many of us have dealt with this word—*prejudice.* Some of us may still be dealing with it, but who cares, right? Everybody does it—treats others according to how they shouldn't be treated," he says, pacing the front of the classroom. "But what's funny is that after we finish treating someone else the way *we* think they should be treated," he continues, his tone becoming a shout, "we turn right around, and yell at the top of our lungs! With frowns on our faces! With clenched fists! With conviction in our voices! Don't call me a nigger; I'm not a nigger! Don't call me a cracker; I'm not a cracker! Don't call me a spick! Don't call me a chink! Don't call me a kike! Don't call me a bastard!"

Dead silence.

Tony frowns at his class. "But who are you to say who or what you are?" He raises the dictionary in the air. "Can *you* write one of these?"

After a moment, Roland raises his hand.

"Yes."

"Wha's uh *kike*?"

Tony frowns at his student long enough to make Roland swallow. "According to this," he finally says, slamming the dictionary on the desk, "a Jew."

More silence.

"Does it make sense to treat people *exactly* the way we don't want to be treated?"

A few look around the classroom. The rest keep their eyes fixed on Tony.

"Then why do we do it?"

Still silence.

Tony grabs the dictionary once more and thumbs through the pages. "The answer is on page eleven forty-five."

Pages rustle throughout the classroom.

"It's listed under the word *stupid*."

A few smack their lips while others groan dramatically. Tony sits back on the top of his desk and scans the room. He focuses on all of the faces staring back at him. They sit—waiting, wondering what he's going to do next. As usual, Richard Brigman nods drowsily, but he fights it off.

Tony clears his throat. "While we own na subjec' uh callin' people out uh dey name, treat'n people hi dey ain' supposed ta be treated—ackin' *stupid*—I wanna let cha'll know hi stupid I been ackin' since I got h'yuh."

The room becomes a giant whisper, but Tony doesn't look up.

"Since day one, I been treat'n uh lot uh you da wrong way. Correctin' hi you talk—hi you ack—wit'out thankin' about hi dass supposed ta make you feel. I been comin' at cha'll la wrong way. Fuh dat, I wanna let cha'll know dat Ah'm sorry. Fuh real."

The whispering continues as a few hands shoot to the air.

"Yes, Marcus."

"Why you ain' let nobody know you knew hi da talk normal?"

"Define *normal.*"

"Like black people talk."

"That's normal?"

"Fuh black people it is."

"All black people?"

"Pretty much."

"People in Africa don' talk like we talk," snaps James.

"Dass 'cause dey from anothuh country—dey'own speak English," says Rodney. "If dey *was* ovuh h'yuh—"

"Dey still would'n soun' like us," insists James. "Check out Malik. He speak English, an he sho'nuff don' soun' normal. Not like *us.*"

"Yo, like, why you say the way you guys talk is normal?" Jose interrupts. "Not everybody can understand what chew guys sayin' when you start flippin'. You guys git crazy wit it."

"How do you mean?" asks Tony, fueling the conversation.

Jose eyes his teacher incredulously. "Sometimes you can't catch everythang they say."

"Why not?" probes Tony, shrugging. "Do they speak too fast?"

Jose shakes his head. "Naw, man. It ain't like dat. They just mess up like just *too* many words sometimes, know what Ah'm sayin'?"

"What chew mean *we* mess up words?" snorts James. "You da one talkin' wit dat jive accent. We'own understan' *you.*"

"Git 'im, Powuh."

"Tell 'im."

Jarek shifts in his desk and says, "So? Why's yo' way supposedly a normal way of talkin'?"

Corey and Jacob are somewhat stunned at Jarek's sudden participation. The three of them made a pact to "ignore the uppity nigger." In fact, it's the theme in all three of their households.

"Most of America talk white, not black," Jarek continues. "*You* da minority in this country. So hi can you be called normal?"

Faith blurts out an exaggerated laugh. "Chile, please. Mr. Avery soun' whituh dan you, wit dat redneck noise ya'll be makin'."

Jasmine Woods, a strong English student, speaks for the first time. "And what's *sounding white?* Roland doesn't sound—quote, unquote—white."

Jarek frowns and says, "He grew up wit 'em." Then he sinks back in his desk, indignantly folding his arms, tired of the conversation.

"Ah'm uh brothuh," grunts Roland.

Jarek, Jacob, and Corey exchange glances as they shake their heads.

"Mr. Avery know which one's right," mumbles Jarek.

Lisa raises her hand and waits for Tony to acknowledge her before speaking. "So, wha's his name?" she asks, motioning toward the back of the room. The entire class looks at Kenny.

"Kenneth Houston," says Tony, arms folded.

"He'own talk much," offers James without looking behind him.

"I would'n say nut'n na ya'll eithuh," says Lisa.

Silence.

"Mr. Avery, which way you think is the right way ta talk?" asks Jacob, ignoring the sudden stillness of the classroom.

"Depends. *Right* for what?"

Jacob frowns. "Fer talkin'."

"That depends on the listener."

"Naw it don't," mumbles Jarek.

Tony smiles. "Jose, does everyone in your family speak English as well as you?"

Jose pauses as if he has to think about it. "No."

Tony addresses the entire class. "For Jose, which 'talk' is right when he's home?"

The class stutters in thought.

"That ain't the same, yo," says Jose. "Some of my family don't speak English."

"So?"

"*So?* So, dass why we try to learn some English. So people don't treat down to us. We know why English is important. We can't just depend on how we wanna talk. So we all learnin' English. Even my gran'mother is tryin' to learn."

Tony nods and says, "How eager would you be to learn English if everyone in America understood most of what you said in Spanish?"

The class encounters a long pause. Everyone waits, knowing the ball rests in Jose's court. Whether through patience or deep thought, the class allots Jose ample time to form an answer.

"Spanish ain't hard to learn after you learn certain thangs," he finally says. "Spanish has a system, just like English. But when black people talk, they mess English up. Dass why it's hard to understand. They don't got no system. Dass why dey should learn English—why everybody need to learn how to talk English . . . *good* English."

"We don't sound the same in Spanish," offers Victor Lawrence, a rather shy student who speaks very little Spanish, despite his grandparents' Puerto Rican-bred fluency. "My parents and I were born and raised in the States, but I know that there are differences. I can't speak Spanish, but I can understand it. My grandparents don't sound like many people do on the Spanish channel, especially the soap opera people and the game show people. It's just different somehow."

Silence again.

Victor starts to feel uncomfortable.

"Spanish *does* have a system," says Tony. "An easy-to-follow-system, come to think about it. Once you learn the rules, Spanish is easy to read. You may not understand what you're reading, but you can read it. That's a *good* system."

He goes to the board and writes a word. "Let's look at the English system for a moment. How do you pronounce this word?"

"Lamp," mumbles the class.

"Louder."

"Lamp."

"*Louder!*"

"Lamp!" roars the room.

"Good! I can hear you!" yells Tony, his back still facing the class.

Giggles and whispers.

"How do you say this word?"

"Stamp!" they yell.

"What about this word?"

"Camp!" they cheer.

"And this word?"

The hiccup in their response is followed by laughter. A few pronounce "swamp" using the same vowel sound as the other words. This invokes more laughter.

"What happened to the rhythm?" asks Tony, spreading his arms.

"You tricked us," says Lisa, beaming.

"No, I didn't. I'm only writing words on the board," Tony says with a grin. "What's the matter? Can't you people follow the system?"

"Dass funny," says Marcus. "Why *do* you say *swamp?* Dat don' make no sense."

"The sound that the *sw* makes causes the vowel sound to change," figures Jasmine, but she sounds a bit unsure.

"It appears so," says Tony. Then, he erases the last letter on all of the words. "Pronounce them now," he says as he points to the top of the list. The laughter starts before they reach the bottom of the list. "Well, which is it? *Swom* or *swam?*"

"That's so weird," says Jasmine as she stares at the board, waiting for the logic to spring off the wall.

"Maybe that was only a glitch in the system," offers Tony as he erases the words. "Let's try it again."

Silence explodes inside the classroom.

"Make sure I can hear you."

Giggles.

"How do you say this?"

"Now!" they scream.

"And this?"

"Cow!"

"What about this?"

"Pow!"

"Okay. And this?"

"Plow!"

"Right. And this?"

Many throw their hands up and sink back in their desks. Their laughter drowns out the few who continue with the pronunciation of the word "flow."

Tony continues to write the words "low," "tow," and "crow," each being a new punch line. "It looks like we've found another glitch in the system," he says with counterfeited frustration. "Let's try this one last time."

Distant traffic is heard.

"How do you say this?"

"Tough!" they yell, laughter in their voices.

"Good. And this?"

"Rough!"

"Right. And this?"

Some manage to yell the wrong pronunciation of "cough" before the class explodes again with laughter, confusion, and submission. Tony continues to add logs to the ignited frolic with the words "bough," "through," and "though." When he motions for silence, the students comply almost immediately.

"Many languages like Spanish have a reliable system, one that's easy to pick up on. Obviously, English can't make such a claim." The class remains totally silent and wonders what he's going to say or do next. He sits back on his desk, legs dangling. "So, why bother learning English?"

"Dass what *Ah'm* sayin'," snorts Rodney.

"Yeah, why we cane juss learn hi da use owuh language?" asks James.

The class mumbles.

Tony springs from his desk and returns to the board. "That's not a bad idea, Powuh. Let's try an experiment. Many of you can speak . . . let's give it an official-sounding name—*Choklish*," he says as he writes it on the board. The class laughs. Tony turns and says, "It's the best I can do on short notice. Now, those of you who don't speak Choklish have, at least, been exposed to it—for some, a great deal. Let's do this. . . ." He pauses in thought. The class silently waits, drowning in anticipation.

Finally, Tony turns back to the board and writes: "I am not the one who is trying to sound white." Then, he turns to face the class. "I'd like everyone—and I mean *everyone*—to take out a sheet of paper and re-write this sentence in Choklish. Pretend Choklish is the only language I know, but I can't read. I need you to transcribe this sentence, so if a person reads aloud what you wrote, I'll understand them. What would you write?"

The class giggles and mumbles, but it's barely heard over the rustling of papers being retrieved, scavenged, and borrowed throughout the classroom. Then, as suddenly as the gentle chaos began, the room drops to a dull silence as pencils and pens hastily meet paper.

What in the hell have I walked into? I've never been around so many blacks before. They're everywhere. Mom'll flip if she ever has to come inside this school to pick me up. That would *really* be the tsunami. Better make sure I keep my bus privileges.

He expects us to know how to write this shit? I've gotta learn to talk like they do to pass this class? That ain't right. If they wanna study their own stupid language, why don't they go back to Africa? I could complain, but who'd listen? It would be my word against the whole class, and obviously, most people in here love him. It's easy to tell he's their favorite teacher. I don't doubt he's buddies with every black in here. After all, they supposedly look out for each other, callin' each other "brother" and "sister" even though they ain't. But a lot of the whites seem to like him too. I don't think the ones that sound like Hank are too crazy about him, but they're still writing. He probably gives them parties and stuff on a regular basis. He's one of those.

What the hell am I supposed to write? *I's not the one who's be a tryin' to sound whitey?* Sounds about as dumb as they do. I am *not* doing this. We're supposed to be learning English. But, now that I think about it, why am *I* in an English class? I already know how to speak English better than most of these fools will *ever* be able to. Here's a better question—what the hell am I doing *failing* English while some of them pass? How in the hell does that work? It's all politics.

TONY NOTICES KENNY'S REFUSAL TO DO THE assignment.
He wants to say something to him, but he figures his new student has
endured enough attention for one day. He can tell by the way Kenny
eyes his classmates that he has an arrogance about him. He'll definitely
be a discipline problem. According to his records, he doesn't go long
without causing trouble, but Tony won't falter, even for someone like
Kenny. If he has to be, he'll be the dose of discipline Kenny is lacking
in his life. Tony has no intentions of catering to the antics of a spoiled,
hot-tempered brat.

Tony glances at the clock, and then claps his hands together. "Okay.
Who wants to be the first to share their translation?"

Hands bloom.

"Roland, come up," Tony summons, pointing at the board. "Write
your translation on the board."

"Git it right, na."

"Represent, Roland."

Snickering.

Roland sashays to the board and writes: "I ain't the one who's tryin'
to sound white."

Applause.

Roland takes a bow. "Hey, Ah'm uh brothuh trapped in uh white
man's body," he says, and then he takes his seat. Marcus gives him a
high five.

Tony stares at the sentence, rubbing his chin. Then, he clears
his throat with exaggeration and reads the sentence as written. The
class pauses as they take a second look at the sentence with informed
scrutiny.

"You ain' say it right," says Marcus.

"What do you mean?" asks Tony with his best imitation of
confusion. "What word did I mispronounce? Isn't that what's on the
board?"

The class pauses again and stares at the board. After a few moments, hands rise again.

"Deborah."

She approaches the board, smiling. "Okay, I'm only guessing about this," she says. "I mean, I don't talk this way—I think this is it—I mean, that this is right, but I don't really—"

"Just write it," urges Tony.

Slowly and nervously, she writes: "I ain't tryin' to be the one who's soundin' white."

The room groans.

Tony smiles at the board and says, "Not bad at all, but you sort of played musical chairs."

Hands fly up.

"Marcus."

Marcus struts to the board with confidence and writes: "I ain't the one who tryin' to sown white."

Again, Tony reads the sentence as written.

"Man, you try'n na be funny," says Marcus. "Dass *sow* wit uh *n* own it."

"Well, in English, you pronounce it as sss . . . *own*," insists Tony. "Look it up."

Pages flip throughout the classroom.

James raises his hand, and Tony motions for him to come up. On the board, he writes: "I'n the one who's trine to sound white."

"This is very good," says Tony.

James grins and says, "Thank you, my brothuh."

Tony smiles and adds, "But the problem lies in the fact that I'm using my understanding of the English language—glitches and all—to read what you write."

After Tony reads the sentence as written, a combination smile and frown comes to James' face. Then, James reads his sentence again, but for the first time. "Well, I'own git it," he finally says with a shrug, and then he takes his seat.

Jarek raises his hand with a grin and Tony summons him to the board. He writes: "I not be de one who's is tryings to sounds white."

After Tony reads it, the class erupts in snorts and wheezes. Jarek's grin melts away. He anticipated a different reaction.

"There may have been a time when that was more accurate than we may realize," Tony says, smiling, "but as with any other language, Choklish has evolved a great deal since then."

Faith raises her hand. "How would you write it?"

Again, the classroom is a silent tomb surrounded by the sounds of distant traffic, birds, and a teacher on the other side of the wall. Tony smiles at his class before turning to face the board, writing: "I ain' na one try'n na soun' white."

Everyone reads it several times before hands fly into the air.

"Jasmine?"

"Why did you change *the* to *na?* What's that?"

"Good question—hold that thought. Roland?"

"Yeah," adds Roland. "An whey yo' *who* at?"

"Hold that thought as well," says Tony. "James?"

"Man!" says James, laughing. "You'own even need da *who!*"

Tony grins. Obviously, James has no problem deciphering Choklish. Why isn't he surprised? Still, he reads the sentence for the rest of the class twice. It seems to satisfy Roland, but Jasmine's hand goes up again.

"Okay," she says, smiling and nodding. "I get it, but why does it do that? That's strange."

"It's not as strange as you may think," Tony says. "In this sentence, it's a lot easier to say *ain' na* than *ain't the* or *ain' the.*" He reads the sentence again. "You see, *ain' na* rolls together better. Many languages do this—even English. In Spanish, they'll write 'Hola amigo,'" he continues, writing it on the board. "But what they actually say is closer to *Holamigo.* That's one of the reasons why it seems people who speak Spanish speak it so fast."

The class pauses. A few look at Jose and Victor, but neither has anything to say as they continue staring at the board.

"So, is that what you did with *trying?*" asks Jasmine.

Tony raises an index finger. "Not exactly," he says. "But I'll get to that in a minute." He looks at the entire class. "So, again—in Spanish, if you have similar sounds, sometimes they're brought so close together that it's pronounced as one sound. And why not? Isn't it easier?"

"English don't do that," grunts Jarek.

Tony smiles and paces the room. "On the contrary," he says, folding his arms. "English does *exactly* this. It's just not taught. English is taught one way, but it's used in so many other ways, many of them subconsciously accepted by 'the majority' as you'd put it. Words bleed together all the time, but this 'bleeding of words' isn't taught much. Diction and articulation is the sermon, but rarely the practice. Oh yes, this bleeding of words is very acceptable in English." He pauses to glance over their faces. "But don't take my word for it. Just try to say the words *don't take* or *just try* by pronouncing the *t* sound both times, the way it should be pronounced—diction, articulation."

The room fills with quiet murmurs and snickers.

"Dass funny."

"No way."

"Man, that's weird."

Tony raises his hand. "When was the last time two people shooting a nice friendly game of pool actually used the phrase *Rack them* instead of *Rack 'em?*"

The class grows silent, and then becomes a giant mumble of understanding.

"And here's an interesting fact," Tony continues, the class hanging onto his every word. "In Choklish, f-o-u-r and f-o-r are pronounced differently. In Choklish, you'd say *I got fo' dolluhs fuh lunch.*"

More mumbling.

"Man!" exclaims James, smiling.

Tony sits on his desk and takes a deep breath. "If I were to write a book, I'd stay away from the friendly representation of Choklish. If a character spoke Choklish, I'd write him speaking Choklish, or maybe I'd write him speaking Standard English, but with a footnote explaining that the person is speaking Choklish. I'd write it one way or the other—Choklish or no Choklish. In many ways, kind depictions of

Choklish fuel ignorance, prejudices, intolerance, and a slew of other social cancers."

"But that's so difficult to understand . . ." says Jasmine as she motions toward the board.

"Fuh real."

"*We* cane even read it dat good."

"I can read it juss fine. Ya'll trippin'."

"We ain' *you*, Powuh—damn."

Tony raises his hand for silence and gets it. "Of *course* it's difficult to understand. You're not used to reading it; this isn't taught. It's unfamiliar to *my* eyes, but that's exactly why I'd use it. It helps illustrate that Choklish is definitely a language. Look at this," he says, motioning toward the board. "It's difficult *not* to call Choklish another language, and that's exactly what it is. Also, if someone reads this aloud, they'd be *reading* the language instead of butchering it, whether they understood what they read or not."

"Just like Spanish," murmurs Victor.

Tony winks at Victor. "Just like Spanish, but if you're familiar with the language—that is, if you can 'understand it but can't speak it,' the way some people are with other languages, then reading it aloud should work for you."

"That's right," says Victor, more confidence in his voice. "That's weird too because I can like understand pretty much everything my grandparents and family say, and since Spanish is—you know—written pretty much the same way that it sounds, I can read it too. I don't read it as well as I understand someone talking, but I'll get most of it. But if I have to say something, I have to kinda think about it. It'll come to me eventually, but I have to think about it."

"Absolutely," says Tony. "As with all aspects of any language, the more you're exposed to it, the more you use it, the more fluent you become. But a lot of rules found in other languages don't change. In Choklish, the *r* sound at the end of a word doesn't happen unless it's necessary to distinguish meaning. In fact, the sound 'are' isn't in the language at all. It's thrown out. The same goes for the *th* sound. It's usually dropped when it ends a word."

Tony points to Jasmine. "Another rule is what Jasmine noticed earlier concerning the *i-n-g*. Typically, if there's a *t* or *d* at the end of a word ending in *ing*, then saying the *n* sound without the *i* is the way to go. For instance, you'd say writ'n instead of writin' or you'd say read'n instead of readin'. Also, if a word ends with a *y* that sounds like the letter *I*—as in the words *try* or *fly*—the rule is the same—you'd say try'n or fly'n instead of tryin' or flyin'."

Tony pronounces *try'n* as "trine" and *fly'n* as "fline" when denoting the difference, explaining that most people would say "try in" or "fly in," regardless of the spelling. And he makes it clear that the latter is not "true Choklish."

Throughout the classroom, eyes wander in thought.

"But it's important to note that, with this rule, the *t* has to be alone," Tony continues. He goes to the board and writes. "In other words, if the word is *blast* or *reject* where the *t* sound is resting next to another consonant sound, the *in'* is used. For instance, you'd say words like *projectin'*, *raftin'*, or *castin'*," he says, writing the words on the board, "but you'd also say *yacht'n* if you're in a yacht club, because the *t* sound follows a vowel sound. Weird, huh?"

The class is dumbfounded.

Tony plows on. "Here's another interesting fact about Standard English. If you know how to make an *s* sound in Spanish, that's all you need to know. In Standard English, we teach the *s* sound, but if we say *Use these shoes*, we use the *z* sound."

Lips move, followed by giggles.

"So, when a person from another country comes over and says *Use these shoes* the correct way, we call that speaking with an accent. Why? Because they're not used to messing up our language? Using a system that has so many glitches? As a matter of fact, it could be argued that Choklish, folk talk, Spanglish, and every other—quote, unquote— dialect in America is actually an honest attempt at consistency, an honest attempt to get rid of the glitches once and for all."

James raises his hand. "Then why learn Standard English?"

Tony scans the room, pausing at every face staring at him. "As we've already proven with Choklish, we don't agree with how it should be represented. This would probably be the case with all of the other different forms of English we have in America. For the most part, *Standard* English has been agreed upon. It is what America wants to be represented by. It's the most dominant. The history is very dark on *why* it's the most dominant, but it doesn't change the fact that it's the most dominant language in our society—not Creole, not Navajo, not Hillbilly, not Choklish."

He pauses for another moment. Every pair of eyes is on him. "Also, there's this belief that the farther away you are from speaking like the majority—not necessarily Standard English—the less intelligent you must be." He folds his arms and smiles. "In other words, if you butcher Standard English the way the majority does, you're less likely to be considered ignorant."

He clears his throat and adds, "We thank we know uh lot about people juss by da way dey talk. Ain' no gitt'n aroun' nat. But learnin' Standard English is definitely uh way you can fight it, to prove 'em wrong. Dey say you cane judge uh book by da covuh. Funny thang is, we *haff* ta judge uh book by da covuh uh l'uh bit—ain't da covuh par'd uh da book? Juss remembuh—if you ain' star'd out in nis world talkin' Standard English, den you juss like Jose—Standard English would be yo' *second* language, not cho' firs'. An everybody, even na ones who'own know nut'n but Standard English, should be proud uh dey language, proud uh who dey is. Learnin' hi da talk an write Standard English ain' about changin' who you is." He clears his throat. "It's about being able to mimic the type of person that most people are more familiar with, are more comfortable with—the type of person who receives, for whatever reason, more opportunities. But it is not—I repeat, it is *not* about trying to be who you're not. It's not about assimilation; it's simply about *demonstration*."

Many flip to the front of their dictionaries as hands fly into the air. Even Kenny has an incredible urge to raise his hand.

"Tammy?"

The bell ending the period startles everyone. To Tony's surprise, students moan and groan at the interruption. Voices ring out with questions and statements from all over the classroom, but Tony motions for silence and gets it. "I'd like everyone to write a reflection on today's class," he says, smiling. "Whatever you'd like to ask, say, or comment on—put it on paper. Have *something* written on paper and turn it in to me tomorrow."

From their reaction to his request, Tony believes he'll receive a paper from at least half of his thirty-four students, and, for the first time, the class drifts out instead of the usual lunging and trampling. More than half the class offers Tony a kind word of departure—a "see ya tomorrow," "take it easy," "peace out," or something to the equivalent. James gives a quick fist and a smile before he leaves.

Marcus and Roland wait on the outside of the door, watching the class spill into the hallway. When Kenny emerges, Marcus jumps in front of him and causes Kenny to flinch into a defensive stance. His tense muscles go limp when he sees Marcus's outstretched hand.

"Mr. Avery tole me da write you uh note sayin' Ah'm sorry—an Ah'ma do it, but I juss wanna say Ah'm sorry fuh messin' wit chew, man. I ain' mean nut'n by it."

Kenny stands and listens, not knowing what to say or do. A few passing classmates slap Kenny on the shoulder, expressing their apologies, but they don't wait for a response.

"You g'own leave me hangin'?" smirks Marcus, hand still offered.

"I'own blame 'im," snorts Roland. "I'd leave yo' ass hangin' too."

Kenny cracks a smile and accepts Marcus' hand, firmly. "We be cool," he says uncertainly.

Roland and Marcus explode with laughter.

"Man! You g'own git picked at fuh *real* talkin' like dat," says Marcus.

"Hang wit us," adds Roland. "We'll straighten ya out."

"Whey yo' nex' class at?" Marcus asks.

Kenny shows them his schedule sheet. "I have History next—Mr. Zimmerman."

"He okay," Roland says. He points down the hall. "He da second doh down nat way."

The three young men stand for an uncomfortable moment before realizing that all they want to say has been said for now. Marcus and Roland leave Kenny with a nod and a slap on the shoulder. Kenny watches them walk away, oblivious of the snickering and laughter offered by students in Tony's third period class.

Well, I'll be damned.

Chapter 23

THE CAFETERIA STAFF DOES A WONDERFUL job with their sweet potato pie, but Tony has learned to trust his eyes and nose. The slightest doubt echoes like a whisper across his taste buds. It's this whisper that has him bringing his lunch every day, brown-bagging it. Today, tuna on white, celery sticks, and Oreo cookies. He can stomach most of the cafeteria food, but he concluded that the extra expense isn't worth the daily gamble. He only enters the lunch line for a drink, usually a large cup of ice water, which costs a dime because of the cup, but the pie cannot be denied.

"I see you've got my pie again, Miss Elsie."

"I got cha right h'yuh," she says, beaming. She hands Tony a specially cut slice. "It's been wait'n fuh ya all mornin'. You know you was g'own git da bess slice."

Miss Elsie reminds Tony of many of his mother's friends, all willing to adopt him in a heartbeat. "Thank you," he says. "I really appreciate your looking out for me like this."

Miss Elsie bats a hand, showing it's the most ridiculous statement she's ever heard. "Chile, please. Dis *my* kitchen, you h'yuh me? If I wanna give my son uh slice uh pie, who g'own stop me?"

Tony flashes her his best smile.

A few students mutter their usual words of protest, words they save for anybody receiving differential treatment in the chow line.

"Ten cents," says the cashier wearing a "Theresa" name tag. She doesn't miss a beat on her chewing gum. Tony hands her a dollar. Theresa two-fingers his buck and drops him his change with the fluidity of a master short-change artist. "Thank you, sir. Come again."

Tony cordially accepts his change, feeling a little guilty about the free pie.

The door leading to the teacher's lounge is on the other side of the cafeteria. Tony has grown accustomed to the ground zero noise of the lunch room—the laughter, the joking, the sudden screams of elation from spirits recently set free—but the lounge still rattles him a bit. There's never any real laughter, and jokes are held in check. By the end of last week, Tony recognized the lounge for what it truly is—a brooding ground for the disheartened.

"Hey! Wha's up, Mr. Avery?"

It's his first time hearing his name called in the lunch room by a student. He almost drops his pie, but it doesn't register beyond a mild twitch. He nods to James and his dining buddies. "Hey, Powuh—Rodney. Hey, Shawn—everybody."

"Uh lot uh us done already star'ded own nat papuh," says Rodney. "Powuh 'bout done finished his."

Tony nods, but the boys are clueless of how good, how melodic their words are. They have no idea how happy he is. "I can't wait to read *everybody's* papers, Rodney. I'm really looking forward to it. I'll probably learn a lot from you guys."

His students, and even the few who aren't, smile and nudge their approval of his response, as though he's just passed some test that none of them agreed to administer, but gave just the same.

"What chew got in na bag, Mr. Avery?" asks James. "Probally somp'm nass uh lot bettuh dan nis crap, huh?"

Tony shows them his pie. "Da pie ain' bad."

"You got *dat* right," says Rodney. He shows his empty pie tin. "Dey juss *got* ta be shippin' nis pie in from somewhe'uh."

The table erupts in laughter, adding to the rumble of the cafeteria.

Tony glances at the door leading to the teacher's lounge. He already hears the slandering and mocking of students. He already senses the politics and tension. He already feels the deflation of it all, making it difficult for those who bother pumping up to stay pumped.

A small syringe filled with a potent dose of attitude punctures his mind. *What the hell.* "Mine if I sit wit cha'll?" he asks without thinking it through, forgetting why he even should.

Everyone at the table pauses and glances at each other, unsure.

"We be cursin' an stuff . . . when we ain' aroun' teachuhs," warns James. "We g'own be ourselves, na."

Tony hesitates, but tries not to show it. "I can deal wit dat. Juss keep it out uh ma classroom." He points a finger. "Ya'll know I run uh respectable business."

"We be talkin' 'bout teachuhs sometimes too," challenges Rodney. "We ain' g'own hole nut'n back. If we wanna say somp'm 'bout cha, we juss g'own say it."

Again, Tony glances toward the lounge. "Ain' nut'n like uh fresh coat uh honesty. You g'own finish dem peas?"

"Hell no!" laughs Rodney. "We'own won't dis . . . *crap!* You won't 'em? Go fuh what chew know. Take mine firs'."

"Take mine!"

"Mine too!"

Tony glances at their trays, food all mussed over except for the peas. The peas remain untouched, in the top left portion of their trays, as if planned. "I already *know* I'own won't 'em," snorts Tony. He thrusts a hand inside his brown bag. "Ya'll ain' g'own kill *me* up in h'yuh."

The table explodes.

Tony studies the cafeteria for the first time. He's contributing to the noise, and it feels good, jubilantly so. He spies Kenny in the far corner sitting with Marcus, Roland, Richard, and a few others. Kenny is already looking at Tony, but without staring. They exchange quick nods before returning their attention to their respective tables. A nod says a thousand words.

"Whey you from, Mr. Avery?"

"Ah'm from right h'yuh."

"Born h'yuh? Right h'yuh in Jacksonville?"

"Born an raised."

"What side uh town you live own?"

"Westside," he says plainly, then bites into his sandwich.

"Fuh real?"

"You grew up own na Westside?"

"Ah'm *still* growin' up own na Westside," Tony admits.

"Damn, you juss full uh suh'prises," snorts Rodney. "Whey you went ta school at?"

Tony flops his sandwich down. "Hi you g'own write dis book wit'out pencil an papuh?"

The boys laugh, Tony included.

"You need da thank about writ'n yo' papuh," says James.

"Yeah, you tell 'im, Powuh," says Tony. He bites his celery.

Rodney rolls his eyes. "Awright, dass awright."

"So, we have an assignment?" asks Shawn Naples, a student from Tony's fifth period class. "What's the paper got to be on? You ain't even taught nothing about writing yet. What do we have to write about?"

"Damn, it ain' all lat, man," says Rodney. "You juss wait an see. Let da man eat." He looks at Tony and grins. "G'own head an keep nibblin' own ya celery stick, Mr. Avery."

"Oh, you real funny," says Tony, but he takes the celery from his mouth and reaches for his sandwich, wondering if there's something wrong with celery nowadays.

"Can I come na yo' nex' period class?" asks Lamar Swain.

"No."

"Why not?"

"You don't have me next period. You're not even my student."

Lamar frowns. "Mr. Tuddles won't care."

"Then I'll care *for* him," Tony shoots back. "You should care for him too."

"Man, dass evil, Mr. Avery," says Rodney. "Mr. Tuddles don' be teachin' nut'n."

"He *need* da juss go ta class," offers James.

"You used ta skip Whitebread's class too, Powuh," snaps Rodney. "You'own like 'im eithuh. Hell, nobody at dis table like 'im." He turns to Tony. "Do *you* like 'im, Mr. Avery?"

Tony shrugs. "What's not to like?" he says, keeping a poker face.

The table stares at him for a moment, like he's just insulted their mothers. Then a snicker is made before the table explodes. The poker face is too difficult to hold, and Tony grins.

"Damn. I was g'own say," Rodney says.

"You ain' ly'n," adds James.

"*Shoot.*"

"Fuh real."

"Seriously, Mr. Avery, what chew thank about da othuh teachuhs h'yuh?" asks James.

Tony reaches into the bag for his cookies, pops one into his mouth, and says, "I'll tell ya if all uh ya'll eat dem peas."

The students shake their heads.

"It ain' all lat import'n."

"Dass uh secret you can keep, dare."

"Dass awright."

"Fuh real."

Tony chews with a grin.

"You awright, Mr. Avery," Rodney admits. "You g'own eat wit us tomorrow, right?"

Tony's grin widens.

This is the weirdest thing. In a school where I'm harassed about my weight more than ever before, filled with the kind of people we don't want as neighbors, filled to the rim with troublemakers like me, I find a friend—two, actually. Neither of which I can ever invite home. Marcus is black, and Roland might as well be. Bringing them home wouldn't exactly be my smartest idea ever. I laugh at the irony. I finally have those friends you're always bitchin' about, Mom. Talk about hitting the roof. That would be the wipeout to beat all wipeouts, the *real* tsunami, a real Shamu splash. Damn shame, too. I think I'm gonna like my new friends. *They be my war dawgs*, as they've told me—or something like that.

"War" stands for "worth all respect," but it sounds menacing on purpose to unnerve teachers. Teachers don't want any "war dawgs" running around in their classrooms. No matter how you say it, it sounds negative, threatening. Yeah. I couldn't be happier being a war dawg. Finally, a name I can deal with and friends to boot.

Right now, Marcus and Roland are laughing at me, but it's a buddy laugh. They're laughing more at my dining blunder. How in the hell was I supposed to know to stay away from the peas? They don't taste so bad. I've had worse—I've had *nothing!* This eating with others is going to take some getting used to.

"G'own, man. Finish ya peas," Marcus says to me. "Ain nut'n ta it. We juss ain' seen nobody eat dese dry ass peas befo', an I can tell by dat look own yo' face dat you done foun' out why."

I finish chewing what's in my mouth, but I give them the facial expressions they're looking for. They're laughing's gonna cause me to spray pea soup if I don't hurry and swallow. Mental note: eat only what everybody else decides to eat.

Marcus hands me his bottle of Pepsi. "H'yuh, wash 'em down wit dis. Milk won't cut it, dawg. Be like pea milkshake."

I've never drunk after a black person before. I never even thought about it. And all of the thinking that I should've done tries to come now, threatening to embarrass me. My mind races with a few crazy thoughts, but I push them out. It's too late now. I grab his drink quickly to hide my hesitation, and I take a couple of swallows, forcing thought after thought from my head, and then set the bottle back down. When he pulls his drink back on his side of the table, I realize he probably wouldn't hesitate to drink after me. I get a little ticked at myself, and then I get ticked at being ticked because I didn't really do anything wrong.

"Is that better?" Richard asks me with his head lying on his arms. "I don't think I've ever seen anybody eat them peas." He talks like he's drunk, almost like he's slurring, but not quite. He's always tired. Works a night job by pretending to be out of school. "And stay away from them damn mixed vegetables too, Kenny. Them ain't nothin' to play with neither," he says with his eyes closed. They were closed before, until I took a mouthful of peas and everybody laughed.

"So you say you ain' nevuh been na William Wells Brown?" Marcus asks me. "Hi da hell you pull lat off? Hi you git h'yuh befo' goin' na WB?"

I just shrug. Hell if I know. Marcus explained that most people at Lincoln went to a detention school called William Wells Brown at least once before finally coming here. Many were sent three and four times. Roland and Marcus have been twice. The second time, they were sent together for the same infraction—destruction of school property. Something involving water balloons. They say it was an accident. I believe them, but I don't count. None of us do. Guess this place is flooded with people who aren't very convincing.

"You should complain, dawg," Roland says, but he's only playing, smiling the whole time. "You should go ta da principal an tell 'im nat you ain' supposed ta be h'yuh yet. Dass what I'd do."

Marcus doesn't agree. "Hi da hell lat g'own work? Da principal ain' sent 'im h'yuh. Besides, you thank Rykuh give uh damn about us? Hell no!" He grabs his Pepsi, squeezing it a little too hard. "Kenny, don' even listen na dis fool. *Go ta da principal.* You muss be out uh yo' damn mine." He takes a big swallow of his drink— no hesitation, as if I never had it in the first place. "Plus, you fuhgit—we h'yuh because we ain' g'own be able la graduate from owuh ole school. We juss hurt'n all aroun'."

Roland fans a hand at Marcus because he isn't too convinced. "I'd still try. Ain' nut'n in try'n. What chew thank, Kenny?"

"I don't know," I say to everyone at the table. They're all waiting for me to say something to settle the discussion, but I don't really care about it. Also, I'm not used to getting this kind of attention—not without a video game in front of me. "I don't really want to talk to the principal," I say. "I mean, if I'm here, I guess. . . ." I stop because I don't know what I wanna say, what I'm *supposed* to say, what I'm *expected* to say. I shrug again. I don't care about it really. I don't.

"What chew h'yuh fuh, anyway?" asks Marcus, but it's not curiosity; he wants to find a different angle to come back at Roland with, a firmer argument.

"Fight'n," I say, as if I've been in a hundred fights, and I say it in Choklish. It sounds better saying it the way they say it. Tougher somehow.

"You musta kicked his ass," says Roland, laughing. "Losers don' usually git in trouble. I guess dey figguh uh ass whoopin's punishment enough."

"Who you was fight'n wit?" asks Marcus. He acts bored at this point, but still he's watching for his angle.

"A guy named Logan."

"See, na I *know* you supposed ta be at WB," Roland says, slapping his hands on the table in triumph. "Fight'n? Dat ain' nut'n na be in h'yuh fuh."

Marcus appears to agree with Roland momentarily, but changes his mind. "Wha's yo' grades like? Bet chew ain' got good grades."

I shake my head. "Nope."

"See, what I tell ya, Ro? I knew it had da be somp'm."

I think I missed the point somewhere. How can all the failing kids in the city fit in one school? Besides, Logan couldn't have been that much smarter than me. He never did homework in Biology. Hell, he never even carried books. Maybe Mom had a lot to do with me not going to William Wells Brown. She fought many battles at my old schools, making sure they didn't screw me over. She obviously was doing a good job too, before she ripped the phone off the wall. After many of her secret meetings with the faculty—those private meetings had to be different from the ones they let me sit in on—she'd come home somewhat relieved, a little bit at ease, like something finally went right, but never right enough to get me off the hook. She would still come down on me—hard. Yelling. Beating. Starving. *Mommy loves you.*

When the conversation moves to the subject of parents, I clam up. I don't wanna tell them about my dad and Amanda dying, or the part about the driver being a nigger, and, luckily, they don't ask. In turn, I learn of Roland's dad leaving his drug-addicted mom, and of Marcus never knowing his dad. Turns out Roland and I are alike—one parent with no brothers or sisters, but he lives in Marcus' neighborhood. Richard raises his head long enough to report he's also living with his dad, no brothers or sisters; his mom's in some kind of rehab.

Marcus, on the other hand, has a brother who's seven and a sister who's four—Taneisha and Colin. I don't blame Roland or Richard for not missing their moms, but Marcus is totally okay about never knowing his dad. He doesn't even mind talking about it, even though there's not much for him to talk about. He knows his brother and sister's dad, but doesn't like him much. He calls him by his first name: Freddie. And Freddie doesn't live with them, and he's hardly ever around, which is okay by Marcus.

"He git own my damn nerves," he says to us. "'Bout da only time he come aroun' is when he won't somp'm na eat, uh. . . ." It's like he doesn't see us for a moment, like something else has his attention.

"What?" I ask.

He snaps back to the lunch table. "Nut'n, he juss git own my damn nerves. Neisha an Cole cane git anuff uh 'im. Dey'own know no bettuh."

"Yo mama don' seem na mine so much eithuh," says Roland. He sounds like he knows a lot more than Marcus is willing to give up. I'm curious, but I know it's wrong to pry. I can't stand it when Mr. Farley does it to me, but I wonder if I make Mr. Farley feel the way I'm feeling about Marcus right now.

Marcus looks more irritated, but with Roland as the target. "You'own know *everythang*, Ro."

"He brought chew dat system and some games," Roland says, but not in a challenging voice. He says it matter-of-factly.

"It was all used," Marcus fires back, more irritated. "I still say he stole it from somewhere. Besides, who you know g'own give up uh copy uh *Conflict?*"

"You have *Conflict* at home?" I ask. I don't mean to interrupt. I was really thinking out loud. They look at me, but it's not a bad look.

"Yeah," Marcus says with a smirk. I think he's happy to be changing the subject. "Plus, I got *Royal Bash, NFL Superstars, Sword of Omens,* an *Rumble House III.*"

"I got *Rumble House II,*" Roland throws in. "But I still can eat his lunch every na an then wit *Rumble House III.*"

"Nigguh, you crazy!" says Marcus, but he's smiling. He actually calls Roland a nigger. Roland's whiter than I am. What's that make me? "You beat me dat one time, dat *one . . . time.* An I what'n even try'n, an you ain' beat me since."

"I'll git chew again," Roland says, but with fake confidence in his voice. "You ain' all lat. Juss wait."

Marcus shakes his head. "You ain' got it, Ro. Maybe in anothuh two uh three years, an only if I stop practicin'. Then maybe. . . ." Marcus turns to me. "I'd probably beat bofe uh ya'll put togethuh," he says with all the confidence in the world.

Mistake.

"You h'yuh dis fool, Kenny?" asks Roland.

"I hear him, Ro," I say with a big grin on my face.

"Well, what we g'own do 'bout his ovuhconfident ass?"

"What *should* we do?" I ask.

"I say we polish dat ass aftuh school," says Roland, rubbing his hands together like an evil villain from some old horror movie or something.

"If ya'll thank you got what it takes, den come wit it," Marcus says, leaning back in his chair, beaming at us. He's cocky, but I can tell he isn't cocky in a bad way. He's not an asshole about it. I almost want him to be better than me. Almost.

IT TAKES A MOMENT BEFORE EVERYONE REALIZES that the roar of the cafeteria has shifted gears somehow. Still loud, but different. Marcus looks first. Roland and Kenny follow the direction of his stare. Richard lifts from his slumber.

Another fight in the cafeteria.

The teachers with Patrol and Surveillance duty in the cafeteria—the worst of all PS duties—move in with rehearsed fluidity. Tony is among them, even though it's not his shift. The altercation ends before it really begins, and the cafeteria enjoys a brief period of quiet murmuring before returning to its normal deafening chord. The fight never happened. Routine.

"So, ya'll comin' ovuh?" asks Marcus, still smirking.

"Where do you live?" asks Kenny.

"Don' worry 'bout it," says Roland. "My daddeh drives us ta school. You can ride wit us, an he'll take you home no problem. He cool like dat."

Marcus nods in agreement.

"You sure it's no problem?"

"You ma dawg!" exclaims Marcus. "You can come ovuh every damn day if you won't. Roland ain' no competition. I git tired uh eat'n his lunch. I won't some *new* lunch. Come ovuh *everyday.*"

Kenny thinks for a moment, and then says, "I can come over on Mondays, Wednesdays, and Fridays . . . if you're sure it's alright."

Marcus lifts his arms in the air. "Whatevuh works fuh you, dawg. Whatevuh works fuh you."

Kenny has now filled the days he's supposed to come home later due to karate. It appears he's in the clear for awhile, but he knows it won't last. Something's bound to give, but he won't dwell on it. He refuses to focus on the negative. He's going to ignore the future as best he can.

He's a war dawg now.

Chapter 24

Roland's dad is a very nice man, and I can tell he wouldn't mind taking me all the way home, but Mom would rupture a kidney if she saw me in this plush Jeep Cherokee. I'm gonna have to get him to drop me off a few blocks away, but I've got plenty of time to think about that. Right now, I'm consumed with a more pressing question: should I let Marcus win at Conflict? At least some games, if not all? That's the million-dollar question. After all, it's his turf. It's not like we're going to Arcade Stadium. It's his house, where he lives. A person shouldn't have to feel uncomfortable in their own home or worry about being ridiculed and insulted, made to feel more worthless than they already are. Home should be a place where you feel comfortable and safe. Home should be your sanctuary. Besides, I don't care about letting him win. I like Marcus. Roland too, but I don't think I can take defeat from someone who's used to losing all the time. That wouldn't feel right, not in the least.

This is a part of town I've looked at many times, but never seen. In the past, I've glanced at it during a distant drive-by, but I've never been here, never seen it up close like this. More than just a glance now. A lot more.

Children play in the middle of busy streets. Lots of people walk every which way. Houses are bunched together, painted in odd colors like pink or puke green. Windows have bars. There're lots and lots of bars. To keep in or out? Unkempt yards—tall weeds and patches of dirt, like lawn cancer. I've seen three stray dogs so far, and no dog-catcher. Where's the dogcatcher? People stand in groups on corners. Are they selling drugs? They look like drug dealers—no, that's wrong. Drug dealers don't have to be black or stand on a corner, and they don't have a look. In my old school, Jonathan Harris didn't have a look. He didn't have a corner either. Moving from one class to the next, after the bell rang—that was his corner. These people on corners could simply be—doing what? I don't know, but it doesn't have to be drugs.

Yes, more than a glance. What is that smell? Musty and heavy. It stinks. And trucks. Huge trucks. Long, eighteen-wheel, cargo-carrying trucks drive through this neighborhood. We've passed two—and I mean barely. They take the whole road. The neighborhood is a lot livelier than what you'd expect.

Too cool.

After Roland's dad finishes his interrogation, putting me on the spot, firing questions left and right, we finish the trip with Marcus and Roland going at it, bragging about how one is going to annihilate the other, but it all comes across as routine. Marcus mentions my gaming skills once or twice, a fake challenge in his voice, but I just smile. I'm not much of a bragger.

We finally come to a green house with white trimming. The yard's decent, but it needs work. Marcus glances back at me with a smirk on his face. "H'yuh we go, Kenny. Da place uh yo' destruction. Ain' no turnin' back na."

"Oh, man," says Roland. "You wait 'til I git out uh my school clothes. Ah'ma show bofe uh ya'll somp'm. I'll be h'yuh in 'bout thirty minutes, Kenny. Keep 'im busy fuh me."

Marcus and I wave at Roland as he rides off with his dad. They live just around the corner, so I don't know why it would take Roland thirty minutes to change clothes. I'm thinking chores, but his dad doesn't strike me as a slave owner.

Instead of going inside his house, Marcus goes next door to his neighbor's house where his sister and brother wait for him to get home from school. They seem happy to see him, because when the bar door swings open with a loud, rusty, horror-movie squeak, they pounce on him, and each grabs a leg as if they've conspired to throw him to the ground, but they just hang onto him. Their mouths move a mile a minute, mixed with statements and questions, but Marcus manages to respond to it all. I'm thoroughly impressed. Next, Marcus takes a few steps with them riding on his locked legs. It's obviously something they've practiced before, but his brother is too heavy for him. He lifts his sister with his left leg, but his brother has to settle for a slow drag.

"Okay," Marcus says, and their release is just as sudden as their grab.

"Wha's yo' name?" his little brother asks me with absolutely no shyness in his voice.

"Kenny," I say, and I smile a little, but I feel kind of awkward. Marcus is still being hammered with a full report from his sister on how her day went at school. I don't believe she's even glanced at me yet. "What's your name?" I ask his brother, because I really did forget somehow.

"Ah'm Colin," he says happily, and then he starts swinging his arms. He's shy after all. "You friends wit my brothuh?"

I simply nod at him because, for some reason, I don't know what to say. I guess a war dawg is a friend. It may be more. Maybe less. I watch Marcus as he loses himself in a conversation with a four-year-old girl, as if I'm no longer standing here. He's so different from the Marcus at school, but he's still the same. Just more of something, less of something else.

"You go ta my brothuh's school?" Colin asks me.

"Yes."

"Why you ain' nevuh come ovuh?"

"We just met today."

"Hi come you juss met if ya'll go ta da same school?"

Kids have all the patience in the world. They always want the whole story and beyond, but don't care how slow it's fed to them. "Today was my first day at his school. I was transferred from my old school into your brother's school—into Lincoln High."

"Switched?"

"Yeah—switched."

"Why you was switched?"

I almost chuckle. I've been known to wrestle with that same question. "Because I'm bad."

Colin sort of shifts his weight on one leg as he looks me over, measuring me up. I can tell by the new expression on his face that I don't fit the bill for what he considers "bad" to be. "You been na jail?" he finally asks me, but he says it almost in a whisper, like he's been told not to say the word.

"No," I say to him, and he seems genuinely confused.

"Wha's yo' name?" his sister asks. She's obviously finished with giving Marcus her report, and speaks to me as if she's aware of me for the first time. "You friends wit my brothuh?"

"Neisha an Colin," Marcus says, "dis my new friend from school—Kenny." Then he leads us to the green house, but he stops short and runs back to the neighbor's bar door and yells, "Awright, Miss Sophie! Lock it up!"

"Awright, Marcus!" a voice yells back from deep inside.

Once we're inside the green house, Marcus instructs Taneisha and Colin to change into their "play clothes." Then, as he heads for the kitchen, he asks me if I want something to drink.

"No, I'm okay," I say, but not too convincingly. He brings me a glass of Kool-aid, my favorite drink, and disappears back into the kitchen. I'm uncomfortable standing in the middle of their living room, holding Kool-aid in one hand, with my other hand stuffed in my pocket. I don't even feel right enough to put my duffle bag on the floor.

Marcus leans his head out of the kitchen. "Turn own na TV. I'll be in nare in uh minute." But I can tell it will be longer than a minute. He's obviously preparing to wash dishes.

"What time does your mom get home?" I ask. I have to raise my voice over the sound of the running water coming from the kitchen.

"Late," he calls back. "She works two jobs."

I look at their widescreen television. The remote rests on the coffee table, along with a lot of other things—small picture frames, figurines, magazines. It's cluttered, but in an organized sort of way. Same with the walls. They have too small a house for the amount of stuff they have, but they've managed to make it all fit, livable. Overall, the place is nice—very clean, very neat—but it smells funny.

As soon as I sit, Colin comes out from the back of the house wearing a blue T-shirt and jeans that have been cut into shorts. He snatches the game console from the bottom door of their entertainment center, turns on the TV, and starts a video game without ever saying a word to me. It's a kid game. The characters are all balloon-headed cartoons. The main character is lost in some sort of fantasy land, filled with evil flowers and sinister marshmallow people.

Taneisha comes out next. She has an entire tea set under her arm. She places the boxed tea set on the floor and beams up at me. "You can have tea wit me," she says. Then she heads back into the back of the house, probably to her room. She returns with a miniature fold-up table and one miniature fold-up chair, but doesn't say another word to me as she carefully and methodically arranges her entire tea set, complete with fancy napkins.

Impressive.

After a while, Marcus returns from the kitchen, and isn't surprised at what he sees. "So, what we havin' na'day?" he asks her.

"Tea wit glazed doughnuts," she answers. She tries to hold back a blush. She's really pretty. For the first time in a long time I wonder what my baby sister Amanda would've looked like, but this time, it hurts to think about it. I never really knew her, but an ache comes over me as if I knew a lot—the sound of her voice, even though she never got the chance to learn how to talk; the way she walked, even though she never took a step; the color of her eyes, even though they'll never open again. Were they blue or brown? I can't remember, and that makes the ache worse. For the first time, I'm missing someone I never got to know.

Then I think about the black man driving the car, but I stop myself before I go too far. Instead, I focus on Marcus who's sitting on the floor, pretending tea and doughnuts are being served. I look at Taneisha, and the ache fades.

"What about Kenny?" asks Marcus.

"Dis his tea right h'yuh," she says, and nudges an empty tea cup in my direction. "H'yuh, Kenny."

She's so pretty, it's impossible not to accept her doughnuts and tea that's not there. So I join, but I don't know what to do besides slide to the edge of the couch. There's no way I can sit in the small space she's provided for me. I lean over to take the tea cup. What next? Don't know. I wait for Marcus' lead, but Taneisha is running the show.

"So, hi was yo' day, Kenny?" she asks. She pretends to take a sip of tea, but she extends her index finger instead of the pinky. She makes it look like the pinky is the wrong finger. Who decided on the pinky anyway?

"My day was just fine," I tell her. Marcus and I grab our tea cups, and we extend our index fingers when we drink.

"Ah'm so happy ta h'yuh dat," she says. Too cute.

"Miss Lafavor, why'own chew tell Kenny hi yo' day was," says Marcus. "Tell 'im 'bout cho' school."

"Kenny, I had uh fabulous day at my school," she says. She takes her time to stress the vowel sounds in the word "fabulous." It's hopeless to try and hold back my smile. "Me an my friends spent uh big par'd uh da day practicin' na lettuhs an numbuhs, but chew probally know all yo' numbuhs an stuff, so I ain' g'own bothuh you wit all uh dat kine uh ins an outs uh my day. But fuh da most par'd, my day was pretty good, if I do say so myself." She says all of this while fanning her hands all over the place, like practiced gestures. She even places a hand over her heart whenever she refers to herself. Too cute.

We spend a good twenty minutes being entertained by our gracious hostess, with Colin still entranced by the plight of his video game cartoon character, who appears to be roaming through a Disney World from hell. Then Marcus informs his sister and brother that it's time for them to get ready for dinner—food he prepares himself, if you can believe that. It takes him about fifteen minutes, but I never hear a microwave. He does it on the stove. It smells good too, but I can't identify what it is. He offers. I decline. So Marcus decides not to eat yet, I guess for my benefit.

He places their plates on the dining table located past the kitchen, while I sit back on the couch and watch the demos of Colin's video game, so I never get a chance to see what Marcus has whipped up. Half of me wants to ask to see the plates, but the other half doesn't want to sound stupid. Then there's a third half asking me what I'm doing here in the first place. And I'm now aware of a fourth half steadily growing inside me, a half I didn't have or didn't know I had only yesterday. That's the half that got me here.

Marcus is good with his sister and brother. I can't imagine their own father doing a better job, and they obviously love Marcus on a level beyond his being a brother. They consider him as more of a—I don't know—something between brother and father. If you ask me, all fathers should be like Marcus. Somewhere between brotherhood and fatherhood. A combination of someone you can talk to about anything and someone you can learn from. A cross between a buddy and a tutor. A classmate and a teacher—no, better than a teacher. Someone who listens, who cares—a super father, dad of steel.

"You ready?" Marcus says. He returns from the kitchen rubbing his hands, a big smile on his face.

I nod.

On cue, Roland comes through the front door. Marcus didn't lock up, but Roland does it for him. Is this their routine? "Ya'll star'ded yet?" Roland asks. He's wearing tattered jeans and a collared pullover shirt with an oil stain on the right sleeve. That's when I realize Marcus hasn't changed his clothes. Advantages of being a father?

Marcus grins at me. "Kenny, you ready?"

"I'm ready," I say, clearing my throat. I make room for Roland on the couch, and then wonder if Marcus will want some of the couch as well.

"Well den, less git dis par'dy star'ded," says Marcus. He bends over the console and replaces Colin's game with Conflict, in a seemingly single motion. Then he sits on the floor next to my feet. Let the games begin.

"Let Kenny play firs'," Roland suggests. "I won't 'im na soften you up uh l'uh bit. Den I'll take you out." He punches one hand in his fist when he says "out," but he's wearing a friendly smile. For a second, I thought this was going to be a mistake, but now I'm back in "Let's see" mode.

Marcus hands me a controller. "Come own, Kenny." He isn't too concerned about my ability. He's cocky, but nice about it. You don't see that combination much. I'm liking Marcus more and more. How can I defeat him in his own home? That wouldn't be right. I take the controller.

"I like dat," says Marcus, grinning at me. Then he turns to Roland. "You see dat, Ro? Kenny ain' g'own do uh lot uh talkin'. He g'own let his game do all la talkin'. Dass what Ah'm talkin' 'bout," he says as he nudges my leg. "Ro be talkin' too much smack when he play."

Roland wants to say something, but he also wants to prove Marcus wrong by being silent for once. Works for me.

The "CHOOSE YOUR PERSONALITY!!" flashes on the screen, and Marcus chooses Coolio. Surprise, surprise. I don't know what I was expecting, but I really am surprised. I choose Spry. Just because.

Roland frowns like he's just been asked to conjugate a verb. "You pickin' Spry?"

"Dass very interestin'," murmurs Marcus. I've surprised him as well. He stares at the game, concentrating. "Very, very interestin'. . . ." he repeats.

We go at it for about sixty seconds before Marcus beats me. I show him one opening and he exploits it like a real professional. Before that opening, it was like the tightest game I've played in a long time. Still, I gave him the opening before spotting a weakness in his game. So I start to wonder.

"Damn!" shouts Roland, jumping off the couch. "Dat was like da most awesome match I've seen, man! Kenny! You can hang wit 'im, man! Play 'im again!"

"You got skills, Kenny," says Marcus. "Ain' no doubt about it. Wanna go again?"

I shrug. "Sure."

The room becomes silent. We choose the same personalities as before. I try a little more, sustaining my efforts, prolonging the fight before giving only the slightest of errors. Again, Marcus is all over the opening, and it's over. I'm aware that I have yet to see an error in Marcus' game. No flaws. No weaknesses. Perfect? I refuse to believe it.

Roland refuses to believe something else. "Hi you hang wit 'im like dat, Kenny?!" he says, jumping off the couch again, only to sit back down. "You see hi he hangin' wit chew, Marcus? Dis boy's good!"

Marcus sits quietly on the floor. He keeps staring at the television screen like he's thinking about something totally different. "Kenny, you ain' got ta keep doin' nat," he finally says. He doesn't look at me or Roland. He keeps his eyes on the screen. "Hi you expect me ta git bettuh if you keep lett'n me win?"

He knows?

I don't know what to say, and I feel uncomfortable in my silence, and a little embarrassed—no, ashamed. In my attempt to respect him in his home, I end up insulting him, assuming that I need to give him an easy challenge, a watered-down test of skills. As if I already know his ability before he has a chance to show it. I'm labeling him, the way people label me—like teachers.

I have to say something because the silence is waiting for me to slice it. "I'm sorry, Marcus," I say, choosing my words slowly. "That wasn't right." I can't think of anything else to say, even though I'm thinking really, really hard. "I'm sorry," I say again.

Roland is the first to snicker at me. "Damn, Kenny. It ain' all lat."

Marcus joins in with a little laugh too. "Yeah, dawg. I ain' mean na git chew all bent up like dat." He shoves my leg with his elbow. He doesn't turn to look at me, but I can tell he's giving me the right smile, a real one. "I juss won't cho' bess game, bruh-man. One mo' time, au'ight?"

"Yeah, Kenny," chimes Roland, nudging me in the shoulder. "Juss kick his ass. He ain' above uh ass whoopin'."

I like the spirit that's in the room. So I go with it. "Let's do it, Marcus," I say, removing all challenge from my voice. "My best game."

"Yo' bess game," says Marcus, but he still doesn't look at me. Is that apprehension in his voice? I hope not.

We pick the same personalities, and Spry and Coolio go at it like never before. I can't believe how good Marcus is, but I don't know why I can't. Is it because no one has ever held out this long with me when I'm in total concentration, or is it something else? This is the longest match I've ever played. Damn, he's good. Still, it can't last forever, and eventually, it's over. Roland doesn't say anything. Marcus also remains quiet. I want to say something, to break the silence and the suspicion in the air.

"You wanted my best game, and that was it," I say, but to both of them. Then to Marcus, I say, "You won fair and square. Good game."

The silence makes it seem as though somebody died, but not somebody we know. A weird silence. The same silence you have when waiting at an intersection for someone else's funeral to pass by. Silence you didn't know was coming, but wish it would hurry up and go away.

Marcus eventually looks back at me, and he's got a big smile. "I beat chew, but chew uh bettuh playuh dan me," he says. "Coolio's my bess man, but when you firs' picked, you ack like you could'n figguh out who da pick. Is Spry yo' bess man?"

I hesitate. I know what he's trying to say, but he's wrong. I pause to think about it for a second, just to make sure I'm right about him being wrong. "I don't really have a best man," I finally say, and that is totally true.

He nods. "Dass what Ah'm sayin'."

"Pick somebody else!" shouts Roland, jumping up like a hot idea just landed in his lap. "Pick Stomp! No, no, no—wait! No—Brain! Pick Brain!"

Marcus is grinning at me. I grin too. Taneisha and Colin come to see what all the commotion is about.

"Play wit Brain if it don' mattuh," says Marcus.

"Yeah, right," giggles Colin. He obviously knows something about the game. He sits on the floor next to Marcus. Taneisha scootches in between me and Roland, but she isn't too involved with what's going on.

"Come own," says Marcus, turning back to the screen. "An remembuh—yo' bess game."

When I pick Brain, Colin snickers. Taneisha leans a little on me like she could fall asleep, but when I look down at her, I see that her eyes are glued to the screen, but with disinterest. She's bored, and I feel sorry for her.

When we start playing, I immediately realize Marcus has had very little practice against what I throw at him. He holds his own pretty good, but it's a terrible mismatch. He's dethroned.

"Dat was da rush!" says Roland, jumping up again, flailing his arms every which way, not knowing what to do with them. "Dat was da ab-so-loot rush! Brain juss—juss mugged Coolio!"

Marcus tosses his controller on the floor. My heart flutters. "You juss got ta show us hi you do dat," he says as he jumps to his feet. "Dat was cole, dawg. You juss stripped me clean. I could'n do nut'n." All of this he says while giving me the right kind of nudges, the ones that say it's only a game.

Roland scoops up the discarded controller. "My turn—pick somebody else, Kenny."

We play with me as Jock and Roland as Coolio. I'm wondering if I'll ever choose Coolio again. The match is a decent one, but I see why Roland doesn't give Marcus much of a challenge—no patience, no discipline. He rushes things. Doesn't think. Still, he's used to losing, so it doesn't matter one way or the other to him.

THEY CONTINUE PLAYING, SWITCHING AMONG the three of them for nearly two hours. By the time Roland's dad arrives to take

Kenny home, they've talked about everything from last summer's escapades to tonight's homework assignment given by their peculiar English teacher. Kenny lets Marcus know what a good time he's had, and he also gets a big hug from Taneisha. She makes Kenny promise he'll return soon. Kenny can hardly wait, and wishes he was scheduled for martial arts lessons on Tuesdays and Thursdays as well. Anything to give him an excuse for coming home late Monday through Friday— a five-day pass.

Roland stays with Marcus to play a few more rounds, so it's just Kenny and Mr. Hess, but Kenny doesn't mind. Mr. Hess proves easy to talk to. Kenny is comfortable with him and speaks freely. But he clams up when Mr. Hess suddenly asks him for his address. He cannot allow himself to be dropped off in front of his house. His mother would go ballistic. Plus, he needs to work up a decent sweat before he walks through the door, which will be very easy to do if he jogs home from a few blocks away. He must be sweating. Otherwise, she'd know.

He could lie to Mr. Hess, but he has enough lies to keep up with as it is. Besides, he likes Mr. Hess, and hates lying to those he likes. "You can drop me off on the corner of Perry Street," he finally tells him. He tries his best to sound like it's no big deal. Perry Street is only about a mile or so ahead, so he figures Mr. Hess will appreciate the convenience.

"It's no big deal, Kenny," Mr. Hess says, obligingly. "Didn't you say you lived on Clayton? If I remember right, that ain't that much farther from Perry."

Panic hits Kenny with a jolt that's almost painful, but he strains to keep it from his voice, even though the Jeep Cherokee is suddenly traveling too fast for comfort. "Really, Mr. Hess, you don't have to go through all of the twists and turns." Then he adds another coat of reassurance: "Perry's close enough." Then another coat for good measure: "Believe me, I've walked a lot farther than that." He almost winces at his last sentence. It didn't come out right; it wasn't the best choice of words.

"I don't want you walkin', Kenny," Mr. Hess insists. "It's dark, and it ain't safe at night."

Fear wraps Kenny in a bear hug.

They approach Perry Street, but Mr. Hess doesn't slow down. Kenny's heart is ready to leap through the windshield. "Here is fine," he says, panic rising in his voice. But at this point, he doesn't care. "Right here, Mr. Hess," he says, grabbing the door handle, but Mr. Hess doesn't slow down.

"Kenny, this is ridiculous," he says with warmth in his voice. His demeanor doesn't make it any easier. "I want to see you home safely. Just tell me—"

"No! Mr. Hess—please!" he shouts, his voice cracking like a whip.

Startled, Mr. Hess almost slams on his brakes in the middle of the road, but manages to make it to the curb before coming to a stop. With both hands on the steering wheel, he pauses without saying a word, and then throws the Jeep Cherokee in park. He stares at Kenny as if he is seeing him for the first time, as if he's a stranger who has materialized in the passenger seat.

Kenny keeps looking straight ahead at the dark road that awaits him, not knowing what to feel. "I'm sorry—I . . . I just. . . ." He has nothing and everything to say, but opens the door instead. He doesn't look at Mr. Hess. He can't.

Mr. Hess grabs him gently by the arm. "Kenny . . . I'll drop you off anywhere you want. Wherever you want me to . . . every time . . . no questions . . . okay? No questions." Mr. Hess' final words come in careful whispers, as if a loud sound could shatter Kenny into a million pieces. Then, he releases Kenny's arm, and Kenny gets out of the vehicle and gently closes the door. He stoops down a little to peer in at Mr. Hess, his eyes saying what his mouth cannot.

"You take care, Kenny," Mr. Hess says, unconsciously wringing the steering wheel, all the while searching for so much more to say—the right questions, a word of comfort, a way in. Anything to help. "Kenny, if you ever—"

A change in Kenny's expression cuts him off, asking him not to go there.

Mr. Hess takes a deep breath, for both of them. "Be safe, Kenny," he finally mutters, knowing he has failed at—what? He doesn't know. But definitely something.

Kenny gives the top of the Jeep Cherokee a gentle tap, and then heads down the black road, bathed in the vehicle's headlights. Mr. Hess watches him disappear into the night, wallowing in emotions he can't describe. All he wanted to do was make sure Kenny got home safely, and he truly believes that by dropping him off here, on a lonely dark street, he has done just that.

After Kenny disappears from sight, Mr. Hess does a U-turn and speeds back to collect his son. He will hold his son in his arms. He will tell his son how much he loves him. And he will promise his son that he'll always be there for him, no matter what.

Dad of steel.

Chapter 25

BEING A TEACHER HAS SWITCHED FROM burden to bliss. That's how Tony would describe the past two days—blissful. Almost overnight, he has evolved. Undergone a metamorphosis. *Transformed.* From an insensitive educator to a thoughtful facilitator. From a callous beginner to a caring apprentice. From a hated teacher to a well-liked person.

Tony is now a *person* to most of his students, and the sensation is both intoxicating and sobering. He has found new energy. In a single night, he read all one hundred twenty-six written responses to Monday's discussion on Standard English. And last night, after reading what they had to say, he decided fourteen minutes after midnight that he'll never again allow his sense of responsibility to waver.

Yes, they are his responsibility.

Their success is partly in his hands. If they fail, he's partly to blame. But even though the blame wouldn't be entirely his, he knows his part in their failure would be the most pronounced. Not the students'—they aren't students by choice, but by law. Not the parents'—many are parents either by chance, by default, or both.

Besides, students and parents don't claim to have majored in their position, or graduated with a three-point-seven-two grade point average while studying to be a student or parent. Students and parents haven't gone through workshops and internships, bent on honing their techniques and skills before being awarded with the title of "student" or "parent." They don't wield a diploma that claims they know what they are doing. They aren't really expected to be professional or even the slightest bit good at what they do, and they can't successfully argue that what they do deserves a paycheck. He'll take the blame from now on because neither student nor parent makes a very good scapegoat—at least, not anymore.

Yesterday, he was amazed at how many students submitted a response to Monday's discussions. Even those who had forgotten to do the assignment scurried to get it done before the class ended. They wanted to be heard, and they knew their English teacher would listen. It made him feel good as a teacher, but the *major* strokes for his ego came by way of students not belonging to him, popping their heads in all day long, asking if they could sit in on the class. Students were actually trying to skip their classes to attend one of his. Some even had notes, supposedly signed by their teachers.

A part of him hated to turn them away, but the idea didn't sit well with his conscience. And though it wasn't explicitly mentioned, he was sure such a move would have violated one of Principal Ryker's "Expectancies." He doesn't want to make more waves. Talk has already started about his decision to eat with the students during lunch, negative talk. Rumors concerning his competency and judgment. So he wants to show he can be just as good as the rest of them. That he, too, is one worthy of the title "teacher."

Yesterday, his students were ready for round two of the discussion. Some submitted their papers and urged Tony to read their words to the class. They wanted to be the first to be heard. A few wanted to be heard even without a submission, while others asked Tony to delay the forum for a few more minutes as they frantically put pen to paper, writing what was needed to enter the verbal fray. But Tony convinced them that it would be better if he were allotted enough time to read all papers first, that it would help him as a facilitator. After some thought and a few moans, every class agreed, and every class gave him one day to read their responses—the same day. Last night.

Still, after the agreement to postpone, the same good question surfaced in every class: "So what do we do now?" In Tony's first class, it was the duo of Rodney Coleman and James "Powuh" Cotner who posed the question. Tony sat on the corner of his desk and folded his arms. "You know, I've been thinking about that myself," he said with a grin. "What do *you* think you should get from this class?"

Rodney's eyes popped open. "Who me?"

"No, not just you. I'm talking to everybody in here. Since this is an English class, I'd like to know what my students expect to get from me. What do you need from me to help you survive, once you get out into the world?"

The room exploded with responses, but Tony mimicked raising his hand, and more than a dozen arms flew to the ceiling as the room fell silent.

"Jarek?"

Jarek flopped his hand down with a smirk. "I think we need to learn hi to tawk *right*."

Someone made a quick comment about "rednecks" before the class threatened to start up, but Tony calmed them down with his hands as though tamping down the air. "He's right. We've already established the importance of learning Standard English, but we also have a better understanding of *why* it's important. So don't sweat it, okay?"

Somebody started clapping, but it didn't take.

Tony went to the board and wrote: "Standard English."

"What else do you really need from this class?"

Hands flew up again.

"Jasmine?"

"We need to be good with Standard English and stuff, but I'd like to know how to do speeches, because to be able to use Standard English is one thing, but you have to know how to stand up and talk the way people who give speeches do it, especially if you end up owning your own company or being somebody's boss. You'll have to talk in front of people."

Tony wrote: "Public Speaking Skills."

"Very well-spoken, Miss Woods."

Hands went up again.

"Marcus?"

"Hi da write."

The class paused, but that's all Marcus had to say.

Tony wrote: "Writing Skills."

"Absolutely—anything else?"

Fewer hands went up.

"Lisa?"

"Read'n."

Tony wrote: "Reading Skills."

"Okay—what else?"

The students continued as the answers dwindled from the unchallenged skills to the highly questioned ones—Vocabulary, Sentence Diagramming, Greek Mythology, Spelling, Parts of Speech, Shakespeare, and so on. In addition to these voiced concerns, the students didn't understand the importance of remembering information that could be easily found almost anywhere. Why take a test on who wrote what? Why should they know the definition of a "predicate adjective" or a "compound-complex sentence"? Were they being prepared for the world or being prepped for a game show?

They also didn't understand the importance of reading a classic novel, and why the same classic message isn't as powerful when told in a text and language more readily understood by today's adolescents. They challenged how teachers can know how good a student's reading selection is *not*, without having read the book themselves. They also wondered why they weren't allowed the same right to judge a classic by its cover, or even by the author. They failed to understand how prehistoric dialect with its "thous" and "nays" could help them obtain and master the dialect America expects. In fact, why read *any* text written in a dialect other than Standard English?

Shawn Naples defended poetry with a passion, almost to the point of walking out of the classroom. That was good enough for some.

Poetry is definitely a medium needed to help a person deal with and express his or her emotions. Tony also explained that poetry falls under reading and writing. That was good enough for everybody else. Poetry was definitely a keeper.

All of Tony's classes ended with the students reminding him that he had only one day to read their papers, that the discussions would be held on Wednesday—today. And as Tony sits at his desk, waiting for the bell to start his first class, not the least bit tired, he recalls his first day here, and how it seems so long ago, even though it's only his second week.

He glances at the clock sign. *Time is either invested or spent.*

The bell rings; he takes a deep breath. "It's time to find out which one *I've* been doing," he tells himself.

As usual, Lisa Boyer and Faith Dunn are among the first through his door. "You muss open yo' doh *way* befo' da bell rang," says Lisa, "'cause you always be juss sitt'n at cho' des' lookin' juss as serious as evuh."

"She flirt'n, Mr. Avery," grunts Faith as she takes her seat. "She need da sit h'uh behine down an git h'uh education—tell 'uh, Mr. Avery."

Tony gives his usual nod with a smile. "Good morning, Miss Boyer—Miss Dunn."

As the classroom fills with bodies and voices, most asking Tony's opinion of their writings, he makes his way to the door with his usual nonchalant stride, anticipating the tardy bell. Kenny, Marcus, Roland, Rodney, Richard, and James are among the last to glide in with seconds to spare.

Tony stands to the side and motions for them to enter. "Hello, gentlemen—Kenny, Mr. Lafavor—wha's up, Powuh." Tony exchanges a newly-created handshake with James, and the tardy bell sounds.

"Thought we what'n g'own make it, did'n ya?" says Marcus. He follows closely behind Kenny, who shoots back a grin before he takes his seat.

Tony shrugs. "I wasn't worried." He closes the door and rests on the usual corner of his desktop. "Besides, Kenny and Roland keep you in line."

Marcus plops into his desk. "True dat."

Tony is very pleased at how quickly Kenny has been accepted by the class, and he has long admitted how wrong he was. Within two days, he's learned so much about how much he needs to learn about *all* of his students, but Kenny has proven to be his greatest miscalculation. So far, the comments on Kenny's transcript don't make sense. *Discipline problem?* No way. *Disrespectful?* Not in the least. *Unmotivated?* Whose fault is that one? *Distant?* Not anymore. And his grades. Tony has also concluded that even his grades are a lie. They don't represent what Kenny is capable of, who he is. He wonders how much more transcripts don't have to say, about *all* of his students.

"You read my papuh?" asks Rodney.

James' hand flies up, as do others. "You read mine?"

"I *know* you read mine."

"Do we get them back today?"

"What chew thank about mine?"

"Have you graded them all?"

"You ain' even write dat much. What chew talkin' 'bout?"

"Dis was fuh uh grade?"

Tony raises a hand and receives silence. "I've read them all, and I've decided to read at least a portion of everyone's paper to the class. I can't read them all in their entirety—some of you had a *lot* to say."

Mild laughter.

"But I tried to highlight what I thought were your most . . . *vivid* points of view. So, we may not have a lot of time for an in-depth discussion, but I think that after hearing what we've all written, we'll have pretty much heard it all, from every angle. At any rate, I'm sure we'll leave here today having learned a little bit more about ourselves, and each other.

"As for the grade—to be quite honest, I thought about it, but got kind of hung up over who should get what for what. After what some of you wrote about grades and such, I realized I have to rethink this thing called grades. With all this talk about fairness going around, how can I be fair about the grades? I mean, some of you wrote about three or four times as much as other people. Some of you spell better than others, while some of you obviously have access to computers. And I didn't really tell you what I was going to be looking for in your writing, so how can I really count off for it not being there? So I thought maybe we should talk about what essays should look like before I start marking you off for not submitting what I haven't asked for."

The class pauses before Jasmine asks the obvious question, the question on most of their minds. "You want *us* to tell you how to grade our papers?"

Tony chuckles. "No, not *tell* me how—help me to decide how. I want us to sit down one day and figure out what a good essay—an A-plus essay—should look like. I mean, what does an A-plus paper look like, exactly? What about a B paper? Or a C paper? How long should an A paper be? And how many points should I take off for each spelling or grammar mistake? Should spelling and grammar count the same? What about punctuation? I just think we should talk these things out so we'll know what to do on the next paper, before I start slapping an *A* on one because I thought it was interesting, despite its twelve errors, but I give another paper with no errors a *B* because I thought it was boring—at least, boring to me. But as I said, we'll get to all of that another day. Today, we listen to what we've all written."

The anticipation in the classroom thickens as Tony reaches across his desk for the neatly stacked set of papers. He has their undivided attention, and he's on cloud nine. Curiosity, a valuable, yet elusive component of the learning process, has never been stronger than it is at this very moment, and Tony's loving it.

As he reads through each selection, the class smiles, frowns, laughs, and scoffs accordingly. Some papers receive shouts and applause, others receive growls and hisses. Tony keeps them from exploding into an all-out argument by constantly reminding them that they only have time to listen to their opinions, that further discussions will have to wait. By the way some react to some of the papers, discussions may have to wait indefinitely. At one point, Tony threatens to discontinue the readings to regain cordiality, to restore academic harmony.

Stephanie Nielson, a student known for her quick temper and Ritalin dependency, is the first to respond to Tony's threat, blasting from her seat. "No, no! We're okay, Mr. Avery! We laxed!" She turns to her classmates. "Ya'll chill out! I wanna hear the rest!"

Her outburst has the desired effect.

Tony gives them a grin and a tsk-tsk. "Now do you see why I'm not reading the names? You people are so high-strung. Brother against brother. Sister against sister. Boyfriend against girlfriend. Lois against Clark. Salt against pepper. Yin against Yang. Bugs against Bunny. Republicans against—"

"Hey!"

"Okay, Mr. Avery! Dawg!"

"We ain' got all day!"

"We runnin' out uh time!"

Tony raises an eyebrow. "Are we going to behave ourselves? Be civilized and courteous beyond the norm of the quote-unquote civilized world?"

"Yes!" they explode. Then laughter.

Tony continues the readings. Their reactions are the same as usual—applause for those they like and disdainful comments for those they don't—but with a lot less intensity and a little more—what? Understanding? Consideration? Whatever it is, the class is a class again.

Tony finishes with Tammy Yates' paper and grabs James Cotner's next. "Here's another long one," he announces. "This person wrote a little over six pages."

The class gives another one of its awestruck gasps, a reaction that becomes more exaggerated with each of Tony's proclamation of a lengthy paper, but respectfully so.

"This person agrees with Monday's class discussion except for the name *Choklish*. Instead, this person gives three other suggestions, complete with—"

"Dat soun' like mine!" exclaims James.

Tony rolls his eyes. "You know, I don't even know why I bother to keep you people anonymous. Over half of you have fessed up."

Laughter.

"As I was saying—*Powuh* gives three other suggestions for Choklish, complete with rationales: Negran, Afrique, or Darcreole—*Darcreole, Powuh?*"

More laughter.

"As with a lot of papers, he makes a lot of interesting points, but I particularly like it when he writes about what's really important in communication. This is how he ends his paper:"

```
Plus, I think people get too wrapped up
a lot about how you say something any
damn way. A lot of teachers for instance
be grading and marking up your paper and
don't even read it. I [am] not saying you
should not care about spelling and all
of that mess but just like in talking
its more what you say not how you say
it. Thats how it should be in writing
something It should be more of what you
write not how you write it. Whats more
important the message or the [messenger]?
If you gonna chop me down at least show
me that you got the message. So what if I
cant use big fat words. I say if you want
to sound smart you should have something
smart to say. Saying something dumb but in
a smart and fancy way don't mean that what
you saying [is] smart. So if you want to
```

```
sound smart all the time have something
smart to say all the time but do they
[hear] you? Hell no. Its like I say about
the [messenger] they be so busy cutting down
the [messenger] they don't even [hear] what he
be trying to get across to them cause they
won't listen and excuse me but there is no
better way to say it but by saying that is
f _ _ _ ed up. Thats all I got to say.
```

The room erupts with more applause than usual.

Tony waits for it to die down. "Well said, Powuh, but let's try and clean up the language from now on. It may turn some people off. You don't want profanity to upstage your message. Like you said, you want them to pay attention to what you're saying, not how you're saying it."

James shrugs. "Sometimes, ain' no bettuh way ta say somp'm, Mr. Avery," he admits. "Can you thank of uh bettuh way ta put it dan nat?"

Tony strokes his chin for a second. "Better? Well, not offhand."

The room erupts again.

Deborah Weems' paper is the next to be heard, and she's one of the few students who wishes to remain anonymous. "This is another brief one," says Tony. "So I'll read it in its entirety."

> *In my opinion, I think that it's a real* [tragedy] *what happened to blacks with slavery, but there still the minority in this country. Why should we sound like them? We all agreed that they can't agree on what they should sound like anyway so I say what's the big deal. We should all just learn good English so we can all understand each other better without any* [confusion] *what so ever about how we should communicate with each other. Good English really isn't hard to learn once you get used to it. In my opinion, I believe we should not be jumping on it the way we are doing because it really does sound better when you want to be honest. For example, if a*

doctor or a lawyer or somebody with a really important job like
that sounded like blacks that just would not be right. Lawyers and
doctors and people with important jobs supposed to sound profes-
sional. Not just any way they want to. I would not even go to a
doctor that sounded like that. It would [not] *feel right. That is my*
opinion on the subject.

Tony interrupts the boos and grumbling. "Remember, people don't have to agree with your opinion. The important thing is that people fully understand why your opinion is what it is. For instance, this person wrote that Standard English isn't difficult to learn once you get used to it. That's fine, but what *is* difficult to learn once you get used to it?"

Rodney Coleman raises a hand, but he doesn't wait to be acknowledged. "Who wrote dat?"

Tony rolls his eyes. "Like I've said a dozen times now, that's not what's important."

The usual whispering starts as Tony grabs Jarek Mitchell's paper. It's only one paragraph, and Tony believes, as with the papers from Jacob Pauls and Corey Watson, these are not Jarek's words. They have an older, more hardened flavor—a *parental* flavor. Corey's paper is the harshest of the three, with words directed more toward Tony's character and competence as a teacher, but all three papers sing in the same key. Still, he has no problem reading them to the class. His real concern is that he's still clueless about the trio's writing ability.

"Here's another really short one," he says, clearing his throat for the hundredth time.

This is what I'm going to say about it. I don't care what you say. The way we talk sounds better so just learn ours and be done with it. Back off sir. Not everybody wants to walk around talking stupid. I think it's a shame the way you people try to push your ways on us and our loved ones. This is not what I come to school to learn. So I'm asking you to stop it. I am hear for good old fashion American English. And I hope I have been clear on this subject and don't have to hear about it again.

The room grumbles again.

"Man! Who keep writ'n nat sh—I mean stuff, Mr. Avery?" asks Roland.

Jose Perediaz stands. "Yo, that's some disrespectful mess, Mr. Avery—know what I'm sayin'? You ain't gotta deal with that *nothin'*. That's some whacked—"

"Again, I want everyone to focus on what's important," says Tony. He motions for Jose to take his seat. "This person makes a lot of statements and claims, but he fails to provide adequate support."

Jasmine Woods raises a hand and waits to be acknowledged, despite the small talk surrounding her. "How in the world is a person supposed to support statements like that?"

Tony shrugs. "Not my statements, not my problem. My concern is to ensure that everyone here understands the importance of supporting what you say, knowing how to deliver a better, more effective message. A message that's more complete. Again, it doesn't matter whether your readers agree with you. You simply want your readers to fully understand where you're coming from. Since you're the one making the statements, it's your responsibility to support them."

The grumbling continues for a few more moments, but they eventually settle down.

"Now, to end on an upbeat—the final paper. This person actually wrote fourteen pages."

The room gasps.

"The paper talks a little about Monday's class, but the writer really goes into an extremely impressive spiel about how Choklish has been represented by many different authors, in many different books, and the positive and negative effects these representations continue to have on our society." Tony flips through the pages. He wishes he could reveal Kenny to the class, but he knows by Kenny's expression that it would be a mistake. He wishes he had time to read Kenny's paper in its entirety. *It's that good.*

But it was more important to make sure every student who wanted to be heard *was* heard. There isn't time to share what Kenny has to say about Daniel Defoe, Harry Crews, Flannery O'Connor, Tony Morrison, Richard Wright, Harriet Beecher Stowe, Alice Walker, and William Faulkner. *And he says a lot.* More than what Tony has to say about some of the authors. In fact, Tony has yet to *read* some of the authors.

Kenny's paper is a little rough around the edges, but, overall, most impressive for a single night's work. "In my opinion," Tony says, "this person's final thought is a particularly interesting one, and it's this section of the paper that explains the title. Yes—it has a title. Titles are important. From now on, everyone should title his or her paper."

Tony writes the title of the paper on the board: *Learnt.* Then he commences with reading Kenny's words.

So I've definitely changed the way I look at language. I think good language is in the ear of the beholder so to speak. For the longest time, I used to think that African-American people (and people who spoke like them too) didn't know how to talk right, but it turns out that I was wrong all along. They know how to talk. I just didn't understand a lot of what they said. I'm not used to the way they talk and I'm not used to some of the things they like to say like dawg and frappin down and terms like that. In other words, I didn't know how to listen. But isn't that my ignorance and not theirs? And isn't it through this ignorance that my mind was made up about their ignorance?

But all of this is starting to change. Recently,

I've spent a great deal of time listening to a couple of my friends talk to each other and me, but now I'm listening with a learning ear. I don't just write them off as needing a good dose of grammar skills. I know what it feels like to be written off so quickly by teachers, so I won't do that any more. Now I just listen, and I'm destroying my ignorance slowly but once and for all. And during this destruction of my ignorance, I've discovered something. As time goes by, I'll probably discover more, but this discovery is worth mentioning now. I noticed that my friends say the word "learned" with a t sound on the end. At first, I didn't notice it, but at some point it hit me that both of them use the t on the end. They say "learnt." They'll say "I learnt this" or they'll say "he learnt that."

Don't ask me why it stuck in my mind, but it did, and when I got home to write this paper, I remembered that word. Out of curiosity, I looked it up in the dictionary. I was very surprised to discover that the word can be said and spelled either way. "Learned" and "learnt" are both right.

So then I got to thinking. White people leave the t off. African-American people add it on. And when I really think about it, I know why white people say it's wrong, but that isn't right. I remember my old English teacher (not Mr. Avery) telling us one day that the correct way to say the word "often" is without pronouncing the t. But we all say the t, so that makes it right. But obviously it isn't right but obvious to who? Nobody. Who cares?

So then I got to thinking about what we were talking about on Monday again, and I agree with

Mr. Avery. As a matter of fact, I'll go as far as to
say that a lot of people don't care about right and
wrong as long as you don't sound African-American.
That's probably why a lot of white people say often
with a t because it sounds more white that way.
Leaving the t out seems more like what African-
American people would do because most of their
language is about leaving letters off. When they say
talking without the g or whatever, that's what they
normally do. So white people see leaving letters off
as a black thing.

So I now say that people should realize that
they can finally say that they "learnt" something
about something and know that they're telling the
truth. And they'll be telling the truth with good
grammar and everything, but it won't be right. At
least, that's what I've learnt so far from all of this.
Right is sometimes wrong, and wrong is "Off-Ten"
right.

Still, a lot of people will never be able to feel
right about saying that they have "unlearnt what
they have learnt." They'd rather stick with the old
way of thinking. For instance, a lot of people are
still strung out on grades and what they supposed
to mean. But when you think about the grades and
stuff like that, they don't necessarily mean that you
know your stuff. It just means you've done what
you needed to do to get the grade. The grade is like
a black belt in karate. The belt doesn't mean you
can really fight. It just means that you've done what
it takes to earn the belt. Isn't it crazy to know that
an idiot can make straight A s?

I say that having the ability to think should

be more important than having something that
just says that you have the ability to think, and
that includes using good English to make yourself
sound like you know what you're talking about even
though nothing but stupid stuff is coming from
your lips. Grades, good English, and black belts are
overrated.

The class pauses and then starts with their usual applause for yet another well-taken paper, but this time, it lasts a lot longer than the rest. For the first time, Tony joins the applause and gives Kenny a quick glance, but is careful not to give him away. Kenny applauds with the rest of the class with a huge smile on his face and something else—*something more*, but Tony can't decipher it.

"Who was that, Mr. Avery?" asks Jasmine.

Tony gives his usual shrug and a smile. "There are a couple of things I want to mention to you before the bell rings," he says to the class, his hand in the air. "Some of you obviously had a lot more to say, but for some reason, you made sure your paper was five paragraphs. Why only five paragraphs when you obviously want to say more?"

"Mr. Tuddles says that an essay has five paragraphs," states Victor Lawrence.

Tony shakes his head. "No. An essay has at *least* five paragraphs," corrects Tony, an index finger raised. "And even that's up for debate. But even with five paragraphs, if you take away the introduction and the conclusion, that leaves you with maybe three points that you want to make. Won't there be times when you'll have more than three things to say about something? For some of you, wasn't this one of those times? Don't limit yourself if you don't have to. Okay—the other thing I want to say is don't get so hung up on grammar, punctuation and all of that junk to the point of your losing sight of what you're trying to say. Like Powuh said—it's the message that's important. You can always go back and spruce it up, but what's the point of saying nothing in a well-organized fashion? Does that create a—"

The bell sounds, startling most.

"In the future, feel free to talk to me one-on-one about any of this, but let's finally lay these open discussions about language to rest—at least, for now. Okay?"

Some moan, but most agree as they filter out the door.

When Marcus, Kenny, and Roland reach the hall, Marcus turns to Kenny. "I ain' know you could write like dat. Can you help me wit writ'n?"

Kenny isn't the least bit surprised Marcus figured out "Learnt" belonged to him. "Sure. If you want me to. No problem."

"Me too," says Roland. "You juss full uh suhprises, Kenny."

Tony sifts through a new stack of papers, preparing for his next class. Suddenly, Corey returns, tosses a small note on Tony's desk without a word, and exits with the same briskness. Tony grabs the tightly-wrapped piece of paper and gently unfolds it—carefully, as if bracing himself for a practical joke.

I did not write that my dad write it. I dont agree with all he say about you and all. I think Jarek and Jacob is not right to. I can tell your not like that. Your a good teacher. I can tell it hurt your feeling when you reading it and Im sorry. I like you for a teacher. Please dont let nobody know I write this to you.

Tony tries to tear the letter into a thousand pieces as he's swept with emotions, and he nods knowingly at the clock sign.

Time invested.

Chapter 26

SARAH WAS WITH MRS. AVERY WHEN SHE purchased them at the neighborhood supermarket. She stomached the smell that seemed to find every corner of the house, while Mrs. Avery cleaned them. When Mrs. Avery placed them over a hot burner, the smell changed to something else—something stronger, and something that, after three and a half hours, is still in the house.

For her last Friday night in Florida—at least for a while—Sarah wanted to provide Tony with one more surprise before she returned to Virginia. She told Mrs. Avery she wanted to learn how to cook Tony's favorite meal and have it waiting for him when he got home from school. Mrs. Avery loved the idea, and, of course, she knew Tony's favorite meal like any good mother would: *collard greens, fried chicken, baked macaroni and cheese, corn bread, and chitterlings.*

Of course, in the Winn Dixie, Sarah overlooked the chitterlings twice, even though the buckets were right under her nose in the meat section.

"Dare dey go right dare, Sarah," Mrs. Avery said.

When Sarah looked down at the buckets, she did a double-take. The buckets read "chitterlings," but she had been searching for "chittlins" the entire time.

The cleaning process was as Mrs. Avery forewarned—excruciatingly tedious, but of the utmost importance. Mrs. Avery insisted more than once that they had to be meticulously cleaned, and because of this, she has always been hesitant to eat chitterlings prepared and cooked by others.

"What are *chittlins?*" Sarah had first asked as they got ready for the trek to Winn Dixie.

"Juss anothuh par'd uh da pig, baby," was Mrs. Avery's only reply as she searched for her purse. Sarah thought she detected a stifled grin, but wasn't sure.

Tony realized the surprise as soon as he stepped through the door—before, in fact. "What's the occasion?" he asked.

"Don' look at me," his mother said, pointing an accusing finger at Sarah. "Dis was yo' fewchuh wife's idea."

Tony couldn't put his things away fast enough before practically running to the kitchen to prepare his first plate. He showed Sarah in more ways than one that she made a good call with dinner—at least in his opinion.

So now, Sarah sits at the table with chitterlings etcetera patiently waiting on her plate. Waiting for her to muster the courage. Waiting for her to dig in. And they've been waiting for a solid three minutes.

Tony is the first to lose it. His explosion of laughter startles Sarah. Her focus has been on the chitterlings. When Mrs. Avery joins in, Sarah smiles awkwardly.

"What's so funny?" she asks, glad to at least be an amusement, if not a dining companion.

Mrs. Avery stands in the doorway of the kitchen and regains her composure just enough to speak with some coherence. "Baby, you ain' gotta eat dem chittlins."

"I'own even know why you put 'em own yo' plate," adds Tony, holding his side in peals of laughter. "But since you juss tossed uh few own yo' plate like dey what'n nut'n, I said da myself—uh-oh, g'own wit cho' bad self. But den, when you looked at 'em wit dat look. . . ."

Mrs. Avery loses it again as she bends over, one hand on her stomach, the other on the counter for support. "She juss *insis'!*" she gasps. "My baby girl juss made up h'uh mine dat she was g'own *eat* h'uh some chittlins!" A vein forms on Mrs. Avery's neck as she fights for air through her giggles.

Tony wheezes.

Sarah blushes bright red. "Well, I thought I could at least give them a try."

Tony gasps and stomps the floor, and Mrs. Avery slaps the counter, tears in her eyes. Sarah releases a small chuckle, happy to amuse them and glad that she isn't expected to swallow a chitterling.

As they all settle down to dinner, Tony takes Sarah's plate and slides her chitterlings onto his. Since Sarah thoroughly enjoys the combination of collard greens and corn bread, their small talk eventually drifts to Tony's classes and his students.

"Well, it soun' like dat James is uh han'ful, if you ax me," says Mrs. Avery. "I unduhstan' his point about all uh yo' classes being mostly full uh black kids, but don't dat boy know white folk ain' g'own stan' fuh dat, even wit juss uh han'ful uh dey chill'un?"

"People would undoubtedly see it as reverse discrimination," adds Sarah.

Mrs. Avery lifts an index finger. "Right—*reverse discrimination.* Dass right. You cane make white kids read all black books an be exposed ta juss black ways uh seein' na world, an tell 'em ney gitt'n uh good education. Dass crazy."

"I know, Mama," chuckles Tony. "But chew should h'yuh dat boy make his point. I would'n be suh'prised if he end up uh lawyuh someday."

"So na you got one tellin' you hi da run na class. You got anothuh one thankin' you should always talk like you was raised—what cha'll say? *Chocolate?*"

"*Choklish,*" corrects Sarah, throwing a hand over her mouth to conceal her upturned lips.

Mrs. Avery frowns. "Yeah—whey you git uh name like dat?"

Tony shrugs. "I combined the word 'chocolate' with the word 'English.' You see, chocolate can be either brown or white."

Mrs. Avery rolls her eyes. "An you got three kids dass always tellin' you what some uh da othuh teachuhs be sayin' behine yo' back."

"I just think that's so outrageous," grumbles Sarah. She folds her arms again.

Mrs. Avery tilts her head to the side. "Baby, like I say—dat don' suh'prise me one bit. You got people like dat everywhey you go." She pauses for a few seconds to let her words sink in. Then she studies Tony. "Tell me dis—you got anymo' *normal* kids who juss wanna mine ney own business? Who juss wanna learn somp'm? Like dat Jasmine girl. Uh dat David. Na *dey* wanna *learn* somp'm. You got anymo' like dem?"

Tony's expression doesn't change, and he answers quickly, as if his mother's words push a name to the top of his consciousness. "Kenneth Houston," he says matter-of-factly.

"Who dat?"

"He arrived Monday. Extremely well-read. Extremely competent and capable. To be honest, I don't even know why he's there. I mean, I feel the same with some of my other students, but he's definitely an advanced student. We've been covering writing skills. With him, if you give him feedback on how to improve his writing in any way, it's done. He immediately understands what you're trying to convey to him. His comprehension level is incredible. Almost creepy." Tony pauses to blink twice. "But . . . there's something not quite . . . *right* with him. I can't put my finger on it, but it's there."

"What?" his mother asks.

Tony shrugs. "I don't know. Maybe students are still bothering him about his size, but not that I've seen. But there's . . . *something*. I don't know. My other students seem to like him, especially Marcus and Roland."

"Well, have you spoken to him?" asks Sarah.

"I've pulled him to the side and asked him how everything's going. He just says everything's fine. But it's like—I don't know—like he's really trying to convince you of it. The way he says it. Like it's rehearsed."

"Well, if you thank somp'm wrong, but he won't say nut'n, what can you do?" asks Mrs. Avery.

"Have you considered contacting his parents?" asks Sarah. "Although I can't imagine what you could possibly ask them. . . ."

"He lives with his mother," Tony explains. "His father passed away when he was young."

"Well, maybe dass it," offers Mrs. Avery.

"I don't think so," Tony says. "Maybe. At any rate, I've been wanting to call his mother to talk to her about his being there. I don't understand how he *could* be there. I just know he's going to blow the AME test right out of the water. Maybe she knows something that's not showing up on the transcript."

"Maybe he was uh bad chile in his othuh school, an ney sent him na Lincoln na straighten 'im out," says Mrs. Avery.

"Supposedly, the students are there for reasons other than disciplinary concerns," says Sarah.

"*Supposedly* is right," says Tony. "But Ah'm findin' out dat ain' na case, Mama. We supposed ta be helpin' nem git back own track—own na right level, an den sen' 'em back ta dey reguluh school, but dat ain' happenin'. Most uh 'em stay dare 'til ley graduate, but Lincoln don' g'yuh reguluh diplomas."

"What dey git den?"

Tony shrugs. "Some kine uh suh'tificate, but dey cane do much wit it. If any of 'em wanna go ta college dey'd haff ta take ovuh two semestuhs uh catch-up classes firs'. An ta make mattuhs worse, ain' too many teachuhs dare who thank dey can *evuh* be college material."

"Soun' na me like dey need mo' teachuhs like you den," says Mrs. Avery, frowning again.

"I agree," says Sarah, flatly.

When Tony keeps his eyes on his plate, Mrs. Avery tilts her head and eyes her son. "You g'own stay, aint cha?"

Tony shrugs without looking up. "I'own know," he says, his voice dropping slightly.

Mrs. Avery drops her fork on her plate. The *clink* sounds throughout the house. "Why not?"

"I juss wanted ta fine uh quick job, Mama," he says, his eyes still down. "Lincoln ain' *nobody's* firs' choice, ya know."

His mother simply grabs her fork and resumes eating. Now it's her turn to quietly stare at her plate, but she's obviously surprised, and even a bit disappointed.

Tony sighs. "You *know* I wasn't planning on staying there," he says, his voice even quieter, softer. "I'll apply to a few high schools this summer, some *real* ones. More than likely, I'll be hired by one of them. From what I hear, the county shuffles teachers and administrators all the time. I might as well put my resume in the mix."

Even though the topic of school is eventually discarded, the chatting doesn't return to its previous mood and tone. Words are left unsaid as the group finishes the meal with less serious talk. Afterwards, Mrs. Avery insists that she do the dishes for a change, and she suggests to the two lovebirds that they enjoy the night air. They oblige by taking a lazy walk around the block.

After they turn the second corner, Tony stops abruptly underneath a streetlight. "Do you think I should stay?" he asks. A fenced dog barks in the distance, and the night wind is chilly enough to give Sarah an excuse to snuggle underneath his arm, though she never waits for one.

She gazes into his eyes. "I want you to be happy," she says tenderly. "Your *mother* wants you to be happy. When you're happy, *we're* happy. Of course, we're disappointed, but we're disappointed that you're not happy there. Lincoln can obviously use you, but so can any other school. You're a remarkable asset to education. How can we be disappointed in you? We *love* you—very much."

They place a gentle hand on each other's cheek, caressing, tracing every curve and contour of the other's face, the way a blind person might handle a priceless work of art. Their lips meet, and their kiss momentarily allows them to abandon all concerns, as they become oblivious to everything but their growing love. For the tender moment, they are the only two on the planet. They maintain their strong embrace, and their eyes say, "I will always love you," before they finally turn for home. Sarah's flight departs tomorrow at 11:40 A.M., but Tony misses her already.

"Do you realize this will be the first time we've spent more than two days away from each other since we became study partners?" he asks as they enter the front yard.

Sarah's only response is a forced smile and another long embrace before they enter the house. Once inside, they find Mrs. Avery on the phone with Sarah's father. The dishes in the sink indicate she's probably been talking since they left for their walk.

"H'yuh dey come na," says Mrs. Avery. "Ain't dat da truth . . . Dass right . . . You do da same, awright? . . . Bye na." She hands Sarah the phone. "Yo' daddeh wanna talk ta you, baby."

Sarah tells her father what a great time she's had getting to know Mrs. Avery, and how much they've bonded in such a short time. She tells of the experience at the Roadhouse restaurant—withholding certain details—and of their newly acquired friend named Amos Garrett. But a large portion of her conversation is spent talking of Tony, Lincoln High, and the "tremendous strides" he's making. Her pride for Tony comes through the phone lines loud and clear.

After twenty minutes, Sarah calls Tony to the phone. "It's for you, sir," she purrs, her voice laced with happiness, the way any typical Daddy's-little-girl might sound, knowing she's indeed loved by her father.

Tony gives her a quick kiss before he brings the receiver to his ear. "Hello, Mr. Parker. How're you holding out without your favorite daughter?"

Mr. Parker chuckles. "I'm managing to keep it together, Tony. Besides, it's something I'm going to have to get used to permanently, right?"

"Yes, sir, I'm afraid so."

"She tells me you're already busy changing the world. We always knew you'd make a great addition to the educational system. I'm really proud of you, son."

Tony pauses to rewind Mr. Parker's last words. *Son?* The Parkers have shown nothing but cordiality and warm hospitality since day one, but "son" still takes Tony by surprise. "Thank you, sir," he manages to say, but realizes he probably should say more, share more of what he's feeling. "I—I mean . . . sir . . . I really—"

"Tony, you've been addressing me and my wife as 'sir' and 'ma'am' for quite some time now. I'm not sure when it started, but we always thought it was a southern disposition. But after talking with your mother, it turns out that that's not the case at all. You don't address your mother that way. Well . . . Claire and I don't expect our children to address us as such, and that includes you. From this day forward, 'yes' and 'no' will do nicely."

Tony pauses for what may be an inappropriate amount of time, but he needs to allow everything to take hold. Suddenly, he's more thankful than he's been in a long time. He's acutely aware of just how sour the reaction to their wedding engagement could've been. How ugly it could've been. How painful and final it could've been. He and Sarah are fortunate to have the parents they have. "Mr. Parker . . . I just want to tell you from the bottom of my heart—thank you . . . so much. For *everything*," he says, but not satisfied with the impact of his words. They're not enough—of what? He doesn't know, but they're lacking. Lacking a lot. "I really do mean it. And I just . . . what I'm trying to say—"

"Tony, my wife and I have spent every holiday and every birthday with Sarah. We've thrown her more parties than we care to remember. And practically every other joyous occasion she's had, we've at least known about, even if we didn't have the opportunity to take part in it. But this, we know for sure—now, Sarah's happier than we've ever seen her in her entire life. Thank *you*, son. Thank—*you*."

For the moment, both men go silent, but the silence says it all.

Chapter 27

MORE THAN TWO WEEKS HAVE passed since he said good-bye to Sarah. Even though they talk every night, Tony misses her a great deal. Absence is supposed to make the heart grow fonder, but his heart simply aches. Still, despite his lovesick blues, he discovers a way to cushion the impact that the distance between them was having on his moods: *Focus on something else.*

On what?

His work. His students. Lincoln High.

Since Sarah's departure, Tony has become more dependent on his routine. He still isn't used to the pace of an educator—the planning that never really ends, the hours which are never really designated—but his stamina is growing, and having a routine has helped tremendously.

Ever since he was late for his first day as a teacher, he arrives no later than thirty-five minutes before teachers are actually required to be at school. Although he now knows where teachers secretly congregate every morning, it's his routine to avoid the politics of wearing the right face for the right people, and the cesspool filled with who's doing what, spiked with an unhealthy dose of "he said, she said." His routine involves saying hello to Miss Edwards in the Main Office, collecting his mail, and shooting up to his classroom on the third floor.

Miss Edwards always says good morning with a warm smile, but he has all but given up on Dean Phillips. Her only response to his morning greetings has been a grunt of some kind, as if she thinks he needs to concern himself with more important matters than meaningless pleasantries. But it's Tony's routine to speak anyway, whenever they happen to pass each other in the halls, although he no longer waits for her grunts. He just marches on by, sometimes with a grin, other times without.

Mrs. Madison, the repressed vice principal, remains as busy and as elusive as ever. Tony has been fortunate enough to see her another three times since his first day. It was on their third encounter when she finally demonstrated she could remember a person's name—given a moment to think about it.

He's only seen Principal Ryker twice since his first-day-of-school reprimand for being late. Both times, it has been from a distance, Ryker looking elsewhere. Both times, Tony has been relieved. Somehow, the principal intimidates him. Ryker is a no-nonsense kind of guy, always monitoring compliance, always on the go, his radio crackling on his hip. And whenever he happens to be in his office, it's always with the door closed, and Tony can't help but picture him chastising someone else with his tough cop routine, someone who's been unfortunate enough to break one of the Ryker rules.

Since reading Kenny's "Learnt," it's been Tony's routine to spend a portion of his planning period reading. Most of his "planning" takes place at home, so reading is how he avoids falling into a fruitless routine. Kenny has shown him just how much he still needs to read, that it shouldn't end after college. Plus, it doesn't sit well with Tony to know that a fifteen-year-old white boy has read titles like *Black Boy*, *Jubilee*, *Maud Martha*, and *Uncle Tom's Cabin* while he hasn't.

Why should it matter? He's asked himself a half dozen times, but hasn't found an answer beyond *It just does*. But he has to admit that, until now, his leisure time was filled with Sarah, and before her, it was the basketball courts. Until now, reading simply for the sake of reading has never had a place in his life.

Even though he tries to make the most of what little time he has in an average day, his tenacity isn't without cost. The routine of being in his classroom at least thirty minutes before the first bell rings, reviewing his lesson plans, preparing the necessary materials before finally burying his head in a book—his current read being an Alex Haley title—has caused some teachers to dub him as anti-social and pretentious. According to Mrs. Moreland, who has been more of a mentor than the elusive Mr. Tuddles—Tony's official mentor—some teachers see him as a typical, snot-nosed, wet-behind-the-ears know-it-all who doesn't have the common sense or decency to get with the program. However, Mrs. Moreland has also told him to keep on doing what he's doing, and that he's been an inspiration to her and others. It's because of him that she, too, insists on eating with the students during lunch.

"I find that I can digest my food better," she said. She also told him that two other teachers have adopted the same habit. Tony had no idea.

And as usual, as he sits at his desk with *Roots* in his hands, it's his routine to convince himself that he doesn't care what a few teachers think of him, that the students are the only ones who matter. Not *them*. Not a handful of teachers who know nothing, but everything about him. Not those who've already written him and most of the students off. He tells himself he no longer cares what they think, but he can't help it. He *does* care. Because true caring doesn't come with an on and off switch. It never stops.

The first bell rings and causes a small rustle in the halls that eventually grows into a soft rumble, filled with the sounds of slamming lockers, squeaking shoes, and scattered bursts of laughter and frolicking. The first period is Tony's planning period, but it doesn't stop his door from occasionally opening, with a student's head popping in to offer a morning salutation. It's Tony's routine to simply glance up from his book and offer a smile or a wave, never really speaking.

As the wave of commotion in the halls recedes, and the soft grumbling of neighboring classrooms percolates through the walls, Tony, again, submerges himself in Alex Haley's portrait of Kunta Kinte's life and his struggles with the "toubob." Although he has seen the television series twice, he's amazed at how much story was omitted from the series, how "edited for television" the televised version now seems.

When his classroom door cracks open, Tony looks up and watches the door curiously. Whoever it is takes a while before deciding to enter. For a moment, Tony thinks the visitor has already had second thoughts, or has realized that this is the wrong room, and the door will again close with the familiar click that echoes throughout the classroom. The moment lasts for a long five seconds before Corey Watson finally enters, but only halfway. He stands with one leg in and the other still in the hallway, while his face asks what his mouth obviously won't.

Tony reads his face like a book. "You're not really disturbing anything," he says. "I'm just catching up on a little reading." He waves the book for Corey to see. Then, his face morphs into a question mark, and his head tilts as if Corey has said something puzzling. "Aren't you supposed to be in class right now?" When Tony sees that the question causes Corey to second-guess himself, he quickly adds, "What can I do for you, Corey?"

With body language alone, Tony actually sees Corey thinking it over, whatever *it* is. Then, he sees Corey change his mind, as if *it* has become a mistake, a momentary lapse in judgment. Corey prepares to retreat, groping frantically for a lie that will explain the awkward intrusion, but he's at a loss for words, now that he's decided his initial words will be a mistake.

Finally finding a plausible lie, Corey reaches for the door. "I . . . I just wanted to say good morning, that's all. I didn't mean ta—"

"I appreciated your note," says Tony, pausing. Not moving. Watching Corey, but trying not to stare. Tony holds his breath the way a poker player does when he waits for his opponent to show his hand.

What do you have, Corey? Then, reading Corey's eyes, calling his bluff: "Is there something you want to talk about?"

Corey looks down at the floor. The eyes don't lie. *Can't* lie. He releases the door and takes a few steps toward Tony's desk, eyes not knowing where to go.

"I had to give it to you," he whispers, but not wanting it to be a whisper. He wants to sound strong, be a man. He clears his throat. "He made me turn it in."

Tony hasn't a clue of what to say or do, but can feel the timer ticking. The ball is in his court, but time is running out. He has to say something, ward off the screaming silence. "Who made you?" he asks, gently—*cautiously*, knowing without a doubt how precarious the conversation is.

"My dad."

Nothing else. Only two words, and the ball returns to Tony's court. Corey's eyes scan the floor, waiting.

Tony takes a deep breath, but softly—a quiet sigh. Inaudible. He senses Corey's discomfort and wishes he could find the words that would whisk it away. "It's okay, Corey," he says, but in his mind he winces at the triteness of the words, the cliché. "Don't worry about it." Winces again.

Corey nods. "If I didn't give it ta ya, he'd've known," he says, but almost as if talking to himself, as if reminding himself of the wisdom in his decision. "Jarek woulda tole his dad, and his dad woulda tole mine. . . ." He stares at Tony now as he says the latter part. "We been talkin' 'bout what you been doin' since you got here," he continues, fumbling with his words. "But it got bad after that stuff about how ya'll talk okay and all of that. Fer a while, it was a joke, but after that day, Jarek's dad got—he was . . . pretty mad about it. I didn't say nothin' about cha, but he called my dad up. They got together like they do—we only live a hop, skip, and a jump away—and Jarek's dad decided ta write it. They both did. I don't think they was gonna ax us ta turn it in. They was just drinkin' and laughin' about it. But then, Jarek's dad tole him ta turn it in with Jarek's name on it. Well, Jarek didn't wanna do the homework nohow. . . ."

His voice drifts as his eyes leave Tony's and find their way back to the floor. Tony glances at the floor also, but looks back at Corey when Corey adds, "I was gonna do the homework. It wasn't nothin' as far as I'm concerned, but my dad said ta give you his too. I don't know how serious he was about it with all of the drinkin'. When he gets ta drinkin'. . . ." His eyes are back on the floor. "When he says do something, you do it. You just . . . do it."

For a moment, Corey stares at Tony, his eyes asking for—what? Answers? Words of comfort? With this, Tony is reminded of what position he holds and is swept with a chilling, splashing sense of responsibility. He is the teacher, but he has never planned for this. He doesn't recall such a happenstance being covered in any of his textbooks or college courses, but he is the teacher. What lesson can he give when he isn't even sure of the need? Indeed, he is learning more from this encounter than Corey is. *But he is the teacher.*

Corey can sense Tony's indecision, can see it on his face. Hesitation caused by uncertainty. A deer caught in the headlights. A face that proves that this was a mistake. After all, what can a teacher do about anything? Corey looks back at the floor, and he tries to swallow the disappointment and regret that suddenly gather in his throat, threatening to rise up, to push unsanctioned words from his mouth. Words that would undoubtedly be coated with frustration. Then, he turns to leave.

"Wait—don't go," says Tony, but he doesn't know what else to say. Still, he realizes that he can't let him leave. At least, not like this. *Like what?* Like he hasn't done his job. "Do you—I mean, why . . . why aren't you more like . . . your father?"

Corey gives Tony a puzzled look, but it fades with the understanding of the question. "He's alright. Just mean sometimes—but not really—just gets out of hand every now and then."

"How do you mean?"

Corey shrugs, eyes downcast.

Tony feels as though he's really in a card game. "Does he . . .?" He stops because he can't find the right words to play.

"No—nothing like that," Corey blurts out incredulously. *Go fish.* "He just can drink sometimes, that's all. Other than that, we're a lot alike. I'm not a drinker. If I was . . ." He pauses, inspecting the words before giving them to Tony. "He's meaner with Mr. Mitchell around than when he ain't."

"Jarek's father?"

Hesitation.

"Yes."

Tony glances down at the book in his hands. Somewhere during the conversation, he felt the need to conceal the title. He places *Roots* on the desk, face down. "You're not like Jarek," he says. Then he folds his arms. "You're not like Jacob either."

"They're my friends," Corey says, voice stronger than it's been thus far, more assertive. *Go fish.*

Tony instinctively lifts a hand, motioning that his words weren't meant as an attack. "I know. I'm just saying . . ." he says, but not really sure what he's saying. Then, another thought: "Did Jacob's father write his paper for him too?"

"No."

Tony can tell that Corey's telling the truth, but he still gives him a curious look.

"Jake go along with anythang Jarek wants," Corey tells him. "But Jake can go too far, too—be mean. He still my friend though. I just don't always go along with everythang he wants to do. Jake don't care none. Jarek tell him about the letters—he write one of his own. Just as easy as that. I just wanna say that I don't think you deserve none of it. You're one of the good ones. You don't get uppity or nothin' like my dad think you do. You're okay." He takes a step toward the door. "I just wanted to tell you that."

Tony watches him leave, unable to stop him. Words fail to come. Deep down, he believes he's just botched one of the most important kinds of conferences. The kind that doesn't come along every day. The kind called by a student.

He sits at his desk, not moving, not reading, thoughts racing. And he stays that way until the bell rings to start his first class.

*   *   *   *

When Marcus, Roland, and I come through the door with our usual few-seconds-to-spare entrance, I notice right away that something's bothering Mr. Avery. He acts normal enough—talking to everybody, saying the usual stuff—but I can tell. I know a good front when I see one. Something else is on his mind. Not too much, but definitely something.

"Hello, Kenny," he says to me as I head for my desk. "How are you today?" He gives me the usual pat on my back.

"I'm fine, Mr. Avery," I say to him, and he still doesn't give me that look that he used to give me after I'd say that. Never could place the look, but it went away after he called my house last week and spoke to my mom. I can't imagine what could be bothering him now. Hell, he's a teacher. I know he's human, and he must have his rough days, but it can't be *too* bad. Not like us. Teachers don't have to deal with what we deal with. They might have to deal with a student every now and then, but we get headaches from them *and* ourselves. Teachers don't have stuff like peer pressure, snickering behind their backs, and a dangerous home life. They don't have pressure and stress at every turn, never having a moment's rest, always on their guard. I'd take the problems of a teacher any day. What problems? No—not problems at all. *Concerns.*

His concern last week was about me being like a fish out of water or something like that. It was kind of difficult to figure out what he was trying to say through all of that careful wording he was shoveling. Basically, he thinks I shouldn't be in this school, but he can't be sure about it because he's just an English teacher, and I could really suck in my other classes. He started saying all of this stuff about the grades I made at Susan B. Anthony. He brought up my fights. Hell, he even knew about the conferences I had with guidance counselors and teachers.

Is there nothing sacred with these people? They call you into the room as if everything is so secret, with all of this bullshit talk of confidentiality. They might as well televise these "confidential" meetings in every teacher's lounge in the city. Maybe they post the whole ordeal in some kind of teacher's newspaper we don't know about—*The Teacher's Tattle Tale* or maybe *The Latest Last Laugh*—but whenever they refer to it with us around, they just call it *Records*. Politically correct. Student friendly. Parent safe.

So, Mr. Avery wants to maybe ignore what *Records* has to say in my other courses because of the misprint he found in the English column. He wants to know what Mom has to say about everything. When he said that, I got a whiff of freedom, but free to go where? Do what? Life sure as hell wasn't better at Susan B. Anthony. Mr. Avery is wasting his time; I'll never be free, but he'll definitely have Mom's support. Mom has been telling the publishers of *Records* to go to hell for a long time now.

She can't wait to see Mr. Avery. She thinks he'll help get me back into a normal school, one she can mention to her friends at the beauty salon, one that'll say she's doing her job as a parent. She sees Mr. Avery as the break she's been waiting for, and I have to admit, for anybody else, Mr. Avery would be a dream come true, an angel sent down by God himself. I say "for anybody else" because Mom still doesn't know Mr. Avery's black, and God doesn't send black African-American angels down to visit white people. I could tell her, but I already have one tsunami to watch out for, and I'm barely treading water as it is.

He's stopping by this Wednesday. That's my day to be at the Northshore Karate Institute, but now it's my video game day. Every Monday, Wednesday, and Friday, I'm at Marcus' house playing games. Marcus and Roland were serious about learning to write, too. So, sometimes, we'll write stuff. Turns out, they need a lot of work with spelling and grammar, but they know how to make sense. I try not to say much about the spelling and stuff because it really doesn't matter too much, and it keeps the writing time friendly.

Even Colin and Taneisha write something for us to read every once in a while. Marcus helps them, and I help him and Roland, but only sometimes with Roland. He doesn't write as much, and I can tell he isn't into it as much as Marcus. Most of the time, he'll write something about one of the video games or some girl that he likes but refuses to talk to, or something like that. But that's okay. Whatever. It's all about just making sense on paper. I'm not a teacher, so I don't really give a damn what he writes about. I don't get paid to stifle what he wants to say. I just wanna help him say it the way he wants it to be heard.

Whatever's on Mr. Avery's mind right now, he seems to be handling it pretty okay. The last few days, we've been working on opening paragraphs and transitional phrases, and he's right back at it. He's been on a kick about goal-setting, and now he's asking us to write a little something or another about our "immediate plans after graduation." I whip up a quick textbook answer—college, a high paying office job, retirement by the age of forty.

"Very interesting plans, Kenny," he says, looking over my shoulder at my paper. "I particularly like the age of your retirement."

I smile. He's weird for a teacher, but he's hard not to like. After he glances at everyone else's paper, he goes back to his favorite spot in the front of the classroom. He likes to sit on the corner of his desk, or stand next to it just in case he feels like sitting on it.

"Being specific is what it's all about, ladies and gentlemen," he says, being the only one of my teachers to refer to us as such. "The more *specific* and *vivid* you can be about a goal, the more real it becomes in your mind. Remember, you can't hit a target you don't see. The more detailed you are about a goal, the better you see it, the better your chance of hitting it. And don't forget to use the transitions we've been discussing."

Jose raises his hand. This is the only class I've got where you have to raise your hand. It's kind of lame. "This for a grade?" he asks. He always wants to know what's going to be graded. You think he'd learn by now. I think Mr. Avery's hiding his frown pretty good.

"What's more important, Jose?" Mr. Avery asks. He suddenly sounds like he's tired or something, and you can tell he's holding back what he really wants to say. "Is the grade more important than the ability?"

That's a good one. We've never heard that one before, right? But obviously, Mr. Avery's been warming up for Jose.

"We've already established as a class that we'll only spend time on things that will truly help us in the real world," he says. When he talks this way, he's never able to sit on his desk. He's standing now. Probably gonna start pacing in a second.

"So, let's deal with this grade question once and for all," he says. "Before anyone asks me this annoying question again, ask yourself what's going to help you the most—the grade or the ability?"

Jasmine raises her hand. This is obviously her favorite class. She does well in here, always raising her hand, but in my math class, she hardly says a thing. She's probably not doing so hot in math. Mr. Avery calls on her and she says, "If you have the ability, you don't need to worry about the grade anyway."

If that doesn't say "teacher's pet," I'm a fashion model for thongs. But we can get away with stuff like that in here. Don't ask me why, but we can. No one looks at you funny, or makes smart comments that make you shut up for the rest of the day.

After all is said and done, and the period comes close to the end, Mr. Avery ends up collecting the papers for a grade after all. Too funny. As usual, he gives us more homework. So far, he's given enough for all of my teachers, but nothing that's really demanding or takes away from your day. It's almost like he doesn't want us to get used to *not* having homework. I wouldn't be surprised, because that's how he runs his class—no down time, always something for us to do.

A few minutes before the bell rings, he asks us for our attention and says, "Before you leave, I need one more thing from you. Lately, we've been focusing on goals—things that are positive. Well, I now ask that you write on a sheet of paper just two sentences," he says, and he holds two fingers up.

He pauses for a moment, and then he sits on his favorite corner. We can tell by his face that he's got something up his sleeve. Then he says, "For the first sentence, I want you to state something that you hate. For the second, I want you to state why. Make sure you stick to only two sentences. And don't use the word 'because.' Instead, use a semicolon. For instance, if what I hate is ice cream, I'd write: I hate ice cream—semicolon—it gives me gas." We giggle and snicker when he says the gas part.

"And finally," he says, "don't bother writing your name on it."

We all look at him funny for a moment, but eventually, we get to writing. The bell rings before all of us finish. Don't ask me why. It's not like he's asking for a term paper or anything. I hand him my slip of paper, and he just shuffles it in with the rest of the pages offered to him. He doesn't even glance down at it.

When Roland, Marcus, and I get outside, Marcus asks me, "What'd chew write, Kenny?"

I shrug and say, "I hate surprises; they usually hurt."

And I meant it, too.

Chapter 28

WEDNESDAY MORNING. PRINCIPAL RYKER waited for Tony to arrive. How long did he wait? Tony doesn't know. For what reason? He hasn't a clue. But as he follows the principal inside the dreaded four walls, the office of doom, his heart sinks to his stomach, and a knot rises to his throat. Tony enters the office with zero enthusiasm, and this time, the surroundings consume him. Suddenly, he realizes the office is one better suited for a detective or a private investigator, not a principal. The only things missing are the ominous, slow-moving ceiling fan and the unexplained shadows of Venetian blinds.

Against his will, Tony's brain compiles a list of possibilities, of all the blunders he may have committed to invoke such an impromptu meeting. Is this about an infraction of one of the Expectancies? He has to admit he still hasn't memorized all of them. Or is this something else? Perhaps this is one of his earlier fears. Maybe one of the fears he used to have as an intern has come to fruition. Did he forget to sign in or out? Is this about his roll book? The sign-in sheet and the roll book have always created their share of anxieties for him, especially during his student-teaching days. His directing teacher, Mrs. Lowell—in his opinion, one of the most thorough people he's ever encountered—always stressed the importance of the sign-in sheet and the roll book.

She didn't give details on the possible consequences of slouching in these areas, but her sermon was embellished with phrases like "required by law" and "legally binding." More than enough to terrify anyone with the slightest imagination.

Indeed, on more than one occasion, Tony's thoughts have drifted back to the sign-in sheet and the roll book during his drives home, especially the roll book. Did he remember to change an absent mark to a tardy mark for students who arrived late? Unlike the teacher sign-in sheet, the roll book is a tentative document. Some students arrive with the punctuality of a partygoer—fashionably late, many times with a note from another teacher in hand, as if it's their invitation letter. They're invited into his classroom by other teachers.

Has he overlooked some of these invitations? Has he been marking late students as absent? Have teachers or parents or both rallied to expose his roll-taking incompetency? *Will I lose my job?* That's another question forcing its way into his mind, but it immediately makes room for *Do I care?*

As he sits in the same chair he warmed on his first day, that final question echoes the loudest, becoming its own chorus, its own melody in his brain. Like a tune that's sometimes difficult to shake no matter how hard a person tries. So he sits, watching and waiting. Watching Principal Ryker make his way around the desk and flop into his plush leather chair. Waiting for Ryker to either fan his ignited fears or set his mind at ease. Watching and waiting with the song *Do I care?* playing in his head.

"How have things been going with you, Mr. Avery?" the principal asks, but in a tone that says the question is really an icebreaker and nothing more—rhetorical.

"Fine," says Tony. He tries to smile, but only manages to force one corner of his mouth to rise.

Principal Ryker pauses, and his eyes rest on Tony like he's trying to read between the lines of that single word. He unhooks his radio from his waist, lowers the volume, and places it on his desk between the two of them. Then, he removes a pen from his shirt pocket and starts clicking it. He seems as though he doesn't care at all about how uncomfortable he's making Tony. "How are your classes?" he asks, in the same tone. "Students doing well, I take it?"

Tony wonders if this is how Ryker talked to suspects and criminals during his years as a police officer. He asks questions with condescension in his voice and contempt in his eyes. He makes Tony feel as if he's on trial and—what? Inadequate? Yes. That's it. As if Tony doesn't even come close to Ryker's idea of a reliable and competent teacher. "Classes are coming along fine," he says, shrugging.

"Allow me to get right to the point, Mr. Avery." Tony's heart starts beating with the irregular clicking of the pen. "For your list of recommendations for the AME test," continues Ryker. "I am told that you named almost a hundred students."

Tony adjusts himself in the chair. "Yes, well . . . I figured I'd give them the opportunity to take the test—I mean, if they pass, they can return to their regular school by the time—"

"I'm quite aware of how the process works, Mr. Avery," Ryker fires back, frowning a little. "What I don't understand is why you would recommend almost a hundred of your students."

A single note from *Do I care?* tickles Tony's thoughts, and then he leans all the way back in his chair and says, "I recommended every student that I have. It seems as though someone has made an error—I have a hundred and twenty-nine students."

Ryker takes a deep breath and exhales like he's counting to ten, like he's undergoing some kind of relaxation technique. If so, it doesn't seem to be working. "Mr. Avery, listen to me very carefully. You're a first-year-teacher, so I don't really blame you entirely," he begins, delicately, as if being a first-year-teacher is a condition that can be cured with proper treatment and time. "On average, teachers usually recommend anywhere from five to fifteen—sometimes twenty of their students. Students they feel will do well on the test, Mr. Avery. When I say 'well,' I'm saying *pass*, Mr. Avery." He takes another deep breath, and forces the air from his lungs, frustrated. "Who is your mentor?" he asks. "Hasn't your mentor explained the situation with the test?"

At first, Tony wants to change the subject and discuss the tone of Ryker's voice instead, but he thinks better of it and simply answers the question. "Mr. Tuddles is my mentor. He's spoken of the testing and such during lunch, but not as a mentor, just in conversation. I didn't even know he *was* my mentor until later. He's only sat with me once, and that was during my planning a couple weeks ago. We didn't really talk about the test," Tony explains. Then, realizing he may be exposing Tuddles in some way, he adds, "He probably hadn't gotten around to it just yet."

Tony can't believe he's actually covering for Tuddles, but at the moment, it seems the natural thing to do. Tuddles has been zero help as a mentor. His only visit with Tony was just short of another lunchtime gripe session. He spoke to Tony as if trying to catch him up with the latest "information" he's been missing in the teacher's lounge, and he asked Tony questions the way an informant might during an undercover sting.

"Teacher recommendations are already trickling in," says Ryker. "When, exactly, would be a more appropriate time for him to 'get around to it?'"

Tony doesn't answer. He hopes the question is yet another rhetorical one.

Ryker shifts in his chair. "I will speak to Mr. Tuddles—of that, I can assure you, Mr. Avery. If he's failing to own up to his end of the mentor-apprentice relationship, I need to know why," he says with a smidgen of apology in his voice.

Tony manages to keep a groan to himself as he listens to how his popularity will undergo further decay.

"No harm done, Mr. Avery." Ryker gives the pen a few final clicks and places it into his shirt pocket. His tone indicates that the conversation has ended, but he doesn't reach for his radio and shows no intention of standing. "You know, Mr. Avery, you still have ample time to make a reasonably accurate judgment. In fact, more than enough time to find out which of your students might actually do well on the AME. There's no need to rush in a panic."

Tony takes a slow, deep breath, and tries to ignore the chill he feels from being bathed with patronizing words and calculating eyes. *What's going on?* he wonders.

Do I care?

Tony shakes his head. "I want all one hundred twenty-nine students tested," he says quickly. He doesn't give himself a chance to rethink his decision.

Ryker's eyes narrow as though he's just been insulted, but he doesn't say a word. Instead, he leans back in his chair, grabs the pen from his pocket, and starts clicking again, but this time, more vigorously.

Tony selects his next words carefully. "From what I understand, the issue is money—to make sure we don't . . . *waste* money on students who won't pass the test." He swallows hard. "Is that right?"

"Money is only part of it, Mr. Avery," growls Ryker, but he doesn't say anything else.

Tony leans forward a little. "What's the other part?"

At first, silence. Not even the clicking of the pen. Then, Ryker takes another long breath, but this time, it seems as though he's stalling. "Mr. Avery . . . to test hundreds upon hundreds of students would require . . . more test administrators . . . not to mention the additional test booklets and answer sheets involved in testing such a large group of students. You have no idea how much a test booklet costs . . . and answer sheets—they cost quite a bit as well. They don't come cheap, Mr. Avery."

Tony shrugs. "I'm still waiting for the other part."

The principal scowls but says nothing. Tony shrinks back into his chair. The words slipped out—thoughts made audible, but he dare not apologize. It would be an admission of having done something wrong, and he doesn't believe that he has. Still, he feels he should say something. He hates the silence. Perhaps an explanation is in order, though he hasn't the foggiest idea why he should have to submit one.

"I . . . kind of understand how . . . *wasteful?*—it is to test students who won't do well on the test," he begins. He rubs his hands, finding it difficult to return Ryker's glare. "I mean, it's definitely a waste of money if a student doesn't take the test seriously—you know—if they Christmas-tree the test." Tony looks down at his sweaty palms, pausing briefly to collect his wits. The click of the pen matches his pulse rate. He forces his eyes to stay on Ryker's face, but he avoids the eyes. He looks at the forehead—an orator's tactic. "So . . . what I did was—you know—talk to the students about the . . . *importance* of the test. Then, I asked those who would take it seriously to write their names on a clipboard I have sitting on—you know—the table next to the back of the room." He shrugs in defense. "Eventually . . . they had all signed up for the test—every one of them."

Of course, he omits the part about his students questioning his ability to have so many of them tested, and that they were well aware of the selection process and had learned to accept it as just another example of how things are in the world. Only after Tony's "discussion" did they develop an itch to challenge the validity of the norm. Only then did they revisit a longing that the norm had effectively suppressed: the desire to escape the walls of Lincoln, return to their regular schools, and perhaps, do something with their lives. And like a reopened wound, the painful reality of their predicament suddenly caused many students to want to attend to the self-inflicted injuries their lives had become. As for the remaining students—the indecisives—they were swept up by the momentum of the now goal-oriented.

The clicking of the pen has ceased. Principal Ryker appears to have stopped breathing. His piercing eyes blink once. It's the only sign that he hasn't joined the ranks of the inanimate objects in the office, which have been offering their tsk-tsks during most of the conversation, the pen included.

With each passing moment, Tony feels more and more like an idiot. More like a naive and clumsy amateur. More like one of Ryker's first-year teachers. Tony has long forgotten about asking the principal which programs would be affected by testing all students, whose purse would be forced to start a diet—not to mention, who'd be outraged. All he wants to do now is escape the office, and maybe lick his wounds before his first class starts.

Ryker finally speaks, and not too kindly. "Mr. Avery, just because a student wants to take the test—just because a student 'signs up,' as you put it—that doesn't magically give that student the ability to pass it. As their teacher, you're supposed to be able to determine who's likely to pass, but more importantly, who's likely *not* to pass. You're supposed to know your students." His eyes become two horizontal slits. "Do you know your students, Mr. Avery?"

Tony listens to the *Do I care?* song again before responding. "I thought my job as a teacher was to teach," he says, not caring the least whether or not he sounds sarcastic. "Not to tell fortunes or predict the future."

"How can you teach if you don't know your students?" snaps Ryker, his voice suddenly rising just below a shout. "All other teachers in this school *know* their students, Mr. Avery. That's one of the many characteristics of a good teacher—*you know*—getting to know your students might—*you know*—be helpful if you expect to teach them. But it seems to me that instead of taking the time to assess your students accurately, you have opted to simply test them all," he says, waving his arms in the air. "Well, as with any school, Mr. Avery, Lincoln High has to adhere to a budget—something teachers don't really have to concern themselves with. That's something that constantly looms over *my* head."

Ryker pauses to take a deep breath, and he clicks his pen a few more times as he gropes for the most effective wording. "I told you that, on average, teachers recommend around ten or so of their students," he continues. "Well, of that bunch of hopefuls, only about seventy percent of those actually pass. In other words, Mr. Avery, only the best of the best—or maybe the luckiest of the lucky—seem to be able to pass the AME test. What that means, Mr. Avery, is there are only ten or so of *your* students who might have what it takes to pass. Certainly no more than fifteen, or perhaps twenty, and that's probably pushing it a bit. But you don't really know, do you?" He gives Tony an intense glare. "Your job is to locate that handful of students and submit their names as soon as possible."

Tony folds his arms, but doesn't make eye contact. "I don't understand. Isn't it my job to increase the percentage? Isn't it my job to turn students who can't pass the test into students who can? I don't mean to sound—I don't know—self-righteous? Is that how I'm coming across? Like some wet-behind-the-ears . . . rookie?—who's out to save the world? If so, it's certainly not my intention, but am I that far off to assume that—"

"Mr. Avery, you're skating on thin ice as it is," Ryker warns. "I suggest you tread lightly."

Ryker's words cause Tony to lose his train of thought as he realizes the meaning behind them; there's more to this meeting than just the AME test. He looks directly into Ryker's eyes, not knowing what he's really searching for. "What do you mean?" he asks. His voice sounds somewhat parched. He could really use a glass of water.

Ryker settles back in his chair. "I've been informed of your supposed preparation antics," he says, more relaxed than he's been since walking into the office. "I must say, I find it extremely difficult to understand how you expect your students to pass the AME when you don't even expect them to use correct grammar—something the AME will definitely be looking for. Students need to have a strong command of English to do well on the test. Tell me, Mr. Avery," he continues, leaning over his desk, his voice almost a whisper, "how can they possibly pass a test that leans heavily on English skills when you insist that they use anything *but* English?"

Tony is dumbfounded. Who's been talking to Principal Ryker about him? His mind swarms with possibilities. It could be anyone. A student. A parent. A teacher. *Anyone.* He barely finds his voice. "I'm not—I mean, it's not like that. I teach them English. I'm not . . . sabotaging their chances for—it's not *like* that," he stammers, caught off-guard by a wave of frustration, confusion, and doubt.

Ryker moves in like a bloodthirsty prosecutor. "You didn't tell your students to embrace bad grammar? That there's nothing wrong with the way they communicate? That bad grammar is just as good as good grammar?"

"Yeah, but we were—I didn't mean it like that—it's not bad

grammar, anyway—but that's not what—"

"Mr. Avery, are you saying that you—an *English* teacher—don't know the difference between good English and bad English?"

Tony doesn't speak just yet. He fears what words and phrases his anger and frustration may concoct.

Principal Ryker takes his silence for something else: submission. And he considers Tony's anguished expression with sudden pity for his new teacher. "Don't worry yourself too much, Mr. Avery," he says, in his best attempt at a comforting voice. "You're a first-year-teacher. You're allowed your share of . . . misjudgments." He places the pen in his pocket. "As I've stated, you have enough time to locate those students who—"

"If it is at all possible, I'd like all of my students tested . . . please," says Tony, flatly, enraged eyes boring a hole in the top of the principal's desk. Then, making eye contact with the same intensity, he asks, "Is there anything else?"

For a second, Ryker seems to toy with the idea of a staring match before he speaks. "As you wish . . . Mr. Avery," he finally says, in a terrible, foreboding tone. Then he clasps his hands, leans forward, and props his elbows on his desk. "But know this, I will make a complete and thorough example of you when this is over, well beyond the typical I-told-you-so's. And let me add that heeding good advice will only help you in future—"

A desperate knock at the door startles them. The principal's expression reveals just how unusual the interruption is. "Yes—come in!" he barks.

The door flings open, and Dean Phillips stands in the doorway with an injured look on her face. "Mr. Ryker, sir. I'm sorry to disturb you, but—your radio was off and—well, sir—I—in the back of the school . . . there's something you should see . . . sir," she says, hastily searching for appropriate words, while her eyes dart back and forth from the principal to Tony.

The principal grabs his radio and storms out of his office, saying nothing more to Tony. Dean Phillips and Tony are on his heels as he marches his way to the back of the school. A crowd of students has gathered around the back corner of the building. Laughing is heard, but it dissipates upon their arrival, and the students clear a path for their principal.

Ryker clenches his fists and looks over his shoulder at Dean Phillips. "Have the custodians been notified?" he asks, his voice suddenly soft and tired.

Dean Phillips nods. "Yes, sir. Mr. Moore is on his way."

The principal walks back inside, not saying another word to anyone. Tony, Dean Phillips, and the students continue gawking at the message scrawled on the wall with neon green spray paint.

PRINCIPAL RYKER IS ONE STUPID NIGGER THAT NEED TO BE SHOT!

Normally, such an act encountered by two African-American males would cause their kindred spirits to bond, the way countless others have been forced to bond throughout the darker side of America's history. And although Tony realizes that being a black principal must be challenging enough for Ryker, even without such malevolence, he cannot empathize with the principal right now. At the moment, he's drowning in the sudden realization that he won't be staying at Lincoln High. The worst part, what really hurts the most, is the fact that he still cares. He feels it, somewhere deep down, like an itch he can't scratch. But to hell with the itch, he's leaving anyway.

And the song *Do I Care?* goes Platinum.

Chapter 29

Somebody really has it in for the principal, but it appears that no one around here knows who that somebody is. The message is a pretty mean one, but I'll bet the principal's angrier about the "nigger" part more than anything. Wonder what he'd do if someone slipped a copy of the dictionary's definition under his office door?

People are already mumbling about possible suspects. For some reason, I find myself standing here, not exactly mixed in with the crowd, trying to look innocent, but how in the hell am I supposed to stand here and do that? If I'm watching, maybe I'm watching my handiwork. If I don't watch, maybe I don't want people to see the guilt in my eyes. If I walk away, maybe the guilty could be trying to leave the scene of the crime before he's noticed.

So, not knowing what the hell to do with myself, I sort of stand here and fidget with my duffle bag. That's when Mr. Avery finally notices me. He doesn't look at anybody else after noticing me, and he walks over to me with an expression that says he's figured out something, and for a second, he's just another teacher again. But the feeling goes away when he tries to smile at me as he gets closer—he actually tries to smile. I can tell that the wall has really got him down, but he tries to smile at me anyway. That says a lot about him as a person. It also tells me he doesn't suspect me. That makes me feel all the more sorry for him and the principal. I can tell by Mr. Avery's expression that they're probably pretty good friends, and that nothing would make him more happy than to find who wrote that stupid shit on the wall.

"Good morning, Kenny," he says to me.

"Good morning, Mr. Avery," I say back to him, but I want to say a whole lot more. I want to tell him I feel bad about what's on the wall. I want to tell him I know how he feels—at least, I think I do. I don't know what it's like to be treated a certain way because you're a black African-American, but I *do* know what it's like to be treated a certain way because you're fat, because you're different. And I want to tell him that. I also want to tell him that if it wasn't for him, I wouldn't be friends with Marcus and Roland, that now we're pretty much insepara- ble. All of this and more runs through my head. All of the ways I want to say thank you to this teacher—this *person*—but all I say back to him is "Good morning," which isn't nearly enough, but I've never really been the type to express myself. I'm not *used* to expressing myself, and I'm sure as hell not used to having someone who'd listen.

"Nothing like a little drama to start the day," he says to me, but he looks back at the wall when he says it. Like he's thinking of something else entirely.

I don't know what to say, so I just say, "Yeah, nothing like it. . . ." I'm so pathetic sometimes.

"You know, Kenny, I'm going to see your mom today," he says, as if I could forget such a thing. "But you're not going to be there, right? Your mom said you have karate lessons on Mondays, Wednesdays, and Fridays. I wanted to come on a Tuesday or a Thursday, but she insisted on one of your karate days."

He says this sort of in passing, like he really doesn't care whether I know or not, like he's only trying to start up a conversation about whatever, but he's still looking toward the wall. He has no idea that Mom never likes me to be around when it comes to me. She used to hate the meetings at my other school that included me. I wouldn't say anything, which was fine by her, but then the counselor or the teacher or the dean or somebody would ask me some kind of stupid question, usually about my attitude or goals or something else I'm supposed to be so concerned about. They'd put me right on the spot, placing all my concerns right there in the room, and I could feel the rage growing inside Mom. I would answer with the shortest response possible, but she doesn't like hearing me at all. Nothing I do is right, and that goes double for what I have to say.

"It *was* karate, right?" he asks, then looks right at me this time. I wouldn't believe me either.

"Yeah, the classes last until kind of late," I say, which isn't really a lie because they do last kind of late. I'm just not in them anymore. I'm with Marcus on those days, but I don't think I can tell him that.

He waits for a second before he says anything else. It's like the sign on the wall really bothers him or something. He looks at the people standing around the wall, and then he looks back at me. "Did you read *Roots* by Alex Haley?" he asks suddenly. His question is so out of place that it takes a moment for me to register what the hell he just asked me.

"No," I finally say.

He gives me a blank face, the kind a person might give you when you've told him a stupid joke or something. Then he nods and stares back at the crowd. Now, everyone's watching the janitor as he cleans the wall with what looks like paint thinner.

"It's funny how I'm actually surprised you haven't read *Roots*," he says with that half smile again. "I mean, *A Lesson Before Dying*? *The Color Purple*? To put it bluntly, Kenny, not many fifteen-year-old white boys decide to read some of the books you've read, not without them being assigned, and even then. . . ."

I can't really tell if he's complimenting me or not. If he is, I really don't deserve it. I end up reading mostly what Mr. Farley gives me, even those I don't like. Every now and then, I'd pick one for myself, but Mr. Farley always has one already waiting for me pretty much every week I see him. So, yeah, I read a lot of different junk. What else am I supposed to do at home? Sure as hell don't wanna be caught lounging in front of the television when Mom gets home. It wouldn't be a good thing to be watching the tube when Mom finds a chore I messed up.

I shrug. "It's no big deal, really. I read all kinds of stuff."

"That's just it, Kenny. You seem to read across the board, and that's very rare for adults—not to mention, someone *your* age." Then he glances at his watch. The bell's going to ring in a couple of minutes. Then he says, "I don't know what to be impressed with more, Kenny— the range of your reading or the insight of your writing."

To this, I don't know what to say, but I don't think he's really expecting me to say anything. He sounds like he just wanted to talk and for me to listen.

"See you second period, Kenny," he says, putting a hand on my shoulder. I see the sadness as it grows back on his face.

"Writing's a lot easier with you," I say before I know I'm saying it.

He stops and tilts his head a little bit. "How do you mean?"

"You let us write about what we think," I tell him. "It's easier to figure out what I think than it is to figure out what a teacher *thinks* I should think."

He thinks about it for a split second and then says, "I know what you mean."

As I watch him walk off, I can't help smiling a little because I know he really does understand. I hope everything goes well with Mom. I just know I should've told her about him being a black African-American and everything, but she'd probably blame it on me. I'm not exactly sure what they can possibly talk about, but I know Mr. Avery is looking for a way to get me out of Lincoln.

Funny. All this fuss to get me out, and I don't really want to go.

SUSPICION ROSE WITH EACH CLASS PERIOD that passed. For the entire day, school was plagued with the Whodunnit question. Every teacher had their list of possibilities, even Tony. But for the rest of the day, he kept the names of Corey, Jarek, Jacob, and a few others to himself and conducted all of his classes as if nothing happened. In fact, after spending the first half of his planning period brooding over his encounter with the principal, he spent the rest of the day contemplating his meeting with Kenny's mother—his first parent-teacher conference.

As a student-teacher, he had the opportunity of sitting in on a meeting between Mrs. Lowell and the parent of one of her "unmotivated" students. That meeting showed firsthand what Mrs. Lowell had professed all along—parents can be overprotective and defensive. Many see the meetings as an assessment of their parenting skills. For the most part, if *they* didn't request the meeting, they didn't want the meeting. Mrs. Lowell also told him that, as a teacher, you should try to be as reassuring as possible, and that the student's performance—not character, personality or upbringing—should be the focus of the discussion.

When Tony called Pamela Houston, he could hear her suspicion and dread turn to relief as he explained the nature of the call. As their brief conversation came to a close, she seemed eager to meet with him, and her eagerness helped alleviate some of his own anxieties.

As he pulls up to the house wearing the address given to him, some of those same anxieties try to reclaim the throne where confidence now reigns, but to no avail. Tony has visualized knocking on the door, introducing himself, offering a handshake and a kind word more than a dozen times. He is more than ready for this, even without the home field advantage of his classroom or one of Lincoln's conference rooms. This is a positive meeting, a walk in the park.

He admires Pamela's Acura as he walks up the driveway, and as he glances around at the various houses, he can't shake the feeling that he's been in this neighborhood before. He has a weird sense of deja vu. He doesn't see their neighbor, Tonya Jacobson, staring at him from the corner of her house.

"Hi you today?" she says in a casual manner.

Tony's eyes dart in her direction. "Fine." He pauses halfway up the driveway. "Is this where the Houstons live?"

"Yeah, dass it," she says, motioning toward the house.

"Thank you," he says, nodding.

He feels the weight of the neighbor's eyes as he makes his way to the front door. He rings the doorbell and glances back at the neighbor, who still watches him with curiosity painted on her face. The sudden clack of a deadbolt lock diverts his attention to the door. He swallows before the door opens, takes a look at Pamela Houston, and swallows again. He recognizes her immediately. Even dressed in loose-fitting, semi-professional clothing, even without the thick layer of makeup, even without the confederate jacket-wearing Watcher by her side, Tony would recognize The Floozy from the Ranch House restaurant anywhere.

Miraculously, he manages to keep the frown on his face from reaching his voice. "Are you Pamela Houston?"

"Yes," she says, a chill in her voice—she recognizes him as well. "You Kenny's teacher?" she asks incredulously. "The one I talked to over the phone?"

"The one and the same," says Tony. Suddenly, he smiles at the sinister humor of the situation.

Unfortunately, his smile splashes Pamela with a wave of resentment and revulsion. She folds her arms and stands steadfast in the doorway. "What's this all about, anyhow?"

Tony wipes his smile away. A part of him wants to leave, just forget about the whole thing, but he wears the cloak of a teacher now, and even though teachers don't recite anything resembling the Hippocratic Oath, he feels something tugging at him, convincing him to finish what he's started. "Like I said over the phone," he replies with a shrug, his face now stoic. "I just want to help Kenny. I don't believe he's supposed to be at Lincoln."

Pamela takes another quick look at Tony from head to toe. "Come on in," she says, with uncertainty dangling from her voice.

Tony steps through the threshold, and for the next following minutes, he's astounded by how easily he makes leeway by complimenting Pamela's neighborhood, her car, her house, and especially her son. She actually relaxes a bit. She even lies to Tony about Kenny, expressing how much he likes him as a teacher, when Kenny's actual response to her question about Tony was a simple shrug, followed by a not-so-enthusiastic "He's alright."

They eventually make their way to the dining room table, where Tony lays out his hunches about Kenny's particular situation. "I just don't think it's a coincidence," he says. "Kenny was diagnosed with the aptitude that makes him a prime candidate for Lincoln High, but during the same week of his run-in with Logan Ellis, the boy he injured prior to his transfer to Lincoln."

Pamela shakes her head. "He hit that boy with a damn book, for crissakes. He's always fight'n like that—just out of the blue, he'll be all over somebody."

"Well, I have reason to believe he was provoked," Tony admits, "but that's neither here nor there. I think it wasn't so much of *what* he did as it was *who* he did it to."

She eyes Tony peculiarly. "What do you mean by that?" she asks.

"I don't know whether you know this or not," he continues, "but Logan Ellis is Susan B. Anthony's all-star athlete. He's very valuable to them in more ways than one. It's possible that retribution may have called for more than Kenny's suspension for a few days, especially if Logan's parents considered moving him to another school. At least on paper, losing a Logan Ellis would've been more devastating to them than losing a Kenneth Houston."

Pamela folds her arms indignantly. "Those sons-of-bitches. I had—I'm sorry, Mr. Avery—it's just. . . ."

"That's quite alright. Of course, all of this is only conjecture, but I don't think that's going to really matter in the end."

"What do you mean by that? Conjecture . . . ?"

"I'm sorry?"

"What's the conjecture you're talkin' about?"

"I'm just saying that what *I* think won't really matter in the long run. What it's going to come down to is Kenny's miscalculated aptitude and faulty assessment tactics. In short, I think Kenny's been receiving poor grades because of his conduct more so than his ability, and that's not enough to get him into Lincoln."

Pamela frowns incredulously, as if Tony has just licked the table. "Well I'll be goddamned. You mean to tell me ya'll—that some teachers git away with stuff like that? How in the hell can you—can *they* give him a bad grade because of fight'n?"

Tony holds back a grimace. "Unfortunately, it's not totally unheard of. Some teachers are very open about deducting points for things like forgetting to write your name in the right spot, not answering questions with a complete sentence, writing in green or red ink instead of black or blue—and yes, for discipline."

"Those sons-of-bitches," whispers Pamela through gritted teeth. "I always knew they weren't givin' it to me straight. And that principal that he had, I could always tell he was a tricky little bastard, comin' at me with all those fancy words and letters like ADH and whatever. That tricky little bastard," she repeats as she taps her knuckles on the table. "And so you think Kenny's smart enough to pass this AME test and get out of your school?"

"Yes," he says, a little surprised that she doesn't know this for herself. "Kenny is . . . unusually well-read for a fifteen-year-old. I'm amazed that no one has realized the kind of head he has on his shoulders." Then Tony thinks to himself, *You included.* How can a parent be so clueless about her own child? How many other parents place their children's education and future completely in the hands of total strangers, never deciding to follow up on their child's progress until their parental neglect comes back to haunt them?

Another question that loiters in Tony's head is how Kenny can possibly be so well-read in a house that doesn't sport even the smallest of bookshelves. In fact, he hasn't seen a single book since he's walked through the door, not even a magazine.

"I've seen him readin' stuff every once in a while," Pamela says, trying to sound convincing. "School books and stuff, I guess. He definitely knows how to read."

Tony manages to conceal his contempt for the parent who sits before him. "He reads a lot more than school books—I can tell you that. From Alice Walker to Richard Wright to Ernest Gaines. But he's into other authors, too—Melville, Steinbeck, Robert Cormier, Jane Austen. He's read *Jane Austen.* His range is absolutely uncanny."

Pamela looks at Tony with glazed eyes, as if he's slipped into a Swahili dialect. She doesn't recognize the names, but she gathers that they are probably writers of books. "He definitely reads sometimes," she manages to say. Suddenly, she feels a little uneasy and a little—what? Out of her element? Like a stranger sitting in on a conversation about someone she's seen, but never met? She ignores the feeling and asks, "So if you think he'll pass the test, what's the problem? He'll be back at his other school next year, right?"

Tony nods. "Absolutely, but the thing is—and I only found this out only recently—he'll be taking a piece of Lincoln with him. You see, his attendance at Lincoln will be on his permanent record. Point blank—from what I'm told—that's not a good thing if you're trying to shine academically. It's like having a stain on your record."

"Those sons-of-bitches. Guess they forgot to tell me that part," she says, looking like she could use a cigarette. "So what can we do about it?"

"You'll have to challenge their original decision to send him to Lincoln."

"I tried to do that to start out with, but they told me it was gonna help him get his grades up. Hell, how was I supposed to know his grades weren't supposed to be down to begin with?"

Tony suppresses a frown. "I did some checking. Many students come to Lincoln by mere recommendation, but that's not enough to get them there if a student doesn't want to go. A student or parent can officially challenge the decision. At that point—to prove themselves worthy of staying in their current school, so to speak—they can take the MRST. I've seen it. It's pretty simple. Most students should be able to pass it with little problem. I know for a fact that Kenny could've passed the MRST in his sleep."

"They never mentioned anything about no MRST to me."

"That's the thing," Tony explains. "As long as the parents go for it, schools can now get students out to Lincoln under a simple recommendation. Now, the test is rarely used. Most people don't know about the test, or that it used to be the *only* way into Lincoln."

"So, all I need to do is call his old principal and tell him to test Kenny?"

Tony twiddles his thumbs. "Well, I'm guessing that explaining how proper procedure wasn't followed—keeping you in the dark about the test—will be enough to keep his record clean, but they may want him to take the test anyway. But, like I said, I'm just guessing on this."

"And you're sure he can pass the MR . . . T test?"

Tony simply nods and holds in his disgust.

They partake in a bit more idle conversation about Kenny's karate classes, the weather, before Tony decides to display the appropriate time-to-go mannerisms. That's when the conversation suffers an unfortunate spill:

"Does your husband work nights?"

After Pamela registers the question, she immediately discards her smile. Stillness sweeps into the room. "I'm not married," she says in a soft voice.

"Oh . . . I thought. . . ."

Pamela shakes her head. "That was a friend of mine that you saw that night at the Ranch House," she says, avoiding eye contact. "Kenny's dad is passed away, killed some years back," she says with accusation in her voice.

Tony calls himself every name synonymous with *bonehead*. "I—I'm sorry." He knew of the first husband but thought she'd found a second.

An uncomfortable silence lingers in the room, but Tony has no idea what to say next. Something about Pamela's new expression has him staring at her face, his eyes refusing to blink. He's never seen such an expression of utter grief, the most accurate portrait of pain and loss a face could possibly produce.

Pamela lets the silence remain for a while, then turns her head toward the front door. "It happened right out there . . . right on the sidewalk," she continues, but it sounds like she's suddenly talking to no one in particular, her voice trailing. "Warren and my . . . my little girl," she says, still gazing toward the door. It seems as though she expects it to open at any minute.

Suddenly, Tony's body becomes rigid with a recollection of a similar incident. "Wait a minute. Did this happen around seven or eight years ago? He was walking a baby in a stroller? A guy lost control of—"

"Lost control my ass!" exclaims Pamela as she suddenly bores her eyes into Tony, her outburst startling him. He sees the tears well in her eyes. "That . . . that *man* . . . wasn't supposed to be in that car! I don't care what they say, he *stole* it—a thief and a murderer!" She stops suddenly, the way a sleeper might stop ranting upon waking from a terrible dream. "I—I'm sorry, Mr. Avery," she manages.

Tony tries to muster a soothing voice. "Really, it's alright."

Again, silence in the room.

Eventually, Tony clears his throat. "I'm going to head out, okay?" He feels the urge to place a hand on her shoulder, but knows he wouldn't dare. "I can't tell you how sorry I am for . . . for your loss." He stands, but she does not. She doesn't even look at him anymore. She keeps her eyes on the table top. "If you have any questions . . . or anything . . . feel free to contact me."

She gives him a quick nod but says nothing. Her eyes stay on the table.

Not knowing what else to say, Tony stammers another apology with a final good-bye, and lets himself out. He leaves Pamela seated at the table. As he walks to his car, he takes another glance around the neighborhood. How could he have possibly forgotten this neighborhood, this street? The story was constantly on the news and was the talk of the town for almost a year. The drama behind that unfortunate day spilled from televisions and into everyone's living room for months, and it seemed that every new week, another interesting fact unfolded that helped fuel the media frenzy.

The original story started as a simple tragedy—a man being struck down by a car while out walking with his daughter. Then, it was reported that both father and daughter were killed, and that the daughter was only a few months old, struck while in a stroller. Then, the story was further modified from his crossing the street to his being struck while walking on the sidewalk in front of his own house. Later, it was reported that the "twenty-seven-year-old-African-American-with-no-prior-record" who was driving had stolen the car. Then, further investigation revealed that the car wasn't stolen at all, that the "black assailant" was driving the car of his lover, a "white-twenty-three-year-old-mother-of-one," who was prominently shown on television, alongside the driver's picture, whenever possible.

According to the driver—who was dubbed by most communities as "The Home Wrecker"—she had advised him to take the car when her husband returned home unexpectedly. Further digging revealed that the husband not only caught them in the act, but had managed to break a chair over the head of The Home Wrecker. In fact, the husband had come close to killing him. How The Home Wrecker made it to the car with keys in hand was highly speculative, but he insisted during the trial that they had always planned for him to take the car if the husband ever came home early, and that she would try to detain her husband while he got away. However, in court and under oath, the wife denied all knowledge of such a claim, and she was most convincing, considering she did *not* attempt to detain her husband.

Unfortunately, as The Home Wrecker sped off, the husband stood in the center of the road, Luger in hand, and squeezed off four rounds—two of which made their way through the back window, reportedly startling The Home Wrecker, who testified that it caused him to careen involuntarily onto the sidewalk, where a man with a stroller was standing.

How could Tony forget such a year? That year, racial tension was like a thick fog that settled on the communities of Jacksonville, as well as those communities found in St. Augustine, Callahan, Keystone Heights, and other surrounding areas. That year, no matter how strong the winds of sanity blew, the fog continued to choke the voice of reason and subdue many acts of brotherhood. Dissension flourished.

Inside the house, still seated at the table, still staring at its top, Pamela deals with her own brand of a recently jogged memory. She was standing in the yard, only a few feet away from the spot where

Warren and Amanda were struck by the car. At least, that's what was reported. She is the only one who knows the entire truth—that she was walking alongside Warren. Father, mother, and the precious baby daughter coming back from a stroll around the block.

More truth pushes its way into her memory.

She was pushing the stroller.

She was the first to see the car.

What happened after that wasn't her fault. Pure instinct, nothing more. It was her instinct to scream in horror. It was her instinct to leap out of the way. It was her instinct to save herself.

Just instinct.

And from the safety of their front lawn, she watched helplessly as Warren's instincts told him to place his arms around the stroller in a protective embrace, as if he knew that the only thing he had time to do was hug his daughter one final time. For Pamela, her instinct meant her salvation—for Warren, his doom.

It's this image of Warren embracing the stroller that causes Pamela to rise from the table, stagger toward the kitchen, and fetch a bottle of vodka. For a moment, she holds the bottle in one hand, reading the label for the first time. Then, without warning, she violently pitches it into the far wall. Glass shards fly, and alcohol sprays everywhere.

She buries her face in her hands and squats down onto the floor in a fit of uncontrollable sobs. After a few minutes, she dries her eyes. She rises to her feet. She collects her second bottle of vodka. She grabs a carton of orange juice and a glass. Then, she retreats to the seclusion of her bedroom.

Instinct wins again.

Chapter 30

Mom wasn't in a very good mood when I got home last night. As a matter of fact, the way she staggered from her room when I got home, I thought maybe she'd discovered something. Like my not going to the karate classes, or maybe my stash in the closet, or my black African-American friend, or even my talking to Mr. Farley, even though I know I've never told him much about me. All of the possibilities raced through my head when I saw her heavy-stepping out of her room toward me, hair sloppy, eyes red.

I had forgotten all about my most recent blunder.

"How come . . . ain't tell me he was nigger?" she asked me.

She had been drinking. Not the usual glass she might have during a weekday. Not the "calm my nerves" drink that helps her make it to the next weekend. This was different. Obviously, to her, last night *was* the weekend, but the drinking was even worse than that. It was more like the kind of weekend-drinking that has a holiday falling on a Monday. It was a Friday-of-the-weekend-when-Monday-is-Labor-Day kind of drinking.

It was bad.

Her words were slurred. "Nigger" was the only polished word that came out of her mouth. And she looked tired. Not the tired-of-me look, but tired of something else. I didn't know how to answer the question, but she didn't wait for one. She wobbled back to her room, shaking her head, as if my not telling her he was a nigger was the dumbest mistake I'd ever made.

I watched her return to her room, asking myself *Can Mr. Avery's being black do this? Would this happen if the Jacobsons set foot in our house too? And Marcus? Upset her like this?* But more than just angry upset, it was anger and something I still can't put my finger on.

I wanted to talk to her for the first time in a long time. Well, maybe not really talk, but I at least wanted to ask her what was wrong, ask her what else she felt besides the anger.

I was curious as hell, to tell the truth.

Normally, Mom would be more than happy to explain why she's mad about something, happy to give you all the answers you could possibly want—and then some. But last night, she gave no answers. Just a question—a riddle.

How come ain't tell me he was nigger?

And then what, Mom? What would you have done instead? Would you have told him not to come, even though you needed an angel sent down from heaven? Would you have hung up on him after calling him a nigger?—"nigger angel" or "angel nigger?" Or would you have met him on another day, when Hank could be around? *What?* What would you have done, Mom? Would you have been the alien or the impersonator?

More riddles.

When I walked in the classroom this morning, I couldn't tell whether or not Mr. Avery was affected by yesterday's visit, but he *did* give me a weird look when he said his hello. It was the look a person might wear when they know your dog was hit by a car, but they don't want to tell you yet. That irritated me a little, but I'm over it. I don't have a dog.

Now, Mr. Avery's going over ways we can respond to literature, but he doesn't care if it's literature or not.

"It's more like a response-to-what-you've-read type thing," he says, and then he sits on his favorite corner of his desk, and hands fly in the air.

"Lisa?"

"Can I write about somp'm I read in *Ebony?*"

"Yes," he says with a bored look. He already told us magazines are okay, but he passes up the chance to say something to embarrass her.

Rodney, a guy who smells like cigarette smoke all the time, jumps at the chance. "He said magazines, girl. Whey you been? Why'own chew go back ta sleep."

Lisa shoots Rodney the finger and says, "Why'own chew write about dis?"

We all laugh and carry on because it's kind of unexpected how punctual her comeback is. Mr. Avery lets it slide, probably thinking Rodney deserved it.

I already know what my paper is going to cover. I was initially going to write a response to Mr. Farley's "topnotch" *Wuthering Heights*. You see, in my opinion, Heathcliff was a punk. There's no woman in the world worth all the grief and suffering Cathy put him through. I might be able to understand it better if he was still a boy and everything, but he's supposed to be a man. Well, real men don't take shit like that in my opinion. No doubt about it, Heathcliff was a punk.

I was gonna write all about it too, but it started to irritate me, so I dropped the whole thing. Now, I'm writing about that diary they published on what Anne Frank went through during World War II and the Holocaust. In my opinion, I think Anne would be majorly pissed off if she knew everybody was reading her diary. At one point, she figured she'd write a book about what happened to her and her family and all of that, but I know damn well no teenager would want her business put out on every street in every city in every country on the planet. Sure, we'd like our stories told and everything, but we'd want to be the one to write what gets out, be the one doing the telling. That way, you'd know only what we want you to know. Not *everything*. So, my paper's going to be about invasion of privacy and public humiliation. Anyone who's read her diary knows what I'm talking about. No doubt about it, Anne would be fuckin' pissed to know we know what she didn't plan on us knowing.

After Mr. Avery finishes all he's got to say about the writing assignment and all questions have been answered, he asks us to be quiet.
Then, he grabs a sheet of paper from his desk, clears his throat, and
gives us the kind of smile a person might have after planting a nasty
note on your back. He's getting ready to read something to us, and
he looks like he can hardly wait to get it out. I don't think I've seen
a teacher who can look so anxious about school and still look casual
about it, like he's not forcing it. Makes us kind of excited about it too,
even though we don't know what the hell's about to go down. But we
don't get crazy about it. After all, it's still school, no matter how you
serve it up.

He fidgets with the paper for a second, and then sits back down on
his favorite corner of his desk. He's got some more talking to do. "I've
been getting a lot of grief from those of you who are poets in disguise,"
he says to us. I could really care less about poetry. "We're getting ready
to make the transition into poetry. In fact, by the beginning of next
week, we should be well into poetry."

Some of us groan a little, and I don't blame them. Poetry really is
stupid. Heart-bleeding shit about loving somebody who's not worth it,
or wordy drool about how pretty trees are or how blue the sky is. What
type of idiot stands around staring at a tree anyway? Robert Frost—
that's who. He wrote a poem about when he bitched over which road
he should take when he came across a fork in the woods. I say anybody
who stands in the woods looking at two paths, as if he's forgotten
where he was headed in the first damn place, has *got* to be an idiot.

"But before we really get into it," Mr. Avery says to us, "I want to
read this poem to you. I don't want you to write a paper about it. I don't
want you to try to evaluate it or decipher it. I simply want you to listen
to it—carefully. Just listen."

We don't say anything.

"I see nothing but blank faces," he says. "Can I get you people to
listen to this poem? Without comment? Without any of your moaning
and groaning? No smart remarks?"

Some of us giggle a little, but the whole class knows we'll give him the attention he's asking for. Most of us know how English teachers get about poetry or Shakespeare or whatever, but we like him. We'll listen.

"The title of the poem is *Hates*," he announces. Then he stands again, wipes the smile off his face, clears his throat, and reads the poem to us.

> I hate changing diapers;
> it's the worst thing in the world.
> I hate the size of my nose;
> it makes me look ugly.
> I hate two-faced people;
> it hurts when people are fake.
> I hate surprises;
> they usually hurt.
> I hate how we don't get enough choices;
> I still don't know what I want to do in life.
> I hate doing homework;
> I already got too much to do.
> I hate my old babysitter;
> she did things.
> I hate loving my boyfriend;
> I don't think he loves me.
> I hate English;
> I'm not good enough.
> I hate my daddy;
> sometimes he hits mama for no reason.
> I hate being poor;
> poor people get yelled at for losing lunch money.
> I hate the police;
> they killed my uncle.
> I hate not having a daddy;
> people supposed to have a daddy.

I hate not knowing stuff;
I always get tested on what I don't know.
I hate racism;
it makes people fight.
I hate growing older;
I don't want to be a grown-up.
I hate people who think they know it all;
nobody knows it all.
I hate having breasts;
you lose so much when that happens.
I hate being scared sometimes;
it's hard to get to sleep scared.
I hate my daddy;
he's in jail.
I hate I don't have a brother or a sister;
I can't make friends.
I hate not being married;
a baby needs a daddy too.
I hate people who use drugs;
if nobody bought drugs, they'd go away.
I hate school;
it makes me feel stupid.
I hate growing up;
you get treated better when you're little.
I hate being late;
I don't want to be pregnant.
I hate being called a minority;
I don't feel like a minority.
I hate English;
we write too much.
I hate having a baby sister;
she gets all of the attention.
I hate being asked what race I am;
it shouldn't matter.

I hate these assignments;
they don't make sense.
I hate my mama's boyfriend;
he tries stuff and she doesn't believe me.
I hate how we always fight each other;
somebody's going to pull a gun someday.
I hate my other teachers;
they hate me first.

I can't even begin to describe how quiet it gets when he finishes the last word. Normally, Mr. Avery would have something to say after presenting something new to us, but even he keeps quiet. He doesn't even look up from the paper, not at first. And the silence in the room gets louder and louder. It's a strange silence. It's as if a deep secret has been exposed, and if any person made a sound, that person would be accused of owning that secret.

No one expected our hates to end up as a poem, not even me. But I like it. I can relate to it. I understand it. I *felt* it. I can't say what it was I felt, but I felt it. I felt something. I felt everyone. I felt the authors of that poem. I felt me through others. Through their words. And some of the words comforted me. Told me I am not alone. And I still feel it. And maybe with sound, the feeling will go away. That's the kind of silence that's sitting in the room. Everybody's feeling it, and no one wants it to go away.

Mr. Avery eventually clears his throat, and the sound startles me. "I hope I've changed some of your minds on the power of poetry."

We don't say anything, but we all know the answer. We were wrong about poetry—some of it, anyway.

"I want everyone to know—"

TONY AND THE CLASS JUMP WHEN Principal Ryker, Dean Phillips, and a police officer storm through the door. Everyone knows why they are there because the principal has been on a school-wide manhunt ever since he read the writing on the wall. Everyone could tell that with the effort he was putting forth to find the perpetrator, it was only a matter of time—inevitable. But they had no idea the hunt would end here, that the guilty person was in their midst all along.

The three intruders glance around the room, ignoring the teacher. Tony glances at Jarek, Corey, and Jacob. All three are wide-eyed and frozen stiff with the rest of the class. A part of Tony hopes Corey had nothing to do with it, that Jarek somehow convinced Jacob, but that Corey insisted on doing the right thing, insisted on not being *mean*. But Corey looks as terrified as Jarek and Jacob, and Tony's heart aches as that fact seeps in.

Principal Ryker finally turns to Tony. "Sorry to disturb your class, but we've found him," he grunts, but he's obviously not sorry for the disruption. Then, back to the police officer, "Take him," he says, pointing to the back of the room.

The entire class watches in silence, eyes wide and unblinking, mouths partly open, as the police officer marches over to Rodney Coleman and stands next to his desk. "Please stand."

Rodney stands and tries to wear a look of strength, but it fools no one. Everyone can tell it's only a matter of time until he succumbs to the severity of his predicament.

"Turn around," says the officer, in a terrible routine-like voice.

As Rodney turns, his face contorts with defeat. He tried to leave with strength in his stride, with dignity in his step, but the handcuffs are too much. His sobs are heard even as they lead him down the hall.

After Tony recovers from the shock of the invasion, his eyes scan his class, and then, he looks at James Cotner. James is the only one not surprised by the intrusion. Tony feels his anger welling inside as James finds it difficult to look him in the eye.

"Look at me!" Tony barks. James manages to snap to attention while sitting in his desk. All eyes leave Tony and fall on him. "Why?!" Tony yells. "All I want to know is why, Powuh! *Why?!*"

James swallows hard. "It . . . It was uh joke," he stammers with a nervous shrug. "Rodney juss won'ted ta git back at 'im—dass all. Fuh real—it was juss uh joke."

Tony's roar travels down the hall. "Get *back* at him? For what? What could the principal have possibly done for Rodney to want to do something as stupid as that?"

James hesitates.

"ANSWER ME!"

James swallows again. "It what'n no secret about Principal Rykuh gitt'n ready ta git in yo' face about some uh da stuff you teach us," he says, softly, as if their knowing what the teachers, faculty, and staff know needs to remain a secret. "Almost everybody knew about it, Mr. Avery. Dey ain' doin' you right." He glances around the room. "We all know it." Then, back at Tony, "Rodney won'ted ta git 'im back." He pauses, takes a breath and then says, "We like you too much ta juss sit back an do nut'n, but like I said—it was juss uh joke."

Tony stands before them, dumbfounded. What the hell does a teacher say to this? "A joke," he finally murmurs.

He stares at James, expecting more, but James says nothing else. Then, Tony scans the classroom and all of the faces staring back at him. Many have worried looks that he's never seen before. He opens his mouth to speak, but pauses. Many of them would give anything to know what's going through their teacher's mind right now. Finally, Tony sighs and then speaks with a tired voice, his eyes closed, "I want everyone here to write a paper . . . that suggests some kind of practical joke . . . that's safe enough not to hurt anybody or get you carted off," he says, and then walks behind his desk and screams, "in . . . HANDCUFFS!"

Somewhere in the classroom, a sob escapes, but all eyes remain on their teacher. Tony collapses in his chair, shoves his face into his hands, and he doesn't look at the class again. No one says anything to anyone, not even when the bell rings and they slowly wade out of the classroom.

Tony stares down at the poem on his desk, and he thinks about all he's been through since coming to Lincoln High. Without thinking, he grabs a pen and writes "I hate" at the bottom of the poem, but nothing else comes to mind, even though the inspiration has seized him by the throat.

With his pen still resting on the bottom of the page, his next class filters in.

"Wha's up, Mr. Avery?" a student asks.

Tony waves a lazy hand, but he doesn't look up from the page.

He's waiting for the hate to go away.

Chapter 31

When we came back on Monday, it was really obvious that Mr. Avery hadn't gotten over the Rodney drama. All through the week, he tried to do his business-as-usual thing that he's supposed to do, being a teacher and all, but you could tell it was a front. He was still bothered. You'd think something like a student getting into a lot of trouble wouldn't upset a teacher so much. After all, practically every teacher at Lincoln was doing cartwheels up and down the stairs when they heard about Rodney. Obviously, Rodney's been a real pain in the ass for a lot of people, and they'd probably been hoping and praying for God knows what—a heart attack, a bolt of lightning, anything that would take care of their Rodney situation. Well, it seems that Rodney's arrest was in that pile of prayers. I must've heard "There is a God" from at least a half dozen teachers. Teachers throughout the school were acting like last Thursday, the day of Rodney's departure, should be declared a holiday. A *Good Thursday*. And all this week, they were still celebrating.

For Mr. Avery, Monday was Monday; Tuesday was Tuesday; and so on. In fact, all week, he conducted class with a sort of sadness behind all of his forced smiles and poorly rehearsed enthusiasm. As if he heard teachers' salaries were going to be dropped to minimum wage, but he was determined not to let it affect his lessons. Hard to believe that

Rodney's predicament could do all of that, but I'll never be one who can say I understand teachers.

On Monday, a few people brought papers they had written on their ideas for good practical jokes, but as usual, Mr. Avery wanted to hold off until he got enough papers in. More came in on Tuesday, but after a whole week's gone by, nobody seems to feel like they've taken the prize for having the best idea for a practical joke. To be honest, I didn't think Mr. Avery was all that serious about it, but he was.

I'm dead serious.

That's what he told Lisa after she was unfortunate enough to ask what many of us were already wondering, and he said it with a coolness that made his calm voice sound like a shout. There had been no other questions on Monday.

On Thursday, Marcus, Roland, and I thought seriously about coming up with a practical joke we could all participate in. We weren't too creative when thinking on our own, and we really did want to impress Mr. Avery with a good practical joke. We didn't care much for the extra credit. We would do it anyway. If the joke was good enough, maybe we could lift his spirits a little, bring a real smile back to his face.

It took a while to come up with something halfway decent. At one point, between the three of us, Marcus came up with the best one. He had the idea of inviting a few classmates over to his house for a video game party. Except he'd only invite people who didn't know where he lived. That way, he could have a group of guys standing behind him while he knocked on the door of a total stranger. Of course, before whoever's gonna answer the door actually gets to the door, Marcus would take off running without saying a word. And the way he figured, it would take the guys one second too many to finally put two and two together, and they'd be stuck with answering the questions of the person who answered the door.

It's funny when you think about how you'd feel standing outside someone's door answering their "Can I help you?" with "We came to play video games with our friend, but he ran off." It's even funnier if you imagine the person who answers the door as a guy holding a beer in his hand, looking at you as if you're trick-or-treating in February.

But one of the biggest problems with that joke is you don't want to be around when the person answers the door—and, you see, not being around makes it kind of difficult to write about how the joke went down. You'd think maybe you could choose a house with bushes or something you could jump behind, but that wouldn't really work because all the guys would simply point toward the bushes, and you'd have to stand up, looking like a dumb ass dork. And the more Marcus thought about it, the dumber the joke seemed. Eventually, we decided it wasn't even that funny.

After tossing all kinds of crazy ideas around in our heads, we finally came up with the idea to do a roadside prank. It took a while to iron out exactly what the prank should be, but once we worked out all the details, we decided to wait until Saturday, the day I leave home for the mall because The Hank comes a-callin'.

So, here we are pulling our stunt right on the side of I-95. A lot of travelers are yelling all kinds of obscenities because they don't like our joke, but we take notes on everything they say and do. We want our essay to cover everything down to the smallest detail so that everyone in the class, especially Mr. Avery, can actually imagine what it's like to do what we're doing right now. One guy even spits at us. This is going to be a great paper.

After we get used to the angry travelers and their wicked responses to our joke, we drift into conversations about school and such. We didn't plan on talking about school on such a sunny Saturday afternoon; it just turns out that way. It all starts with Marcus mentioning what I've been thinking all along:

"I thank Mr. Avery's g'own leave," he says out of the blue.

Roland and I look at him, but neither of us appears surprised or anything.

"I think you're right," I say.

Roland grunts something to let us know he agrees, and then a guy driving by in a Jeep yells something at us, and we all give him the same finger we've been giving all of the mean and ugly commuters. Nasty comments no longer distract us from our conversation, but our fingers have developed a reflex.

"I thought he was g'own be one nat lass uh while," continues Marcus. "But I'own thank he g'own hang—not no mo'."

I think about what he's saying, and then I add, "I've seen it before—my old school. You see it a lot with new teachers, but it can happen to veterans too, I guess." Nobody says anything, so I add, "It's not really his fault. I guess even veterans can mess up their pace once in a while, tire themselves out."

"Dass what I say," Roland chimes in. "He tired. Like he came out uh da star'd'n block too fass, an he done ran out uh steam uh somp'm."

Marcus and I shake our heads the same way people do after being told an acquaintance has cancer, and it's only a matter of time.

"It's uh damn shame when you thank about it," adds Marcus. "We supposed ta be able la put up wit da principal, right? Mattuh fack, we put up wit uh lot mo' dan nat strick nigguh. Mr. Avery ain' got it like we got it. Da way he star'ded out, I thought he'd be able la hang wit Lincoln no problem."

"He kine uh remine me uh Mr. Higgins," adds Roland. "Marcus, remembuh Mr. Higgins? All fired up? He came out wit all lat hype an stuff in his classes talkin' 'bout *knowledge is powuh* an all lat stuff? He ack like he was try'n na kick uh crack habit, like he juss got off dat pipe. Kenny, some days dat nigguh ack like he was ready ta walk own na ceilin'."

I give Roland a grin, but I'm always fascinated at how he says "nigger" around Marcus without hesitation, and how Marcus never even flinches. Marcus explained that it's important to drop the *r* sound, but I don't wanna start a nasty habit that I may not be able to quit. It's like Mr. Farley once said, *Don't grab hold of somethin' you can't let go.* But I think he was talking about cigarettes at the time.

"Yeah," says Marcus, "but Mr. Avery ain' come out all crazy like dat, Ro. Mr. Higgins ack like he ain' nevuh teach befo'."

"I'own thank he did," argues Roland. "Mattuh fack, I thank I remembuh somebody talkin' 'bout hi dat was his firs' time teachin'."

Marcus frowns at him with the frown that's especially for Roland. "Dat what'n his firs' time teachin'."

"Yes, it was, Marcus. I swear I heard dat."

Marcus thinks about it for a second, not sure whether Roland's telling the truth or trying to sound like he knows what he's talking about. Roland gets that way sometimes. Even I've developed that look for Roland, but I don't use it much.

"Well, I ain' suhprised if it was," Marcus finally says with a shrug. "But Mr. Avery ain' like no dumb ass Mr. Higgins, so I'own even know why you brought 'im up."

Marcus gets a little irritated with Roland, but it'll fade before you know it. Always does. Sometimes, listening to them talk about stuff reminds me of John Steinbeck's Lenny and George in *Of Mice and Men*. Roland is like Lenny, and Marcus is like George, even though George was white. In the book, George always got mad at Lenny, but the love was obviously there, even though George never once said it. Guys ain't supposed to say it, not to each other.

Roland doesn't say anything else.

A guy driving a Mercedes honks his horn at us and gives us the finger. We flip him back.

We've never really talked about Mr. Avery before, so I want to take advantage of this opportunity. I want to know more. "How long has Mr. Avery been at Lincoln anyway?"

Roland jumps in. "He juss came right befo' you did."

"Juss uh week befo' you," adds Marcus.

I give them my Roland look because it doesn't make sense for Mr. Avery to have been there only a week before me. It sure as hell didn't seem like it. I know what a week-on-the-job teacher looks like, and Mr. Avery was not it, not by a long shot.

Marcus notices my look. "Fuh real. He what'n nare but uh week befo' you came."

"Dat was da bad week too, Kenny," Roland adds. "Mr. Avery was trippin' nat firs' week."

Two guys in a pickup truck yell something at us that we can't quite make out, so we give them the finger to be safe.

"Mr. Avery was uh real Unca Tom nat week," says Marcus. "He was fuh *real* trippin'."

I've read *Uncle Tom's Cabin* by Harriet somebody, but I have no idea what Marcus is trying to say. Uncle Tom was a very religious slave. Whatever his master told him to do, he would do it because he believed that's what God expected him to do. Did Mr. Avery preach to the class at some time or something? Tell them a lot of stuff about God? Mr. Avery hasn't brought up God or anything like that since I've been at Lincoln. He doesn't seem much like an Uncle Tom to me. "You mean like the Uncle Tom from the book *Uncle Tom's Cabin*?" I ask Marcus.

He looks at me as if I just gave him a pop quiz, and his face goes blank for a second.

"Yeah, I guess so," he says. "Dey wrote uh book about uh Unca Tom?"

"Yes."

"You read it?"

I nod.

"Is it about some jive ass nigguh who done fuhgot whey he came from?" he asks.

Uncle Tom was a slave who was eventually taken away from his family, even though his owner said he would never sell him and separate him from his family. He was sold and taken far away from the only place he knew, the only place he could really call home. I don't think he would've been able to remember his way back home even if he had a map, so I nod again.

"Well, lass hi Mr. Avery was when he firs' got ta Lincoln," says Marcus. "One uh da bigges' Unca Toms you could evuh meet."

I still don't get it, but I don't want to sound ignorant, so I let it go.

"You gotta admit," says Roland, "he done straightened up pretty good since den."

Marcus nods, so I nod too.

"Ta be honest," continues Roland, seeing that we agree with him so far, "he 'bout one uh da bess English teachuhs I've had. 'Cept I'own like all lis homework we be doin'. But Mr. Avery awright if you ax me."

A lady goes by in a station wagon filled with kids, and she shoots us an extra mean glare. We stare back at her, but no one gives her the finger.

"All la good ones always leavin'," grunts Marcus.

He says it as though he's seen dozens of teachers like Mr. Avery. He probably has, but then again, black African-American teachers tend to favor black African-American students. At least, that's how it seemed to me in my old school. Now, I'm not so sure. There aren't many black African-Americans at my old school. Maybe they favor the minority in the class, regardless of whether the minority's black or white or whatever. After all, Mr. Avery kind of stuck up for me in the beginning—favored me. And I'm a minority even when I'm around nothing but white people. Maybe black African-American teachers look out for any type of minority because it's their instinct. Maybe they really know what it's like to be the fattest person in the class.

I'm thinking about all of this, so I have to ask, "Are all the good ones usually . . . not white?"

Roland and Marcus look at me as if I'm sprouting antlers and farting at the same time, eyes wide and faces scrunched. "I've never seen any other good ones—not like Mr. Avery," I quickly explain.

"Oh," they say with a little relief in their voices.

"I'own thank culluh got nut'n na do wit it," offers Marcus.

"Me neithuh," agrees Roland. "Long as dey care 'bout chew learnin' somp'm."

I was thinking that their idea of a "good one" was one who cares about you as a person. If a good one is simply one who wants you to learn, then almost all new teachers are good ones—at least, for the first few months. I've seen three rookies turn from good to bad, all in less than three months. It's like it takes a little time before the veteran teachers fill them in on who's who, which students to like and which to hate. Well, to me, Mr. Avery's a "good one" because he seems like the type of person who makes up his own mind, no matter what *Records* says about you. Personally, I've never met a good one until Mr. Avery, and he's starting to not be so good after all. Just better than the rest.

"I never thought Mr. Avery was the type to quit," I say, but I'm not really talking to them as much as I'm just thinking out loud.

"Who *did?*" says Marcus.

"Well, he ain' g'own yet, ya'll," Roland says. "It's still uh chance he might stay."

An eighteen-wheeler honks at us, but we can't see the driver's face, so we ignore it.

"He might," says Marcus. "He juss might."

I don't say anything. I'm not too big on hoping.

"I mean, he *did* go ovuh yo' house ta help you git out uh Lincoln," Roland says to me. "Dat ain' na kine uh stuff teachuhs who gitt'n ready ta dip end up doin'. What cha'll thank?"

Even though we hear Roland's forced optimism, Marcus and I don't respond to the question. Roland goes silent for a second as we watch the cars go by, not really looking at them, three minds momentarily someplace else. The sounds and smells of traffic are gone.

Marcus is the first to talk again. "Who he talked to anyway?" he asks me. "Yo' mama? Yo' daddeh? Uh bofe?"

I've never spoken of home to them. Even when I told them of Mr. Avery's intention to visit my home and help me leave Lincoln, I only spoke of his intention to visit and help. I didn't really speak of home, not once. "He spoke to my mom," I say, and I want to change the subject, but I'm still new at holding a conversation. I can't think of anything to say to get out of it.

"He shoulda talked ta bofe," adds Roland.

"He ain' talk ta yo' daddeh?" Marcus asks. "Seems like he woulda wont'ed da talk ta yo' *daddeh* befo' yo' mama. He ain' talk ta yo' daddeh?"

The question irritates me. I just told them who he spoke with. "No," I say, and before my attitude gets any worse, I say a little more. "My dad's dead." I don't say "passed away" or anything like that because that's not how it feels.

They stare at me.

I stare at the traffic, feeling more irritated because they keep staring at me. I'm nervous and feeling uncomfortable. I want to change the subject, but I don't know how. Everything that's on the tip of my tongue is about the stuff I don't want to talk about, waiting to come gushing out.

I swallow.

It's still there.

Marcus speaks first. "I ain' know yo' daddeh was dead."

I nod because it's the only thing I can think to do.

Marcus pauses, probably deciding whether he should say he's sorry or something stupid like that, the way people do when they find out someone only *you* knew is dead, offering their social reflexes, their on-the-spot concocted words of comfort and sympathy. "So, do you thank Mr. Avery g'own be able la git you out?" he finally asks me.

I shrug, even though I really want to thank him for not pushing it. "They seem to think I'll be gone after I take the AME test, but I hope I can at least finish out this year," I tell him, but my words come out kind of broken. My voice gives me away.

"Hi yo' daddeh died?" Rolands asks.

Lenny strikes again.

Marcus watches me intently because he probably wanted to ask the same question, but knew better. It's obvious he wants to know just as much as Roland does.

Three guys wearing University of North Florida T-shirts go by in a Volkswagen, laughing and pointing and cheering at us.

Roland waves.

Marcus smiles.

I just look—and *think*. Think hard. Think fast. Think through the cloud.

When they turn back to me, I open my mouth, and it all comes rushing out. I tell them about my dad and my sister being run over by a guy who stole a car in my neighborhood. I tell them about how he killed them when he drove the car on our sidewalk. I tell them how a stupid car wasn't worth the lives of a dad and a baby sister. I barely notice that I've raised my voice a little, and that I'm talking kind of fast, forcing it out, so that both can see it for themselves, that certain something that's been lodged in my throat for so long. And they silently stare at me as I cough it up.

I leave out the part about the driver being a black African-American. I guess it's because whenever I think of him, I think "nigger," and I don't care that I think "nigger." But I'm thinking "nigger" with Marcus standing next to me, and for the first time, it hurts that I'm thinking "nigger," but the hurt makes me angry because I want to keep the man who killed my dad, the man who made my life what it is today, a nigger forever.

The *nigger* that killed my dad.

The *nigger* that left me with Mom.

The *nigger* that's not a black African-American.

Frustration builds up inside me until my head starts throbbing. My eyes water, and they notice it, but they turn away and act like they don't. Marcus eventually says how sorry he is that my dad's dead, and I want to fuckin' scream. In my mind, I *am* screaming, and I can't stop.

MARCUS PLACES A HAND ON KENNY'S SHOULDER and the screaming in Kenny's mind stops abruptly, and the sound of the traffic returns. Kenny faces Marcus and Roland, and they look him directly in the eyes. Their eyes show their empathy. Their postures offer their condolences. Their facial expressions and their close proximity are the best they can do for Kenny, without actually attempting to give him a caring embrace, thus violating the all too familiar buddy code that tends to exist among young men, a code that finds its way into every generation.

Kenny wipes his left eye as a tear slides down his cheek. This, too, causes Marcus and Roland to adhere to the code, momentarily glancing away, which is the right thing to do. And then, suddenly, Kenny gives his two friends a slight smile after a small sniffle.

They smile back.

Kenny gives them a nod.

They nod back.

Words could never do what the exchange of their nervous glances and self-conscious smiles have done. *Never.*

Marcus gives Kenny a gentle shove before the three young men turn to watch the traffic for a few minutes, not saying a word.

Kenny breaks the silence. "This is going to be a good paper," he says, keeping his eyes on the traffic.

Marcus glances at Kenny, then back at the traffic, nodding. "Yep."

Roland speaks, but he doesn't take his eyes off the vehicles going by. "What we g'own do aftuh dis, ya'll?"

A pause.

"Let's go to the mall," Kenny says. "I usually go to the mall on Saturdays."

Marcus grins. "*Conflict?*"

Kenny shrugs. "We could, but there's somebody I'd like ya'll to meet, too."

They grow silent again, and another five minutes or so go by before Roland notices a police officer on a motorcycle making his way through the congested traffic and down the side of the shoulder.

Roland points and yells, "Police!"

Marcus and Kenny glance in the direction of Roland's outstretched arm, and then all three take off through the brush, escaping through an opening in the fence that runs parallel to the Interstate.

The police officer parks his bike on the side of the highway and picks up the large sign the three young perpetrators left behind. He frowns as he reads what has brought traffic to a crawl for nearly a mile.

ATTENTION: RUBBERNECKS!!!
THE REASON YOU ARE IN HEAVY
TRAFFIC NOW IS BECAUSE YOU
CHOOSE TO READ THIS SIGN!!!

The police officer looks in the direction of the perpetrators' escape route, and then back at the cardboard sign. Then, for another minute, the officer holds up the sign and waves at the traffic.

Protect and serve.

Chapter 32

Tuesdays suck. Thursdays aren't so hot either because, like Tuesdays, I have to be here working on the house and yard like a good little slave when Mom gets home from work. Still, at least Thursdays are closer to Fridays and Saturdays—Fridays being Marcus-and-Roland days, while Saturdays are now filled with Marcus, Roland, Mr. Farley, and Arcade Stadium. Tuesdays really suck.

At least I can get into my supplies before Mom gets home. I usually have about two hours before I hear her car pull into the driveway, which is good because being sprawled out on my bedroom floor like this, junk food everywhere, reading *Lord of the Flies* and munching on snacks, can't be filed under "Kenny's brightest ideas." But I have to nibble once in a while. Otherwise, these cookies, doughnuts, and candy bars would pile up and eventually go to waste. There's nothing worse than biting into a moldy doughnut when you're starving. When you're not so hungry, you'd catch the foul taste on the first doughnut, but when you're starving, you can get down to your last two before you'd notice it. But if you're *really* starving, what the hell, right?

On Mondays, Wednesdays, and Fridays, I've been eating at Marcus' house, for over two months now, but I still have to eat when I get home on those days, just not so much. Don't want Mom to think I'm eating someplace else. I know she's noticed me eating less, but she hasn't said anything, not one word of praise. Probably because she's also noticed that even though I appear to eat less, more of me is appearing. Oh yes, I've gained a few more pounds. Not really a lot, but enough to make her wonder. Maybe enough to make her want to do away with the refrigerator, but she needs it for her orange juice. So, I try not to stash too much stuff because I end up eating it, but I have to stash something away because—I don't know—just because.

Marcus is another problem. Turns out that he's an awesome cook. His mom taught him well. He said he had to learn everything a man usually avoids—how to cook, how to wash clothes, how to clean the house—because his mom said a man shouldn't have to depend on a woman, just like a woman shouldn't have to depend on a man. As soon as he said that to me, I thought about all the things Marcus does while his mom's working her second job. Marcus is more parent to Colin and Taneisha than she is. Hell, I've never even met the woman. She depends on Marcus for a lot of things. I guess she's gonna stop depending on him once he's a man.

Marcus doesn't like doing housework, but he's good at that too. He cleans as good as I would, and I don't even think his mom would get upset if she came home to a little clutter once in a while. Still, he doesn't clean half as good as he cooks. Not that I've eaten all his meals, but most of the food he cooks is better than what I've ever been used to. Mom doesn't cook much, and when she does, it usually involves the microwave or something straight out of a wrapper that you plop into the oven. Some of the food Marcus cooks is stuff I've never heard of, but it's still good. "Neck bones," "fatback," and "ham hocks" sound so gross, but it's a whole different story when you smell them.

Still, there *are* certain things I can't see myself sinking my teeth into. For instance, there's certain parts of a pig I won't touch with a cattle prod, but to black African-Americans, swine is divine. I mean, there are some things even Roland and his dad stay away from, and I don't blame them. For example, pig ears. I'll never eat another pig's ear. They didn't smell too bad when Marcus cooked them, so I tried one, after seeing how Colin and Taneisha were ripping into them, but I only took one. I bit down on it, and as my teeth sank through the skin, they eventually cut through something that felt like—I don't know, but it really grossed me out. I almost vomited right there on their kitchen table, but I managed to swallow it down. Marcus and Colin really cracked up that day. Taneisha gave me a motherly pat on the forearm, asking me if I was okay.

The day Marcus cleaned "chittlins" was the only day I didn't totally enjoy being at his house. They stink up every room, and they're the worst things I've ever seen a person eat—pig intestines. How a person can eat the pathway for pig shit, and not give it a second thought, will forever be beyond my comprehension. On that day, it was *my* turn to laugh at them as they ate. Marcus offered me an alternative meal—leftover fried chicken—but I was no longer hungry, and that was the truth.

I'll never eat a foot either—pickled or otherwise. But even Roland eats pickled pig's feet. And he doesn't even mind the strands of hair that are sometimes found on the knuckles. Too funny. Too gross.

I'm going to miss having Roland and Marcus as friends. (Hell, I'm gonna miss having friends.) We don't talk about it, but we all know that after we take the AME test tomorrow, we'll be officially prepped for segregation; I'll be back at my old school, and Marcus will probably be back at his. We're still worried about Roland. He still has serious trouble with his reading comprehension. He tries hard, but reading isn't anything you can really fix over a short period of time. It takes a while. All the years he's neglected his reading can't be made up the way we make up a hundred and eighty days of school in just three weeks of summer school. In summer school, people can give you a passing grade if they like you enough, but they can't give you ability. You have to get that on your own, and they've rigged it to where it takes ability to get out of Lincoln. The AME test wants ability. Not effort. Not attendance. Not personality. Not the cleaning of erasers.

It's kind of funny when you really think about how it works. You can be the best behaved, hardest working student in the school, who actually does well in all your classes, but if you fail the test, it doesn't matter that you're a model student. On the other hand, if you blow off every assignment given to you by every teacher and get on their bad side, but prove you already have the ability by getting a perfect score on the test, you still fail. Funny, right? Don't even try to figure it out. It doesn't have to make sense; it doesn't have to have a point. It just is. Is what? Senseless? Pointless? Of course it is, but that doesn't change the fact that it—still—just—is.

But Roland's not the only one having problems in English. There are others. Of course there are, but there's a rumor going around that all of Mr. Avery's students are under a microscope. There's not much detail, but everyone thinks it has something to do with the meeting he had with the principal. So, Roland and a few others are afraid they're gonna make something negative come Mr. Avery's way. We don't really know what it could possibly be. Maybe his salary is based on how many students pass. Maybe all teachers are paid that way, and we just don't know it.

Regardless, Mr. Avery has loosened up a bit. Not a whole lot, but he seems to be better than he was two months ago. The practical joke papers may have had something to do with it—at least, that's what a lot of people are thinking, but I think it was more. I don't think it was so much the papers. I think it was more the attitude everyone had toward making Mr. Avery feel better. A lot of us were trying to give him a joke that would put a smile on his face, and all of us have been on our best behavior since. It's like we're trying to help him survive whatever he's going through. Like we're pulling for him without knowing what it is we're pulling for. Still, it was good to see him happy again.

Hard to believe it's been two months since that highway joke. Our paper was eventually voted number two. Number one was a joke from another class involving a car wash. When Mr. Avery finished reading what we had titled *Life in the Dunce Lane*, the whole class laughed, cheered, and applauded us. Mr. Avery gave us a thumbs-up sign and a genuine smile. He liked the joke. Of course, we left out the part about the police trying to arrest us. That cop must've been madder than a cat getting a bubble bath when he found out what was holding up traffic. My heart hadn't beat that fast since . . . well, anyway, it was really beating fast. The last thing I needed was for Mom to hear I was in jail. Mr. Avery wouldn't have felt too hot either. Knowing him, he would've blamed himself.

A lot of people are still nervous about the AME test tomorrow. Yesterday, Mr. Avery tried to deal with all of the last minute questions. A few of us still have problems with stuff like thesis statements and transitions. Call it a coincidence that they're also the same few who've always griped about homework assignments on a regular basis, even about the ones that weren't going to be graded. But Mr. Avery never cares. If you ask a question—even a tired, stupid one—he'll give you an answer. It's the rest of the class that can make you feel like an idiot, with all of the groans and exaggerated sighs that can accompany a question about thesis statements or transitions, concepts Mr. Avery has covered at least a hundred times. Even Richard Brigman, the guy who sleeps half the time because of his night job, has grasped most of the concepts. Mr. Avery does more than simply cover a lesson; he beats it into the ground.

I don't want you to learn it, he keeps telling us about everything he teaches. *I want you to master it.*

He said we don't need to be taught something over and over. Things should be taught only once. Then, after we've been taught something, the training should come next. He gave us the example of how a professional boxer is first taught how to box, but after the technique, the training always follows. And a boxer has to keep doing it over and over if he's going to master it. So, we never really leave anything that Mr. Avery has taught. While he's teaching something new, we're still in training on lessons long gone.

And the way he spoon-feeds it to us is what Mr. Farley would call "bringing the hay down so the mules can get to it." Mr. Avery doesn't teach like you're already supposed to know a whole lot. In fact, he teaches like you're stupid and know very little, which is good because a lot of people really aren't into that raising of the hand bit for clarification.

Today, Mr. Avery gave us our final pep talk before taking the AME test. Tension was high, even though he tried to lighten the mood with a few of his usual lame remarks that only he thinks are funny. It was obvious that even *he* was worried about the test, and that worried us even more. But what can we do except what he's taught—I mean, *trained* us to do?

Well, Mom'll be home in an hour or so. I still have time to eat the watermelon she has allowed me to slice open today. This is her new food fad. She probably figures if I eat watermelons, it can't be too far from simply drinking a lot of water. Of course, this idea comes from the alien who probably couldn't name the food groups. I'll slice an extra small slice for myself, and then put the rest back in the fridge. That way she'll know I'm not overzealous about watermelons. But I'm still gonna have a few more doughnuts, another candy bar, and rinse everything down with another tall glass of Kool-aid. I call it brain food for tomorrow's test.

Chapter 33

PAMELA HOUSTON HEADS FOR HOME early today. She left work two hours before quitting time by playing the not-feeling-well card. Now, she's tearing through traffic, tempting the travel gods, rushing home to deal with her son. She doesn't even see the traffic—not the cars, not the four-by-fours, not the big rigs. All she sees is Kenny, the son who has been playing her for a fool.

She is furious.

Yesterday, after work, Pamela got a glimpse of her ex-friend, Beth Travers, leaving for the parking lot with the rest of the crowd. From habit, Pamela almost called out to Beth, but she remembered they were no longer friends. So, Pamela simply watched Beth navigate her way through the four-thirty-whistle stampede with the mastery of a fifteen-year veteran of Florida Transtech, the telemarketing giant of the Southeast.

It was then, watching Beth leave with a flood of strangers, that Pamela realized they were never really friends. They had never visited each other's houses, never spoken to each other at odd hours over the phone. In fact, other than the phone call to Beth's husband to get the details on the karate lessons for Kenny, they had never attempted contact outside the walls of their workplace.

No, they were never friends, but whatever they were, they weren't any longer. And Pamela knew they had been something. She knew of Beth's first husband who broke parole. Beth knew of Pamela's deceased husband and child, and Beth never asked too many questions about what happened. Pamela knew of Beth's four-month affair two years ago. Beth knew of Hank and their weekend rendezvous.

They were never like sisters, but they were never like strangers on a crowded elevator either. They used to be like any two people who found they had a few things in common—not necessarily bosom buddies, but, at the very least, up to date with each other, always familiar. Indeed, they shared the way friends might share, but they weren't friends. Still, they had been *something* at one point, and that something disappeared. So, yesterday, as Pamela lost sight of Beth in the afternoon rush of people, after having second thoughts about calling out to her ex-whatever, she decided she'd at least try to find out what happened to their semi-relationship. Something didn't seem quite right. But instead, she thought, *Tomorrow. I'll ask her tomorrow.*

This morning, Pamela went to work determined to find out why her ex-whatever was avoiding her. She saw Beth twice before lunch, but both times were from a shouting distance, and Pamela didn't want to shout. She didn't want to call attention to their conversation. She didn't know why, but felt it better if they talked without much chance of being overheard. When lunchtime came, Pamela decided that the best time and place to talk would be in Beth's cubicle, right after lunch. So, a few minutes before lunch was over, she stole away to Beth's work area, where she stood and waited by her desk, resisting the urge to fold her arms and tap her foot.

As she waited for her ex-whatever to return from lunch, she noticed that Beth had, yet again, replaced some of her many photos of Michael, her cherished son. Beth was always very proud of Michael. Of course, she had a right to be. Beth and Wayne Travers had a perfect son, one who did wonders for their image as parents.

Five years ago, Pamela didn't mind how much Beth carried on about her twelve-year-old wonder boy, who was about to make brown belt in his father's karate dojo. She didn't mind how much Beth went on about how fit and strong Michael was turning out to be. Five years ago, Pamela wasn't bothered by all the new photos Beth would bring to work, usually on a monthly basis, to ensure her Michael shrine was always as current as possible. Pamela didn't care because she also had a son to speak of, and even though Kenny didn't compare to Michael—what son could?—Kenny was nothing to be ashamed of. Even though Kenny couldn't score five touchdowns in a single game or do a "jumping spinning crescent kick," he was a good boy.

However, the constant comparisons that were never really comparisons—Pamela never spoke much of Kenny—eventually got the best of her. She began to tire of all the Michael jubilations Beth served whenever their conversations stumbled into the "what's new on the home front" category. Eventually, Pamela began to see her own son with new eyes. She began to notice that Kenny didn't have the friends Michael had. In fact, to her knowledge, Kenny had no friends at all. The constant comparisons that weren't comparisons also helped Pamela notice how lazy Kenny had become, how slothful. And as far as personalities went, Kenny never seemed to manifest one, which never really bothered Pamela until the night she confronted him about his shortcomings. That night, his quietness and laziness—his Michael deficiencies—finally irked her. Kenny didn't understand the importance of parental image. So from then on, she was determined to make a better son of Kenny. She didn't expect to make him into a Michael—a feat she knew was impossible, anyway—but she didn't want Kenny to remain a Kenny either. She simply wanted something comfortably in between, something to cushion the impact of never having a Michael, of never being a perfect parent.

That reality was floating around in her head when Beth finally returned from lunch. "Hello, Pam," she said, and it was clearly not the same "Hello, Pam" from a few months ago.

"Hi, Beth," Pamela returned, trying to match Beth in tone and demeanor, stride for stride.

There was an unexpected silence, and then Pamela realized that

Beth was waiting for an explanation for the intrusion. "I want . . . to talk to you," Pamela muttered meekly, but she really wanted to sound nonchalant, as if she was only passing by, which was, of course, ridiculous considering the location of Beth's work area.

Beth frowned. It seemed involuntary, but a frown just the same. "Okay," she said, and then walked around Pamela to sit at her desk.

Pamela was surprised by Beth's expression, and it caused her heart to shudder. "Is everything alright?"

Beth looked at Pamela incredulously, as if she couldn't believe Pamela had such audacity. Then her expression changed to dread. Dreading what? Pamela didn't understand what she could've possibly done to cause such an expression. She thought for a moment, scanning the possibilities. Found none. Then, without warning, one came to mind—a good possibility. "Did you want me to start payin' for Kenny's karate lessons or somethin'?"

Originally, after discussing the difficulties she was having with Kenny, Beth had offered to approach her husband for free lessons, knowing Pamela's salary would otherwise nix the idea. Beth had returned to work the following day and happily told Pamela that Wayne agreed to give free lessons for a year, but she also told Pamela not to worry; she was confident about getting the year extended whenever the time came.

That was the spirit of the offer at the time, but this morning, Pamela questioned the endurance of the offer. The question caused Beth's facial expression—whatever kind it was—to intensify.

"If that's what the problem is, Beth," continued Pamela, convinced by Beth's silence that she was correct in her assumption, "I can start paying. All you had to do—"

"Why would I ask you to pay for something you haven't been using?" Beth said—snapped, actually.

Pamela looked at Beth, puzzled. "What do you mean?" she asked, tilting her head. And then, "Kenny's still goin', ain't he?" But she already knew the answer. The answer was there on Beth's face, in her eyes. Then, Pamela nodded with understanding. "I'll get him to start going again," she said, straining to keep her voice calm, despite the impact of the startling discovery. "I'll get him back if I have to—"

"No!" Beth actually launched from her chair, but still kept her voice discreet. "We don't want him back," she hissed, with rage on her breath. "Why in the hell would we want him back? Your damn boy attacked my son, or didn't you know that? You can't control your son, at all. We had to take him to get stitches, Pamela. We had to take Michael to the *hospital*," she said, with the word "hospital" coming as a quiet shout.

Pamela's mouth dropped open, confused and shocked. She wanted details. She didn't need details, but she wanted them. However, after seeing how Beth's eyes welled with tears of frustration and anger, showing Pamela's intrusion for what it was, she thought better of it. So, standing in Beth's work area, feeling awkward and dazed, not knowing what else to say as anger, frustration, fatigue, and embarrassment assaulted her all at once, Pamela retreated without uttering another word, leaving Beth struggling to regain her composure.

Pamela returned to her station with the intention of finishing the day, but thoughts of Kenny consumed her, making it next to impossible to breathe, let alone work. All she could think about was Kenny, and how she was going to deal with him. And the more she thought about her son, the more paralyzed with rage she became. Eventually, she gave Mr. Yarger, her Floor Supervisor, the story of not feeling very well, which wasn't far from the truth. And since it had been a while since Kenny caused her to miss work, Mr. Yarger chose to believe her—or, at least, not to care very much. Besides, part of him could tell that Pamela would no longer be effective on the phones.

That's how Pamela's workday went, and that's why she's aggressively weaving in and out of lanes, chancing collision, just to get home to her son. Yes, she's extremely ticked. Very angry. Completely mad.

She finally pulls into the driveway, and the bumper of her pampered Acura dings the garage door for the first time, but she doesn't even notice. She ejects from her car with just enough awareness to remember to remove the keys from the ignition, but she forgets her purse as she stomps toward the front door. Her trembling hands make it difficult for her to fit the key into the lock. This frustrates her even more. She shoves the door in anger before she turns the key, but once the door is unlocked, she shoves it again and almost trips upon entering, wincing after slamming her little toe into the door frame.

Once inside, she slams the door with all the rage she has to offer. The sound of the door echoes throughout the seemingly empty house, but the door doesn't stay closed. It stands ajar, wounded by Pamela's abusive tantrum.

The sound of shattering glass reports from Kenny's room.

And he's broken something! she thinks to herself.

Her rage leaps to another plateau, then she notices the kitchen. An entire watermelon lies splattered on the floor, as if Kenny lifted it off the counter and spiked it. Juice is everywhere, but it's obvious that Kenny intended to slice it because the butcher knife is on the floor as well.

Pamela's heart threatens to pound out of her chest. "What the hell? *Kenny!*"

No answer.

She throws her keys on the floor and steps into the kitchen to survey the disaster, but she miscalculates the traction of her high heels on wet linoleum. She slips, slamming violently to the floor, twisting her ankle. A vein appears on the side of her neck as she roars at the top of her lungs. "Damn you, Kenny!" she screams. "Damn . . . *YOU!*"

She clambers to her feet with the largest chunk of watermelon in one hand and the butcher knife in the other. She throws the watermelon toward the trashcan. It bounces off the lid and back to the floor. She intended to place the knife in the sink, but in her eagerness to get to Kenny, she skips that part.

"Kenny! I know your fuckin' ass hears me callin' you!" she yells as she marches toward his room, knife clamped in an ice pick grasp—a stabbing position.

Kenny's door is not only closed for the first time in years, it's also locked. Nevertheless, Pamela's anger gives her more than enough strength to deal with an inexpensive plywood door. She opens the door with a single slam of her shoulder.

Kenny is sitting on the floor, staring up at his mother. In his hand is the shirt he's been using, frantically trying to get the purple Kool-aid stain out of the carpet. Pamela sees where he dropped the glass on the side of the nightstand. She also sees where he tossed doughnuts, cookies, a half-eaten Snickers bar, and a bag of pretzels into the closet, but it's obvious that he couldn't conceal his stash by closing the closet door because a very large box of books is in the way.

Kenny's hands tremble, and his bottom lip quivers as he watches his mother, standing frozen in the doorway, drinking in the entire scene with eyes refusing to believe. When his mother releases another bloodcurdling scream, he notices the knife in her hand.

She lunges toward him with unparalleled rage, still screaming, but Kenny no longer sees his mother. All he sees is the beginning of the end. And as the word "no" gently makes its way to his lips, it's another word that consumes every part of his inner being.

Tsunami.

Chapter 34

AFTER THE TARDY BELL SOUNDS, TONY LOOKS over at Marcus and Roland. "Where's Kenny?"

They shrug.

"He usually h'yuh befo' we git h'yuh," reports Roland.

"His mama drop him off early," adds Marcus. "He be one uh da firs' people at school, but he what'n up front dis mornin'."

"Well, did you see him after school yesterday?" inquires Tony.

"He come ovuh my house own Mondays, Wednesdays, an Fridays," explains Marcus. "We ain' nevuh seen 'im own uh Tuesday—Thursday eithuh."

Tony recalls that Kenny's martial arts classes are held on the same days, but he doesn't develop any suspicions about it, let alone conclusions. All he knows is that Kenny has never been absent, but he's absent today of all days. Of course, Kenny never seemed enthusiastic about the AME test, but he didn't seem to fret either, not like some of the other students. He should be here.

Tony glances at the door again, as if trying to will Kenny's last minute arrival. He's also trying to ignore the thoughts now hammering at his mind: Kenny has never missed a day. Kenny has never been late. Kenny should be here by now. *Kenny is not coming.*

He turns back to the class and stares at everyone for a moment, wanting to stall, knowing he can't. The students look from teacher to the door and back to teacher.

"I guess we'll just get started," he announces, but it comes as a mumble.

Suddenly, someone grabs the doorknob, and every pair of eyes darts to the opening door with such quickness and synchronicity that the act is almost heard, like the almost-noise of thirty-two butterflies taking flight all at once. Principal Ryker marches in, gives Tony a tight-lipped nod, and then scans the room. After the same amount of time it takes to count thirty-two students, the principal grabs the chair that's always next to the table adjacent to the door, and he carries it to the back of the room where he takes a seat with a mild grunt.

Tony is just as surprised as the students, but his surprise switches to irritation, and eventually anger. Principal Ryker, with all of his rules, "expectancies," and by-the-book demeanor hasn't set foot in his classroom since he abducted Rodney, and he has never given Tony a formal, clipboard-in-hand evaluation, even though new teachers are required to have several during their first year. But now he wants to watch Tony as he administers the AME test.

With his frown intact, Tony reaches for the stack of answer sheets, divides it in half, and hands the portions to Justin Giles and Jasmine Woods, who distributes the answer sheets to their classmates without a word.

The principal finally speaks. "What are you doing, Mr. Avery?"

Justin and Jasmine freeze in their tracks and turn back to Tony, who has added a look of confusion to his frown.

"What do you mean?" Tony asks. "What's wrong?"

The principal gives a small, obnoxious chuckle. "What's wrong, Mr. Avery, is that you're allowing your students to handle everyone's testing material."

Tony glances at his two standing students, then back at the principal. "This is our procedure for taking exams," he explains. And then he thinks, *If you or my supposed mentor were to stop by sometime, you'd probably already know this.*

"This is no mere exam, Mr. Avery," the principal explains, patronage sounding off loud and clear. "This is a 'standardized' test. We *proctor* standardized tests, Mr. Avery. *We* do, not our students."

The entire class again turns from the principal to Tony, wondering what's going to happen next. Tony stands in the front of the classroom, arms folded, as he peers over the heads of his students to glare at the man sitting in the back of the room. He's tired of this—whatever *this* is.

"Go ahead and take your seats, guys," Tony finally says in a lowered voice. He reaches for the answer sheets and says, "The principal doesn't trust you."

The class giggles a little, which is a welcomed relief from the tension already caused by the test, and now, the principal's sudden intrusion. Tony doesn't look at Ryker to see what reaction he may have to his remark, and he really doesn't care what the principal's reaction may be.

The English portion of the AME test only consists of two short articles for the students to read, but each article has seven multiple-choice questions and an expository question. The multiple-choice questions check for mere comprehension—understanding of what's read—while the short essay questions check for thinking and communication skills—whether you can construct a thought about what you've just read, and, if so, how clearly you can present that thought on paper. The students have only forty minutes to complete the test. There's no time for figuring anything out; you have to know what you're doing.

Five minutes into the test, well after every student's head is buried in the AME test booklet, and well after Tony returns to his desk, arms folded as he surveys the class—the way he believes the principal would want him to—Ryker suddenly grunts to his feet and leaves without a word, never looking in Tony's direction.

Everything in the classroom breathes again. Even the textbooks on the shelves seem to breathe a sigh of relief. Then, the thought hits Tony again: *Where's Kenny?*

Every other teacher in the building finishes their AME testing during their first class period. Typically, the few students "identified" as likely to pass the exam are shuffled to a teacher's first class, while that teacher's actual first class is babysat by any available warm body—a librarian, a coach, a not-so-busy clerk—in either the library, gym, or lunchroom. However, because Tony opted to test all his students, he'll be stuck testing for the entire day, and the principal will be there for every class—always sitting in the back of the room, always leaving without a word—although he'll arrive at different times so that Tony cannot anticipate his arrival.

Tony will never ask Ryker for an explanation for the visits, which he feels only he receives. He already knows the answer: intimidation. Ryker wants to instill in Tony the fear of discovery, should Tony have any ideas of tainting the results of the test by providing inappropriate accommodations for his students. Any type of assistance is disallowed. Even if the students have questions concerning the way a problem is worded, they're on their own.

These and other actions by the principal and staff make it a bit easier for Tony to think about applying for a transfer to another school. The constant sneering from those who know him without knowing him, the incessant bad-mouthing of students, and the sabotaged apprenticeship program for new teachers—the hallmarks of Lincoln High—should be reason enough for anyone to seek greener pastures. Of course, he doesn't believe he'll ever find the Utopian High he may have envisioned at some point in his college career, but that's okay. He's willing to settle for less than perfection. Anything to get away from Lincoln. All he wants now is a place where most of the teachers and administrative personnel get along with each other. A school where all the teachers believe in their hearts that every student in the building can learn something. The type of school with a polished induction process for new teachers, so they don't flounder about, hoping they're doing things right. He doesn't need extraordinary or flawless. A "typical" high school will do just fine.

During the beginning of his lunch period, Tony calls Kenny's home twice. Both times, no answer. Try as he might, he can't make sense of Kenny's sudden absence, today of all days. Kenny and his mother knew the importance of the test, and they never showed any signs of welshing on the initial plan. Tony *knew* they were going to follow through, and it makes Kenny's no-show all the more perplexing.

At the end of his lunch period, Tony contacts Pamela Houston's job. When the voice at the other end reports they haven't heard from Mrs. Houston today, it finally hits Tony: *Something is definitely wrong.*

As the day winds down, he considers telling someone of his concerns—but who? Mrs. Moreland is one of the few who'd really care to listen, but he knows she'd simply suggest speaking with someone in the Guidance Office. Mrs. Moreland has a propensity for following procedure.

Tony knows that the people in the Guidance Office are accustomed to problems—*real* problems, not probable problems. On a daily basis, they deal with parents who are disgruntled about their child's grades, class schedules, and so on. They constantly deal with teachers who're flustered with many of the contractual accommodation plans designed to offset certain students' learning deficiencies. Then there's the horde of students who storm their office every class period, with gripes ranging from a simple course change to accusations of being touched inappropriately by a teacher. Amongst the confusion found in their office, Tony's concern would be treated like a report of a kitten that just *might* be stuck in a tree found in the center of a thousand-acre, raging forest fire.

How about the principal?

Certainly not. Ryker would merely ask him if Kenny was the only student absent today. The smug look would be fixed on his face long before Tony confessed that a total of five students were absent, and again, Kenny's absence would hardly be considered a crisis.

At the close of the school day, and after he dials Kenny's number once more and gets no answer, Tony decides to swing by Kenny's house on the way home. He doesn't really know why, but something inside goads him into going beyond the call of duty yet again. When he pulls up to the house, he's relieved to see Pamela's car parked in the driveway. There has to be a logical explanation for Kenny's absence today, and all he needs to do is ring their doorbell to discover what it is. Maybe there was a death in the family. That would explain a lot. During his last visit, Pamela never mentioned relatives, but if there *was* a death in the family, their relatives may live far enough away to warrant air travel. They may have taken the first flight out of Jacksonville, meaning the house is indeed empty. If this is the case, Kenny will be allowed to take the make-up exam whenever he returns.

On the other hand, if they *are* home, what then? What explanation could they possibly give for Kenny ditching school on a day as important as today? Maybe an injury? A broken leg? The flu? Perhaps a faked fever? Then, a terrible thought shoves its way to the front of the line: *If there's no good reason for his absence, could he—would he dare—do it again?* The AME test only provides one make-up day, unless circumstances—as with a death in the family or car accident—prove to be extreme.

Yes, hearing of a death in the family or seeing Kenny in a cast would be better than hearing that Kenny didn't want to take the test today, but Tony still tries to keep himself from hoping for such reprieving tragedies such as an uncle's heart attack, a grandmother's stroke, or Kenny's broken hip due to a fall. There's got to be a better way.

He reaches for the doorbell—at least, he prepares to reach for the doorbell—but the door is already slightly open. Instead, he does a quick shift of the head, trying to see inside. "Hello?" he calls, leaning toward the opening. "Mrs. Houston?"

No answer. No sound.

He rings the doorbell, and the melody echoes inside the seemingly deserted house. He turns to again verify the Acura in the driveway, front bumper touching the garage door, and then looks back through the narrow opening of the front door. "Hello?" he calls again, but louder, trying to be heard through closed bedroom or bathroom doors. "Mrs. Houston? Kenny?"

Again, no answer. Again, no sound.

He thinks about pushing the door open, but he's stopped by a vision of Pamela and Kenny working in the backyard—a garden, maybe. However, when he walks around to the back, he sees that the backyard is just as empty as the house seems.

He returns to the parted front door and gives it a nudge with an index finger, causing it to open another six inches or so. "Mrs. Houston?" he says, but this time almost in a whisper. So he says it again with more assertion. "Mrs. Houston?"

Nothing.

He pushes the door completely open and steps in before he has time to consider the consequences. He spots the watermelon mess first, and it shocks him. His mind races with all the possible reasons why a person would drop a watermelon on the floor without bothering to clean it up, and none are promising. What's worse, he can tell by the dried stains that the mess has been there for a while. When he spies the keys, it adds to the riddle, to the creepy conundrum of the Houston home.

Where could they be with the car keys on the floor and the door open? This doesn't make the slightest bit of sense. He can't shake the feeling that something is terribly wrong.

This is not the scene of an empty house.

He steps no more than twelve inches at a time, forgetting to call out to anyone for fear of—what? He can't say, but it's definitely fear he's feeling. Not the run-for-your-life fear. Not even the what-was-that-strange-noise fear. It's closer to the fear a child might have when he swipes cookies from the cookie jar, and his mother is in the next room. That's it. The fear of being discovered, doing something you're not supposed to be doing—that you know better than to do.

The fear isn't as strong as his curiosity.

What's going on here? he wonders.

He eventually makes his way to the entrance of Kenny's room. He gasps, but he doesn't scream.

Blood is everywhere. On the floor, on the bed, on the closet door, on the nightstand, and on the two bodies at his feet.

Are they dead? It's the first thing that enters his mind. Not "What happened?" Not "Who did this?" Not "Oh my God."

Are they dead?

He's seen enough movies to know he shouldn't touch anything, not even the bodies to see if either is alive. Frankly, he's seen enough movies to know he should run out of the house, screaming his head off.

But he needs to know if they're alive.

"Kenny?" he whispers. Then he clears his throat. "Kenny! Mrs. Houston!"

Kenny springs to life, but he doesn't look up at the voice above him. Instead, he crawls toward the bed—cowers, really—like he's trying to squeeze underneath it, raking his forehead over the bloodstained carpet, murmuring the words "no" and "please" repeatedly through a dried throat.

Tony quickly recovers from the jolt Kenny's sudden movement gave him. "Kenny, it's alright," he says, but doesn't step into the room. "Kenny, it's okay. It's okay. It's me—Mr. Avery."

"Mr. Avery?" Kenny asks, not turning back to the voice, still cringing, as if the voice may be a hoax.

"Yes," Tony says gently, a hand reaching to touch Kenny, even though he knows he won't step into the room. "It's me, Kenny. It's Mr. Avery."

"Mr. Avery?" Kenny repeats. Then, he lifts his head from the floor and turns toward Tony. "Mr. Avery?" he asks again, fear smeared all over his raspy voice.

"Yes, Kenny. It's me."

Kenny stares at Tony for a moment, still in disbelief. Then, he looks down at his mother who rests at Tony's feet, and he plunges into a fit of uncontrollable sobs and tears. Tony can tell by Kenny's face that he's been crying off and on for a very long time.

"Oh my God. . . ." he whispers, and then leaves Kenny to find a phone.

When the police, rescue unit, and ambulance eventually get to the

house, they'll find that Pamela Houston is dead—a fatal knife wound
to the throat. They'll ask Tony questions, and he'll explain everything
from the AME test to his finding Kenny and his mother on the floor.
When one of the investigators asks Tony, for the record, his relationship to Kenny, he'll say, "This is my student."

It will be the first time he's ever uttered those words.

Chapter 35

WHEN TONY GETS TO SCHOOL the next morning, he can tell that everyone knows about Kenny and his mother. The story monopolized the six o'clock news, and he imagines that it did the same for the eleven o'clock spot, as well as this morning's news segment. The way the students whisper among themselves when they see him, and the way faculty and staff members give him a double-take—not unlike how most people would react to seeing a celebrity or the U.S. President walk into a high school—tells him they've either seen or heard what's been on the news.

Tony caught the news, and it angered him to see how easily the newscasters placed such worry and concern in their voices when reporting what "transpired at the Houston home." Yesterday, when they had pummeled him with questions, they were everything *but* worried and concerned. He repeatedly told them that he just wanted to go home—he had forgotten to use the "no comment" line—but they didn't care that he was exhausted from the day's occurrences and the rigorous police interrogation. They didn't care about anything. And of all the questions they hammered him with, no one asked him if they could place his face on the news, not one single reporter.

He also didn't like how the story was told. Yes, they simply reported the facts, but the facts turned Kenny into a boy who could kill his mother. The word "murderer" was never broadcast, but it didn't need to be. By the way the story was told, you heard it anyway.

Kenny Houston, the Mom Murderer.

The news showed Kenny being escorted away in handcuffs, and even though it also showed him covered in bandages due to superficial knife wounds, he was still Kenny Houston, the Mom Murderer—or maybe at that point, he became the boy who killed his mother, even though she fought her deranged son valiantly.

Kenny Houston, the Mom-Who-Put-Up-A-Good-Fight Murderer.

They took Kenny to jail. Not to the Youth Crisis Center. Not to the Juvenile Facility for Boys. *Jail.* When the newscast told of how they were taking Kenny, a fifteen-year-old boy, to a real jail, Tony's heart sank as an image of Bone flashed into his mind. A month ago, Cletus reported that Bone was in jail once again. Watching the news, Tony wondered about the chances of Kenny ending up in a cell with Bone. Maybe the thought was preposterous, but it stabbed at him just the same, and after such a trying day, he didn't want to think about Kenny sharing a cell with Bone.

When Tony enters the Main Office, he sees that the principal's door, the one usually closed because of his compulsive patrolling of school grounds, is wide open. The crackling of the principal's radio reveals that Ryker is in his office. Tony gives Miss Edwards his usual smile as he signs in and checks his mailbox.

"Good morning, Tony," she says, which surprises him because she usually whispers her morning greetings. Then, she nods her head toward Ryker's office. "He wants to see you."

Principal Ryker's voice leaps from the office. "Is he here?" he asks, sounding like he's grunting to stand. Then, he steps out of his office. "I want to see you, Mr. Avery," he says, and then fades back into his office, not bothering to check whether Tony is following him.

Tony stands in Ryker's doorway and watches him plop back in his comfortable chair, the way only an ex-police officer with a private investigator's office would.

Ryker eyes Tony peculiarly. "Close the door behind you, Mr. Avery."

Then, seeing Tony's hesitation, he adds, "Please."

Tony gently closes the door, and the loud click speaks to both men. He remains standing, not taking the slightest step forward, and he returns the principal's stare.

Ryker motions toward the seat. "Go ahead, have a seat, Mr. Avery."

Tony takes a deep, tired breath before he does, but he doesn't say a word, and he doesn't take his eyes off the principal.

"You had an interesting evening yesterday," Ryker says.

Tony says nothing.

The principal settles in his chair and rubs his hands together. "I don't really blame you for not liking me." He sighs and looks away from Tony for the first time. "Sometimes, I guess I don't even care for myself much," he says with a chuckle, but it's brief and inappropriate. "The things I have to deal with and do sometimes," he says, shaking his head, sounding as if the real conversation hasn't started yet. "It's difficult sometimes, Mr. Avery—this job I have."

Tony suddenly notices how tired the principal appears, how drained.

Ryker stares back at Tony, and he holds his stare long enough to make most people look away, but Tony doesn't even blink. Then, the principal smiles at him, admiring his composure. He leans back in his chair and reaches for his pen. He grins as he starts with the clicking and says, "I really admire you, Mr. Avery. Not many new teachers can just march in here and do what you've done—not at Lincoln High. It's incredible, actually—very commendable. Your kids, and even some who aren't yours, really respect you." He leans forward. "And I can tell you, Mr. Avery, respect is very difficult to come by with these kids."

Tony just blinks at the principal.

Ryker leans back again. "You see what little respect *I* get," he continues, "with that violent wall message left by Rodney Coleman, and that's not the worst of what I've had to endure here, I assure you."

Tony breaks his silence. "What happened to Rodney?"

The principal pauses at the question, trying to measure Tony's interest in Rodney. "Rodney Coleman is no longer your concern," he finally says. "You are his teacher no longer."

Tony says nothing.

"I take my hat off to you, Mr. Avery. You really know how to handle these kids. I've never seen a first-year-teacher do what you've done in the time that you've done it. They like you—I *know* they like you." He leans forward again. "Ever since the reports of you teaching them how to stay away from correct English, I've been watching you, Mr. Avery—listening in on you, outside your classroom door."

Tony cannot conceal his surprise, but he says nothing.

Ryker seems satisfied with his English teacher's reaction. "I never caught any of your lessons that allegedly taught them how to speak poor English," he continues, "and for the life of me, based on what I can attest to your doing in your classroom, I find it difficult to believe a person of your upbringing would conduct such lessons." His pen clicks with agreement. "But you, my friend," he continues, pointing the pen at Tony, "had their attention every time I stopped by. If I didn't know better, I'd swear you knew I was coming."

Tony blinks twice, but he says nothing.

Ryker doesn't seem bothered by his silence. In fact, he seems to prefer it. "Many of my veteran teachers are still struggling to get the control that you're enjoying in your classroom, Mr. Avery—my *veteran* teachers," he says, smiling. "It makes you wonder what the word 'veteran' means, doesn't it?"

Tony doesn't respond.

The principal places his pen back in his shirt pocket, then rests his clasped hands on top of his desk. He eyes Tony for what most would consider an uncomfortable amount of time. Again, Tony doesn't blink. "I rushed the results of your students' tests yesterday, Mr. Avery," he confides. "I couldn't wait to find out how they did. I just couldn't wait." He pauses, as if for dramatic appeal. "You know what, Mr. Avery? Forty-eight percent of your students passed the test—*forty-eight percent*, Mr. Avery. And another twenty-four percent came *close* to passing. These results are absolutely astounding, considering the amount of time you've had to work with them."

Tony looks at his lap, taking his eyes off the principal for the first time. He has disappointed many of his students, and it doesn't sit well with him.

Ryker thinks Tony is blushing. "Yes," he continues, "you have good reason to be proud, Mr. Avery. What you've done is amazing, but the most incredible thing about your students—something I haven't seen in a long time, I might add—is that every last one of them *tried* to pass. For some reason, Mr. Avery, your kids really wanted to do well—all of them." He tilts his head to one side, grinning. "How do you teach something like that, Mr. Avery? How do you get a kid to care about learning, to care about anything, for that matter?"

Tony doesn't respond, and he doesn't look up from his lap. He's wondering which students failed, and he's also wondering what he'll say to them, what words he could possibly use to ease their pain.

Principal Ryker takes a deep breath. "Right. I don't blame you if you end up leaving. I never expected you to stay, anyway." Then he pauses for a moment, searching for the right words. "But I wouldn't be doing my job if I didn't ask a teacher of your caliber to stay."

Tony lifts his head but remains silent. His expression hasn't changed, and, in a way, his expression says it all.

Ryker frowns for the first time. "Regardless of how you may feel about me or anyone else here, Mr. Avery, you need to realize that you are one person, and that you can't do it alone." His hands fidget, as if crying out for the pen. "There are other teachers here, Mr. Avery—*good* teachers, and they work just as hard as you do to make a difference. Many may not have the results you have, and in a way, that means they work even harder than you do because of it—and for what? Only to obtain the small victories they have to settle for? Something to help them hang on for another day?" Then, his face becomes more intense, sterner. "It's easy to hang tough when you're winning," he continues, "when things are going your way. But the truest test, Mr. Avery, is what you do when you're down to your last shred of hope, when your tomorrows look just as bleak as your yesterdays." His eyes bear down on his quiet English teacher, demanding Tony's attention. "There are teachers here who continue to tough it out, Mr. Avery. It seems they'll never be able to control a class the way you do, but they endure. Even knowing that the kids hate them, they still show up in the morning—*every* morning." Then, Ryker pauses for another moment. He can tell that Tony is thinking about his words, tossing them around in his head.

Suddenly, Tony clears his throat and stares down at his hands. "If what you say is true, why make it worse by not acting and operating as a team? Why make it more difficult than it already is?"

The principal takes a moment to consider Tony's words carefully. Then, he rubs his chin and says, "College taught you how to teach English, Mr. Avery. It taught you how to write lesson plans. It probably gave you some insight on how to manage a classroom, how to talk and deal with the kids." He leans forward and gives his English teacher a genuine smile. "When did college teach you how to act as a team member? Which course was that? You don't even have to take a business course to become a teacher, Mr. Avery, but we wonder why schools aren't more 'businesslike,' a well-polished, corporate machine where every cog knows its function, where every member of the team is reading from the same play book."

Ryker takes a deep breath, and then leans back in his chair, studying Tony with calculating eyes. "I don't know anything about your home life, Mr. Avery, but I'd wager that you come from good stock—a loving mother and father who always had high expectations, and who've probably been fostering a sense of responsibility since you were potty-trained. But I don't really know—maybe I should know, but I don't." He releases a small chuckle, slaps a hand on his desk, and says, "Maybe if we all knew more about each other, we wouldn't have to make so much up. Maybe we'd all be much better off."

Tony nods at the comment. "Maybe."

The principal loses his smile, and he studies Tony for a moment. "I don't know how well you know this Kenneth Houston, Mr. Avery," he says suddenly, "but I believe he could use your help right about now."

This catches Tony off guard, but Ryker ignores his surprised expression. "He isn't eating, Mr. Avery. Can you imagine a boy that size not eating? I sure as hell can't, but he's not eating."

Tony's concern is evident. "How is he?"

Ryker shrugs. "He's fine for the moment, but he won't be much longer if he doesn't get something in him. He won't even talk. He just sits on his bunk, staring at the floor. He doesn't acknowledge anyone."

"What's going to happen to him?" asks Tony, sitting forward in his chair.

Ryker leans all the way back, clasping his hands behind his head, and looks up toward the ceiling. After a deep breath, his eyes back on Tony, he says, "Based on what I've been able to find out, it looks as if the boy was actually defending himself—of course, it's not official yet. The investigation has to run its course, but it's definitely pointing toward self-defense. They still have to keep him in a cell until they're sure—maintain the 'zero tolerance' image that the public is expecting nowadays— but it shouldn't be too long before he's released." Then, Ryker looks at Tony with concern in his eyes. "Still, none of that will matter much if he doesn't start eating—now will it? Of course, there's also the matter of where he'll live after this is all over. They haven't been able to locate any relatives." Then, he lifts an eyebrow and asks, "Do you know a Mr. Farley?"

Tony shakes his head.

Ryker rubs at his chin thoughtfully. "Probably some nut, anyway," he mumbles. "He's being checked out, but he stormed the police station yesterday, wanting to speak with Houston, even offered to post bail. He was babbling on about wanting to be the boy's foster parent, if you can believe that." He shakes his head. "He'll probably turn out to be a psycho pervert or something. How many people would volunteer to keep a kid who's just killed his own mother?"

Tony bites his bottom lip, and then asks, "Can I see Kenny? I mean, is it possible for me to see him?"

Principal Ryker smiles. "Your classes have already been covered for the day. Go to your student, Mr. Avery."

Chapter 36

THE POLICE STATION SMELLS OF copy ink and coffee. After going through all the routine safety measures, Tony is escorted by an Officer Bartley to Kenny's holding cell. He doesn't look at the occupants of the cells they pass, and when they reach Kenny's, Tony is relieved to see he has a cell of his own.

Kenny is sitting on his bunk, feet flat on the floor, wearing a bright orange jumpsuit—criminal attire. Still, it's better than the blood-stained clothes he was wearing yesterday. His shoulders are stooped, and his head is bowed, as if he's staring at the floor. It's obvious he's tired. In fact, it seems like he could topple at any moment. He hasn't slept for two days, and it shows.

An untouched breakfast tray rests on the table next to his toilet. According to Officer Bartley, Kenny has refused to eat or sleep, and he's ignored everyone who's attempted to break his coma-like silence.

Tony grasps the bars with both hands, surprised by how cold they are, and he brings his head within an inch of them. "Kenny? Kenny, it's me—Mr. Avery. Can you hear me?"

Kenny lifts his head to Tony and Officer Bartley. The officer shows mild astonishment, but quickly regains his stoic professionalism.

Tony glances at the officer. "Is it alright if I go inside?"

Officer Bartley stares at Tony incredulously, as if surprised he'd even ask such a question. "Of course," he says, but he remains at the entrance with a ready-for-anything posture.

Tony sits on the bunk with Kenny. "How are you doing, Kenny?" he asks, even though he feels it to be a rather absurd question.

"I'm okay, Mr. Avery," Kenny murmurs with a terribly coarse voice.

The sound of Kenny's voice causes Tony to wince a little. It reminds him of yesterday—Kenny's bedroom. "Your voice . . . sounds pretty dry, Kenny." He steps over to the tray and grabs the small carton of orange juice. "Here, drink some orange juice."

Kenny takes the open carton from Tony and takes a few swallows. "Isn't that better?"

Kenny nods but looks back at the floor.

Tony takes the orange juice from him, fearing it may hit the floor otherwise. At the same time, he gropes for something sensible to say. "You won't be here much longer, Kenny," he says, but doesn't know what to say next. He doesn't want to upset Kenny.

Kenny looks up at Tony. "Where will I go, Mr. Avery?"

Tony walks back over to the tray and grabs the biscuit. "Don't worry about that right now," he says, offering Kenny the biscuit. Kenny accepts it and takes a bite. Again, Tony sits on the bunk. "We'll figure all of that out later. Right now, I want to make sure that my best student is okay."

Kenny slows his chewing and looks at Tony. "I'm your best student?"

Tony gives a soft smile. "Without a doubt, Kenny." He allows Kenny to finish the biscuit, and when he offers him the juice, he finishes that as well. "When I come back, I'm going to bring you some *real* food," he says, trying to put light humor in his voice, but it doesn't really work. "Just tell me what you want."

Kenny seems ready to cry, but he doesn't. "I'm an orphan," he says suddenly, eyes on the floor.

Tony is stumped. He has no clue how he should respond, and his aching heart makes it all the more difficult. He looks at the floor, following Kenny's eyes, and is surprised at how clean the floor is. "Do you know anyone named Mr. Farley?"

Kenny lifts his head and looks at Tony, but this time, with a slight spark in his bloodshot eyes. "Yes."

Tony studies him curiously. "Who is he?"

"He owns a bookstore in the mall," Kenny says, eyes back on the floor. "We're friends."

Tony chooses his next words carefully. "Do you . . . *trust* him?"

"Yes."

Tony looks up at Officer Bartley, who seems particularly interested in what Kenny has to say. Then, he looks back at Kenny. "I'm not sure, but I think he's trying to get you to stay with him for a while, but if that doesn't pan out, we'll work something out, Kenny. Don't worry."

Kenny keeps eyeing the floor, but some of his sadness seems to fade—at least, that's what Tony believes.

Silence returns again, and Tony looks back at Officer Bartley, who's now leaning against the bars. His concern for Kenny is smeared all over his face. Then, Tony looks back at Kenny. "Marcus and Roland told me you were helping them with their reading and writing," he says, bringing a nervous smile to his face.

Kenny nods, keeping his eyes on the floor. "Yes."

"Aspiring teacher, huh?"

Kenny turns to Tony, and it's the saddest face Tony's ever seen. "Are you gonna stay at Lincoln?"

Tony's little smile melts away.

"Everybody's been wondering and wondering if you're gonna stay," Kenny admits softly. "Will you?"

Tony looks at the floor, shaking his head. "I . . . I don't know, Kenny." He takes a deep breath and adds, "As you can probably guess, things haven't been going too well for me there." He takes another breath. "And I'm not exactly loving it there," he says absently.

Kenny looks back at the floor. "I love it there," he murmurs, and for a moment, the cell goes silent again, and then Kenny adds, "But you said I don't belong there. So, I believed you. You said that where you're supposed to be isn't necessarily where you *want* to be. That's what you told me."

Again, silence. Tony's mind races, trying to find words to whisk away the silence, but his emotions make it difficult.

"I'm alive because of you," Kenny says suddenly. Tony looks over at him, but Kenny keeps eyeing the floor. "There was a time I would've just let it happen," Kenny continues, slowly shaking his head. "I wouldn't've even cared." He pauses, and, for a moment, Tony thinks he's finished, but then Kenny says, "You changed that, Mr. Avery. You made me start caring. And you gave me the only friends I've ever had, too—Marcus and Roland. *You* did that." Another pause, and then he adds, "It's easy to see why so many people like you." He looks directly at Tony. "A lot of us would've written that message on the wall if we'd've known about it—how the principal was treatin' you." Then, he again focuses on the floor. "I know I would've."

Silence returns, and they bathe in it for a while, lost in their thoughts.

Finally, Kenny looks over at Tony. When he sees that his teacher has tears rolling down his face, he looks back at the floor because it's the right thing to do. "If you don't belong at Lincoln, nobody does. You may not like it, but that's where you're supposed to be."

The silence returns for a longer period. Then, Tony finally wipes his face on his sleeve and stands. "I'll be back later today," he says, clearing his throat. "Can I bring you anything? Maybe something to read?"

Kenny slowly looks up and stares at his teacher. "Something to read," he says, nodding, without energy.

Tony offers a weak smile. "What would you like—*War and Peace?*"

Kenny's expression doesn't change, but he shakes his head. "I've read it. Didn't care for it too much."

Tony's expression turns somber again. "I'll bring you whatever you want to read, Kenny," he says, tenderly.

Kenny considers the offer for a brief moment, and finally, he says, "*The Little Red Wagon.*"

Tony tilts his head. "*The Little Red Wagon*? Isn't that a children's book?"

"Yes."

Tony waits for Kenny to say more, but he doesn't. "Okay, Kenny— *The Little Red Wagon.*" He stares at Kenny for a second, trying to think of better parting words, but nothing comes. He glances at Officer Bartley, and then back at Kenny. Finally, he says, "Finish your breakfast, okay?"

Kenny looks over at the tray resting on the table, then back at the floor. "Okay," he says with another tired nod.

After Tony and Officer Bartley leave, Kenny remains seated on his bunk for another twenty minutes or so, and then, suddenly, he struggles to his feet. His legs ache terribly, but he ignores the pain and makes his way over to the bars. Holding onto the bars with one hand for support, he begins delivering the front kicks he learned at the Northshore Karate Institute. Due to his lack of nourishment and sleep, he finds it excruciating just to lift his leg off the floor, but he does it anyway, struggling with everything he has. He tries not to count because he remembers how counting made it worse.

After four minutes, when he can't deliver another kick, he kicks anyway, trying to ignore the pain. Tears begin to fall down his face, but they are not because of the pain in his legs; it's the pain in his heart. He cries because his mother is gone. He cries because he can no longer camouflage what has always been resting inside his heart—his love for his mother. The feeling was always there, he knows, but, until now, he's always managed to ignore it, suppress it, but not anymore. Since the hope is gone, the love is all he has left, and it burns with renewed life and brilliance. Even now, he kicks for her because of the love that blazes inside him. Yes, he still loves his mother the way a boy is expected to love his mother, because true love doesn't come with an on and off switch. And when his right leg gives out on him, he'll switch to his left. And again, he'll kick for her over and over, giving everything he has.

All of his strength.

All of his will.

All of his love.

Snap. Pop.

About the Author

Edward M. Baldwin, a former high school English teacher and literacy coordinator, is a graduate of the University of North Florida. He started *Learnt*, his first novel, during his junior year at UNF. It took three years to complete. However, he wrote *Victims of Shakespeare* (his second novel) in half that time, quickly followed by *Teacher Deficit Disorder*. He's currently writing *Gun Point Average*, his fourth Duval County novel.

With an arsenal of "classroom dramas" to complete, he aspires to become "America's Education Novelist." He lives in Jacksonville with his wife and three children.

For more information about the author and his work, including draft pages of future books, visit online at www.EdwardMBaldwin.com.